THE DEEPEST OF SECRETS

THE DEEPEST OF SECRETS

A ROCKTON NOVEL

KELLEY ARMSTRONG

MINOTAUR BOOKS
NEW YORK

First published in the United States by Minotaur Books,
an imprint of St. Martin's Publishing Group

www.minotaurbooks.com

Library of Congress Cataloging-in-Publication Data

Names: Armstrong, Kelley, author.
Title: The deepest of secrets: a Rockton novel / Kelley Armstrong.
Description: First edition. | New York: Minotaur Books, 2022. |
    Series: Casey Duncan novels; 7
Identifiers: LCCN 2021039558 | ISBN 9781250781734 (hardcover) |
    ISBN 9781250830203 (ebook)
Subjects: LCGFT: Novels.
Classification: LCC PR9199.4.A8777 D44 2022 | DDC 813/.6—dc23
LC record available at https://lccn.loc.gov/2021039558

Our books may be purchased in bulk for promotional, educational,
or business use. Please contact your local bookseller or the Macmillan
Corporate and Premium Sales Department at 1-800-221-7945, extension 5442,
or by email at MacmillanSpecialMarkets@macmillan.com.

First Edition: 2022

10 9 8 7 6 5 4 3 2 1

For Jeff

THE DEEPEST OF SECRETS

INTRODUCTION

If you're new to the Rockton series—or if it's been awhile since you've read the last book—here's a little introduction to get you up to speed. Otherwise, if you're ready to go, just skip to chapter one and dive in!

Welcome to Rockton. Population 171 and dropping faster than we care to admit. Located in the Yukon wilderness, we're a hidden town where people go to disappear. Residents come here under false names and false histories, and they must stay a minimum of two years. Extensions can stretch that to five years, but those extensions have become impossible to get. The council is shutting us down. They just refuse to admit it.

Rockton was born in the 1950s as an exercise in idealism. It's a place for people who needed refuge, and in those earliest years, it was often their ideals that brought them here, fleeing McCarthyism and other political witch hunts. When the town struggled in the late sixties, a few wealthy former residents took over management and organized regular supply drops. That's when the town began evolving from a commune of lost souls into a for-profit institution. While there are still people here who genuinely need sanctuary, there are also white-collar criminals who've bought an escape hatch from the law. And there are an increasing number of hardened criminals that the council sneaks in to increase the profit margin.

The council runs Rockton from afar. We've never seen them. We only speak to a council liaison on a satellite phone. There's also a board of directors, including Émilie, one of those "wealthy former residents," who still believes in the philanthropical ideal of the town. We believe in that ideal, too. We're the people of Rockton.

We live off the grid, with no access to the outside world. No roads. No phones. No internet. We're cut off from the world, and we need that to keep everyone here safe. You won't find Rockton on any map, and we stay that way with the help of camouflage, both structural and technological. That's easier than it seems when you're in the Yukon—a northern Canadian territory the size of Texas with fewer than forty thousand people.

There are a handful of key residents in Rockton. I'm Casey Duncan—known here as Casey Butler—the lone detective. Eric Dalton is the sheriff and my common-law husband. We also have a deputy, Will Anders, and an honorary canine officer, Storm, my Newfoundland dog.

The town's council representative is Phil, who used to be our liaison before he was exiled here, and he's still adjusting to that. Technically, Phil and Eric are the town leaders, but really, the most powerful person here is Isabel, who runs the bar—the Roc—which doubles as the brothel.

My sister, April, is our doctor. My former best friend, Diana, is training to be her nurse.

Petra doesn't have any such "essential" job in Rockton— she's a comic-book artist who works in the general store. Or that's her cover. She's actually Émilie's granddaughter and a former operative for an organization that shall never be named.

Mathias also holds a nonessential position—as the town butcher—belying the fact that he's a psychiatrist with an expertise in criminal pathology, both professionally and personally. His current project is Sebastian. At twenty, Sebastian is Rockton's youngest resident. He spent seven years in prison for killing his parents. He's a certified sociopath determined to overcome his diagnosis, and we're willing to give him that chance.

Kenny is our carpenter and head of our militia, which also includes Jen, my self-appointed nemesis. Devon and Brian are a couple who run the bakery—my favorite shop in town.

We are a secret town and a town of secrets. I don't even want to guess how many residents are actually here because of crimes they committed down south. I am, and Anders is, and I hold out hope that most are like us—people who made mistakes, desperate to get back on the right track and repay any debt we owe. Only Dalton knows everyone's history—he must, for the protection of all. As his detective, I get that information only when I need to know it, or when someone tells me their story.

There are also people who live outside our boundaries and our jurisdiction. When capitalism moved into Rockton, a group of residents moved out and formed the First Settlement, which is now in its third generation. The First Settlement is run by Edwin, one of the earliest settlers there. His granddaughter, Felicity, is expected to succeed him.

The next exodus from Rockton began in the seventies with nature-loving residents. They formed the Second Settlement, a more commune-like, nature-faith-based nomadic community.

There are also people who choose not to join a settlement, like Eric's brother, Jacob, and former sheriff Tyrone Cypher. They're twenty-first-century pioneers, living off the land.

There used to be another group, the most dangerous one: the hostiles. A few months ago, I solved the mystery of their existence, and most have been taken south for rehabilitation. My reward for that? The council is shutting us down. We know they are. They just haven't made it official yet, and we don't quite know what to do about that.

ONE

It's July in the Yukon, a gorgeous night that's perfect for a camp-fire. Or, in this case, a game of campfire Dungeons & Dragons. Having suffered an untimely demise, I'm tossing a ball with Storm while keeping one ear on the game as my friends—sorry, my *questing party*—wriggle through an ink-black tunnel.

"Caves," Marissa grumbles. "Why is it always caves with you?"

Anders grins over at his new girlfriend. "Because caves are awesome."

"Could you lighten up on the setting and just get to the monsters? They're a lot less terrifying."

The dungeon master tonight is our local deputy, Will Anders. The games started because he used to play as a kid. It's not an image he fits these days, as a six-foot-two, brawny former military man. Give him a twenty-sided die, though, and that suburban teenage geek surfaces in all his shiny-eyed glory.

Marissa is a relative newcomer to Rockton. I'm delighted to have her join our games. Even more delighted to see Anders settling down. There's nothing wrong with enjoying the hookup scene, but there'd always been a touch of the frenetic to the way Anders went about it. Losing himself in sex the way he'd lose himself in a bottle. Both have steadied as he finds his footing and finally boxes up his past.

Beside Anders is Eric Dalton, the local sheriff. I've been working as his detective since I arrived and living with him for the past eighteen months. When his gaze flicks to the ice cooler, I toss the ball again for Storm and then play a little fetch myself, getting a beer.

As I pass the bottle over Dalton's shoulder, he catches my wrists and tugs me against his back. I loop my arms around his neck and kiss his cheek, which suggests I've reached my two-tequila shot limit for the evening. Public displays of affection are not my thing.

"I'm up against a beholder," Dalton says. "Any advice?"

"Hey!" says Kenny, head of our militia. "No tag-teaming."

"Eric's a necromancer, right?" I say. "He can consult with the dead."

"Shit, I forgot that," Dalton says. "Fuck, yeah. Casey's my spirit guide or whatever."

"His elven ranger love," I say. "Taken too soon from this world. Stabbed in the back by her own sister."

"I am not your sister in-game," April says. "Nor did I kill you. That was the orc you insisted on facing down single-handedly. I simply chose to use my shamanic skills to slay the beast rather than resuscitate you. I acted in service to the greater good. Your death, while tragic, was not undeserved."

"Harsh," Kenny murmurs.

My sister is a brilliant neuroscientist. She's also almost certainly on the autism spectrum, and learning to deal with her undiagnosed condition. Even sharing an evening game with friends is new for April. Back home, she'd have spent the night as she spent the day: working. I know what that's like, though my relentless drive can be chalked up to a demon of my own summoning.

Dalton pulls me onto his lap, which proves he has also hit his alcohol limit. This is a rare chance for us to relax, hidden from public view behind our chalet.

"We're in a cavern, right?" Dalton asks. "Lots of loose stones?"

"No, Eric," Anders says. "You can't throw rocks at a beholder. Also, being a necromancer, you could barely lift them. Your strength lies in your dominion over the undead."

"So where the fuck are the undead?"

"Ooh!" I say. "I can be your zombie soldier. Resurrect me."

"Your corpse is twenty miles away," Anders says. "Also, it was decapitated by the orc's ax, which is why Eric couldn't resurrect you at the scene."

"*Conveniently* decapitated," Dalton mutters. "Fine. Lots of dead things in a cave. I'll raise a few."

"There are no animal corpses nearby," Anders says.

"Dead bodies, then. I'll summon them, and they'll crawl from their final resting place—"

"No dead bodies within twenty miles."

"Huh," Kenny says. "Must not be near Rockton then."

Everyone laughs. Everyone except Marissa, who glances at Anders.

"Remind me why I'm a fucking *necromancer* again?" Dalton says.

"Because April expressed an interest in playing the shaman, and you agreed to switch roles."

"In other words, I was being nice. Let this be a lesson to me. Nice guys get stuck in a forest, facing a beholder, without a resurrectable corpse in sight."

Anders sighs. "Fine. I'll give you a rabbit. A very mangled, very decomposed dead rabbit is now at your command."

"One killer bunny is all you need," I say.

Dalton is considering his play when footsteps pound beside the chalet. I jump off Dalton's lap so fast I nearly end up in the fire. When I see who it is, I expect a sarcastic comment, but Jen doesn't seem to notice my lap-sitting or my stumble. She's focused on Dalton.

"There's a problem," she says. "We need you in the square."

Anders rises. "Conduct issues come to me, Jen."

His correction is gentle. He has endless patience with Jen, as if he's made it his mission to take the town's biggest law-breaker and turn her into proper militia. I expect Jen to snap back, but her gaze shunts his way, and there's trepidation in it before she returns her attention to Dalton.

"Will should stay here," she says. "Enjoy the rest of his night off."

Again, I know how Jen should say this, her voice dripping with sarcasm, as if the three of us—and Kenny—taking a rare night off together is first-order slacking.

"What the hell is going on, Jen?" Dalton says.

Kenny lifts a hand. "Let me handle it. Eric can take over my barbarian."

"As the dead player, I can duck out easily," I say.

Dalton and Anders both still hesitate, but Marissa puts a hand on Anders's leg, murmuring that he doesn't need to break up every town brawl. My look to Dalton says the same. We've had a shitty month. Dealing with the council shutting down Rockton while we tackle a seemingly endless stream of minor crimes. It's been three days of relative peace, and so I declared us all in need of a break. One evening off, and we couldn't even get through it without a fresh fire to put out. Hopefully not an actual fire.

★ ★ ★

I see the problem as soon as I get into town. Or I think I do. There's a crowd in the square long after there should be gatherings anywhere. It's past midnight. Anders had insisted on working until ten, so we'd gotten a late start to our game. This being a weeknight, the Roc shut down about fifteen minutes ago. If there'd been trouble, Isabel would have warned us.

That's when I spot Isabel herself, marching from the Roc, one end of a ladder in hand. Phil carries the other end. Both their faces are set in grim determination.

"Move away from the pole." Isabel's voice rings out. "Anyone who does not get out of my damn way earns a month's suspension from the Roc."

Only one resident—a guy named Conrad—dares turn on her. Before Conrad can get a word out, Phil grabs him by the collar. Conrad straightens, but Phil is younger and taller, and Conrad backs away with a few parting grumbles.

Jen, Kenny, and I are still heading toward the square, and no one has spotted us yet. Jen's in the lead, and Isabel sees her first.

"What the hell is this?" she says, waving at the pole. "Were you just going to leave that up there?"

"I couldn't reach it," Jen says.

"Then find someone to help you. This should have been taken down the moment—" Isabel spots me and stops. Her gaze shoots to Kenny, who follows on his crutches. "Is Will still at your place?"

"Yes. What's up? Did we have another avian accident?"

The pole was erected earlier this month. It looks like a basketball-net backboard. It's a projection screen for "midnight movies in the square." My idea. We strictly limit our electricity use here, but the long summer days keep the solar batteries juiced up, and we hold weekly movie nights in the community center. Now that the sun has started dropping before midnight,

I thought it'd be fun to show movies outside instead. Kenny rigged up the aerial screen, only to have a gray jay fatally hit it last week.

No one answers my question. No one even seems to hear it. They're all watching Isabel climb the ladder. As Phil holds it, he darts a look my way, one I can't quite read through the reflection off his glasses. His mouth is taut, brow furrowed.

I shoulder through the crowd just as Isabel reaches her goal. It's looks like a big sheet of paper plastered on the projection-screen panel. I catch the words "Will Anders" before she rips it down.

"Do you think that's going to help?" someone says.

It's Conrad again. As I glare at him, I remember back to a time when I thought he was such a nice guy, an asset to the community. After he arrived, he'd worked for a few months stocking shelves while running a weekly dental clinic. Then he went to Phil and asked to be the permanent town dentist with essential-worker privileges. Phil informed him that we didn't require a full-time dentist, and the town already paid him handsomely for his professional services. That's when the real Conrad appeared.

"We've all seen the sign," a woman says. Jolene. I don't know her former occupation, but it had something to do with caring for animals, and she's temporarily working at the stables while Maryanne is down south for dental reconstruction surgery.

"We all know what he did," Jolene continues.

"Do you?" Isabel says from her perch on the ladder. "This is the equivalent of writing on a bathroom wall. I could put anything I like up here. Doesn't make it true."

"So it's *not* true?" says a balding man. Ted. Another of our permanent malcontents.

"How would I know?" Isabel says as she folds the paper. "I have no idea what anyone did before they came to Rockton.

That is, I believe, the point of being here." She turns a laser gaze on Ted. "How about you come up here and tell us why you're in Rockton? Since you're so interested in other people's stories."

Ted sputters that it's none of anyone's business. Isabel's aim is dead on, though. She knows why he's here. So do I. While Dalton only shares on a need-to-know basis, he's come to realize that, in some instances, I need to know even before a crime is committed, so we can protect our residents.

In Ted's case, he'd been a college dean who blackmailed female students for sex. Why does Isabel know that? She also runs the local brothel, and I make sure she's warned of predators. I don't give her any details, but she does require a heads-up.

"Anyone else?" she calls. "Anyone want to come up here and share their story?"

"Only if Will goes first," Conrad says. "Tells us whether he really shot his CO."

I stop midstride. A couple of people notice, and I cover my reaction quickly with, "What the hell?," my voice ringing over the buzz of conversation.

Jolene turns toward me. "Oh, you didn't know you're working with a killer, Casey? Where is Will, anyway? Better not have left him alone with Sheriff Dalton. Apparently, he has a thing for murdering his superior officers."

"Casey has no idea what Will has done or hasn't done," Isabel says. "She only knows—as we all do—that Will Anders is a good man. A good deputy. A trusted member of this community who has never had a word of complaint against him—"

"He nearly broke my jaw two months ago," Ted says. "It's still sore."

"He hit you because you went after him with a steak knife," I say.

"I was drunk," Ted whines.

"And then, when Eric wanted you to spend twenty-four hours in the cell, Will was the one who argued that a sore jaw was punishment enough." I stop at the bottom of the ladder. "I have no idea what's going on here, but if anyone has a complaint about Will—or me—you can bring it to Phil, who will see that it is properly addressed."

"Note she didn't include Eric," Kenny says. "Please see Phil if you *don't* have a complaint about the sheriff. That line will be much shorter."

A few laughs and a few more chuckles, the tension easing as the crowd backs up to let Kenny through.

"It's past midnight," Kenny says. "Most of you have work tomorrow. I'm going to suggest you all head home. I'm sure Casey will address this tomorrow with a town meeting."

"I will," I say.

"Are you going to investigate?" Conrad asks.

"Absolutely," I say. "I don't know whether this was someone's idea of a prank or a deliberate attempt to undermine Deputy Anders's authority, but I will find out who posted this and take the appropriate action."

"I mean investigate whether your deputy did this. Whether he killed—"

"I am not going to address the nature of the accusation further. I'll refrain from comment until I know what the hell I'm talking about, and I would suggest you all do the same."

"Is that a gag order?" a woman says.

I look over. It's Jolene, her cool gaze fixed on me.

"If it was, it'd have been worded as such," I say. "But I'm going to hope that, knowing most of you have had nothing but positive interactions with Will Anders, you will grant him the benefit of the doubt until this matter has been sorted. Rumor and speculation will only make it tougher to get to the truth."

"Will we get the truth?" Conrad says. "Or will you cover it up?"

"Oh for God's sake," Isabel says, still on the ladder. "Everyone knows you were chasing Marissa before she took up with Will. And Jolene? You vow revenge every time Will kicks you out of the Roc for drunk-and-disorderly. You're both embarrassing yourselves here. Go home. Both of you. *All* of you."

I turn to Kenny and Jen. "Can you please disperse this crowd while I find out what's going on?"

They nod and set to work.

TWO

Find out what's going on.

Except I already know, don't I? Someone has accused Anders of killing his commanding officer in the army. Which he did. Shot and killed his CO and injured two others. I uncovered the full story during my first case here.

When residents come to Rockton, Dalton gets their backstory. Sometimes it's even the truth. The council is honest when the resident is a victim or a white-collar criminal.

For the serious criminals, though? The violent offenders? The council lies to him. When Dalton discovered that, he started researching residents he suspects are guilty of violent crimes. I've been able to help him refine his methods, but even before I arrived, he was doing a damn fine job playing private eye.

Being offline here, Dalton needs to conduct that research on his supply trips to Dawson City. He'd kept a journal, using only real names and no connections to actual residents. When I needed to solve my first case, he gave me the journal, but he'd removed a few pages. I later found those pages in a copy made by a former officer. Taking those missing pages, together with what I knew of Will Anders, I'd figured out the identity of "Calvin James," a military officer who'd killed his CO and injured two other officers. At the time of the shooting, Anders was being treated for stress. He'd been on medication with adverse effects, but his concerns were ignored. One night, he dreamed he shot his CO. Just walked into his quarters and opened fire.

It hadn't been a dream.

Most people would say it wasn't his fault. Blame the stress. Blame the medication. Blame the culture and the lack of appropriate mental-health care. After all, Anders had done everything right. He'd admitted he was having trouble. He'd taken the prescribed medication. He'd alerted his doctor to side effects. He has every reason to say it wasn't his fault, and yet he does not. This is the nightmare he fights with alcohol and sex—the knowledge that he killed a man who'd done nothing to deserve it. The knowledge that, maybe, in the theater of war, that wasn't the only innocent victim whose life he took.

After the crowd disperses from the town square, I get the sign from Isabel. Then I take it aside to read privately, in case my reaction gives away more than I'd like.

It's four sheets of paper taped together as a makeshift sign. On it, someone has written in block letters.

WILL ANDERS IS A KILLER. HE LOST HIS MARBLES AND KILLED HIS ARMY COMMANDING OFFICER AND ESCAPED TO ROCKTON BEFORE THEY LOCKED HIM IN A LOONY BIN.

I stare at those words, my hands shaking with rage. The ones I'm staring at, though, aren't the ones about killing someone.

LOST HIS MARBLES.
BEFORE THEY LOCKED HIM IN A LOONY BIN.

There is such derision in those words, as if a mental breakdown is more damning than murder. The issues Anders suffered explain behavior that is otherwise completely out of character for him. Here, they aren't an explanation. They're an accusation.

He's not only a killer; he's crazy.

"Hey," a voice says behind me.

I spin, slapping the sign to my chest as Anders walks over.

"Uh, okay," he says, his gaze dropping to the paper. "I came to see if you needed help. Do I dare ask what that is? Not another hot-tub petition, I hope."

His lips quirk, but the smile doesn't reach his eyes. "Hmm. Jen didn't want me handling this, and now you're clutching that paper like it's an X-rated photo. If it's me, they better have got my good side."

I don't speak. I can't.

"Casey?" he says. "That look on your face is kinda freaking me out."

I turn the sign around. I don't know what else to do. I just hold it up, mutely.

Anders takes it and reads it. He rocks back on his heels. There's a split second of disbelief in his eyes. Then acceptance. The resolute acceptance of a man who has lived with an ax poised over his head, knowing it must eventually drop.

I know that feeling. There have been times when I wished my ax *would* drop, just so I could stop waiting.

"I'm sorry," I say. My eyes fill with sudden tears, so uncharacteristic that I wonder what that prickling sensation is. "I'm so sorry, Will."

I reach for him, tentatively. I'm not a hugger, and the first sign of rejection will have me stumbling over myself to retreat. But he drops the sign, opens his arms, and I fall into them, wrapping mine around him and hugging fiercely.

"We'll figure this out," I say. "We'll get through it."

"I know."

"I'm just . . ." My throat closes, and I push out the words.

"I'm so sorry. I keep saying that, and it doesn't seem to mean much but—"

His hug cuts me short as he brushes a kiss over my forehead. "It's okay, Case. *I'll* be okay."

A rustle in the trees. We turn to see Marissa. I startle, very aware that I'm in the arms of her lover. Anders only tightens his grip, reminding me we're doing nothing wrong. Then he releases me and steps back.

"Hey," I say.

"Hello," she says, her voice chilly as her gaze moves between us.

"We got some bad news," I say. "Upsetting news and—"

"And it's fine," Anders says. "It's all fine."

His tone challenges Marissa to say otherwise, and I bristle on her behalf. She's in a new relationship with a guy who isn't known for commitment. Of course she's going to be wary.

"Is Eric around?" I say.

"Nope," she says. "Luckily for you, he's still back at the campfire."

"Luckily for me?" It takes a moment to realize what she means. I shake my head. "I would not be the least bit worried if Eric walked in on me hugging Will."

"Ah, so it's that kind of relationship, is it?"

"Oh, for fuck's sake, Mari," Anders says, and there's real anger in his voice. That startles me. Then I realize it's not anger at Marissa. It's for what he just read. Fear and fury zeroing in on the wrong target.

Before I can intercede, he continues, "If you're going to get jealous every time I hug a woman in town, you're going to spend a lot of time being jealous. I get a lot of hugs."

I ease between them. "Something happened tonight, Marissa. Something we need to discuss with Eric right away. Once that's out in the open, this will make a lot more sense."

"I shouldn't need an excuse for—" Anders begins.

I turn a look on him. He bites off the rest, but the anger roils behind his eyes. Then I realize we *can't* let Marissa walk away. She'll hear about the sign, and that should come from Anders. Right now, though, he's in no mood to talk to her. He's not ready to discuss it, either—she's going to ask whether it's true, and he'll need time to figure out how he's going to handle that question.

"Marissa?" I say. "Can I have a moment with Will?"

She blinks at me. "Seriously?"

Anders lets out a Dalton-worthy string of curses. Then he says, "Here, let me make this easy for everyone." He snatches the sign from the ground and holds it up for her. "Someone posted this in the town square."

She reads it. Then her gaze shoots to Anders, anger vanishing in shock. "Someone posted *that*?"

"Yep, and by morning, everyone's going to know about it."

"This is what we're dealing with," I say, my voice steady. "I brought Will here to show him in private, and then I gave him a support hug. That's what you saw."

"But it's not true, right? He didn't . . ." Her gaze goes to Anders. "You didn't . . ."

"Go home, Marissa," he says.

"What? Go *home*? I just found out that my boyfriend might have—"

"Not your boyfriend. Not anymore. I'll make that part easy for you."

Her jaw sets, and I back away fast. I don't need to hear this. Anders waves for me to stay close—he wants us to talk to Dalton together—so I stop after a few paces and turn away. I can still hear them.

Marissa says, "You're cutting me loose so you don't need to explain."

"Right now, I'm not sure an explanation even matters. I'm not sure the truth matters. The problem is the accusation. That shit's gonna stick, and we need to figure out what to do about it. That means me, Casey, Eric, and Phil need to get together and discuss it. That's the priority at the moment."

"Not me," she says.

Anders hisses an exhalation, one that brings him back to himself.

"Yeah," he says. "I'm sorry, but yeah."

"All right, then," she says. "I guess I know where I stand."

Part of me wants to smooth this over. Soften the blow. But honestly, my own annoyance meter rises here. Of course the town takes precedence over the woman he's been dating for a month. Even Dalton needs to weigh his responsibility to me versus Rockton.

That's not what Marissa is feeling, though. It's her versus Anders's friends. I can say I expected better, but that's judgmental. She is understandably unsteady in this new relationship. I'm sure dozens of people have warned her it won't last, that Anders won't stay, that he's just trying something new and he'll revert to form soon enough. I've been keeping out of it. I don't know her well enough to reassure her without sounding like that annoying happily married person, eager to see all her friends paired off.

Still, I'm going to interfere here, just a little. I walk back and say, "I'll need to call a town meeting in the morning to discuss this, but we'll make sure you have the official statement before that, Marissa. You'll know before everyone else does." I glance at Anders.

He sighs, just a little, but nods. "I'll talk to you before that, Mari. I know this is going to be tough on you, too. I'd suggest you let someone walk you home. I can have the militia deliver your breakfast so you don't need to go out."

"I'm not hiding in my apartment, Will."

"And I'm not asking you to. I'm giving you the option." We catch sight of a figure, and Anders calls, "Sebastian?"

A young man jogs over, wolf-dog at his side. "Hey," he says with a grin. "I thought I heard voices. I was trying to sneak past with Raoul so we didn't interrupt. It's his pre-bedtime elimination run."

"Could you do me a favor?" Anders says. "Walk Marissa home?"

"Sure."

"You might get waylaid," Anders says. "There's been . . ." He lifts the sign. "This was posted in the town square."

Sebastian reads it.

"Huh," he says. A moment's pause. "People are upset, I take it?" A wry smile. "Dumb question. Normal people get upset when they think there's a killer in their midst." He looks at Anders. "If you did it, I'm sure you had a reason. If not, then posting that is a really shitty thing. Well, it's shitty either way but . . ." He shrugs. "You know."

Marissa stares at Sebastian as if she's not quite hearing him right. Or he's failing to process what Anders has been accused of. He isn't. We get all kinds in Rockton and, honestly, I trust Sebastian a hell of a lot more than I trust the white-collar criminals who bilked people of their life savings. He knows what he is, and he's committed to fixing it, which is more than I can say for most of them.

Dalton's voice rings out just as Storm bursts through and tackles Raoul. "So the party moved into the forest, huh. You guys find anything dead for me to raise?"

"Just my career as a Rockton law-enforcement officer," Anders calls back. He holds up the sign.

"Fuck," Dalton says.

"That about sums it up," Anders says. "Sebastian, if you could walk Marissa home, please. Eric, Casey, and I have a few things to discuss."

We're in the police station. We considered taking this conversation home, but that could look as if we headed off to bed, ignoring the situation. Better for people to see a light shining in the station window.

When we enter, Dalton goes straight for the desk. He pulls out a sheet of paper, writes a sign of his own, and sticks it on the door.

Meeting in progress. Knock & we'll let you listen in from the cell.

"Not even the 'fucking' cell," Anders says. "You mean business."

Dalton grunts and puts the full kettle over the fire before lighting it.

"Marissa caught me hugging Casey," Anders says. "Possibly also kissing her forehead."

Dalton stops short. "She posted that sign because of it?"

"No, no. The hug came after the sign, but Marissa kinda made a big deal out of it, so I figured you should know, in case she spreads stories."

Dalton snorts. "Any chance that story would drown out this other one? If so, you two better start hugging all over town." He straightens. "Is that seriously Marissa's concern right now?"

"In her defense, she was upset before she learned why I was hugging Will," I say. "I don't think you need to worry she'll say anything."

"Wouldn't be worried if she did. Anyone who'd believe you two are screwing around isn't someone whose opinion means shit to me. I'm a little more worried about this." He picks up the sign. "Fuck."

"Let's focus on who wrote that," I say. "Will's going to need time to figure out how to handle it. We all are. So we'll start with the crime."

"It isn't slander if it's true," Anders murmurs.

I lower myself to the floor beside Storm. There's only one chair inside, and I don't feel like dragging in two from the back porch. "Revealing the details of a person's previous life violates the rules of Rockton. It's on the form I signed before I got in. I am dissuaded from sharing my own details and forbidden from seeking out or sharing the details of others. That makes it a crime." I look at Dalton. "Yes?"

"Yeah. It's not on the books as a law, but fuck, nothing is. We make it up as we go."

"I'd rather not make this up. Any precedent I can use?"

His eyes roll up, accessing the law-enforcement archives. "Had a case maybe ten years ago where a woman told her boyfriend that she came here after her husband killed their kid. When she broke up with the boyfriend, he tried to blackmail her with it. Gene didn't want to pursue it. He figured since she'd been the victim, it didn't matter."

"It mattered because she didn't want to be labeled a victim," I say. "She came here to get away from being the woman whose husband murdered their child. Also, it's no one's damned business."

"Yep," Dalton says. "Gene let me run with it, and I prosecuted the guy. So that's a precedent. Then there was the asshole who left just before you arrived—"

"Oh!" Anders cuts in. "Larry, right?" He looks at me.

"Total asshole. He made a point of getting personal details from people and then sharing them. Eric thought it was a game for him. I argued it was social currency. We shut him down. Charged him with something like violating the expectation of privacy."

"Have there been times when people shared residents' backgrounds and you *didn't* prosecute them?" I ask. "We don't want to seem like we're picking and choosing when to enforce the law."

Dalton shakes his head. "Definitely none in the past five years, which is as long as anyone except me has been here. More often, people share their own stories. There have been a few cases of drunken oversharing, but that happens in the Roc, with witnesses."

"Okay," I say. "So the crime was posting the sign. If the person who had that information felt it was a security threat, they should have come to us."

Anders shakes his head. "They'll argue that Eric might bury it, being my boss."

"Then it could have gone to Phil," I say. "The point is that we agree posting anyone's information is a direct violation of the terms of residency, and therefore I have the right to investigate."

"You do," Dalton says. "No question. As for who knows, though . . ." He looks at Anders.

"No, I haven't got drunk and told anyone. Haven't pillow-talked and told anyone. I drink to forget what happened, not share it. The only people I've talked to about it are you and Casey, and only after Casey figured it out."

"Okay," I say, uncapping my pen. "Eric and I know. Mick had a copy of the journal with Will's page still in it. That's how I found it."

"Because Isabel found the journal after Mick's death," Dalton says. "If there's any chance he knew it was Will, she might too."

"She'll be at the top of my interview list, which I'm sure she expects. I can't see her telling anyone. That leaves Mathias."

"Mathias?" Anders's head jerks up. "I sure as hell never told *him*."

"He has hinted that he knows both our secrets," I say. "As for where he got them, I'd presume the council told him."

"Shit," Anders mutters. "Here I thought the leak was obviously that journal."

I shake my head. "We destroyed both Mick's copy and Eric's."

Dalton nods. "Yeah, finding out Mick got hold of it made me realize I shouldn't be keeping notes."

I lift my notebook. "Nothing in here either. Once we've figured out someone's story, we destroy the evidence. No amount of safekeeping works in Rockton, where hiding something only tells people it's important."

"I'd underestimated that," Dalton says.

"Mick was a cop. He was concerned. But, yes, it's likely that the leak came from his notes. Or someone else got to your journal before you removed Will's pages." I lift a hand. "I know you kept it secure. Mick only got it because he had access to the station."

"I wasn't going to argue. I screwed up, and if that's what caused this, then I'm sure as hell not going to duck the blame."

I tap my pen. "Will was the last person left from your journal, right? As I recall, everyone else in it is gone."

"Yeah, no one's around from those days except Will."

"Lucky me," Anders mutters.

"While it'll be cold comfort to *you*," I say, "at least we don't need to worry about other targets." I snap my book shut. "Okay, that's how we'll handle the investigation. Now the question is how we'll handle the revelation."

"That's up to Will," Dalton says. "He should take some time."

"No need," Anders says. "I already know what I want to do."

THREE

It's morning. The announcement is scheduled for 8 A.M., which is the optimal time for a town meeting of any urgency. Most people won't be at work yet, but they're already up and can't complain we held it too early, hoping for a small turnout. Not that I've ever done that . . .

I would gladly have tackled this with another 6 A.M. "free coffee and pastries" meeting. I suggested it last night but wasn't surprised when Anders vetoed the idea. He's not letting anyone accuse us of trying to bury this in a two-inch column on page six. It's headline news, and we must treat it that way.

We posted notices last night. This morning, the militia do the rounds, employing the town crier method—they walk up to a building and shout the announcement, and whoever didn't catch it can ask a neighbor.

I don't join those rounds—I'd be stopped constantly for questions. Instead, I'm outside the bakery when Devon and Brian come by to open up. When I'd first landed in Rockton, they were relative newcomers themselves. They'd arrived a month apart and moved in together shortly after that. They're still together—a rarity in Rockton relationships—and are due to head back south next month. Both have applied for extensions, and both still expect to get it. They won't. No one does these days.

I haven't told them that. I'm still arguing their case. Still hopeful that the council will reverse course, while knowing I'm reaching the point where hope is sliding into delusion.

When I see the guys walking into work, I brace for the inevitable question about their extension. Instead, Devon says, "Early town meeting?"

"Eight A.M." I hold up a sign that says the bakery is closed until nine, but free coffee and pastries will be available at the meeting. "Yes?"

Devon smiles. "Stick it up, and we'll switch to catering mode."

"Lot of signs going up these days," Brian says.

I must tense, because he grimaces. "Sorry. That sounded snarkier than I intended. We heard about the one last night."

"I will refrain from asking whether it's true," Devon says as we walk through the bakery rear door. "Though I'm glad to be closed until post-meeting, so I don't spend the next two hours telling everyone I don't know any more than they do."

Devon has a reputation as the best source of information in town. Some would call it gossip, but he draws a line between innocent chitchat and malicious rumor. It's fine to say Jane was seen moving her stuff into John's place. It's not fine to say Jane is allegedly messing around with Jill while living with John.

"Will's going to speak at the meeting," I say. "My concern is who posted that sign."

Brian pulls carafes from the shelf as Devon starts up the industrial coffee machine. The bakery has some of the few solar panels in town. Solar power may seem the obvious way to go, especially during long summer days, but the reflective surfaces interfere with the structural camouflage that hides us from passing planes. Minimal panels only, mostly for large-scale cooking operations like this one. They'll start the coffee with the electric brewer and then switch to fire-heated water when demand subsides after the morning rush.

It's only after they've gotten the stove and coffee maker started that Devon says, "I haven't heard anything about who posted it yet, but I'm sure I will. I'll pass it all on. I wouldn't want anyone knowing why I'm here, either. It's not *that* sort of thing, but it's still no one's business."

Brian grunts his agreement as he sets out ingredients for baking. He's the real baker, and I suspect that was his down-south job. Devon is the prep guy and barista. He sets about tending to the coffee and grabbing things for Brian as we talk.

I lean against the counter. "Something tells me 'none of their business' won't apply in Will's case. But we'll work it out. I just want to talk to whoever did this, in case they know other stories."

A little fear works in my favor here. I'm not going after the person who hurt my friend; I'm protecting the privacy of all.

I continue, "Do people ever ask for that kind of news? Whether you know what brought people to Rockton?"

Devon's nose scrunches. "Yeah. Oh, they always have an excuse. They just started seeing someone or they switched jobs or moved into a new apartment, and is there anything they should know about their new girlfriend, coworker, neighbor? I shut that down fast. I remind them that no one's here because they did anything dangerous so . . ." He pauses and glances my way. "Well, that's what I did tell them. Not so sure that's the truth anymore."

He says it in a level tone. No accusation. I still feel the accusation, because it's legitimate. People came here to escape something, often violence, and now they need to worry that others have come here to escape the consequences of *committing* violence?

I don't answer. He doesn't seem to expect one, just checks the progress of the coffee.

Then he continues, "You're also going to ask whether I've heard any of those stories—what brought people here. Sometimes, yes. There are people who don't hide their reason. There are people who drop enough hints that they might as well scream 'I embezzled company funds.' There are people who get drunk and confess that they double-crossed their drug dealer. Line the locals up, and I could make an educated guess at stories for a quarter of them."

"None of those ever suggested violence?"

He pauses. Then he sighs. "Not many, but some, and no, I didn't automatically dismiss my suspicions while wearing my Pollyanna rose-tinted glasses and chanting 'no one here has done anything bad.' I know we have rotten apples, whether they snuck in or bought their way in. I also know Will isn't one of those rotten apples. If he did this, well . . ." Devon shrugs. "I won't pretend I'm not salivating for the full story, but I'll reserve judgment until I get it."

"Have you ever heard anyone talk about why Will's here?"

"Never. You guys are different."

I frown. "Different how?"

Devon shrugs. "You've come to do a job. Like people who go to work on the oil rigs for two years and take home a pot of cash for it. We figure that applies to all the professionals—you, your sister, Will, Isabel, all the essential-services workers. Even Mathias. Everyone grumbles about why he gets a chalet when he's only the butcher." Devon snorts. "Only the butcher. Right.

Guy's obviously a shrink watching the rest of us for signs of isolation-induced mental breakdowns. So, no, people don't ask what Will's here for. They figure he's just doing a job."

I nod, and he can interpret that however he likes. Then we chat a little more before I steal a thermos of coffee and head off to find Dalton.

Down south, I was one of those annoying people who showed up for a 2:00 P.M. meeting at 1:55 and expected it to start by two. I have no patience with those who think "two o'clock meeting" actually means you start hauling your ass out of your desk chair at two and maybe take a bathroom break on the way to the meeting. It's a matter of training people. If they know it never starts on time, they have no incentive for arriving on time.

Today, I'm climbing that podium a couple of minutes early, as if we can somehow zoom through before the late arrivals make it.

You snooze, you lose.

Except the only thing they'll lose is the chance to hear the story firsthand. The version they get will be the warped one, several iterations down the telephone line. I don't want that. So while I'm up there early, I wait until exactly eight before I begin.

If there's one advantage to the town shutting down, it's that fewer incoming residents means less time spent explaining protocol for new arrivals. No one has arrived since the last two meetings, so I can launch straight in without mentioning the coffee and pastries or asking people to hold questions or reminding them that they won't be counted as late for their shifts.

I go straight into the story of what happened last night.

Someone posted a sign right here on the movie screen, and this is that sign.

Hold up the paper. Read the paper. Make damn sure no one can later claim they couldn't see it themselves.

When I'm done, I turn the podium over to Anders.

He doesn't waste a moment on preamble. "You all want to know whether I did what it says on that sign. Whether I shot my commanding officer. The short answer is yes."

He waits for the inevitable exclamation to subside. It does, quickly, because everyone knows this isn't the end of the story, and they don't want to miss a word.

"I would be happier ending my confession there," he says. "Yes, I did it. Now let's deal with that. But if I do, Casey will get back up here and fill in the rest. Eric will remind me that it is my duty, as law enforcement, to take your concerns seriously and therefore provide the entire story. Since I'd rather not have them defend me . . ."

He takes a deep breath. "Here's the story. These aren't excuses. There are none. The gist of what that sign says is true. I killed my CO. As for the mental breakdown part, yes, I was having trouble coping with the stress. I was on medication. It was causing side effects that concerned me."

He catches my eye. "Casey will want me to point out that I mentioned those concerns to my doctor. I should have stopped taking the medication but . . ."

He shrugs. "As Eric always says, I'm a good soldier. I do as I'm told, and I trust those in charge. I took the medication despite my concerns. One night I dreamed I shot my commanding officer. As you can guess, it wasn't a dream. I sleepwalked in and shot him in what the doctors called a fugue state."

Someone grumbles, and someone else snorts. Dalton and I both turn sharply, visually identifying the offenders and mentally noting names. Anders only glances their way and shrugs.

"Yep, that sounds like an excuse," he says. "Which is why I'm uncomfortable giving it."

"Mental illness is never an excuse," Isabel calls from her porch. "It's an explanation, and anyone who cares for a mini-lecture on what Will is describing can join me at the Roc an hour before opening. I'll even throw in a free drink." She pauses. "*One* free drink."

A chuckle ripples through the crowd as people relax.

"The point," Anders says, "is that I did kill a commanding officer, and I had no motivation for doing so. This wasn't a movie, where I heroically shot a tyrant. I temporarily lost my mind."

"Lost your mind *because* of medication," Isabel says. "Which has not been a concern since that time."

I catch her eye and shake my head. I know she's trying to help, but Anders has asked us to stand down. Everyone knows we're Anders's friends, and having any of us defend him doesn't help. We need to trust residents to work this out for themselves.

"That's the sum of it," Anders says. "Now I'm sure you have questions . . ."

"Let me get this straight," Conrad says, moving forward. "You were a soldier who murdered his CO and fled to Rockton? Escaped justice?"

"He never said that," someone else says. "It happened in his past. He killed his CO accidentally—"

"Accidentally? He walked in and shot him."

"He wasn't in his right mind."

"Is he now? What if he snaps again?" Conrad looks up at Dalton. "I demand Deputy Anders be removed from his position and shipped out immediately."

Dalton surges forward, but I grab his arm.

"We will consider all possibilities," I say. "We'd like residents to take a bit of time to digest this and—"

"Then you'll form a committee to devise a poll, another committee to conduct the poll, a third to interpret the results, and maybe a task force or two thrown in there, too, so by the time you declare Anders unfit for duty, we'll all be gone and no one will be left to give a shit?"

"No," I say slowly. "We're asking for a couple of days to investigate—"

"Investigate what? Find the whistleblower and ship *them* out before we can ask more?"

"Let Casey talk," Devon says. "She's trying to answer your questions and you keep interrupting."

"You got a problem with that?" Conrad turns on Devon. "Sticking up for your friends? Or hoping this all blows over before *your* real past comes out?"

"My real past would put you to sleep."

"That's not what I heard. Got caught with your hand in the cookie jar, I hear. And by cookie jar, I mean 'the pants of a twelve-year-old boy.' "

"What the hell?" Devon says. "That is—"

"Homophobia," says a French-accented voice as Mathias strolls forward. "Pure and simple homophobia. Pedophilia is a common accusation leveled against gay men by the wretchedly ignorant."

"Who the hell asked you, old man?" Conrad says. "We can guess what you're here for. You're a little too handy with that butcher's knife."

"Many years of practice carving up my victims," Mathias says. "Most of which were never found. If you cut the pieces small enough—"

"That's enough," I say. "Don't get him going, please."

"How about you?" It's Jolene this time, piping up from the back. "What did you do, Casey? Shot some kid, right? Pretended you thought his cell phone was a gun?"

"Casey and Will were brought to Rockton for their policing skills," Isabel says.

"Which includes shooting innocent tourists," Jolene says.
"Two months ago, you *both* shot that woman from the woods."

"You mean the bitch who tried to murder a resident?" Jen
walks from the crowd. "You want to accuse Casey and Isabel
and Eric of being Will's friend? Well, I'm no one's friend, and
I still call bullshit on you and Conrad. Deputy Anders confessed. He didn't have to. It's not like anyone can look it up
on the internet. He confessed, and I accept his explanation."

"Why? What'd you do?"

"Fuck you." She looks between Conrad and Jolene and
then up at me. "Can we lock these two idiots in a cell and let
the adults finish this conversation?"

"No," a voice says quietly from the back. It's Gloria, a shy
woman who has never caused any trouble. "I have concerns,
too. I'd like to hear everyone's opinion. I don't think this is
the time for silencing voices."

A few others agree, and when anyone voices support for Anders, Conrad or Jolene turns on them with "And what did *you*
do?," leaving only Anders's allies daring to take his side.

"This isn't working," I murmur to Dalton.

"Shut it down," he says.

And we do.

We've retreated to the Roc. At first, it was the police force
plus Phil and Isabel, but others have trickled in. April. Petra.
Kenny. Sebastian, slipping in cautiously, as if we might kick
him out. Even Mathias joins us, though he pretends he's just
keeping an eye on Sebastian.

"So that wasn't what I expected," Anders says. "I didn't think anyone was going to congratulate me for telling the truth, but I did hope it'd win me a few brownie points."

"Then you do not understand human nature," Mathias says as he sips his coffee. "You are a popular man in town. You are respected. You are liked. You have many gifts that others lack, and they will smile at you and be friendly while they must, but once you show weakness?"

"Like when a celebrity stumbles and people gleefully pile on," I say.

"It doesn't help that he's a Black man," Sebastian says.

Everyone turns to look at him.

"What?" Sebastian says. "Am I wrong?"

"You are not," Mathias says. "Even those who would insist race is not a factor will consider it subconsciously. It appears to reinforce bias. William is a Black man, therefore he is violent. He is a Black man, therefore he should not hold a position of authority."

"Well, I'm not going to lay all the blame there," Anders says. "But yeah, it doesn't help. As usual."

"As to my original point," Mathias says. "There are those—a minority but a vocal one—who will be, as Casey said, gleeful for the chance to pull William from his pedestal. They have discovered, too, that the situation provides the perfect accusation against his supporters."

"If you support him, then it's because you've done something, too," I say.

The door opens, and Jen walks in. She stops and looks across our faces.

"You guys do realize people are talking about this meeting," she says. "They've noticed every face that came in here, and you've all joined the Friends of Will Anders shit list. They think you're conspiring, and they aren't going to listen to a single word you now say in his defense."

"Well, then, if you were telling the truth on that podium, maybe you should leave," I say. "Give him one antagonist supporter."

She snorts. "Fuck that. I spoke out in his defense, so they've already labeled me a fangirl." She looks at Anders. "Your actual fangirl, Marissa, was conspicuously absent out there."

"I talked to her earlier. She's digesting it."

"Who leaked the information?" Sebastian says. "I'm not exactly eager to have my own past come out."

Petra rolls her eyes. "What'd you do, kid? Jaywalk?"

"We don't know where the leak came from," I say. "But understandably residents are going to be concerned about that, too, so if no one minds, I'm going to slip out and start chasing leads." I glance over at Isabel.

She gets to her feet. "That would be my cue. As the local bar owner, I will be at the top of Casey's suspect list. Phil? Please lock up after the meeting. I'll be at the station."

FOUR

"Yes, I read Mick's notes," Isabel says as I close the station door behind us. "You already know that. In retrospect, I remember reading Will's story. It was under another name, of course, and I never made the connection to Will. While I'm not above blackmail, I like and respect Will, and I think he's good for Rockton."

She takes the chair as I perch on the desk. "That's my declaration," she says. "I'm not certain how to prove it, though."

"Has Phil ever discussed residents with you?"

Her perfectly manicured brows shoot up. "If you can imagine any circumstance where Phil gossips about residents, then your imagination far outstrips my own."

"I don't mean gossip. I mean has he said anything that suggests he knows residents' backgrounds?"

"Ah, so you don't know whether he even *has* that information."

"He does in some cases. I'm not sure that extends to everyone."

"Then I would suggest you ask him, rather than place his

lover in a very awkward position. You don't trust him to give a straight answer. He will, Casey. I will also answer the question because I can say, without hesitation, that he is one of the most circumspect people I know. I suspect he knows most of the backstories, but he hasn't so much as suggested he knows mine. He will not be your leak. Nor am I."

"But someone else could have found Mick's notes and figured it out."

"Who? The only person still here from those days is Mathias."

"He's next on my list but, yes, I know I'm grasping at straws."

"We both realize this is a waste of time, right?" Isabel says.

"Because Will's the only person still in Rockton from Eric's list? No one else is in danger, which makes my investigation smell like revenge, rather than preventive policing."

She shakes her head. "That's not what I mean. We know who did this, Casey. Who's behind it, at least."

I lift my pen from the notebook.

"You don't want to seem paranoid," she says. "But in this case someone really is out to get us. We've established that."

I set down my pen and exhale. "You think the council is behind the leak."

"If you tell me you haven't considered this, I'll be insulted that you think I'd buy such nonsense. Also insulted that you don't trust me enough to discuss it, but the wound to my intelligence always stings more."

"Yes, we've considered it. Obviously. And yes, it feels paranoid."

"So you're eliminating the obvious suspect to avoid seeming paranoid?"

"The council may be the ultimate source of the leak, but they didn't write that sign. I need to find out who did that and then see whether it leads to the council."

"It will."

When I don't answer, she fixes me with a look. "Really, Casey? The council has realized you know we're shutting down, even if they're pretending it's temporary attrition. They've tipped their hand, and they need to hurry this along. What better way to do that than to undermine Eric's authority by disbanding the police force?"

"All the more reason for me to find who is behind this."

"Whoever wrote that sign is getting their information directly from the council. There's no point tracking down potential sources in Rockton." Her eyes narrow. "Which you knew. This was about getting me to independently voice your own theory. Making sure you weren't being paranoid."

"You'd make an excellent detective, Iz."

She mouths a profanity at me. Then she settles back in her seat. "I suppose I should be flattered that you value my intelligence so highly."

"I do. Also, it'd seem very odd if I *didn't* question you first, you being the keeper of secrets."

She snorts. "That'd be Mathias. I am but a student of the master."

"That's why he's next on my list." I close my notebook. "I also do need to keep other sources in mind, in case the council isn't behind this. Imagine if I blamed them, and it turned out that the actual culprit was someone who found Mick's notes?"

"Understood. Eliminate the obvious first. Ultimately, though, since anyone could have found those hypothetical notes, it doesn't narrow down your search."

I smile. "But it does give me an excuse for questioning anyone I like, without the council realizing I'm looking for their spy."

★ ★ ★

A council spy. That should make it easy. They have three in town that we've already identified. The problem is that all three were in that meeting with us earlier: Mathias, Petra, and Anders himself.

Dalton flipped them long ago, though he'd say it was the town that flipped them. They came here promising to keep an eye on the sheriff, only to realize the true threat to Rockton is the council.

Even if I didn't trust their loyalty, I can't imagine any of them being behind this. Anders certainly didn't expose his own crime. Petra's true allegiance is to her grandmother, who is firmly against Rockton's closure.

Mathias is always the wild card in any situation. The one least wedded to our cause. Still, he wouldn't do anything as gauche as post a sign in the square, nor as ignorant as those mental-illness insults.

So who is the spy? Whoever wrote that sign, and that's the way I need to approach this investigation. Find out who posted the sign.

I let Phil handle the council. One of their residents has been identified as a killer, and they must be notified. Phil is better equipped to handle this, because he knows the council lets in less-than-innocent residents.

They tell Phil to convey the message that Anders's skill set outweighed any other concerns.

The council isn't happy that Anders admitted to his crime. They wish they'd been consulted first. As for what should be done about it, they aren't demanding his head on a platter. Or his ass on a plane. They will reserve judgment and see how we handle this unfolding situation. They hope we can win back our residents' trust.

We have twenty-four hours.

I spend the day chasing leads while watching the portcullis slowly close in front of me. At first, people come forward— those who support Anders and want us to find the perpetrator. They tell me who they saw out last night, who has a grudge against Anders, who has expressed far too much interest in resident backstories.

But I'm not the only one making the rounds. So are Conrad and Jolene, who seem to have teamed up as the opposition. They've brought in others, too, like-minded individuals who just want to see justice done and clean up a corrupt system. Bullshit. Mathias is dead right here, at least for Conrad and Jolene. They're in this for their own petty reasons, and the at-tention they're garnering doesn't help.

If you're slavering to bring down a popular guy, it follows that you envy his popularity. If bringing him down also means building yourself up? Win-win.

While Dalton and Kenny and Jen canvass for potential leads, Team Conrad-and-Jolene are getting the word out— the word being that if you're helping my investigation, you must want the whistleblower caught before they expose *your* secrets.

Jen's suggestion to lock them in the cell becomes increas-ingly tempting. Yet it would only suggest we're silencing pro-test. Normally, we could at least find ways to stop them from interfering with my investigation. That doesn't work when the person under threat is one of our own. Without the option of bringing in outside investigators, I spend my day racing against time, speaking to as many people as I can before they decide to stop talking.

It's nearly midnight, twenty-four hours since that sign went up in the town square, and I'm no closer to finding out who did it. I've interviewed every witness who'll talk. No one saw who posted the sign.

Whoever did it picked the perfect time. Petra left the Roc at eleven and says the screen was empty. I suspect the sign went up around eleven thirty, when those lingering at the Roc didn't plan to leave until Isabel kicked them out at twelve. A brief window of time when the streets would be empty. Then one last burst of activity when the Roc closed, during which someone was bound to spot the sign.

I've spent the last couple of hours dusting for prints while expecting nothing. Paper isn't the best source for fingerprints, and a half dozen people handled the sign after it was taken down. I should have been more careful about that. At the time, I'd been focused too much on the message and too little on finding who posted it.

When I do manage to lift prints, they're all from people I know touched it: Isabel, me, and Anders. Either the poster wore gloves or their prints didn't adhere.

The paper is cheap all-purpose white sheets, bought by the ream in Dawson and sold in our general store. The marker used to write the message is standard black.

Phil has made improvements in the inventory system, which means cracking down on store staff whose idea of inventory control is to make daily notes of what they remember selling. Itemized receipts in duplicate are the new standard. I have a list of those who bought paper or markers in the last few months. That doesn't include everyone who bought it earlier and has a stash at home, which is probably everyone in town. Nor does it account for the other businesses that purchase it or the fact that you can grab a few sheets of paper free at the community center.

Lifting footprints from the scene is out of the question. By the time I got there, the entire area had been trampled. I still checked last night, but it'd been a mess of smudged prints.

The better question is how someone got the sign on the movie screen, eight feet off the ground. Whoever posted it must have brought a chair or step stool. But who'd risk lugging something like that through town? Even at near midnight, it'd be noticeable.

I'm at the scene of the crime, pacing as I try to figure out how the sign got up there. The podium is nearby, but it's fixed to the ground. There's a basketball net. A couple of trees, too far to be used. Nothing that could be easily dragged over and climbed on.

Am I sure that's what they did? What if the tool was something used to reach up instead?

Was the sign haphazardly affixed? Or firmly taped on?

And what difference does it make, really? I'm grasping at straws here, and they aren't even solid straws.

As I wander through town, I tell myself I'm working the case. This is close to the same time of night. What do I see? What do I hear? Who's out and about? Whose apartment light is on close enough that they might have seen something?

There aren't many lights. People adjust to the patterns of sunlight in the north. A month ago, they'd have been awake, even out on porches, taking in the midnight sun. Now they've gone to bed. When I do see a flicker of distant light, it comes from a chalet on the edge of town. The small houses are our premier living quarters, a perk for essential-services workers. This particular chalet, though, should be dark and empty.

It's Anders's.

I'd asked Anders to sleep over at our place. Last night, he'd agreed without comment, still lost in the shock of that sign. Tonight, he'd argued, but Dalton insisted. Anders might be on light duty, but we can't function with a police force of two, meaning he needs to be well rested in case of an emergency. Or that made a good excuse. The truth was that neither of us wants Anders being alone right now.

Just a few days ago, he was telling me how good he felt, how stable and steady his life had become. He had close friends, a job he enjoyed, a town he considered home, and the beginnings of a solid relationship with a woman he really liked.

He's already lost Marissa. He told her the truth before the town meeting, and she agreed he was right to end it. That'd been a blow, as much as he tried to pretend otherwise.

So he's spending the night at our place. He's there now, with Dalton and Storm, and if I squint across town, I can see light in our living room. I'd popped by there an hour ago, and they'd been deep in conversation, so I'd slipped out again.

Now there's a light at Anders's place. A light on the move, meaning someone carrying a candle or lantern.

It could be Anders popping back to grab something he forgot. Yet that light looks dim, as if stifled, and he has no reason to do that in his own home.

I flick off my own light and head toward the chalet.

Someone is definitely moving through Anders's chalet. Searching for something?

The light has disappeared, but when I circle around back,

the door is ajar. I creep up to it. Before I slip in, my hand drops to my gun. Then I hesitate.

Having my gun in hand is always the right move for entering into a dark and unknown situation. Even in Rockton, where we don't need to worry about anyone opening fire, we take our guns out as a warning.

Sure, you thought it was okay to break into the general store for a pack of matches—you'd have repaid them in the morning—but what if we mistook you for a bear?

After what happened today, though, an unholstered gun could be mistaken for a show of police power. Local law enforcement threatening an innocent resident who just popped by to tell Anders they support him.

I leave the gun in my holster and ease open the back door. It's quiet inside. I slip in and shut the door behind me.

I keep my flashlight in hand as a potential weapon, but I leave the light off. Enough illumination shines through the windows for me to see. All of the chalets also follow the same blueprint. I could move through Anders's with my eyes closed.

The back door opens into the kitchen. A visual sweep tells me it's empty. I slide out of my shoes and creep forward in stocking feet. When a board creaks overhead, I stop. Another creak, paired with a soft footfall.

I continue out of the kitchen and into the living room. The stairs are to my left. Before I turn that way, I peer around the living space. This is the biggest room in the small house, and even the furniture arrangement is similar to ours—sofa to my right, chairs across from it, and a fireplace on the far wall. Anders has a coffee table where we have a bearskin rug. When I notice that dark shape, I think, *Oh, right, the coffee table.* Then I realize there's something lumpy at the base.

I squint, but the window light hits the room wrong, casting

the table into shadow. I take a step that way. Something protrudes across the floor.

An arm. I'm seeing someone's arm.

A figure lies beside the table, half hidden behind it.

I ease back on my heels. The figure isn't moving. Do they see me? Do they think they're hidden?

No, if they were trying to hide, their arm wouldn't be splayed across the floor.

It isn't Anders, come home and jumped by an intruder. The light brown skin confirms that.

Someone has broken into Anders's chalet. Someone who is currently upstairs. And there's a second person motionless on the floor.

I don't rush over to help. Even if I did think it was a victim, I'd need to secure the scene first. With my gaze fixed on the supposedly unconscious figure, I reverse until I reach the base of the stairs.

I climb the steps sideways, gaze swinging between the prone figure and the darkness upstairs. When I'm at the top, I pause to consider my options. The chalets have three upstairs areas. Bedroom, bathroom, storage. A tiny hall connects the three. I need to swing around to face the other direction, while not forgetting the person downstairs.

As soon as I'm where I need to be, something rattles in the bedroom. The intruder is going through Anders's things, drawers opening, objects inside shuffling and shifting. I lift my flashlight, ready to flick it on as soon as I'm through the doorway.

One step, two steps—

A floorboard creaks behind me. My brain screams that I've forgotten the person downstairs, but I haven't. This creak comes from the storage closet.

I spin, but the intruder is already lunging from the closet. Hands slam me into the wall. I recover fast and smash my heavy flashlight into a dark jaw. I catch a glimpse of a face and see only a black mask.

The figure stumbles back. I kick, and they hit the ground with a masculine "oomph." Then someone slams into my left shoulder.

The intruder in the bedroom.

I swing, but the one on the floor grabs my leg and yanks it from under me. I manage to hit the second figure with the flashlight and then I kick.

I'm reaching for my gun when a blade stabs me in the leg. A flash of pain. A fist behind my knee.

I stumble. Hands shove at me as I fight them off, and a memory ignites. Me in an alley, falling under a rain of blows and kicks. I lash out, but these blows aren't an attack—they're a defense, my attackers shoving me aside as they make their escape.

A hand grabs my shoulder and elbows hard enough that I spin, losing my balance, that pain in my leg buckling my knee. By the time I get turned around, they're already clambering down the stairs.

I pull my gun and take off after them. I'm at the bottom of the stairs when the figure by the coffee table rises. I catch the movement and spin.

"Hands up! Now!"

The figure continues rising unsteadily. A face turns toward mine, brown hair hanging over it. A slender hand brushes the hair back, and I'm about to repeat my order when I see Marissa's face.

"Casey?" she says, her voice slurred. "Where's Will?"

Shit.

I tell Marissa I'll be right back. I'm already in flight, already racing toward the back of the house.

Marissa calls after me. I ignore her. I fly out the rear door and . . .

And there's no one in sight.

FIVE

I still go after them. Try to, at least. I run around the front of the house and look for signs of movement in the dark streets. Seeing none, I jog into the forest behind the chalet. There I listen for the crash of escape.

Nothing.

In this darkness, they could be hiding ten feet away. I need to get Storm and track them, but Marissa is in the doorway, groggily calling after me.

I get her to lean on me, and I take her to April as quickly as I can. I ask my sister not to release Marissa until I've returned. April doesn't let me get away that easily. She insists on checking my leg. The pain hasn't let me forget that I've been stabbed, but it's not slowing me down any more than my old leg injuries.

"There is blood *dripping* down your leg, Casey," she says when I grumble.

She says more than that, but I tune it out until I get the magic words.

"You seem fine," she says. "But come back as soon as you're done so I can reassess and clean—"

I'm already running for home. I'm halfway there when I spot Dalton and Storm. I change direction and sprint their way.

"I lost track of time," Dalton calls as I draw near. "You were counting on that, weren't you? Letting you work into the wee hours of the morning. Should have at least insisted you take the dog—"

He stops, as if I'm finally close enough for him to see the blood. "Casey?"

"It's a scratch," I say. "April's looked at it. I foiled a break-in at Will's. I lost the intruders. I need Storm."

If he answers, I don't hear it. I'm already jogging back to Anders's place with Storm at my side. Dalton calls that he'll warn Anders and then conduct his own tracking while I handle Storm.

Two years ago, Dalton bought Storm for me with the excuse that Rockton needed a tracking dog. Newfoundlands are hardly world-renowned trackers—they just happen to be my favorite breed.

Only later did I realize that even saying Rockton needed a tracking dog far oversold the matter. We already have Dalton. Between the two, they cover all the bases. Storm follows scents while Dalton tracks the visual signs I'd miss. A scuffed print here. A broken twig there. That spot where, if you look closely, you can see that the undergrowth parted as someone ran through.

The biggest advantage to using Storm is that no one can accuse her of framing them. Also, people trust a tracking dog over a human tracker. Everyone's seen movies where the dog tracks a month-old scent through a snowstorm and finds the missing hiker. When it comes to dog noses, people truly do believe in magic.

Working independently, Dalton and Storm arrive at the

same destination: Conrad's door. The two intruders ran through the woods. They stopped about twenty feet away and hid in the bushes when I came out. Once I was busy helping Marissa, they continued on and circled the town, exiting near Phil's chalet and then weaving through the shadows to Conrad's place.

With the trail clear and fresh, Storm gets there first. I hear Dalton not far behind, and I wait for him to arrive. When he sees where the trail leads, he snorts.

"Didn't need trackers for that," he mutters.

"No, but it's good to have supporting data. I'll suggest I talk to him, and you join me afterward. Give Storm all the credit."

He pats the dog's head. "Agreed."

I set Storm back on the trail and follow it to Conrad's door. Being a dentist gives him an edge when it comes to residences. That's the true recognition of his status here and our appreciation for the work he does. He may spend most of his time stocking shelves, but his dental skills earn him half a duplex, while his fellow shelf stockers live in apartments. He also gets extra credits, and I can see he's put them to use. He has a custom-made porch chair with quilted cushions and a side table. There's even an empty wine glass left on the table, alongside a brand-new hardcover novel. Maybe he just forgot them outside, but it feels staged to me—the Rockton equivalent of parking your Mercedes on the front lawn.

I climb the steps and knock on his door. I need to knock three times before he opens the door, rubbing his eyes and yawning.

"Detective?" he says through another very fake yawn. "What are you doing here at . . . ?" He lifts his arm and blinks at it, as if expecting his watch to appear.

Anger flares as I remember Marissa unconscious on Anders's floor. I want to tell him to cut the shit and get his ass down to the station. I want to shoulder past, check his bedroom and prove he wasn't asleep. That won't help. It took three knocks before he answered because he was racing around setting the scene. If I barge into his room, I'll find his bed unmade, every sign indicating he just left it, and that will not help my case at all.

"It's one in the morning," I say. "There was a break-in at Deputy Anders's place."

His face screws up, overdoing the confusion by fifty percent. "What does that have to do with me?"

"Storm followed the intruder's scent from his back door to your front one."

He crosses his arms and leans against the frame. "Convenient. Deputy Anders is revealed to be a killer, I voice my concerns, and suddenly I'm being accused of breaking into his place. On the word of your *dog.*"

So much for no one being able to accuse Storm of framing them.

I look at Conrad. He's in his late forties, tall and thin, with glasses and receding brown hair. A slight paunch. Otherwise trim and tidy, with the air of a middle-aged professional, a guy you'd trust to work on your teeth and not overcharge you too much for the service.

That's the image he projects. Yet if you cross him, he gets this glitter in his eye, the malicious ugliness of a man who's tired of being dismissed as a nice guy, a man who wants you to know he's more dangerous than he looks. Is he? That remains to be seen, but in my experience, that gleam usually means he *thinks* he's a lot more dangerous than he actually is.

I wouldn't be surprised if he's the one who cut my leg. Even with two big men against one small woman, they'd hightailed it out as soon as my fists and feet started flying.

Speaking of blows, I recall the one I landed to his jaw. That will leave a bruise. I don't see a mark on Conrad's face, which means if he was one of the guys in the house, he *is* the one who stabbed me.

At the thought, my leg throbs, and I shift my weight until it stops. I don't need the reminder that this guy gleefully stabbed me. It'll bias my interview.

"My dog is a trained tracker," I say. "I invite you to come out and watch her follow the trail back to Deputy Anders's place."

"Because you trained her to do that. You'll give her commands to pretend she's sniffing the ground straight from my place to his."

"That'd be a helluva trick." Dalton's voice cuts through the night as he ambles toward the house. "Can we do that, Detective Butler? Maybe train Storm to plant evidence, too? Save you from actually needing to investigate."

Conrad shrinks back before realizing he's doing it. He straightens fast, his jaw setting. Guys like Conrad are smart enough to realize they're intimidated by Dalton. They also need to prove they're not, which means getting their back up every time Dalton is near.

"Storm *wouldn't* walk straight to Deputy Anders's place," I say, "because you didn't. You and your companion cut a winding trail, which she will demonstrate."

"My companion?" He steps back. "Come in and find that person, please. I'd love to know who my partner in crime is."

"If you do not wish to watch Storm follow the trail, then we will have independent corroboration."

"By who? One of your buddies?"

"We will provide a list for you to choose from—"

"I walked around the perimeter of the town earlier today. Unless you've changed the rules, that isn't a crime. I entered over there." He points. "Which may be near Deputy Anders's place. Not like I know where he lives. I entered there and walked over there." He points in the other direction. "Then I returned home."

"Huh," Dalton says. "First you blame the dog for framing you. Now, if she did find a trail, it's because you went for a walk."

"I forgot that. It's one in the morning, Sheriff. I can't be expected to think straight. You're free to get your 'independent corroboration' but if it does suggest a trail, I've provided the reason."

"All right then," I say. "Eric? Would you mind getting a witness while I have a look around Conrad's place?"

"You got a warrant?" Conrad says, moving to block the doorway as Dalton leaves.

"We do," I say. "It's the paper you signed when you came to Rockton, which acknowledges that we have the right to enter or search your quarters at any time."

"I don't remember that clause." He waves toward the station. "Go get it."

"Sure," I say. "I'll run and get that and give you time to hide whatever you wish to hide. You may escort me to the station—"

"Forget it. I'm not letting you in because I just cleaned and you're dripping blood. You'll make a mess of my floors, and I sure as hell don't want you sitting on my sofa."

I tamp down a flare of outrage and look at my leg. "The bleeding's stopped. I won't sit down, and it'll be fine. When I find who did this, though, they definitely owe me a new pair of jeans. These are ruined. That's the worst of it. Barely a scratch underneath. Guy gave me a little scratch and then ran like a scared rabbit."

He flushes, and that erases any doubt about who stabbed me.

"On second thought," I say, "let's wait for Eric to find that witness. I have a feeling if I locate any evidence, you'll claim I planted it. So why don't we both stay right here until they're done checking the trail, and then they can corroborate my search as well."

"Fine. Let me get properly dressed first."

"Nah, you're decent. Stay where I can see you until we have our witness."

Our witness is just a regular resident Dalton found slipping back from his lover's place. Poor guy nearly had a heart attack thinking he was being rousted for . . . Well, I don't want to know what he'd been doing that he thought might get him in trouble. Point is that we have ourselves an independent witness. He verifies Storm's work and then comes inside to watch mine.

I find a black balaclava in the closet. Conrad claims it's his standard-issue winter wear and he hasn't worn it in months. I bag it.

I also find dark clothing shoved into the laundry basket. The shirt has splotches of what looks like blood on the sleeve. Ah, yes, Conrad recalls cutting himself shaving this morning. I bag that, too, and tell him I'll be testing it.

"Knock yourself out," he says. "It's my blood."

He thinks I'm bluffing, that I wouldn't send it for DNA testing to solve a mere break-in. He's right. Except I don't need DNA testing. I'll make sure it's blood first. Then I can test for blood type. If it matches my own and doesn't match his, then it's evidence against him, even without the DNA.

I check his shoes and find damp clots of mud. He says he forgot he'd also been out for a another walk just before bed. Guy seems to take a lot of walks, considering I've never seen him do more than travel from point A to B.

I check drawers in his bedroom, bath, and kitchen, looking for what cut my leg. I don't see the knife. Whatever he used, he isn't stupid enough to shove it back into the drawer with blood on the blade. Most likely it was a pocketknife. Everyone is issued one. I ask for his. He tells me he lost it.

Yes, he's blocking me. Inwardly smirking about it, too. I see that from the gleam in his eyes. This is the truth of policing, though, whether it's down south or in Rockton. I can find all the circumstantial evidence in the world. I can have my dog locate a trail from his house to the crime scene. Without an eyewitness or irrefutable evidence, I'm screwed.

Even those things are mostly useful for convincing a suspect that *he's* screwed and should cut a deal. That won't happen with Conrad. I could have five people who saw him flee Anders's house, bloody knife in hand, and he'd claim it was a mistake and force me to decide exactly how far I want to push this.

"Marissa didn't do anything wrong," I say. "She was hit over the head and left unconscious for being in the wrong place at the wrong time."

I don't know what I hope to accomplish with this. He won't be seized with guilt and confess. I guess I'm just hoping he has enough humanity to feel bad about what he did to Marissa. That he'll realize breaking into Anders's place had unexpected consequences for an innocent person.

"Yep," he says. "She's a good woman. She doesn't deserve any of this. Doesn't deserve to find out her boyfriend is a killer. Doesn't deserve to have people whispering about her, wondering whether she knew. Doesn't deserve to get knocked out for being at his place. But this is what's going to happen, Detective Butler, if you leave that murderer in town. People will get hurt."

"That sounds like a threat."

"It's an observation. Whatever happened to Marissa, she didn't deserve it, and it wouldn't have happened if your boyfriend agreed to ship Will Anders out. He didn't. Now everyone needs to deal with the consequences. Marissa got hurt. You got hurt. I got woken up at one A.M. to be accused of assault. People are angry, and it's only going to get worse. I just hope our sheriff realizes that before it's too late."

SIX

I want to throw Conrad's ass in the cell. Forget stabbing me or even knocking out Marissa. I want to lock him up for what he said before I left. He might claim it wasn't a threat, but on behalf of my friends and my town, I feel threatened.

I interview Marissa. She's groggy and in shock. Earlier, I'd told her she'd been attacked, but I don't think she'd been in shape to fully process it.

"I went over to talk to Will," she says. "I . . . I have things I wanted to say. I thought he was on his usual midnight shift, so I was waiting. The back door opened. I figured it was him. I turned and saw a dark figure. I still thought it was Will. And then . . ." She blinks. "I don't remember the rest."

She got to Anders's place at 11:45 P.M. She'd used her key to enter the back door and believes she left it unlocked. She'd turned on a lamp in the living room and settled in with paperwork.

Having a law degree, Marissa had been offered a choice of jobs in Rockton, including a managerial position. To our surprise, she'd picked a server position at the Red Lion. She'd put herself through school working at a cocktail bar and had joked that during her most stressful trials, she sometimes fantasized about trading her suits and sensible shoes for miniskirts and high heels. She'd happily thrown herself into the work, quickly becoming the Lion's most popular server, while picking up extra credits working at the library.

Those choices got my attention. Made me decide I liked this woman, and I liked her even more when she started dating Anders. That's what stings the worst. I can't write her off as a flighty twit who chased a hot guy and dumped him at the first sign of trouble. I only hope that going to Anders's house means she's reconsidered their breakup.

As for the paperwork, she's recently been headhunted by Phil for a special project. He's analyzing and documenting Rockton's infrastructure for future town leaders. Of course, we both know there will be no future leaders. He's really doing it for us. Learning everything he can about how Rockton operates so we can launch our own version if we can't reverse the council's decision. To Marissa and the council, his project is simply filling in gaps in the scant documentation. Because he's Phil—the guy who memorizes policy documents in his spare time—no one suspects him of having an ulterior motive.

Marissa had been working on that paperwork when the break-in occurred. Seeing a light on, the intruders had known someone was at home. Did they expect Anders? Did they intend to attack *him*? I don't know. While I'm interviewing Marissa, Anders and Dalton check the chalet, and they find signs of a search, but nothing is missing.

What would the intruders have been searching for? They hardly need proof of Anders's crime, since he confessed. That makes me think they really did plan an assault. Break in, surprise Anders, and show him he was in danger if he stayed in Rockton. I wish it *had* been Anders in that room. If so, the perpetrators would be taking Marissa's place in the clinic, as

April tended to their wounds and I informed them they'd be spending the night together in the cell.

Anders hadn't been home, though. So they lashed out at Marissa. April suspects Marissa knocked her head in a fall. With her conveniently unconscious, they'd decided to search the place. Not really looking for anything, just doing some damage, sending a message.

Whatever their plan, they hurt an innocent woman. Maybe that's the way for me to go after them. They assaulted one of the town's most popular residents. Get a little outrage on my side and help me solve this case. The sooner we shut down Conrad, the better.

I invite Phil to breakfast the next morning. Well, second breakfast for me. I ate with Dalton and Anders, and then left them at the station and grabbed egg sandwiches and coffee, which I took to Isabel's door. She accepted the offering and let me borrow Phil for a breakfast meeting.

We convene at his place. I tell him about the break-in and my plan to conduct the blood test, for which I will need access to Conrad's blood type. What he fails to see are the implications of me requesting that. Even after I explain them, he's exasperated bordering on annoyed.

"A crime has been committed," he says. "You are investigating that crime. Of course you may have access to his blood type."

"Right, but the fact he broke into *Will's* place suggests I might be making this a personal vendetta."

"What it *suggests* doesn't matter. A woman was injured. A property was entered illegally."

"Marissa is fine, and nothing was taken."

"Crimes were still committed. In pursuing the offender, you are doing the job we hired you to do. You cannot allow that to be influenced by how residents may react."

We debate this, but I can tell I won't get anywhere. Phil is the ultimate corporate manager. Brilliant at his job, a true wizard at analyzing and tweaking systems to achieve maximum output for minimal cost. CEOs and boards of directors love someone like Phil. Employees stick his photo on the wall for dart practice.

He's getting better at understanding the human cost, but mostly as another vector to consider. An unhappy workforce produces inefficiently. While he *has* come to see residents as more than "the local workforce," he analyzes this situation and decides that a few malcontents will not affect the system as a whole, and therefore should be ignored. What he fails to take into account is the contagion of discontent. Conrad, Jolene, and their ilk are already spreading their disease as fast as they can.

"Let me talk to Marissa," I say. "We can stoke a bit of outrage on her behalf and then—"

A rap on the door cuts me short. Phil checks his watch.

"Office hours," he says with a moue of displeasure. "I have not been looking forward to this today."

Office hours are something Phil recently instituted, in recognition of that "resident satisfaction" component to the efficiency equation. Isabel convinced him that it would help if people could speak to him directly about their concerns. He argued that most of their "concerns" are the result of poor critical-thinking skills, like complaining about powdered milk and creamer without working through the logistics of transporting and storing fresh milk and cream. The rest is just garden-variety whining. He doesn't have time to listen to that. So, as she argued, does he have time instead to be waylaid with questions and complaints every time he steps outside? He conceded the efficiency issues, and now has office hours. One hour, twice a week, and it ends on the hour, even if that means cutting someone off midsentence, I suspect.

He opens the door. "Oh, Marissa. Did we have a meeting this morning?"

"No." Her voice wafts back to me. "I needed to talk to you. There are others waiting, so I won't jump the line—"

"No, no. Come in. We wanted to speak to you, and your timing is impeccable."

Marissa steps in. When she spots me through the hallway, she stops short. "Casey. I didn't . . ." She takes a deep breath, audible from here. "Well, this is probably for the best. Saves me explaining twice." She walks in Phil waves to a seat, but she stays standing.

"I'm here in an official capacity," she says. "I've been asked to represent the residents calling for Will Anders's removal from Rockton."

I rise. "What?"

She turns to face me. "I've been asked—"

"Got that part," I say. "I'm waiting for the second part, where you tell us that you refused them, and that you're here to warn us that they'll be making this request official."

She shakes her head. "I accepted their offer. I will be making that request. I came to ask Phil how to do that."

I open my mouth, but she cuts me off. "This isn't about Will. I think he's a good person. Finding out what he's done doesn't change that. We might no longer be in a relationship, but I am firmly pro–Will Anders."

"Yet you want him gone?"

"For the good of the town. He made a mistake, and I believe—I know—he has paid the price for that. He deserves better. The problem . . ."

She sinks into a chair. "The problem is that we need to remove 'Will' from this equation and focus on 'Deputy Anders.' As a resident in a position of authority, his record must be spotless. People must be able to trust him implicitly."

"What he did happened before he came to Rockton. If we discovered he'd committed a crime here, that would be different."

"I disagree. Again, we aren't talking about Will. We're talking about the perception surrounding a figure in a position of power and how this revelation will affect the comfort of the residents."

"Comfort?" Phil says. "By that measure, Marissa, Sheriff Dalton should not be in his position either. He makes many residents uncomfortable. It's part of his effectiveness as a sheriff. These people enforce our laws. They aren't meant to be the residents' friends. The question for me is whether Will Anders performs his job. He does, very well. The other question would be whether he presents a danger. He does not. He's been here four years without a single strike on his record."

"No one is disputing Will has been an excellent deputy. But he cannot continue to hold that position after this revelation."

Phil glances at me and then says, "Would your clients be satisfied with a temporary suspension, pending a full investigation?"

She shakes her head. "He must leave Rockton. That's the only solution."

I keep my mouth shut. I must or I'm going to explode and say things I can't. Like how we have at least a dozen killers in this town, including me, and they're rarely the ones who cause the problems. An ordinary resident, here for an ordinary reason, is just as likely to lose control and hurt someone. It's the nature of this isolated, insular life.

"Will Anders will be leaving Rockton when his term ends," Phil says. "It is up at the end of the year, and any request for an extension would likely be denied. I propose that he be allowed to remain here, in an administrative capacity, until that time."

"No," she says. "I'm sorry, Phil, but my clients—"

"Your clients knocked you out last night," I say, unable to hold back any longer. "You do realize that, right? Conrad is the one who broke into Will's place."

"I am aware that he is your lead suspect. He has also retained me to represent him in that matter."

I sputter, unable to find words.

"Conrad is not a likable man," she says. "I acknowledge that. He has made things difficult for Phil, as I've witnessed firsthand. However, I believe that has influenced your investigation, Casey, along with the fact that he's leading the coalition to remove Will."

"Fuck you."

She blinks in genuine surprise. "What?"

"Don't pull that lawyer bullshit here, Marissa. I've investigated my colleagues when the evidence even slightly pointed in their direction. I've given the benefit of the doubt to people who pissed me off far more than Conrad ever could. Hell, I argued to allow Jen in the militia. Questioning police competence is a textbook defense attorney tactic, but don't you dare pull that here. Conrad is my main suspect because the evidence points to him. His trail goes from Will's to his place."

"Someone's trail does. Can Storm prove it was him?"

"Yes, she can and she did last night, in front of a witness. There's also the bloody shirt."

"His blood, as he said."

"I intend to prove otherwise."

"If you do, then we only have your say-so on that."

"Excuse me?"

She gives me a look, as if I'm a not-too-clever child. "You're the one conducting the test. You're the one receiving the results. Don't expect us to allow that into evidence."

"Then someone else will conduct the test."

"Who? The doctor, who is your sister? The nurse, who is your former best friend?"

I meet her gaze. "You know Conrad did it. He attacked you. He stabbed me. And yet you're going to defend him? How much is he paying you?"

"This isn't about money, Casey. It's about doing what's right for this community. Whoever did those things did so out of fear."

"Fear?" I choke on the word. "Fear of what?"

"Will Anders. I will argue that the break-in was committed by someone who feared for their safety."

"And wanted to hurt Will? Kill him before he kills them? You do hear what you're saying, don't you, Marissa? That Will deserved to have his chalet broken into, and if he'd been killed, he brought it on himself."

"I said nothing of the sort. I understand you're upset, Casey, but I'm asking that you not allow your feelings to interfere with your job."

"Marissa," Phil says, his voice heavy with warning. "Casey's right. You're attempting to discredit her. I presume you're practicing for a jury, as your only audience here is me, and I am well aware of Detective Butler's record of performance. The only person you're lowering in *my* estimation is yourself."

"I'm calling into question the dynamics of this particular case. Also, while Casey has been an excellent detective in Rockton, I have no way of knowing how she performed down south. I don't even know whether she was actually a police detective there."

"Do you really want to go there, Marissa?" I say. "Think carefully."

Her eyes harden. "Don't patronize me, Casey. I'm making a valid point."

"I was exactly a detective on a major crimes squad, actively employed when I came to Rockton to help Diana. Since you insisted on going there, though . . ." I look at Phil. "I presume you're aware that Marissa was under threat of disbarment before her arrival in Rockton."

At her sharp inhale, I turn on her. "How hard was that hit on the head? I asked if you wanted to go there. I warned you."

If looks could kill . . .

No, that's not right. The look in Marissa's eyes isn't anger. It's hurt, and I'd prefer the former. While I don't know what happened to her down south, she did confess she's been in danger of losing her career. So yes, telling Phil is a shitty thing to do, but obviously she isn't the person I thought she was. Conrad has promised her something, and she's willing to throw Anders under the bus to get it, and there is no justifying that.

"I think you should leave now, Marissa," Phil says, his voice low.

"I came to inform you—"

"Consider us informed."

Her jaw sets. She looks between us for a moment, and then turns on her heel and marches out.

SEVEN

Marissa isn't dropping the matter there. Later that morning, she files an application to speak to the council. There is no such application process, just as there is no formal judicial process. She knows that. If we pointed it out, though, she'd only use it as proof of a corrupt system.

I warn Anders before he hears it through the grapevine. His only response—after ten seconds of stunned silence—is "Well, I guess I don't need to feel so guilty about her getting clocked on the head at my place."

True enough. I have no idea what to make of this. I expected better of Marissa. I really did. But it's hardly the first time someone here has disappointed me. That's the true reveal in Rockton. Not discovering someone lied about their background or committed a crime in their past. It's finding out they aren't the person you thought they were, their underlying character hidden behind a false front.

As outraged as I may be at the thought that Marissa is defending—literally defending—the guy who attacked her, I have other concerns. I do run the blood-typing test, with April overseeing the procedure and a random resident called in to witness the result. It's my blood type, and it's not Conrad's. He stabbed me.

So what do I do with that? Not a damn thing. If Marissa doesn't care that her new client attacked her, that's her problem, and I don't care enough about punishing him for attacking me.

I want to focus on who put up that sign. They're the real enemy, especially if the council is behind it. Find the culprit, and I can discredit their intentions and help Anders that way.

Which puts me right back to square one, admitting I have zero clues to lead me to that culprit.

I spend most of my day interviewing potential witnesses, based on the lists Dalton and Kenny drew up yesterday. Half of them have changed their mind about what they saw.

Did I say I spotted a person near the podium after eleven that night? Sorry, I meant I saw someone there the night before. Or maybe even the night before that.

I want to shake people and tell them to grow a backbone. Don't be intimidated by Conrad and Jolene and their flunkies. Yet fear is a powerful thing, and fear in a small community spreads like wildfire. I remember doing a case study on a town in Saskatchewan where the police charged a dozen people—including fellow officers—in connection with a so-called Satanic cult based on zero evidence. It'd been panic, pure and simple. The devil was at work, their children were at risk, and if you disagreed, then maybe you were part of it.

If you see a problem with someone revealing Deputy Anders's crime, then maybe you have something to hide yourself. Even if you don't, well, a few whispers in the right ears will change that. You'll be a suspect, and you don't want that, do you?

What if I were a resident, someone who barely knew Anders?

What if someone threatened to reveal my past for supporting him?

I wouldn't be cowed into silence, but that's more stubbornness than courage. I could not let someone hold such a threat over my head, or else they'd never stop holding it, and I'd hate myself for allowing it.

I will not judge these people. I understand that the situation is complicated, and to many, the whistleblower didn't really do anything wrong.

When I do get a hit, I should be thrilled. Finally, a resident willing to stand up to the bullies and defend a good man. Yeah . . . Not exactly.

I rap on Ted's door. Ted is the guy Isabel singled out at the town meeting. The dean who'd been accused by multiple female students of trading academic favors for sex.

You're facing disciplinary action for drunk and disorderly behavior? I can fix that. You've been accused of cheating on an exam? I can fix that.

Ted had been very particular with his victims, selecting those who were already trouble. Those who wouldn't be believed if they complained. He's a predator, and I've had my eye on him since he arrived in Rockton.

He's been careful, though. It probably helps that he works in cooking prep, with no power over anyone. Also, the youngest female resident is in her mid-twenties, and Ted liked them on the cusp of legality.

Yep, I'm not a Ted fan. But with this case, I need to take my leads wherever I can get them.

Ted opens his door, takes one look at me, and says, in a booming voice, "I have nothing to say to you, Detective Butler."

I inwardly wince at his community-theater performance,

but I grit my teeth and force myself to stick to his script. "I am legally permitted to search your apartment."

"On what grounds? I haven't done anything wrong. I have an alibi for last night, when Deputy Anders's house was broken into, and the night before, when someone posted that sign."

His voice echoes along the street. Making sure everyone knows he isn't a suspect, and he doesn't want to speak to me.

"I know," I say, still following the script. "But you did purchase paper last week, and I need to follow up on that."

"Fine. Come in and see my paper. Twenty sheets. All present and accounted for."

He lets me in then and shuts the door behind me. "You could have spoken louder."

"You were speaking loud enough for both of us. If anyone asks, I'll stick to your story. I came to check your damned paper supply. Now, what have you got for me?"

As he leads me into his kitchenette, I take a better look at him. Is that bruising on his jaw? He hasn't shaved, which makes it hard to tell. Not shaving because he's hiding a bruise?

We sit at the table. Then his voice drops low enough that I have to strain to hear it.

"I want immunity," he says.

I tense. "For what?"

"You're lucky I don't sue this town for breach of contract. I came here with the promise that my past would remain sealed. I paid very well for that, and then I stood in the town square while the local *bartender* called me out."

"As the bar *owner* and the *brothel* owner, Isabel receives the names of anyone who has been accused of a sex-related crime. It's a watch list. She has no idea what you did. She was needling you, and I have spoken to her about that. It was unacceptable, and I apologize."

"So she was given my name as a *sex offender*?"

"No," I say carefully. "She was given your name as someone who had been accused of a sex-related offense."

"Nothing was ever proven."

Because you fled to Rockton before it could be. I don't say that. I force myself to nod semi-sympathetically. "That's why it's a watch list. If you were convicted, you would have been barred from Rockton. You may feel misled, Ted, but I can bring out the forms you signed. They state that anyone requiring knowledge of your past will receive the minimum data needed, protecting your privacy as much as possible."

He leans back in his chair. "It's a ten-page form. You didn't expect me to read it, did you?"

"The point is that Isabel only knows you were accused of something sex-related. You said you want immunity. I'm presuming you had something to do with that sign. Or the break-in?"

"Of course not," he snaps. "I mean I want immunity from those accusations. Someone out there has a hit list. Will Anders was the first, but he won't be the last."

I stiffen. "Who's saying that?"

"It's obvious, isn't it? This is just the first step. Everyone knows it. That's why I'm talking to you. To shut it down before it gets to me. I spent the last six months living like a goddamn monk. I don't know what you expect straight guys to do, when there are three of them to every woman, and some of those women aren't even straight."

"One, access to sex isn't covered under the Charter of Rights and Freedoms. Two, that's why there's a brothel."

"Do I look like a man who needs to pay for it?"

No, you just coerce eighteen-year-old girls into giving it to you free.

He continues, "I finally have a girlfriend. Frieda. She's not exactly my type." *Being over eighteen and not under your control.* "Beggars can't be choosers, though, right?"

I'm sure she's thinking the exact same thing.

"The problem," he says, "is that she's a bit of a feminazi."

"Uh-huh."

"Just last week, she was telling me about this friend of hers who lost her job after accusing her boss of harassment. I said she should consider the possibility that her friend lost her job because she was a lousy employee, and she'd been screwing the boss to avoid getting fired. Frieda . . ." He gestures wildly. "Blew up. Walked out. Stayed away until I apologized." His face gathers in a scowl. "How humiliating was that? I had to lie and say I was sorry."

"Uh-huh. So what you're saying, I think, is that you're afraid if she hears your backstory, the sex pipeline is going bone dry."

"Exactly. Obviously, if you catch the person behind this, I don't have to worry. But if you don't get him—or get him fast enough—and my story comes out, I want Sheriff Dalton to say it isn't true. I want him to say that the evidence proved that my accusers banded together in a concerted effort to oust me from my position."

He looks at me. "Sheriff Dalton has always struck me as the sort of man who understands these things."

I have no idea what that means, other than that it proves Ted may be the world's worst judge of character.

"I'm not sure that would be necessary," I say slowly. "I'm not sure you'd even want it. Having Eric blame your accusers could turn every, uh, 'feminazi' in town against you. Which would be a problem."

He nods. "There seem to be a lot of them here."

"Right. It would be better if—were you accused—Eric simply said the whistleblower's information is wrong. Phil would confirm it. They obviously confused you with someone else."

"That'd work," he murmurs.

"All right then. We have a deal. If your past is revealed, Eric and Phil will claim it's incorrect. Now, what do you have for me?"

What Ted has for me is less than I'd hoped for. I'm not sure it's worth the price I paid, but I remind myself that we'll almost certainly never need to make good on our end of the deal. Even if the whistleblower has a list, from what I know of Rockton's residents and their pasts, Ted's case would be at the bottom of it. Worst scenario, the asshole gets his immunity, and I find a way to suggest to Frieda that there might be some truth in the accusation.

What Ted gives me is a lead. A tiny one, but that still makes it bigger than anything I have so far.

It starts off even more promising.

"It's not a secret who did it," he says.

I straighten. "So you have a name?"

"No, I just mean that people know. That's the scuttlebutt— that some people in town know exactly who's responsible because he's taken credit."

"He? You know it's a man? Or are you just picking a pronoun?"

"*I'm* not picking one. Others could be, but I definitely get the sense they're being specific for a reason."

"You've heard this directly from people who know a name?"

He sniffs. "I don't travel in those circles, Detective. I wasn't chopping vegetables down south. I had a position requiring multiple postgraduate degrees. I didn't come to Rockton to *party.*"

While he sneers the last word, envy shines in his eyes. It's easy to place himself above the "popular" crowd. He's too distinguished, too respectable, too educated for that. Truth is that the troublemakers are usually people just like him. Either they're taking advantage of the opportunity to cut loose or they're reliving their frat-boy days, acting like twenty-year-olds at a kegger.

"The culprit is part of *that* crowd, then?" I say.

"Part of one of them. There are many cliques here, Detective." Another sniff. "It's like high school. I can't say exactly which one your culprit belongs to, but word is that he's taken full credit with his cronies, basking in the warmth of his fifteen seconds of fame while positioning himself as a modern-day Robin Hood, bringing down the corrupt Sheriff of Nottingham."

I frown. "They're targeting Eric?"

He waves off my words. "I mean 'sheriff' figuratively. It's a literary analogy."

"I see. Well, do you have anything for me to go on? Anyone you know has heard this confession firsthand?"

"As I said, I don't travel in those crowds."

"Then can you tell me who you heard it from?"

"Two people, and no, I will not divulge their names. I am a man of honor, Detective, not a common stool pigeon."

I pause, both to keep from making a smart-ass remark and to figure out a way to get that information. Before I can speak again, he says, "However, knowing this isn't enough for you to go on, I made some discreet inquiries. I know how the culprit got the sign in place without being spotted."

He pauses, as if for dramatic effect. Then he says, "It was there all day."

I shake my head. "That's impossible. I went by earlier that evening. There was just the usual . . ."

As I trail off, Ted smirks.

There was just the usual sign. The one that tells residents about the next movie showing.

"The whistleblower put his sign behind that one," I say. "Then he rigged the movie sign to come off somehow?"

"Nothing so dramatic. He affixed the movie sign loosely. Eventually, it just fluttered away."

I can grumble about the drama of that. Also the inefficiency. It was just as likely that the old sign would have hung there, half fastened, until someone climbed up to fix it and found the other one, which would have been a lot less impressive.

That plan was both to make a scene and to set up a mystery. To have us all—especially me—wondering how the sign got there when no one saw it being posted.

Yet someone still put it up. Not only put it up but needed time to affix the covering sign just right. They had to find a ladder or sturdy chair, drag it into the town square, and do the work without being spotted. That might be possible in the middle of the night, but it only takes one person hearing a noise to foil the plan.

Then the answer hits. The dead-obvious answer, and with it, a suspect.

The person who put up the sign must be the same person who posted the movie-night poster. They could take all the time they needed fussing with it and not raise a single eyebrow.

The last movie was five nights ago. The new sign would have gone up the following day. The problem? The person who puts it up is Devon.

EIGHT

"The movie-night sign?" Devon says as he takes a pan of cookies from the oven. "Sure, that's my job." He glances over. "You think whoever posted the sign about Will used my ladder. I borrow Kenny's. That's a good lead, though. Everyone uses his when they need to climb up somewhere, so he keeps it inside. Otherwise people would just borrow it and leave it wherever. He should be able to tell you who took it out the other night."

He pauses as he sets down the pan. "It's weird he didn't mention it being borrowed that night. Maybe someone broke in and took it? Returned it before morning?"

"Sources tell me Will's sign wasn't put up that night. It was *behind* the latest movie poster."

Devon frowns and stops, spatula in hand. "Someone climbed up and stuck it behind the poster? Why? They'd still need to pull off the poster later. That doubles the chances of being caught. I think someone's messing with you, Casey."

"Apparently the movie sign was loosely attached. They were waiting for it to fall off, and then I'd zero in on *that* time frame to figure out who posted it."

He scrapes off a hot cookie and sets it onto a plate for me. "I guess that's semi-clever. Still, they'd need to get up there in the first place, not just to stick up a sign but to remove the top one, put on the new one, and tape the original over it. Lots of opportunity to be spotted."

"Not if you're the person putting up the movie sign."

He pauses. It takes a moment. Then he says, "Wait. You think whoever posted Will's sign *also* posted the movie sign. That's why no one would have noticed. They were doing their job." He hands me the plate with the warm cookie. "Then I'm really glad I wasn't the one putting up the sign this week."

I exhale. "Thank you. That was awkward."

He grins. "You still get a cookie, despite thinking I tried to destroy the nicest guy in town."

Devon lifts a hand as I open my mouth to protest. "I'm teasing. You were following up on a lead. You had to ask. Putting up the sign *is* my job as head of the movie committee. This week, though, Gloria offered to do it. She had trouble reading my handwriting from a distance and wanted bigger letters. I suspect someone needs new glasses. She's on the movie committee. No reason not to let her try her hand at sign writing. I offered to post it, but she said she'd do that, too."

Gloria. The quiet woman who spoke up at the meeting when Jen tried to shut down Conrad and Jolene. Gloria, who'd said she wanted to hear all opinions.

I don't know her well, other than that she's always seemed kind. She's one of the last arrivals, and she works at the general store. She's quiet, barely says a word to anyone.

In other words, perfect council-spy material.

I thank Devon, take my cookie and head out.

★　★　★

Gloria isn't at the general store.

"She took a sick day," Petra says, when I find her closing up alone. "Killer migraine, apparently. Hungover, if you ask me."

"Gloria parties? I got the impression she was something of a loner."

"Mmm, I wouldn't say she's a partier or a loner. I do know she got herself a boyfriend recently. Don't ask me who. She's not volunteering that information, and I don't pry." A roll of her eyes. "You know what this place is like. Secrets, secrets, and more secrets, most of them not worth the effort of digging."

Petra would know. In Rockton, she's a comic-book artist turned part-time artist and shop clerk. In her former life, she was a spy. A professional one.

She continues, "In a town with so many secrets, people should get tired of them, but I swear, it just makes them want more. The way Gloria acts, you'd think she was secretly hooking up with Eric."

"Maybe she is."

"Yeah, and I'm dating Isabel." She shakes her head. "No, this is just a secret for secrecy's sake. When Gloria finally reveals her mystery lover, it'll turn out to be someone like Ted." She makes a gagging noise.

"Ted's dating Frieda."

"What?" Her lip curls. "I need to have a talk with that girl. But yeah, Gloria is an odd one. She asked for this job, but her customer-service skills suck. She's not rude. It's like dealing with a self-serve checkout. No chitchat. No welcoming smiles. No 'have a nice day.' We moved her into the back fast." She eyes me as she puts away the inventory list. "Wait, she's a suspect then? For our council-spy whistleblower?"

"No one said anything about council spies."

"Right." She gives me a look. "Well, not that I have any

experience in these matters, cough-cough, but Gloria would make a shitty spy. Sure, she passes under the radar, but she's not going to get intel in Rockton by listening at doors. Here you need to be part of the conversation."

"So you say she stayed home today."

"Way to bring me back on track, Case. Fine. Yes, she stayed home. I suspect a hangover because ever since she's hooked up with this guy, she's been coming in bleary eyed."

"Did she work yesterday?"

"Nope, it was her day off."

"Did you see her at all today? Or did someone deliver the message that she wasn't coming in?"

"She stopped by. Holding her head. Wearing sunglasses." She shoos me toward the door and then stops. "While I figured she was hungover, it's also possible she was faking it. I just wouldn't expect that from her. I did bump into her yesterday. I missed the meeting—figured you guys would catch me up—and I was heading into the bakery as she was coming out. I asked if she'd been to the meeting, and she jumped like I'd accused her of skipping work. She reminded me it was her day off. I said yeah, I know, and I was asking about the meeting, since I wasn't at it. She mumbled something and got out of there fast."

"Interesting."

"I thought so."

After that, I break for dinner, which is more about sharing my leads with Dalton than needing to eat. When I'm this involved in an investigation, I tend to forget everything else. Today, though, I want to talk.

We pick up dinner and dine alone at the station. My investigation so far seems straightforward. Not much to bounce off

Dalton, really. Gloria taking over the movie-poster work this week would seem to confirm what Ted heard—that someone posted the Anders sign behind the regular one. Gloria might not be prime spy material, but she's definitely acting like someone with a guilty conscience.

Is the new boyfriend the key here? Gloria finds a boyfriend and starts getting secretive. A boyfriend who doesn't want anyone to know they're dating . . . because he's setting her up. She's on the movie committee, and he wants access to that poster.

What I really need from Dalton is data. Well, no, I also want some time with my guy, time to decompress and prepare for another long night of work. But, yes, data, too. Is there anything in Gloria's background I should know about?

Dalton considers long enough that, in the past, I'd have jumped in with apologies for putting him on the spot. I know better now. I'd only be putting him on the spot if he felt obliged to share private details with his detective because she's also his lover. While Dalton *can* overdo it trying to please me, that means puppies and chocolate, not breaking resident confidentiality. If he's quiet, it's because he's accessing his mental file on Gloria and deciding what might be pertinent.

"If someone wanted to woo her," he says, "alcohol would be a good way to do it."

"She's a drinker?" I frown. I've never seen her in the Roc, and residents can't purchase take-home in any significant quantity.

Before Dalton can answer, I say, "Oh. Wait. You mean she's a former drinker. An alcoholic. She meets a guy, admits she has a problem, and the asshole takes advantage."

Dalton doesn't confirm. He doesn't need to—he's given me enough of a hint. Such a scenario only reaffirms that I need to take a closer look at this boyfriend, whoever he might be. It could be unconnected to the sign—just some horny guy like Ted, willing to seduce a recovering alcoholic with booze. I still want to know who it is. We have ways of turning off that particular pipeline.

The fact that her lover seems to be plying her with booze means he has access to it himself. Stealing it is impossible. Nothing is locked down tighter. Either her boyfriend has the status to purchase more or he has the credits to buy others' allotments. Either way, it means he has a high-ranking job.

We come up with a short list of suspects. Then dinner's over, and I'm off again, leaving Dalton on full-time patrol. Not his favorite place to be—especially when most of the issues are people wanting answers about Anders—but with our deputy on desk duty, we don't have much choice.

I stop at Gloria's apartment first. She's home but not answering the door. When I knock a second time, I catch a faint click and think she's unlocking it. Nope. Apparently, she crept over to *lock* it.

I move to the window and shade my eyes to peer in. I don't need to check. I know she's there. I just can't resist letting her know that I know. There's an advantage to making her even more nervous. The cops are closing in. Time to give up.

While I could call in Dalton and his skeleton key, I decide to drop it. Let her stew tonight and confront her in the morning. Maybe I'll get lucky and she'll confess. If not, though, I need more than one person saying she volunteered to put up the sign.

Next step: confirm Devon's story.

I find Kenny in his workshop. April's there, too, sitting on a chair and talking to him as he works. That's almost enough to make me back out.

My sister is taking an evening off! She's socializing! She's with a guy she likes, who likes her back!

Yeah, all very exciting for sister Casey, but detective Casey has a job to do. I slip in with an apology for the interruption.

"Yes," April says. "You should be more careful when Kenny has a saw in his hand. He could hurt himself."

Kenny smiles. "If I cut myself every time someone walked in, I'd have bled out long ago. What's up, Case?"

"The movie-night folks use your ladder to put up their poster, right?"

He leans against his workbench. "Yep. I thought of that, but no one borrowed it that night, and I had the workshop door locked."

"Devon's the one who puts it up each week, isn't he?"

"Normally, yes. Gloria took it this week, though."

"Did anyone help her?"

He shakes his head. "I offered, but she said she was fine, and it's a bit awkward with my crutches, so I didn't insist."

"She was alone when she returned it, too?"

"It was outside the shop the next morning."

April looks over. "I don't see what the movie-night sign has to do with Will's sign, Casey."

"I'm presuming there's a connection," Kenny says. "Yes, Gloria borrowed the ladder alone. She put the sign up alone, too. I spotted her when I was heading home. She seemed to be having some trouble sticking it on. I asked if she needed anything, and she nearly fell off the ladder. I must have startled her. Felt bad about that. She said she was fine and seemed flustered, so I didn't want to make a big deal of it."

"Okay, well, my next step is finding out who she's been dating."

April frowns. "She's no longer seeing Conrad?"

We both turn to look at her.

"Conrad?" I say.

"Yes. She came to see me about a confidential matter, which

I will not divulge, of course. It doesn't pertain to your case. Then Conrad came to see me about the same matter, and I realized their situations were related."

"Ah."

"Which is not why I say they are a couple. That would still breach confidentiality. It only put the thought into my mind, and then I saw them together in an intimate tête-à-tête, while I was taking my morning walk along the town border." She pauses. "Or perhaps, given that I formed my initial opinion based on confidential appointments, telling you about the tête-à-tête is inadmissible. Fruits of a poisonous tree."

I try not to smile. My sister's reading has recently moved from police-procedural mysteries to court-drama thrillers.

"That's debatable," I say. "However, having no court here, there's no one to argue the point, thankfully."

"I didn't realize their relationship wasn't common knowledge," she says.

"Which helps. It was a secret. Now it isn't. And you may have just cracked my case."

Conrad? Oh, hell. Part of me *loves* this solution. The whistleblower's biggest fan is actually the whistleblower himself? That'll lob a cannonball through his campaign against Anders. Yet it won't detonate it entirely. Not unless I can prove Conrad is also a council spy sent to discredit local law enforcement.

No one in Rockton is a council supporter. Oh, they certainly arrive that way. After all, the council let them in. Saved their lives and gave them refuge. Then they arrive and realize they're just widgets on a shelf, stashed in Rockton for what is, in some cases, a king's ransom in gold. The only people committed to making sure they have a safe and comfortable stay are the innkeepers: us. The council is the corporation that owns the inn, purely interested in profit.

That's the key then. Flip the narrative. Conrad isn't a whistleblower. He's a traitor.

Except half the town is already convinced I'm out to get Conrad. Sure, he's an asshole, and they're fine with me harassing him over the break-in, but accusing him of posting the sign? Of being a council spy? That's taking a reasonable vendetta five steps too far.

I can't accuse Conrad until I have proof. Gloria is the most likely source of that proof. While I have a feeling she'll break under very little pressure, I don't want to start there.

I want to start with Conrad. Stop by and claim to believe I was wrong about the break-in. From there . . . Well, from there, I have a plan.

As I rap on his front door, I rehearse my gambit. I must be careful here. He's smart enough to lawyer up at the first hint of trouble. This isn't usually a problem in Rockton. Our justice system is too streamlined for lawyers, and on the rare occasions someone recruits one, the lawyer ends up overcomplicating matters and turning a minor case into a major one, with potentially major consequences.

Technically, because we're operating outside the Canadian legal system, I could refuse to let Conrad speak to Marissa. Yet I must avoid anything that even remotely smacks of totalitarianism. If he asks for his lawyer, I must stop talking until he gets Marissa, who will then see exactly what I'm up to and shut down this friendly meeting in a heartbeat.

I'm so busy rehearsing my lines it takes a few moments to realize Conrad hasn't answered his door.

"He's out," a voice says behind me. I turn to find Jen standing ten feet away.

"He left about ten minutes ago," she says.

"Any idea which way he went?"

"That way?" She vaguely gestures. "That's all I noticed." She shifts her weight. "You got more on him?"

Several people have slowed to eavesdrop.

Thanks, Jen. Really the conversation I want to have shouted across a ten-foot gap.

"No," I say, as I walk to her. "I was just confirming something."

She nods. "So he's still a suspect?"

Really, Jen?

I clear my throat. "He has not been officially cleared."

"But you're moving in that direction?"

I peer at her. This isn't a Jen-like conversation. She hadn't been herself the night the sign was revealed and hasn't been since.

Before I can decide how to pursue it, the community center door opens and Gloria steps out. She looks both ways. Sees me and backs inside.

I glance toward Jen, but she's moved on. I hesitate. Consider. Then I stride off to confront Gloria.

NINE

"You do know that's an emergency exit, right?" I say as Gloria slips out the community center rear door.

She looks from the door to me and then laughs nervously and hikes up a stack of books under her arm. "Guess I missed the sign."

I look pointedly at the sign, red block letters six inches tall. Then I wave her back inside. She hesitates, but obeys. I shut the door behind us.

"You're dodging me," I say.

She shifts the books. "You make me nervous. You all do, after finding out what Will Anders did."

I say nothing.

She readjusts the books again. "It's like living in a police state. You're out there, rousting the usual suspects, accusing Conrad of assaulting an officer." Her gaze drops to my calf. "Your leg seems fine to me."

"How'd you know it was my leg?"

She hesitates. Another book shift. "Everyone knows. Someone broke into Will Anders's place, knocked Marissa down, and stabbed you in the leg."

"Huh. Well, the message we sent out was that the intruders disabled Marissa and attacked me with a knife. The only people who know where I was stabbed are Dalton and my sister. Well, except the actual person who stabbed me. Your boyfriend got a bit chatty, huh?"

She startles back. "Boyfriend? I don't have—"

"Conrad."

Her laugh takes on a rabbit squeal of nervous fear. "W-what? Conrad? N-no."

"So you're *not* involved with Conrad?" I meet her gaze. "Remember who you are speaking to and answer carefully. Very carefully."

She isn't on a witness stand. I haven't read Gloria her rights. Still, when I say that, she quivers as if a lie will smite her with a lightning bolt from the heavens.

She finally lifts her chin. "There's no law against keeping our relationship a secret. You know what this town's like. People love to drag out everyone's laundry and wave it around for a few moments of entertainment."

"Like posting it on a sign for the whole town to see?"

She has the grace to color at that. "That's different. Deputy Anders committed murder. We trusted him, and he betrayed us."

"No, the *council* betrayed you when they hired him knowing his background. But let's not split hairs. You're dating Conrad, and he asked you to post that sign under the movie poster."

"What?" Another rabbity shriek, her built-in lie detector giving her away again. "I-I don't know what you're talking about."

I sigh. "You volunteered to put up the movie sign. I have confirmation of that and confirmation of you borrowing the ladder and of you putting it up. The sign about Will was underneath. You affixed the movie poster loosely, so it'd fall off."

Her mouth works. "How-how—"

"I'd love to claim awesome detective work, but the truth is that, like so many wannabe criminal masterminds, your boyfriend can't resist bragging and laughing about how you did his dirty work for him. If anyone goes down for it, it'll be you, and since no one knows you two are a couple, he can deny everything. Hilarious, isn't it?"

Her mouth works, and I feel a little sorry for her. There isn't a split second where she thinks I'm lying. This is what she expects. What she's learned to expect. And maybe, deep down, she knew Conrad was using her, but she told herself otherwise. I'm confirming her worst fears, and that's a shitty thing to do, but putting up that sign was a shittier thing.

"You thought you were doing the right thing," I say, my voice softening. "If our deputy killed someone, then people should know about it. Conrad convinced you he was seeing justice served."

She doesn't reply, just keeps her gaze down, her body quivering under my words.

"I can understand that, Gloria," I say. "But the part that bothers me most is the message itself. Will was a soldier with a mental-health issue brought on by war. Saying he 'lost his marbles' and should be in a 'loony bin' is ignorant and insensitive and—"

"Conrad wrote it," she blurts. "He worded it like that. I . . ." She shivers. "I told him it was wrong, and he laughed and said . . ." Another shiver. Then her gaze lifts to mine. "What do I need to do now?"

TEN

Well, I have my witness. I find one of the militia outside and ask him to escort Gloria to Phil, who can take her statement. My job is to find Conrad before he catches wind of our conversation.

For that, I get a tip from Gloria. I could feel guilty about tricking her into thinking he mocked her. But from the way she believed it—and the way she talked about him mocking her over the sign wording—I suspect my lie hadn't been far off the truth. Conrad used booze to seduce a recovered alcoholic and then set her up to take the fall for his crime.

Gloria had been with Conrad earlier when he'd gotten a note from a fan who had dirt on two more residents. The meeting was supposed to take place in the forest at eight. When I check my watch, it's 7:56.

I collect Storm and ask Dalton to witness Gloria's statement with Phil. He'd rather go with me. I need that witness, though, and we obviously can't ask Anders to do that. Nor can I ask Anders to accompany me. He must remain outside this investigation to avoid impropriety.

"I'll snag someone to come with me," I call as I jog off with Storm.

"You better!"

As I run with the dog, I survey the town. It's still a few hours from dark. Plenty of people about. None suit my needs. I need a militia member or Petra, even Mathias would do. Hell, I'd settle for Diana, who isn't much in the way of backup, but she's really good at screaming for help.

I have Storm. She's at least as good as half my human options. I'm sending up a silent apology to Dalton for contravening his order when a voice says, "Casey? We need to talk."

I turn to see Jen.

"Perfect," I say. "Walk and talk. I need backup."

She pauses. "What?"

I wave her over, not pausing my jog. She catches up, and says, "We need to talk, Casey. Now."

"Does it have something to do with Conrad meeting a mysterious informant in the woods?"

"No."

"Then it can wait." I slow outside Conrad's place and ask Storm to pick up his trail. She does so readily. His trail had been important to me last night, and so she understands what I want.

As she snuffles about, people slow to watch. I ignore them. I can no longer worry whether it looks as if I'm zeroed in on Conrad.

"What's this about Conrad and an informant?" Jen asks, her voice low, uncharacteristically discreet. I motion that I'll explain once we're out of town. Storm finds the scent. It goes exactly where I expect, making a beeline for the first path to the town border trail.

If there's a cardinal rule for Rockton residents, it's "Don't go in the forest." That may seem to oversell the danger, but experience has taught every Rockton sheriff to enforce that rule above all others. If you want to explore the wilderness, then join a hike or a fishing trip or a logging crew. Otherwise, you are restricted to this trail, which meanders around town, granting privacy while remaining within shouting distance of help.

There's no one in this particular section, so when Storm pauses to tease out Conrad's scent, I turn to Jen.

"Conrad—" I begin.

"It's him," she blurts. "He's the one who made up the sign."

"Please tell me that is the result of keen detective work, and not that you've been sitting on it this entire time."

Her flush answers for her.

"God*damn* it, Jen. Really? What? You wanted to make me work for it? Earn my keep?"

"Of course not," she snaps. "I wouldn't—" She bites off the rest and eases back. "Fine. I've pulled shit like that before. I wouldn't with this, though. Will's . . ." Her voice roughens. "He's been good about me being on the militia, and he's had every reason not to be."

I check Storm, who's still sniffing. Then I look at Jen. "We'll discuss this later. For now, is this a rumor? Or do you have evidence?"

"I can't be sure he posted the sign, but I know he's the one who got the information."

Storm has the scent now, but I motion for her to wait as I turn to Jen. "Do you know where he got it?"

"Yeah." Her gaze shifts and her hands shove into her pockets. "From me."

"What?" My voice rises loud enough to startle a couple turning the trail corner. I motion for Jen to follow and for Storm to resume tracking.

Once we're into the forest, Jen whispers, "It was during dental work. He gave me something for the pain."

And while under the influence, you revealed Anders's secret.

Even for Jen, I'm shocked. Yet this isn't following the usual Jen-bad-behavior playbook. First, she'd make me figure it out. Then she'd deny it categorically. Finally, if she couldn't weasel out of it, she'd find some justification and stick to it, never showing a moment's remorse. None of that is happening here, and so I must listen, as much as I want to ream her out loud enough for all of Rockton to hear.

"Whatever he gave me," she says, "it made me loopy. It was just a filling, and he was using freezing, so I didn't need the drugs. But he gave it to me before I realized what it was. Then he started asking about you guys."

"Us guys?"

"Eric, Will, you, Phil, Isabel . . . His personal hit list."

"People he thinks have done him wrong. By not letting him be a dentist full-time."

She nods. "You and Will don't have anything to do with it, but he's casting his net wide and including anyone who might have had a say in the decision. I thought I didn't tell him anything. I only vaguely remember the conversation. It was like something I dreamed, you know?"

I make a noncommittal noise.

"Afterward, he asked me a few questions about what I remembered, and I didn't think much of it until the sign. As soon as I saw that, the memory slammed back. Conrad had asked me about you guys, flattering me, saying I should be part of the inner circle and you guys are all keeping me out, and you don't realize how smart I am."

She rolls her eyes, the old Jen returning. "Fucking asshole. I wish he'd tried that shit when I wasn't drugged up. I'd have told him where to get off. Treating me like some kind of loser wannabe."

Jen *isn't* a "loser wannabe." And yet . . . Well, there's always been a hint of that. She's not sitting on the outside, looking in forlornly, but she has resented her status, responding by grabbing the mantle of "outsider" and wearing it proudly, making herself difficult and unlikable. You can't be accused of wanting to join the cool kids if you've given them every reason for excluding you. That makes it a choice.

Yes, in her right mind, Jen *would* have told Conrad where to stuff his flattery and insinuations. When she'd been drugged, though, his seeds found fertile soil.

"How did you know about Will?" I ask.

She rolls her shoulders in obvious discomfort. "I was listening in once when Val was talking to the council. I'd . . . kinda snuck into her chalet."

"You broke in."

"I was out of shampoo, and I knew she got special stuff, and I wanted to try it."

I'm not going anywhere with that. It makes sense, though. Val was Phil's predecessor. She must have known about Anders and been discussing him with the council.

Jen continues, "If I'd found out Will was stealing booze, I'd have used that for all it was worth. But this?" She shakes her head as she moves aside a branch. "This was offside, you know? Out of bounds."

"Not to Conrad," I murmur.

"Fucking asshole. Can we tattoo that on his forehead?"

I follow Storm a few more steps. Then I say, "Are we sure Conrad obtained it from you?"

"Yeah. What he wrote is what I remember of Val's conversation. Will shot and killed a commanding officer during a mental breakdown."

We continue on. I'm ready to let this lapse for now. I don't want Conrad and his informant overhearing us. But after a few steps, she continues, in a voice soft enough for only me to hear.

"You're going to ask why I didn't come forward," she says. "I panicked. I didn't think you'd buy that I forgot what I'd told Conrad until I saw the sign. You might not even believe I'd been doped up. I spent the next day trying to decide what to do. I hoped Will would deny it, and it'd all go away. But of course he had to do the right thing."

Twigs crackle in the distance, and I motion for quiet. Then I catch the faint outline of a distant caribou making its way along a game trail. We resume walking, and Jen continues speaking.

"When I heard Marissa was attacked—and Conrad was the main suspect—I headed to the station to confess. Then someone said Marissa hopped sides. That she was leading the charge to get Will kicked out while defending the guy who attacked her. I decided she wasn't nearly as smart as I thought, and so fuck her. I wasn't putting my neck on the line. But later I realized that if I confessed, I might lose any shot at an extension. If you tracked me down, though, I'd definitely lose it. I needed to tell the truth."

"Which also could prevent more people from being hurt, as well as being the right thing to do."

"Yeah, yeah. So does my confession help your case?"

"It does."

It also means that this has nothing to do with the council. It's a personal vendetta, unleashed by a guy who thinks the world owes him special treatment. When the world doesn't deliver, he set his mind on revenge. Because ruining a guy's life is fair payback for whatever tiny role he might have played in keeping you from a temporary job placement.

Fucking asshole indeed.

As for the lack of a council connection, maybe I should be

disappointed, but this resolution to the mystery will be easier. I don't need to worry that the council will insist on exiling Anders. Nor do I need to worry that I'll be next on the hit list.

I look over at Jen. "Is there any chance you divulged more than Will's story?"

She hesitates.

"Jen . . ."

"I had some dirt on Diana, okay? I know you came here to help her out and she double-crossed you. I remember starting to tell Conrad that. He didn't even hear me out. Said it wasn't the sort of stuff he wanted, and how the hell did it help his cause to prove you were a nice person who got stiffed helping a friend? Personally, I think it shows you're too nice. Gullible, even. And a shitty judge of character."

"Thank you."

"You're welcome. That's all I said. Conrad was only interested in you five, and I've got nothing else. Phil's too up-tight to do anything wrong. Isabel might have, but she's sure as hell not telling anyone. Eric inherited his job. No secret there. And you're Saint Casey, who came here to support her double-crossing BFF and didn't even send the bitch packing when you learned the truth."

I'm glad to hear Jen didn't have anything more to give Conrad, but it's only a temporary reprieve. Conrad is meeting another source right now. He's desperate for dirt on those he thinks have wronged him. Someone wanting to catch his ear just needs to claim they have information on Phil or Dalton. How do we fight lies? That's one reason Anders admitted to his past. Nothing he said would convince people he was innocent.

Even if he were innocent, it's not as if he can show proof. Part of that is the lack of internet or phones, but part, too, is just the difficulty of proving a thing did *not* happen. If someone says Dalton murdered a resident ten years ago, how does he prove otherwise? They could claim Phil was a serial killer, and it would be our word against theirs, ours counting for very little these days.

I'm fretting about this when I catch the murmur of a male voice. I go still. Storm lifts her head and sniffs. Then she whines, tail wagging, and my heart sinks.

Whoever Conrad is meeting? It's someone Storm likes.

ELEVEN

This is the hell of working in a tiny town, one that has become home. With every case I investigate, there is a very good chance that the perpetrator will be someone I like. I will never forget the pain of arresting a friend, something I likely would have never experienced in big-city policing.

Residents may think I'm going after Conrad too hard, and I suspect they're partly right. It isn't malicious glee fueling my pursuit. It's the relief that my culprit is someone I'd happily see gone. Everyone wants the bad guys to be assholes. Especially me.

Storm likes whoever's ahead, and she does not like Conrad, which means she's hearing or smelling whoever set up this meeting.

Damn it.

I motion for Jen to wait with Storm. I'll never rival Dalton for tracking, but Jen is about as stealthy as my hundred-and-thirty-pound Newfoundland. Storm side-eyes Jen, considering my request. I motion again, telling her it's not actually a request, and a sigh ripples her jowls.

Jen is not a dog person. Bad early experience, according

to the bare minimum she told me to explain why she once kicked Storm away. I could say that's why Storm doesn't care for her, but I held that grudge far longer than my dog. Storm just isn't keen on people who aren't keen on her, which is an understandable choice, whether you're human or canine.

Storm takes up position beside Jen, and I continue into the forest. I catch two voices, male and female, too far for me to make out more. The male must be Conrad, meaning the woman is his mysterious supporter—and the resident Storm likes. My mind wants to run through a checklist of possibilities, but I pull it up short. I'll see soon enough. Speculation only muddies the waters.

I apply all my Dalton lessons as I creep through the forest. Stay downwind. Even humans can notice unusual scents on the breeze. Don't walk through open areas, or you might be spotted. It's better camouflage to squeeze through saplings and bushes. Also, foliage above the ground is usually alive, meaning you don't need to worry about the crackle of dead branches and leaves. That comes from underfoot. If you must step down on dead flora, slide into it.

I can see the figures now. They're walking on a path, one behind the other. Moving and no longer speaking. Heading toward Rockton.

Shit. I'd hoped to catch them talking. That gave me a reason to confront them. This way, they'll only claim they were out for a walk, and if I want to fine them for leaving the border trail, go ahead.

I ease back the way I came. I'm getting ahead of them in hopes I'll hear something incriminating while they walk. There's nothing, though. Just the tramp of feet. Then a woman's soft laugh.

I know that laugh.

The male voice says something low and almost inaudible.

The woman murmurs that she thought she saw a snake, and it was just a tree branch, obviously, because there are no snakes in the Yukon.

I know that voice. It tugs happiness in its wake. I like this person, and I associate their voice with good things. Shit. Not what I want.

When I can't make a connection, I creep closer, hoping to see more than dark-clad figures. Then the man speaks again, teasing the woman, and I stop short as I break into a grin.

I ease back in the other direction and then slip out behind them on the path. I creep up almost close enough to tap the man on the back before he wheels, eyes widening.

I sigh. "You're supposed to go for your weapon, Jacob." I nod at the woman in front of him, brandishing a knife. "See, Nicole knows how to do it. You are a shitty survivalist, and I am totally telling your brother on you."

Jacob grins and catches me up in a hug. Dalton's younger brother looks enough like him that there's no mistaking the shared DNA. Yet I'm not surprised he didn't go for a weapon when he sensed someone at his shoulder. There's an innocence in Jacob, a gentleness that his brother shares but keeps well hidden.

I hug Nicole next. At first, I'm careful not to squeeze too hard, but she pulls me in for a fierce embrace.

"I'm just pregnant, Casey," she says.

I look down at her stomach. She's five months along and was supposed to have her first prenatal appointment six weeks ago.

"So you finally showed up," I say.

"I'm *fine*. We were taking advantage of good hunting." She glances at Jacob. "At *my* insistence. I reasoned that we should hunt while we can, stock up on food and fur, and then overwinter near Rockton, as planned." She looks at me. "Acceptable?"

"If it means you'll be here for the birth, yes."

Jacob says, "I wouldn't have it any other way. We'll be as close as we can, in case of complications."

"Oh, I don't care about complications," I say. "I just want to be around when the baby comes. I'm going to be an auntie. It's all about me."

Nicole laughs and hugs me again. "It's good to see you."

"I'd say the same, but then I might also be forced to give you more shit for not coming around sooner."

"I know, I know." She backs up against Jacob, and his arms go around her. "We were busy honeymooning."

I look down at her stomach. "I see that."

I'm about to say more when I remember what I'm supposed to be doing.

"Shit," I say. "I'm out here to foil a secret meeting, and then my targets turned out to be you guys, and I forgot the whole damn thing."

"Blame us."

"I will. That's what happens when it's so long between visits."

"Well, if it helps, we did hear someone," Jacob says. "We caught a man's voice maybe a quarter mile back. They were off the trail, and the guy was whispering. Nic thought it might be a couple sneaking away from Rockton, so we kept quiet as we passed, giving them privacy."

"Did you hear what was being said?"

Nicole shakes her head. "A guy was talking. That's all we caught."

I turn to the forest and raise my voice just a little. "Jen, are you out here?"

Storm appears first, barreling through to see Jacob and Nicole, and we need to drag her off before she knocks Nicole flying. I stand over Storm to hold her still while Nicole pets her.

"Riding your dog now," Jen says as she steps out. "The sheriff hasn't bought you enough motor toys?" She nods at Nicole and Jacob with a gruff greeting that softens a little for Nicole.

"Could you escort Nicole and Jacob into town?" I say. "They heard someone a quarter mile back. If I'm lucky, that's far enough away not to have overheard us. I'm going to check it out."

"By yourself?" Jacob says.

"I have Storm."

"And you have me," he says. "My brother would kill me if I let you chase down bad guys alone."

"Minor-league bad," I say. "But yes, since you know where you heard that voice, I'll take the help. Jen? Escort Nicole straight to April, please. I don't want her sneaking off before she's had a full prenatal exam."

Nicole rolls her eyes, but follows Jen down the trail.

As Jacob and I head out, it's a struggle to keep from peppering him with questions. They really have been away too long. I understand it. They're a new couple. Part of me is envious. Dalton and I have been permitted a handful of weekends off. I dream of an entire week alone together. I'd take a month, maybe even a summer. More than that, and we'd both be jonesing for outside conversation. Neither of us is overly sociable, but we love our group of friends, and our brains need the extra stimulation of conversations and debates that go beyond our echo-chamber-for-two.

Jacob is accustomed to a very different kind of life. He lived in the woods with his family until Dalton was taken, and then with just his parents, who'd died when he was a young teen. He's introspective and introverted by nature, and I think his short visits to Rockton are all the socializing he needs. As for Nicole, she spent a year being held captive in a cave. She's more sociable than Jacob, but she finds a serenity in the wilderness with Jacob, the two of them bonded tight and happy together.

Any catching up will need to wait.

Jacob leads the way off-trail. The longer we walk, the more certain I am that I've missed my chance. The forest is silent, and Storm isn't perking up to show she's caught a live scent. Conrad and his "fan" must have seen Jacob and Nicole—or he heard us talking—and they've bustled back to town along another route.

Jacob slows and cocks his head. I listen, but I only catch the faint burble of a stream over rocks. He mouths *Too far,* and I realize the stream is what he'd heard, an audio indication that we've walked past the point where they heard the voice.

He considers a moment and then reverses course. I fall in step behind him. Storm snuffles the air but only lightly, as if scenting something other than her target. We're on the opposite side of the path from where Jacob heard someone, meaning there's no trail here for Storm to follow.

After a few moments, Jacob slows. He motions for me to wait, and he slips back to the path, presumably to check landmarks. When he returns, he whispers, "We're in the right area, but it's quiet."

I gesture that I'm going to check it out, while asking him to stay back with Storm. He nods. They're close enough to come to my aid if I need it.

I creep to the path. Then I stop and listen. It's thick brush here, the kind of spot where I could be a foot off the path and have someone pass by without seeing me.

When I hear nothing, I ease across the path and into the brush on the other side. I make my way through, stopping every couple of steps to listen. Still nothing to hear.

Okay, that's not exactly true. If I strain, I can pick up the distant rustle of some critter in the undergrowth. A red squirrel scolds. The wind whispers through the evergreens, perfuming the air. But immediately around me, all is silent. Any birds or animals know I'm here and they're waiting for me to move on.

What I don't hear is a human sound. Not a voice. Not a footfall. Not a cracked branch.

I've missed my chance—possibly through my own carelessness, happily reuniting with Nicole and Jacob when I was supposed to be working. It's easy to do that here. Too easy, the line between Detective Butler and Resident Casey blurred often to invisibility.

Down south, I'd worked with a detective who'd moved from small-town Newfoundland, and he'd always said it had been both rewarding and restricting working and living in a community of a few hundred people. At the time, I didn't really understand either part. Now I do. This way of life and of policing suits me better than I ever imagined, but I still need to work harder on separating my roles.

I've lost my chance to catch Conrad with his informant, but I still have one hope. The scene of the crime, or in this case, the scene of the meeting that I consider criminal. I very much doubt either participant left behind incriminating evidence, but at least I might be able to get shoe prints.

I call for Jacob to rejoin me, and Storm picks up Conrad's

scent on the path. He'd snuck out of town off-path, but once he felt safe, he'd followed the trail to meet whoever sent him that message. Then they left the path to tramp along a game trail and ended up in a clearing.

Storm snuffles around the clearing while I search for clues. I find and mark two partial prints from the same tread.

"Hey," Jacob says. "Someone tried to cover their tracks here."

I glance over to see him looking down at a scuff mark. Someone left a footprint and then tried to rub it out. It's a laughable attempt, so obvious that it draws our attention to a footprint that might otherwise have gone unnoticed. The hasty erasure leaves enough for me to get an idea of both the shoe size and tread pattern.

When Storm woofs, I'm bent over the print, sketching the tread in my notebook. She gives another woof, and I'm on my feet, turning to find her. The sun has started to drop, and it gets dark faster in the forest. Spotting a black dog isn't easy, and she gives a third woof before Jacob and I locate her, ten feet away.

I make my way over and find her nosing at the ground.

"It's been disturbed," Jacob says. "Something digging. Bear maybe? Wolverine?"

That's where his mind goes first. What animal could have done this? I'm thinking of the humans who'd been nearby. Especially when I notice that a large branch has been dragged over the disturbed earth, in a pitiable attempt to hide the digging.

So what could Conrad or his informant have buried? A notebook with additional resident backgrounds? That's my guess. Whoever contacted Conrad has more stories, and they realized— with the police already searching Conrad's residence—nowhere in town is safe for that information. Stick it in a box and bury it.

Jacob pulls off the branch, and I immediately see my mistake.

I see how big this patch of disturbed earth is.

I drop to my knees and start digging. "Get back to Rockton, Jacob. I'm going to need a shovel. And Eric. Bring Eric quickly, please."

"There's a shovel here," he says, walking back with one in his hands. "I saw the glint of it. Do you want me to dig while you get Eric?"

There's a calm in his voice. The calm of innocence. He hasn't figured out what I have, only that I want something dug up rather urgently.

I'm about to tell him to give me the shovel, when my digging fingers touch flesh. Warm flesh.

I claw at the dirt, pushing it away as fast as I can, pale skin appearing between the dark clods. An arm. A still-warm arm. I brush madly now, up higher, aiming for the face. Instead I get a throat. And my fingers feel something else. Movement. A pulse.

"Shit!" I say. "He's still alive."

"W-what?"

Jacob steps closer, and I glance up just in time to see his eyes widen as he realizes I've uncovered a person. He drops on the other side and starts digging.

"His face," I say. "Help me find his face. Clear his airways."

It's a man. That'll all I know, from the arm. I've already found his head, and it takes a moment to be sure he's faceup. Jacob grabs the man's shoulders and yanks, pulling him upright out of the dirt. There's a danger in that—if the man's spine was injured—but Jacob doesn't know better, and under the circumstances, it's the right choice. We don't know how long this man has been buried. How long he hasn't been able to breathe.

The man is sitting up now, as limp as a rag doll, with Jacob supporting him. Damp earth clings to the man's face. As I brush it off, my brain insists I know who this is. Yes, I do. I just need to be sure. One last swipe, and I am.

It's Conrad.

TWELVE

I keep clearing the dirt from Conrad's face, faster now, my heart thudding. There are no residents I wouldn't frantically try to save, no matter what they'd done. I do not need more deaths on my conscience, and I would never want to look back and question whether I really did all I could.

I'm also suddenly very aware of how it will look if he dies. Residents won't care *who* buried this man alive. They'll only know that I found him and failed to save him and maybe, just maybe, that was revenge for what he did to Anders.

One advantage to Conrad's upright position is that I'm not fighting gravity to clear his airways. I lean him forward, face tilted down. Then I open his mouth and hook a finger inside. Nothing falls out, and my hand comes back clean. That means he hadn't woken up under the earth, clawing and gasping. A small mercy there. He's unconscious now and has been since someone dumped him into a very shallow grave.

"There's blood on the back of his head," Jacob says.

I nod and hope it's not too curt. At this point, injuries are irrelevant. The man isn't breathing. That's all that counts.

"I need him on his back," I say.

Jacob helps me get Conrad into position. I bend over the unconscious man and begin rescue breathing. I get maybe a half dozen breaths in when Conrad convulses and sputters. His head jerks, as if he's trying to get upright, but it's only a cough. His eyes stay closed.

"He's breathing," Jacob says. "That's a start, right?"

I nod. "Can you run to town and get help? Please?"

He rises. "Your sister and Eric, right?"

"And a couple of strong residents with a stretcher. Tell Eric we have an unconscious victim in need of emergency attention. He'll know what to do."

With Jacob gone, I put Storm on watch. I'll be too focused on Conrad and the scene to notice if there's trouble, and out here, trouble could be anything from a curious bear to whoever failed to kill Conrad.

My sister will remind me that "failed" is a premature judgment. I don't know what his injuries are. I do a quick assessment on that right away.

As Jacob said, there's a wound on the back of Conrad's head. A wide and shallow dent, high on his skull. When I check, I find a second strike lower down. Hit from behind. He falls to his knees and then comes the killing blow.

It's supposed to be a killing blow. It is not. Did it render him unconscious and his killer said "good enough"? Dug a shallow trench and covered him up to let nature take its course? Or did they think he *was* dead? Either way, it was a spectacularly half-assed job, like covering the footprints and burial site.

A half-assed job that still would have killed him. It'd have been tomorrow before we realized Conrad was gone, and even then, we wouldn't have rushed a search, presuming he fled after being tipped off that I knew he was behind the sign posting. We'd have eventually found this shallow grave, but by then, he'd be dead, any evidence gone.

Speaking of evidence . . .

We have a shovel. That suggests premeditated murder. There wasn't enough time for the killer to fetch it from Rockton after knocking Conrad out. This wasn't a supporter wanting to help the cause. Someone wanted Conrad stopped.

Stopped before their own secrets were revealed?

Lure Conrad into the woods. Hit him over the head. Have the hole pre-dug with a shovel brought for that purpose. Bury him, cover it up, and accidentally leave the shovel behind.

When I find blood on the shovel, I start cursing myself. I almost used the murder *weapon* to dig out the murder *victim*. Of course, at the time, all I was thinking was that someone was buried here, and I needed to get them out.

Technically, it's a spade. All-metal construction. Definitely Rockton issue. From the wound, the killer hit with the spade part. The second strike had been focused on power rather than aim, and there's a cut in Conrad's scalp where the edge bit in.

Hit twice with the spade. No other obvious wounds. Those two are nasty enough, and it's a miracle he didn't die of that second blow. Whoever hit him used all their force to do it.

With my flashlight out now, I see drag marks in the dirt. He'd been struck close to the hole. Had he noticed it? Come to investigate and been struck from behind?

That's all I have for now. Partial footprints. A possible scenario. The murder weapon. And a living murder victim, who can hopefully recover and point his finger at his killer, and all this will be supporting data only.

At the sound of voices, I rise, and I'm halfway up when my swinging flashlight beam catches something in the hole. Fabric.

I lean in to see a hat of some kind. It must have fallen off Conrad when he stumbled. Just before the second blow.

I use a stick to pull it up without touching it. Since I've already, you know, touched the damn murder weapon. As I lift the hat, I frown. I've seen it before. A dark gray baseball cap that honestly doesn't look like anything I can imagine Conrad wearing. The man is really more the fedora type.

The killer lost their hat? Buried it with the body? Oh, that would be too good. The ultimate half-assed murder.

There's an insignia on the front. I shine my light as I twist the baseball cap on the stick.

It's a Canadian military hat. One I know very well, because I bought it as a joke. That's why this cap seemed so familiar.

It belongs to Will Anders.

THIRTEEN

April and Dalton have come, with Jacob leading the way and two militia members following. April does an onsite assessment and declares Conrad fit for transport. The militia and Jacob carry him on the stretcher, with April keeping watch over her patient. As they leave, Dalton sets up a battery-operated floodlight for me to process the scene. When he turns, I'm holding Anders's baseball cap in one gloved hand.

"I found this in the grave," I say.

"Fuck." He sighs and throws up his hands. "Well, that's it. Case solved. I'll go arrest Will."

"Funny man." I lift the cap higher. "Though I might be tempted to actually laugh if I wasn't rolling my eyes hard enough to hurt. Is this actually supposed to incriminate Will? When he was with you at the time of the murder? With you the entire *evening*?"

"We aren't dealing with a criminal genius," he says, taking out my camera. "Although, to be fair, given the inexact science of determining time of death, it would have opened up a window of doubt if we didn't know exactly when Conrad died."

"One would hope that Will, being a police deputy, wouldn't

let his baseball cap fall into the shallow grave as he's burying the body."

"Still reasonable doubt."

"Agreed, which is why I wasn't waving it in front of the others." I look up at Dalton. "I do *not* want to suppress evidence, Eric. In an actual investigation, police keep lots of things from the public to help us narrow down suspects and weed out crackpots. Up here, it's not as if I publicly report every finding, but this . . ."

"If we don't mention it—and residents find out—they'll scream cover-up, even if you've noted the cap and filed it as evidence."

"Yep. And even if you and I agree this doesn't introduce an iota of reasonable doubt, given Will's ironclad alibi."

"The guy providing that alibi is his boss and his friend. I can say he's been with me all evening, except for a two-minute piss break, and they'll argue he managed to attack Conrad then. Or that I'm outright lying."

"I don't want to put this burden on you."

"I'm the sheriff. It's my call. And my call is . . ." He runs a hand through his hair. "Fuck. My call is that we can't be accused of covering it up. I'm not walking back to town waving that hat over my head, but it needs to go out in a public message." He shakes his head. "I can't believe I just suggested you do one of those damn statements."

"It's the only way to handle it. Full statement first thing tomorrow about what happened to Conrad, and as part of that, I will mention the baseball cap. You will alibi Will. Before any of that happens, Will needs to be warned and we need to figure out where the baseball cap came from. Presumably the break-in."

"Which is awkward when we think Conrad did that."

"He could have brought it along as a souvenir. Showing off

for whoever he was meeting. Or whoever summoned him was his accomplice that night. Or it was stolen later, when we had Will's house open as a crime scene. Our best bet, though?"

"Hoping Conrad wakes up to identify his attacker?"

"Yep."

We set Storm on the would-be killer's trail. She follows it back to town, where she loses it in the web of scents. I wish I could ask her whether it's the same scent as the one at the break-in. If there's a way of doing that, we haven't trained for it. Another thing to add to my endless list.

We warn Anders next. He's shaken, more than we were. To me, it's a truly eye-rolling frame-up job. To him, though, a killer has actively tried to pin a murder on him.

The last time he wore the baseball cap was a week ago. Since then, it's been in his front closet with all his outerwear. After the break-in, he checked valuables, but he didn't look through his clothing or other everyday items.

We stop in at the clinic next. Yes, Anders was our priority, and I will feel no guilt about that. Conrad is in my sister's hands, and he couldn't receive better care.

I walk into the clinic. Dalton peeks over my shoulder, sees Diana there and murmurs that he'll meet me back at the station. I'm sure he's retreating because four people in the tiny room is too much, but yes, if he doesn't need to deal with Diana, they're both happier for it.

My sister is busy with Conrad, who's unconscious on the table.

Diana slides over and murmurs, "I haven't had time to talk to you in person lately. How's Will doing?"

Anders and Diana had a one-night stand shortly after she

arrived. She'd hoped for more, and when it didn't materialize, she'd blamed me—I must have said something to Anders or batted my lashes and lured him away. That is Diana.

Is it more accurate to say that *was* Diana? I think so. She's changed. I know that if she hadn't, we wouldn't be the semi-friends we are today. We'll never be best friends again. I came to recognize the toxicity of our fifteen-year friendship and decided I deserved better. She's given me better, and I must acknowledge that.

"Will's managing," I say.

"In other words, he's as well as can be expected. If there's anything I can do to help . . ."

"Just stay on his side. Please."

She nods. "I'm there. Always. He doesn't deserve this."

"Are you two done chitchatting?" April says as she prepares an IV for Conrad. "If you aren't, I'll ask you to leave, Casey. I require my nurse's full attention."

"I'm your nurse now?" Diana says. "Can I get that in writing?"

"Certainly. As soon as you can provide your nursing degree. Now, do you think you can help me with this, Diana?"

"That depends. Two minutes ago you shooed me away."

Diana brings the IV tube over to April. Diana's nursing background comprised one summer when we'd both been candy stripers. My parents had insisted I take the job, still holding out hope of a medical career for me. As for Diana, she just wanted to meet cute interns.

She'd stumbled into nursing here. Knowing Diana from before, April is comfortable with her. And by "knowing her," I mean that April was aware Diana existed and thought she was a waste of space in my life. I believe her opinion has changed. I'm not actually sure.

Whatever their personal opinions of one another, they

work well together. I wait while they get the IV inserted. Then April turns to me. "When I started here, I was assured that baby and prenatal care would not be required, given that children are not permitted. Yet I have treated one baby and now I will be delivering another. *Delivering.*"

"Don't forget, Jen can help. She was a midwife."

Diana mutters, "I'd sooner deliver the poor baby myself."

"Speaking of which," April says, "I need a full team of medical professionals, and you've given me . . ." She peers at Diana. "What are you again?"

"Human?"

April waves her hand. "Whatever Diana did for a living. You bring me cases such as this. A man brutally struck over the head and buried alive. Buried *alive*? You don't think that's a bit excessive?"

"I agree in principle, but you'd need to ask the person who buried him."

"It is one trauma after another. One unique situation after another."

"One *challenge* after another?" I say. "I know you love puzzles. And before you suggest it, I did not bury him alive to give you one. It isn't your birthday yet."

"I realize that is meant to be a joke. It is not funny."

I walk over and pat her back. Not the most affectionate gesture, but it's one she'll allow. I understand the reason behind this outburst. It has nothing to do with her questioning our medical hiring practices or even railing against inadequate staffing. This is how April deals with stress.

My sister does enjoy a challenge. Just not the ones where someone's life is in her hands and her hands alone. She feels inadequate to the sheer breadth of work she's asked to do in Rockton, and it isn't in her to simply say she's done her best and rest easy. In that, we are truly sisters.

"I take it the prognosis isn't good," I say when she turns back to Conrad.

"I don't know yet," she says curtly. "I don't know how long he was buried for. I don't know how much damage was done by the blows to the head versus the suffocation. What I can tell you right now, Casey, is that he is unconscious and has shown no signs of reversing that condition."

"He's alive," I say.

"For now," she says. "For now."

Without an MRI or CT scan, April can only guess at what's keeping Conrad from waking, which completely freaks her out, as much as she tries to hide it. I bring in help. She might rail at the lack of medical professionals here, but as a psychiatrist, Mathias has his medical degree. He's just never practiced medicine. There's Anders, too, who'd been pre-med in university and started his army career as a medic. While I am not a medical professional—at all—growing up in my family means I have stellar first-aid skills. For this, we decide to leave Anders out of it. Covering *his* ass in case anything goes wrong.

Mathias suspects intercranial swelling from the blow, but again, there's no way to confirm that, especially when Conrad is unconscious. For now, that's the best thing for him—being unconscious. His body is resting, and his brain is healing, and we need to leave him be, which means I'm not interviewing Conrad anytime soon.

I'm in the forest with Dalton and Storm. We're going over the trails again in hopes that if we reinforce the scent of Conrad's attacker, Storm will be able to unweave that web of in-town scents. Better yet, we'll return to town and she'll race to the killer, barking madly. Yeah, if there's a way to teach her that, I haven't found *it* either.

It sometimes feels as if I don't do enough tracking work with Storm. *Think of all the incredible applications it has to Rockton police work! Tracking lost residents! Tracking fleeing criminals! Identifying killers!* But even if she could run up to Conrad's attacker and bark, no one would accept that as proof. I've already seen how quickly skeptical residents dismissed her work tracking Anders's home intruders.

What I'm hoping for is not that she'll expose the would-be killer to the world, but that she'll expose them to *me*.

Show me whodunit, Storm, and let me take it from there.

That doesn't happen. She seems to get the scent in town, and then loses it. Picks it up again. Loses it again. By that point, it's time for the town meeting.

The crowd is smaller this time. I'm not sure what to make of that. It's later in the morning, with little excuse not to be there, and surely "resident found buried alive" is a bigger deal than Anders's sign. My fear is that fewer people means they're losing trust in us. They want to know what happened to Conrad; they just don't trust us to give them the truth.

I explain what I discovered last night. I say that I had reason to believe Conrad went into the forest, and that concerned me so I followed with Storm and discovered him in a shallow grave. No mention of the fact that I knew he was meeting someone there, someone who sent a note. I don't want to spook his attacker.

What I don't withhold is the baseball cap. I display it in a baggie and explain where I found it. Then Dalton gives his alibi for Anders, and the grumbling begins. It's quiet at first, an angry hornet buzz that finally erupts in a single word.

"Figures."

When Dalton surges forward, I subtly block him with a hip and shoulder.

"Would you care to elaborate on that?" I call into the audience.

"Do I need to?"

"No," I say. "But I thought you might want the opportunity to step forward and say it, instead of hiding in the crowd." I shade my eyes and squint for emphasis. "Is that you, Arnie? You're questioning the validity of Will's alibi. We anticipated that. Eric has compiled a list of everyone who stopped by the station or otherwise saw them yesterday evening. We will be confirming that with the people involved. In the meantime, if anyone saw Will alone or with someone other than Eric, please come forward. I will investigate—"

A loud snort from someone lost in the audience.

"I will investigate the attempted murder of Conrad."

"Despite the fact you already know the killer?"

"Yeah," Dalton drawls. "Because obviously, if a career law-enforcement officer murders someone, he's going to leave behind his most identifiable baseball cap. He's going to put his victim under three inches of dirt. Make no attempt to cover his tracks when he knows his colleague has a fucking *tracking* dog."

"Will doesn't need to be careful. He has you guys to cover for him."

It's definitely Arnie talking. When he began, he got nods and noises of agreement. But with each round of this conversation, the support dies down, and by this last line, he's lost his cover, too, people shifting away from him, leaving him standing there, alone.

No need to say more. They're angry and suspicious, but they get it. This was a poor frame-up job, and they aren't buying it.

"With any luck," I say, "Conrad will be awake tomorrow to identify his attacker."

And with that, the meeting adjourns.

FOURTEEN

I spend the rest of the morning compiling evidence in Conrad's attempted murder. There's a lot of it, a shocking amount really, all of it further proof that I'm dealing with a rank amateur. That describes most killers, even those who've done it before.

I got away with murder once, as a stupid nineteen-year-old who went to confront her ex-boyfriend with a gun. When we'd been attacked in an alley—because of something he did—he fled and left me to a presumably fatal beating. So I took a gun to confront him. I had no intention of firing it, but instead of apologizing, he blamed me.

Even as I pulled the trigger, I hadn't intended to kill him. My rage reacted for me, zero forethought involved. I didn't hide his body. I didn't clean up the crime scene. I walked away without even checking to see whether I left footprints. All I did was dispose of the gun, my police cadet training giving me enough insight to do that. The rest was dumb luck.

My ex obviously hadn't told anyone he was going to see me, and I hadn't told anyone I was going to see him. Either I didn't leave footprints or there were too many to choose from.

He'd been a small-time drug dealer—a privileged college kid who swiped dope from his dad's pharmacy. In his arrogance and stupidity, he'd pissed off dangerous people, and it was presumed one of them killed him.

Dumb luck for me, yes, but not unusual. Of the murders I investigated down south, at least a third of the time they were only solved because the killer talked to someone who talked to us.

With the attack on Conrad, people are happy to talk. Gloria for one. I reinterview her, and she gives me everything she can. She doesn't know who his accomplice was, but she can confirm that Conrad himself broke into Anders's place.

She can also confirm that, as far as she knows, he doesn't have any other resident backgrounds. He got Anders's from "a reliable source"—in other words, Jen under the influence. His entire plan had been to expose Anders in revenge for jealousy and various trifling offenses, like warning Conrad about "accidentally" dropping litter and warning him about "borrowing" from a neighbor's woodpile. In other word, Anders had the audacity to call him out—very politely and respectfully—on minor offenses, none of which resulted in charges.

Conrad had asked doped-up Jen for dirt on any of the inner circle of Rockton. What he got was too good to reserve for mere blackmail. It was a chance for petty revenge.

When Conrad had Gloria post the sign, he won Rockton's variety of fame, with the town buzzing about how someone "exposed" a cover-up. His revenge became the act of a crusader, and he quickly gained fans. The smart thing to do at this point would have been to remain the masked avenger. Bask in the accolades without revealing his identity.

This is where the superhero stories get it wrong. The true power of all those heroes must be the bulletproof egos that allow them to go about their everyday life, enduring everyday injustices, and not scream "But I'm really a superhero!" No way in hell was Conrad's ego letting him do that. So he allowed a few people into his confidence. He started his own fan club.

The problem with fans is that they want more from you. *That was great, but what's your next act?* Conrad pretended he had more when he did not. That's why he jumped at that note luring him into the woods.

As for the note, I have that, too. It was in Conrad's damn pocket. I'd planned to search his apartment for it this morning, because clearly he'd have the sense to hide it. Nope. The note was still in his pocket, neatly folded.

Talking to Gloria was first on my list. Next up is examining the note and those boot treads found at the scene. I'm heading back to the station when Nicole hails me.

"Hey!" I say, giving her a quick embrace.

"Two hugs in less than a day?" she says. "Clearly I need to disappear into the woods more often."

"Yeah, yeah. Did you get to see April?"

"I did, and your sister is as endearing as ever."

I laugh. "Makes me look warm and cuddly."

"She does indeed. Were you heading to the station?"

"I was."

"I'll walk with you then."

We continue on. No one stops us. A few look askance at Nicole, only to decide she's just another forest dweller allowed into town for medical help.

"How quickly things change," she murmurs as someone gives her a vague nod. "When I came back after my ordeal, I marveled at all the new faces. There were plenty I knew, though. This time it's barely been a year, and there are only a handful of faces I recognize."

"They're shutting us down."

She looks over. "What?"

"It isn't official yet, but it's coming. No one's getting extensions. We've gotten less than a half dozen new residents in the past few months. I was new when we got you back, and now I'm the old guard."

"What are you guys going to do?"

I shrug. "Whatever we can. Right now, we just want the council to admit they're closing us down, so we have something to fight. We're boxing shadows at this point." I inhale. "So, on a happier note, I'm guessing April gave you a clean bill of health?"

"She did. I felt as if everything was fine, but I'm past thirty, first baby, and there was the . . . one I lost."

The one her captor beat out of her. I don't let my expression change, just nod in understanding. This is how we bonded. We had our ordeals—hers so much more horrific than mine—and we just want to move on. To live as regular people, our pasts put behind us.

She continues, "No issues that April can see, although she reminded me—not less than three times—that she isn't a gynecologist."

I sigh. "She does that."

"With a laundry list of qualifications and conditions, she is 'allowing' us to return to the forest. Which is why I caught up. There's a lot going on here, and Jacob would prefer not to linger. You guys are obviously busy. We'll be back in a few weeks—April wants twice-monthly checkups—and hopefully things will be calm enough for a proper visit."

I want to protest. I don't. The atmosphere in town right now will make Jacob uneasy. Dalton won't be pleased about them leaving so soon. Yet they are right about the timing. We don't have any attention to spare. Not right now.

"I think I'm wrapping up the case," I say. "I know who

exposed Will's background. I have enough evidence on his attacker that I can expect to make an arrest soon. Yes, you should go, but do come back. Please."

She puts an arm around my shoulders. "We will."

I've ordered Nicole to stop by the bakery for a takeaway care package before she goes, on my tab. Same for the general store Get what they need, and we'll settle up with fur and meat trades later.

Dalton will tell them the same and probably strong-arm his brother into the shop to be sure he takes advantage. Jacob might hesitate; Nicole will not. She'll make sure it's accounted for and repaid, but she knows that anything they remove from the store will be replaced, and so they should avail themselves of the opportunity.

Once I've said my goodbyes, I'm in the station with the note Conrad's attacker used to lure him into the forest.

> I appreciate what you did with Deputy
> Anders. I have more stories for you if you
> want them. Meet me at fishing site 2 at 8pm
> tonight. Tell no one, please. If anyone finds
> out I have this, my life would be in Danger.

Fishing site two. I'd seen that earlier when I read it, and my brain has been idly turning it over. We'd found Conrad about fifty feet from fishing site two. His attacker must have met him there and led him to the clearing. The significant part of that only creeps into my consciousness now. His attacker knew site two. Conrad also knew it. But for his attacker to *know* Conrad knew it suggests they'd been in a fishing party together.

We keep records of all trips outside town. Part of that is in case of contact with anything toxic. Part of it is so we know the experience level of the participants. If someone volunteers for a hunting expedition and says they've been on two fishing trips, Dalton wants proof.

I bring the logbook to the desk. As I do, I see the note again. It's written in block letters, nothing distinctive, but it keeps bringing to mind a sign. Apparently, after the one accusing Anders, I have signs on the brain. This lettering is nothing like that one.

I flip through the logbook and insert stickies on pages with fishing trips to site two. I find six trips there this year. Obviously a popular spot. Six trips, with between six and ten residents per outing. Of those, Conrad went on four.

Damn. That is not as helpful as I might have hoped.

The door slaps open, and I glance up to see Dalton entering with two steaming boxes.

"Tell me that's lunch," I say.

"Tell me you ate lunch at lunchtime."

"Uh . . ." I look at my watch. It's nearly six. I glance up. "Thank you for dinner. Also, did you let Conrad go on extra fishing trips?"

He frowns, trying to make sense of that segue.

I lift the book. "I have reason to believe his attacker joined him on a fishing excursion. However, he's been on four since May, which seems excessive."

Dalton sighs and sets down the food. "Yeah. He was whining about the dentistry thing, and Phil decided to give him extra fishing privileges as a bonus. Easy way to shut him up. With fewer residents, we don't often have a full group. Guy likes his fishing. Shitty at it, according to Brandon, but he likes it."

Brandon—Isabel's bartender—is in charge of fishing excursions, having taken over from Sam. I write out a list of everyone who was on the same trips as Conrad and add "talk to Brandon" to my list. I don't know whether Conrad would have interacted with his future attacker on the trips, but it's worth knowing whether there was any animosity.

"Is this the note Conrad's attacker sent?" Dalton says, picking up the evidence baggie from my desk.

I nod and keep jotting in my notebook.

"I've seen this writing before," he says. "On a sign, I think?"

I look up at him.

"Not *that* sign," he says. "Another one. Around town." He lifts the note higher into the light. "It's not a distinctive hand, but it looks familiar."

"If I gave you a weird look, it's because I thought the same thing. That it reminds me of a sign. I just figured I had signs on the brain."

Dalton unpacks dinner, and we eat as we talk. I still have more evidence I hope to process tonight: the footprints and the shovel. First, I want to speak to Brandon and see if he remembers Conrad being particularly chatty with anyone on the excursions to fishing site two.

Once we're finished eating, Dalton pulls on his hat. "I'm going to do a round looking at handwritten signs. It might be long gone, but the surroundings could jog my memory. Mind if I take this?"

"Go ahead." I check my watch. "I'll swing by the Roc and see whether Isabel will let me steal her bartender for a chat."

I'm outside the Roc. It's open for the evening, and people are streaming in. If they see me on the porch, they nod, the degree of friendliness telling me how they feel about the current situation.

I gaze up at the sign announcing I've arrived at the Roc.

There's a painting of a bird, which is supposed to be a mythical roc but is actually a rook. That's what happens in a town without internet to double-check these things. Of course, it's not like the average person knows their rooks from their rocs anyway.

A few months ago, Dalton admitted the bar name is entirely his fault. Back when he was a kid, the place was known as the Rockton Arms. A lightning strike split the sign at the K. The bar owner wanted to fix the K and call it the Rock, but Dalton told him about rocs, and the guy decided to go with that, either to humor the kid or because—as I would agree—it's a much cooler reference. So the bar becomes the Roc, and the next owner decides to paint the bird on it. Dalton offered to help, but no, the guy knew what he was doing . . . and painted a rook.

"You still thinking about asking Petra to fix that?" says a voice behind me.

I turn to see Dalton and Storm.

"No, just looking at it," I say, as Storm lumbers onto the porch and begins snuffling around.

He steps up beside me and leans down to my ear. "We'll get her to paint a new one for the new town."

Tears prickle at my eyes, and I blink them back. The new town. Our backup plan. It seemed so obvious when I first arrived. If we were forced out, we'd create our own Rockton. Only now, as that possibility looms, have I realized why Dalton didn't do it years ago. It's a Herculean undertaking. While we *are* making plans for that possibility, I fear that it's like children making plans to run away, entertaining impossible and naive dreams.

A couple pauses to check the sign at the door and be sure it's a non-brothel night. When I first came to Rockton, it was always brothel night. Oh, sure, many of the customers came just to drink, but the presence of sex workers kept other women away, fearing uncomfortable conversations with would-be johns. Isabel didn't see the problem, because Isabel is the kind of woman no one approaches with that mistake. She just figured women preferred the Red Lion.

We originally instituted pre-brothel "early hours." Now it's alternating days, and more women show up even on brothel nights as men learn that a woman drinking there is not necessarily a sex worker.

"We won't need that either," Dalton says, as if reading my mind. "If someone wants to trade on the side, fine, but no brothel. Isabel has agreed."

I nod. Dalton shifts. He's trying to figure out why I'm standing here. It's not pure nostalgia. I have a job to do, and I wouldn't let myself get lost in melancholy thoughts. I need him to see it himself. Independent corroboration.

He could just ask what I'm doing, but the man has never met a puzzle that he didn't want to solve on his own. He glances around and then . . .

"Fuck."

I follow his gaze to the sign beside the door.

Wednesday at the Roc

The only thing on offer tonight is our
alcohol, including delicious semi-chilled
beer and watered-down cocktails.

Evening special: raspberry vodka lemonade
(and no, it's not on sale)

Isabel didn't write that sign. The fact that she even allows it to be written is proof that she likes her new bartender enough to permit this gentle mockery of her business practices.

Dalton looks at me. "That's it, isn't it? What you were looking at."

I nod.

He holds Conrad's note beside the sign. "Fuck."

That's why the writing looked familiar. Because we see it almost daily on Isabel's signs.

"It's not a distinctive hand," I say. "As you pointed out."

"It's not. However . . ."

His gaze turns to Storm, who is still snuffling, taking far more interest than usual in the layers of scent outside the Roc's door.

"Still not proof," I say.

"Nor is the fact that they've been on the same fishing trips multiple times."

I slump against the wall. "Fuck."

"That's what I said."

"I like Brandon," I say. "He's always seemed like a decent guy."

Dalton nods, and we move away from the front door. Storm snuffles for a moment, and then joins us. I glance back at the sign.

"Is there anything you can tell me?" I say. "Concerns in his background?"

He steers me farther from the Roc and then lowers his voice to say, "I think his backstory is fake."

"What?" I glance up at him. "Sorry. That sounded shrill."

"I didn't know it when Isabel hired him, or I'd have said something. It's actually Phil who suspected it and brought it to me to research when we're in Dawson next week."

"He's concerned about Isabel. Protecting her."

"Yep. We aren't quite at the stage where Phil would bring random concerns to me. But he knows Brandon's alleged story, which Brandon must not realize. Recently, in talking to Brandon, Phil noticed discrepancies."

"Between what Brandon says and the backstory the council gave him."

"None of it suggests the guy's real background, so I can't help you there. It could be white-collar crime. Or it could be violent. For now, Phil has just been keeping a close watch, both on the stockroom and Isabel."

"If Brandon does have a secret background, that gives him a reason to silence Conrad—the person promising to reveal those backgrounds."

"Take him in for a proper interview." Dalton glances back at the Roc. "We should do that now."

"We should."

FIFTEEN

Dalton stays outside with Storm. Having both of us walk in wearing our work clothes would be a sure sign we aren't there for a post-shift drink. Dalton sticks close, though, to help escort Brandon to the station.

I walk in and the burble of conversation rises to greet me. It's just after seven, a couple of hours from peak drinking time. Most of the customers are on the back deck, enjoying their beer or wine al fresco. I spot Isabel through a window. As I pass the bar, a bearded guy in his late twenties looks up. I pretend not to see Brandon. My poker face is decent, but I'd rather not test it tonight.

I step onto the deck. Isabel doesn't see me. She's deep in conversation with Phil.

This has become a common sight, early in the evening. Isabel and Phil sharing a tiny table, leaning over it as they drink, enrapt in their discussion and oblivious to everything else. It's rare to find anyone else with them. If Dalton and I come in later, we might share a drink. A few others are occasionally invited to join them. Mostly their table is a private one. A private table for private people.

Early in my Rockton stay, it'd come as a shock to realize Isabel doesn't have many friends. She's the most powerful woman—possibly most powerful person—in town. She's
charming and easy to talk to, a first-rate conversationalist. I
wouldn't call that an act, but it is part of her public persona.
The therapist turned bar-and-brothel owner. Get to know her
personally, and the conversation is even better, but the privacy
shield goes up. I'm probably her closest friend in Rockton, yet
that only means she seeks out my company now and then.

I'm glad to see her with Phil. I liked Mick, but this is more
a meeting of the minds. Sharp minds and sharper ambitions. I
only hope . . . Well, Isabel has made it clear she's joining us if
we start a new Rockton, and Phil has made it clear he'll help
us, but has no intention of being a pioneer. Another reason I
hope it doesn't come to that, for their sakes.

As I move toward their table, Phil notices me first. Sensing
business in the air, he nods and motions to ask whether he
should step aside. I shake my head and continue approaching.

"Hey, Iz," I say. "Any chance I can steal your bartender?"

One split second of confusion, and then her shoulders slump
as she sighs. Phil must have told her something. A vague warning about her new bartender.

"Anything I should know?" I murmur, too low for other
tables to overhear.

"He had last night off," Phil says.

"And no," Isabel says, "we saw nothing suspicious in that, or
we'd have mentioned it. It's his usual night off. He was at work
on time today and has been fine."

I nod. No alibi then. Damn, I was really hoping I had the
wrong guy.

Isabel rises. "Is Eric around?"

"Out front with Storm."

"All right then. I will speak to Brandon and ask him to step outside with me to check the cistern. If you and Eric meet me there, that should minimize the drama. I would appreciate that."

I know her well enough to understand this is as much for Brandon's sake as hers. She's allowing him the courtesy of a private arrest.

"I would prefer to handle this," Phil says. "If you insist, Isabel, then I'll ask to be there when you do it."

She nods. "I don't expect trouble, but yes, I will accept the backup."

"I'll join Eric . . ." I begin, trailing off as they both go still, their gazes traveling past me.

Isabel recovers in a blink with a smile and a nod. "Hello, Brandon. Please don't tell me we're out of tequila. That will not make our detective here happy."

I turn to see Brandon approaching with a bottle of tequila and a shot glass.

"No," he says, with an answering smile of his own. "We have plenty. I just saw Detective Butler and thought she might like a drink." He lifts the bottle and the shot glass. "Good call?"

Around us, tables have gone quiet. They'd ignored me chatting with Phil and Isabel. Just town business, and from our relaxed expressions, not interesting town business. Now, though, there's a crackle in the air that raises the hairs on my neck.

I could play along. Smile and take the tequila shot. Or smile and say, *I'm working, but thank you.* No need to explain why I'm talking to his boss. Between her and Phil, I have plenty of reason to do so.

That crackle in the air is what stops me. A sixth sense that everyone else here feels. Is there an edge to Brandon's words? To his smile? Either way, he hasn't come out here to offer me a drink. He's come out because he tried to kill Conrad, and he knew he'd been caught the moment I walked into the Roc.

I glance at Isabel. She lifts one shoulder in the faintest shrug. Any fancy footwork now might be mistaken for subterfuge by the witnesses. As if we spared Brandon a public arrest because we secretly applaud him for trying to kill the guy who outed our deputy.

"I'm going to need to speak to you down at the station, Brandon," I say. "I just have a few questions."

He sets the shot glass on the table. "Ask them here. I have nothing to hide. Also, considering what's going on in the police department, I'm not sure I trust you to question me in private."

There's the tiniest smirk on his face, and between that and his words, I no longer feel bad about learning he's our would-be killer. Both tell me that Brandon isn't the guy we thought he was, and beside me, Isabel shifts, as if thinking the same thing.

Great. It took her nearly two years to replace Mick as bartender, and once she does? The "nice guy" she chooses turns out to be a killer *and* a dick.

"All right," I say. "Do you have an alibi for last night between the hours of—"

He smashes the bottle. It happens so fast that if I hadn't suspected trouble, I wouldn't have gotten out of the way in time. I twist aside as soon as I hear that crack. He's smashed the bottle on the table edge, toppling it, and then he's slashing at me. I avoid that slash, but tequila sprays my eyes, and I stagger back, blinded.

There's a sharp intake of breath, and I spin, blinking madly, to see Brandon slashing at Isabel. Still blinking, I dive for them, but Phil's already there. He throws himself at Brandon, and knocks him flying clear across the patio. Chairs and tables clatter, people jumping out of the way. The two hit the edge of the patio and tumble off it, and by the time I get there, Phil has Brandon on the ground.

Has him on the ground, while completely ignoring the broken bottle in his hand.

"Phil!" I shout. "Watch—!"

I don't even get the first word out before Brandon is slashing. Phil tries to roll aside, but Brandon has his other hand wrapped in Phil's shirtfront. I leap off the patio edge and kick Brandon's hand as he slashes. It's too late, my hasty kick lands off center. The bottle still slices Phil. Blood sprays.

I grab Phil by the back of his shirt and yank. Phil flies free of Brandon's grasp, but Brandon scrambles after us, slashing again. Someone grabs him from behind and I think, *Thank God, someone's actually helping.* Then I catch a glimpse of the face. Dalton. Of course.

I heave Phil back, and Dalton has Brandon. The armed man twists and tries to slash at Dalton, but a smack to his arm sends the bottle neck flying.

Dalton's move costs him his grip on Brandon. The man dives for the dropped bottle. Dalton kicks it aside as Brandon goes for it. Dalton grabs Brandon again. The man falls limp, head shaking in defeat.

Too easy. I'm opening my mouth to say that when Brandon lashes out. Dalton blocks, and then hisses in pain, and his palm splits in a bloody line. I'm there then, charging at Brandon. He sees me coming and barrels into the forest.

I pause, my gaze going to Dalton. He lifts his bloody hand. "Got it," he says. "Go on."

"Casey!" Isabel's voice calls behind me. "Please!"

I turn. Isabel is on the ground beside Phil. I lowered him onto it and then ran at Brandon before I could see Phil's injury. I do now. A deep cut on his arm spurts blood.

Shit! I am not going anywhere.

SIXTEEN

I race to Phil. As I do, a familiar voice calls, "I'll get April!," and I look up to see Diana taking off.

"No!" I shout. "Tina, can you get my sister please. Diana, get Will."

I don't know where my sister will be at this time of day. Eating dinner at home? At Kenny's? Out with him for a walk before returning to her comatose patient? I can't take a chance that she isn't around, and I don't trust anyone here except Diana to get Anders.

"Shirt!" I shout. "Jacket. Belt. Anything!"

Again, it's Dalton who's there first. Oh, the others move this time, once they figure out what I'm asking for. But he's first. Always first.

He passes me his shirt, but I wave it off, saying, "Your hand," and instead grab a light jacket thrust my way. I take a belt, too.

I wrap the jacket arms tight above Phil's wound. Spurting blood means an artery. I need to cut off blood flow immediately. I yank the sleeves as tight as I can and then affix the belt over them, yanking tighter still.

"Are you trying to take his arm off?" Isabel says, with a

shaky half laugh. Then she catches Phil's expression and bends down to whisper an apology. I'm not sure he hears it. His face is ashen.

"Keep talking to him," I say. "Keep him engaged. I've stopped the blood. Biggest problem is shock." I raise my voice. "Hear that, Phil? The danger is shock. Stay with us."

He nods. Dalton is beside me, asking what he can do. I motion for him to hold the tourniquet. Then I quickly check for other wounds.

I'm still checking when April and Anders both arrive. Anders comes at a full-out run. My damn sister walks as if her patient suffers no more than a broken arm. To her credit, when she sees the amount of blood, she breaks into a jog. By then, Anders is already kneeling beside Phil.

"Deep cut to the underside of the biceps," Anders says, words machine-gun fast as April bends. "Looks like it's at least nicked the brachial artery. Blood flow has stopped. Did you bring—?"

April is already opening her medical bag. Her face is impassive, as if this is indeed a simple broken arm, and on a complete stranger. Yet she flexes her fingers as she reaches inside, as if to calm a quiver I can't see.

"Casey?" Fingers rest on my shoulder. I look up to see Isabel, with Dalton standing behind her, Storm at his side.

I rise and nod abruptly. "April and Will have this. We should go after Brandon."

"You should," Isabel murmurs. Then, "I had to stop you. Even if it meant he got away."

"Obviously." I meet her gaze. "Phil was the priority."

Her chin dips in a nod. "Yes, but if I appeared slightly panicked . . ."

"It's because you were hiding the fact that you were *completely* panicked?"

Her mouth opens, as if to protest that no, she wasn't *that* worried. Then she closes it and says, "Yes."

"Just make sure you tell him that when he's ready to hear it."

Another nod. Another glance toward the woods. "I really should be a better judge of character. I'm a psychologist and a bartender. Reading people is my job."

"Shall we list the number of times nice people in Rockton have turned out to be assholes? Or killers? Or both?"

I wipe my bloodied hands on a piece of cloth that Dalton wordlessly passes me.

"That's one of my linen serviettes," Isabel says.

"Do you want it back?" I hold it out.

She sighs and waves for us to get going. We do.

There really was no question of whether I should have pursued Brandon or stayed behind to help Phil. I also wouldn't have wanted Dalton to take off alone, not with his injured hand.

The biggest danger is that Brandon will flee into the forest, only to circle around and grab a hostage. I've wagered on that not happening. Possibly wagered an innocent life, but that is the job out here. Constant choices. Not that different from police work down south.

Police make mistakes. So many mistakes. Sometimes they arise from an ugly place—an emptiness in the soul filled by a gun on your hip and the law on your side. I won't pretend I haven't seen that. Seen it so often that when I first saw Dalton's swagger and heard his bluster, I'd been sure—so sure—that's what I was witnessing. Another cop who makes me want to surrender my badge and take up social work. I'd been wrong, thank God. But the fact that I'd jumped to that conclusion proves just how often I'd seen officers who fit the stereotype he seemed to embody.

Beyond those mistakes—which are, let's be honest, the mistakes of a system that allows such people to become law-enforcement officers—there are the everyday errors. Do I let a teenager off with a warning and trust he won't steal another purse? What if I do, and he escalates to worse? What if I don't, and that solidifies his path in life and tars his feet to it?

Save the man with a possibly severed artery? Or stop the one who attacked him?

I played the odds here. Now that he's in the forest, I'm betting Brandon doesn't circle back to take a hostage.

Storm picks up his trail right away, and it heads straight into the forest. It's still at least a kilometer before I can relax, certain he didn't loop back.

Brandon is running full out and making no attempt to disguise his trail. By now, I swear everyone in town has figured out that the way to lose a tracking dog is to run through water. Plenty of streams around here, and at this time of year there's no risk of frostbite. Brandon ran alongside one without ever setting foot in it.

"Still not a criminal genius," I say as we jog along the path Brandon took. It isn't even a game trail. It's an actual path.

Dalton grunts. "Never was any kind of genius."

Brandon was exactly what Isabel looked for in a bartender. Good-natured, easy to talk to, and bright enough to mix a drink but not clever enough to pilfer the alcohol safe. With the high turnover rate here, there isn't time to establish that level of employee trust. Best to just hire someone who isn't smart enough to rip her off.

"Should I be hoping he doesn't run straight off a cliff?" Dalton mutters. "Or hoping he does?"

He shoots me a look that is seventy-five percent exasperation and twenty-five percent guilt. Sometimes we wish our worst criminals would just take a convenient tumble. Saves us from arguing with the council to get them removed. With Brandon, the council will claim that no one actually died, and we should just lock him up. We've done that before. It didn't go well. People did die.

"Mmm," I say as Storm veers onto a side path. "Not a fatal plunge. Too many questions. I vote that he is just gravely injured and requires immediate transport down south."

"Unless he claims we pushed him off." He glances back at me. "How fast can April induce a convenient coma?"

"Fast enough. That's the best bet then. He runs straight off a cliff, and we dope him up before he can tell the town we—"

A distant bellow brings us up short.

"Was that a moose?" I say.

"Sure as hell sounds like it."

"Tell me he didn't disturb a moose."

Dalton throws up his hands. Then he pinpoints the source of the sound. I map the trajectory between where it came from and where we're standing.

"The path veers that way up ahead," Dalton says.

"Suggesting it's not a coincidence there's an angry moose in that direction?"

"Yeah." He squints. "Fuck."

I wait, and after a moment, he sighs. "It'll be faster cutting through here."

I nod and follow.

SEVENTEEN

We're tramping through the forest. The brush here is sparse, leaving open spaces between the towering pines, and Dalton weaves through them at a slow jog. All has gone silent up ahead. Has been silent since that bellow.

We've run about a hundred feet when a snort has Dalton slowing. He cocks his head to listen. I pick up a second snort, lower pitched, more of a grumble.

"Moose?" I murmur.

Before Dalton can nod, Storm leans against my leg, and that confirms it. She's had bear encounters, and they don't bother her as much as large ungulates. Last year, she was kicked by one, and while it wasn't serious, I think her canine brain has decided caribou and moose are irrational and dangerous creatures.

Ask me whether I'd rather encounter a moose or a grizzly, and I'll take the ungulate every time. That doesn't mean they aren't dangerous. One only needs to witness the result of a moose-vehicle collision to have a healthy respect for the damage such a large beast can do. In the wild, they'll avoid humans wherever possible—especially when we usually come bearing rifles—but if surprised, they'll charge.

Dalton considers options and then slides forward, step by step. I keep farther behind and motion for Storm to stay with me. We've gone about ten feet when Dalton gives another grunt and waves for me to approach.

I get up beside him and follow his gaze to see a massive bull moose under a tree. The beast stamps the ground and shakes its head, showing off a truly impressive antler rack. I'm torn between admiration for a gorgeous animal and thinking how long that much meat would last. Yes, I've become a hunter. I wouldn't pursue it down south as a sport, but up here, where hunting provides our key source of protein, I can't help mentally breaking the poor moose down into steaks and roasts.

Dalton's fingers tap his gun, and I know he's thinking the same thing. We aren't equipped for hunting, though, and five kilometers is a long way to drag that much dinner without proper tools.

"What the hell did you do, Brandon?" Dalton mutters.

It's only then that I jerk from visions of grilled moose steak to realize there must be a reason why the moose is stamping at the base of a tree. I glance up and, sure enough, a shoe dangles through the boughs.

"You're kidding me," I say.

"Right? It's not rutting season. Takes some serious ingenuity to piss off a bull moose midsummer."

Startling one is possible, if you come from downwind. In that case, most will just turn and run. In Brandon's defense, this is a bull in its prime and more likely to get territorial. That bellow we heard was the moose before it charged, and Brandon—in a lifesaving display of intelligence—climbed a tree rather than try to outrun it.

At this point, the moose should be satisfied and lumber

away. It has not, which suggests Brandon has indeed done something to piss it off.

Storm pushes closer, asking me very politely if we might leave the angry moose and let Brandon deal with it.

"Tempting," I murmur. "Very tempting."

Bears might kill more people a year, but moose attacks are more common, often resulting in serious injury.

"Much as I'd love those steaks," Dalton says, "I'm going to try shooing it off. Should tell Jacob it's here, though. That'd get them through summer and fall."

It might seem that one moose isn't that big a deal in a forest teeming with game. While the large ungulates are common enough, that doesn't mean we see them daily or that we can even find one when we go hunting.

Two hunters like Jacob and Nicole could easily spend days tracking this single moose and waiting for the right opportunity. A lot of work with no guarantee of success, but with them living near Rockton, they could trade the meat to us and earn two seasons' worth of varied foodstuffs in return.

"You and Storm stay here," he says. "Find a thickly wooded spot in case it charges. Also have your spray ready."

Bear spray instead of my gun, which may sound humane, but it's just common sense. My chances of fatally shooting a charging moose are not good, whatever my marksmanship.

Dalton starts forward. Storm and I follow at a distance. While I will get into thicker tree cover, as he asked, I also want to be close enough to help if things go wrong.

We slide into a patch of older saplings. Then I peer out to watch as Dalton approaches. He's staying in the trees, making a lousy target for a full-out charge.

"Brandon!" he says, his voice echoing.

The shout is more for the moose than Brandon, and the beast swings its huge head Dalton's way. It snorts and licks its lips, which is never a good sign. It's agitated and unhappy, and having a second human appear isn't going to make it any happier.

The moose doesn't charge, though. It peers at Dalton through nearsighted eyes, and its chest quivers as it inhales his scent.

"I'm right here," Dalton says. "Not coming any closer. I'm no threat to you."

His voice is firm but gentle, a tone designed to avoid startling the moose. It still paws the ground and swings its antlers in Dalton's direction. He's less than ten feet from the beast, close enough to make my heart pound.

I swear I will never see a moose and not think, *Holy shit, that thing is huge!* I come from southern Ontario, the land of white-tailed deer. Up here, ungulates start at mule deer and get bigger. The moose towers over Dalton. Its knobby legs make it look clumsy and awkward, but if it charges, Dalton won't be able to outrun it. It'll knock him down and trample him under a thousand pounds.

I adjust my grip on my gun. I have the bear-spray canister exposed in my holster, but if it charges, it'll go after Dalton. Bear spray won't help him from here.

The moose licks its lips again, telling Dalton he's too close. He backs up a step. I watch for any sign of a charge, but the moose seems to relax, its lowered ears rising.

"Shoot it!" Brandon shouts.

"Yeah, that'll only piss it off more."

"You need to do *something*."

"Actually, best thing we can do is nothing. Let it calm down and wander off."

"You're kidding, right?" Brandon's voice rises, and the moose flicks its ears in irritation. "It's the size of a fucking bus, and it *charged* me. I could have died."

"You didn't. Now stop shouting, or you'll piss it off more.

I have a gun, and I have pepper spray. If you really want to do something, come down from the tree and we'll see what happens."

Brandon lets out a stream of profanity.

"I'm not joking," Dalton says. "There's a thick trunk on that tree. While climbing it was a good idea, you'd have been fine just getting behind it. A moose isn't agile enough to dart around and attack you."

"You want me dead."

Dalton sighs, a sound deep enough that the moose looks over. "Nah. I mean, sure, you nearly killed two people in the last twenty-four hours. I wouldn't be saying the eulogy at your funeral. But your death right now would be inconvenient. People already expect the worst of us. If we go back and say you died? Attacked by a *moose*?"

Dalton shakes his head. "No one's going to buy that. You're not going to die, Brandon. I'm here with a gun and pepper spray. Casey is nearby with both those plus a very big dog. All this moose wants is for you to go away. Can't say I blame it. I'd like the same. Not if it means being blamed for your death, though. Now climb down, and stay on the far side of the tree."

They go through a few more rounds of "You want me dead!" and "No, I don't." I keep hoping the moose will lose interest and move on, but if anything, it seems fascinated by the human drama unspooling around it.

Finally, with great caution, Brandon lowers himself to the other side of the tree. The moose doesn't even seem to notice. It's looking from him to Dalton as if waiting for them to resume that fascinating exchange of noises.

"There," Dalton says. "You're on the ground, and the moose doesn't care. Unfortunately, it isn't moving on either. So what we're going to do is come over to your side—"

Brandon wheels and runs into the forest. The moose lets out an odd little noise of surprise but only watches him go.

"You honestly didn't expect that?" I say.

Dalton sighs again, loudly, as he retreats toward me. "I tried to give him credit for being a little smarter, but figured my chances were low."

Dalton continues my way. Through the trees, I watch the moose, which has lowered its massive head to the ground and started eating, as if nothing happened.

"You okay splitting up?" he says. "I think I can run him down."

I nod, and he loops around the moose. I follow. Brandon is still running. Running loudly, barreling through the forest making more noise than any moose. By the time Storm and I are past the beast—giving it wide berth—Dalton is long gone.

"Follow the crashing," I mutter to Storm. "No need to bother with a trail."

I break into a jog, and she does the same. I pick up speed once I'm sure our own crashing won't startle the moose. Soon I'm at a full run, which for me isn't exactly lightning fast, given the old damage in my leg. This is why Dalton took lead.

I've barely hit full speed when Brandon shouts, "Stop right there!," and I start skidding to a halt before realizing he's obviously not talking to me.

I tap my hip, telling Storm to stay close. Then I start a slow jog as the two men ahead begin verse two of their abandoned dialogue.

"Stop chasing me, or I'll run," Brandon says.

"You know, I'm tempted to respond with 'Stop running, or I'll shoot,' but it seems a bit cliché. I *will* shoot, though. With this bear spray. You're three feet downwind of me, Brandon. That's not going to tickle."

"No, it'll kill me. If it kills grizzly bears, it'll sure as hell kill me."

A pause. A long one, as if Dalton's working this one through.

"It's not bug spray for bears," I call. "It's a deterrent. Pepper spray."

"Pepper spray? You're going to blind me?" His voice rises, as if this is somehow worse than death.

"Temporarily," Dalton says. "But only if you move from that spot."

I step out to where I can see them. One more step, Brandon's still half hidden in the trees, and then he screams "Bear! Behind you!" and runs.

Dalton's finger moves on the spray trigger, but it's too late. Brandon's on the run, his back to Dalton, who gives yet another deep sigh.

"Is it too much to hope he actually had the intelligence to try tricking you?" I say. "Because I don't see a bear. Or did he spot Storm?"

"Nah," a voice says. "It was me."

We turn as a huge, grizzle-haired man steps out.

"Hey, Ty," I say. "Thanks for scaring off our quarry."

"Serves you right, since you scared off mine. You see a big ol' bull moose around here?"

Dalton's already gone, running after Brandon. I walk up to Tyrone Cypher. It's a running joke that someday someone will mistake him for a grizzly, a joke Brandon just made good on. Cypher is about six four and big, broad shouldered and brawny, as befits a proper mountain man. Long hair. Beard. Hide clothing. Yep, it's a wonder he doesn't get people fleeing in terror more often. Which is a good call with Cypher, considering he's a former hit man. Also a former sheriff of Rockton.

"Moose . . ." I muse. "Was it about this tall?" I rise onto my tiptoes and reach up. "Biggest rack of antlers I've ever seen? At least a good fourteen hundred pounds. Or four hundred juicy steaks?"

He glowers at me.

"Yeah, sorry," I say. "We've got a guy on the run from the long arm of our law."

"What'd he do?"

"Attempted murder. Two in the last twenty-four hours."

"Fucking amateurs."

"Right?" I nudge Storm. "You stay with Uncle Ty, okay? We've got a runner to catch."

Cypher puts out a hand for Storm, who heads over for petting. I turn, getting my bearings.

"That way, kitten," Cypher says. "My hearing's not what it was, but even I can hear him."

He's right. Once again, Brandon is crashing through—

A scream cuts me off midthought.

"Great," I mutter. "He's found that killer rabbit, hasn't he?"

"Go on," Cypher says. "I'll catch up. Something tells me this will provide my evening's entertainment, even if I'm not forgiving you for the moose."

EIGHTEEN

We follow the sound of Dalton's voice. Verse three, apparently, of this very tedious conversation with Brandon. When I catch up, the first thing I'm doing is grabbing the guy. Second thing? Gagging him.

When I hear the sound of running water, I wince and pick up my pace. A few landmarks tell me where I am. Near a river I know well. I burst from the forest to see only Dalton looking down.

Looking into a canyon. A canyon I'd once clung to as I'd tried to get down and rescue the body of a fellow resident.

"Well, this looks familiar," Cypher says. "Remember when you—"

"Yes, I do. Thank you."

He snickers. "Looks like another rescue mission. This one should be easier, though."

I see what he means. We're downstream of the spot where I'd fallen, and the cliff sides here are about half as high. Still high enough to kill you if you took a tumble but unless Dalton has learned to speak to the dead, that isn't Brandon's fate.

"Please don't tell me he ran clear off the edge," I call as I approach.

"Yep."

"Please tell me his feet wheeled in midair for a few seconds before he dropped."

Dalton lifts a brow, but Cypher chuckles, getting the cartoon reference.

"Please tell *me* he ran off it on purpose," Cypher says. "Pulling a failed Thelma and Louise. Because otherwise?" He looks up and down the wide-open space atop the canyon. "I don't see how you can miss that big ol' first step coming up."

"Well, he did."

"Damn. That's embarrassing." Cypher moves past me to the cliff edge and shouts down. "Embarrassing, you hear that? Kinda like mistaking me for a bear." He peers over the edge. "Wait. Aren't you the new barkeep? You served me and Jen just last week when I stopped by."

Yes, Cypher is still seeing Jen. Which I think explained her sudden zeal for an extension this past spring, but I knew better than to even suggest that. They make an interesting couple. That's all I have to say.

"Back off, or I'll jump!" Brandon shouts.

I look over the edge.

"I'm not kidding!" he says. "Leave me alone, or I'll plunge to my death and everyone will think you pushed me off the cliff."

Cypher looks at me and murmurs, "You want to tell him, kitten?"

"Nope."

Brandon has landed on a ledge. The cliff isn't a sheer drop, and from the skid marks, he went off the edge and tumbled onto the narrow strip where he now lies, fingers clutching for dear life. Beyond that ledge, there's a drop of about eight feet.

He'd need to swan-dive into the shallow river below to even risk serious injury.

"You know," Cypher says to us, "you kids have gotten yourselves into a lot of harrowing situations. This isn't one of them."

I grumble under my breath.

He continues, "I do believe the quality of criminals in Rockton is on a fast decline. Probably best they just shut the place up before it becomes downright embarrassing."

I glower at him.

Dalton crouches. "You're gonna kill yourself, Brandon?"

"I am. Back off, or I jump."

Cypher pulls back fast to stifle a snicker.

"Well, that's your call," Dalton says. "But before you do, you need to confess."

A pause. "What?"

"Well, you know Casey and I can't just leave you out here. We need to come after you, which means you need to jump, and if you die, you need a clean soul. I don't know if you're a religious man."

"Not really."

"But you want to go someplace good, right? That means you need a clean conscience. We saw you try to kill Phil, so that one's obvious."

"I didn't *try* to kill him. I was *trying* to get away."

"All right. We also know you tried to kill Conrad. We have your fingerprints."

"On the shovel?" A note of satisfaction. "Now I know you're lying. I wore gloves."

Dalton and I look at each other. He shakes his head.

"Brandon?" I call down. "You do realize you just incriminated yourself, right?"

A long, long pause. "Fuck."

Cypher is now moving away from the edge as fast as he can, sputtering with laughter.

"We also have the note," I say, "which handwriting analysis will match to the notes left on the door of the Roc. Plus boot prints, which I'm sure match yours. Conrad isn't going to sleep forever. He'll wake up and identify you as his killer."

"But he didn't see me. I snuck up behind him."

Dalton drops his head face-first into the dirt.

"All right," I say. "So having established that you are the killer—"

"Wait, no. I never killed anyone. He's still alive."

"Attempted assassin. Is that better?"

Pause. "I like assassin."

"Which is what you are," I continue. "You cleverly lured Conrad in and then tried to stop him. Like a vigilante hit man."

Cypher looks over sharply, offended at the comparison.

I ignore him and continue. "Were you trying to stop Conrad from ruining other lives? Did he threaten someone specifically?"

"He threatened *me*. He's been blackmailing me for weeks. Even before he said that stuff about Deputy Anders. He told me he knew what I'd done, and if I didn't give him booze, he'd tell the whole town."

Booze. Shit. I remember the wineglass on his front porch and the fact that he'd wooed Gloria with alcohol. I'd assumed he'd gotten the extra legally. If I'd dug deeper . . .

Well, if I'd dug deeper, I might have only set Brandon off sooner, and Conrad would probably appreciate skipping his premature burial, but I feel less bad about that than I should. If I questioned Isabel about Conrad having extra alcohol, she'd have questioned Brandon, and that might have been dangerous for Isabel.

Brandon is still talking. "He paid me for the bottles. He had extra credits, so the only problem was the limits. That meant Isabel didn't notice anything wrong. All the credits were there. But when that sign went up about the deputy, I knew it was Conrad. I confronted him and said if he kept blackmailing me, I'd turn him in. But then everyone started talking about him like he was some kind of good guy, and it went to his head. He started saying he'd expose my secrets unless I did what he said. First, he made me break into Deputy Anders's place with him. Then he said I'd have to get him as much free booze as he wanted. Otherwise I'd be next on his hit list."

"And you couldn't have that."

"Of course not!" His voice rises. "I saw what happened to Deputy Anders. Everyone hates him."

"Everyone would hate you if they knew your secret."

Down south, we'd call this leading the witness. Hell, down south, a lawyer would have told him to shut up ten minutes ago. Fortunately, Brandon is the kind of guy who never asks for a lawyer.

I have no idea what Brandon's true backstory is, and I want it, if only so I can figure out where Conrad was getting his intel. My best hope of getting those answers is from this guy, before he hurls himself over the edge and twists his ankle.

"Of course they'd hate me." Brandon's voice rises. He's infuriated by this line of questioning, possibly because my tone suggests, very gently, that he may have overreacted. "I ripped off hundreds of people. Innocent people."

Dalton and I exchange a look.

"That's . . . not good," I say.

"It wasn't my fault. I believed the guy. It sounded like an awesome investment opportunity."

"They always do," I murmur.

"It was easy getting people to buy in. I didn't even need to understand the money stuff. I just drove around in a nice car and told all my friends that I'd invested money in this thing, and then they put in money, and it doubled, like the guy said. They sent their friends to me, and I set them up with the guy and it all seemed great. Right up until the cops busted him."

"Uh-huh."

"Then he sent me here. Paid a lot of money to protect me from getting arrested."

Prevent him from being a witness. From naming names. From running off his mouth and getting "the guy" in even deeper trouble.

Brandon isn't exactly a dangerous offender. His story, sadly, makes sense, though. Well, up to the part where he'd been so freaked out over exposure that he'd tried to kill Conrad.

This is one reason Isabel picked him as her new bartender. Everyone liked Brandon. That's what he had going for him here. Popularity. If his story had been made public, it'd hardly be catastrophic, but to him, it'd be a death knell.

He doesn't see the difference between his crime and Anders. He only sees his certainty that he'll be hated for it. Like Anders, he'd go from homecoming king to town pariah.

"Do you have any idea how Conrad obtained this information?" I ask.

"No!"

"Did you tell anyone your story?"

"What? No. I'm not stupid."

"Maybe by accident?"

"No. I didn't tell *anyone*. The guy said if I did, he'd kill me. You notice I'm not even using his name? He made it very clear what would happen to me if I said anything. He knows people who can do terrible things."

Ah, here is the true root of Brandon's panic. He's been

threatened with death if his story comes out. While I doubt "this guy" even knows a hired killer, all that matters for Brandon is the threat. He believed his former boss about the investments, and now he believes him about the horrible death that awaits if he opens his mouth.

"No one knows, then?" I say.

"*No*. The guy said if he paid enough money, the people who run Rockton wouldn't ask for details or ID or anything like that. Money was enough."

Money is always enough. In this case, I can't imagine Brandon's "guy" forked over millions. He'd said enough to convince the council that it was a white-collar crime rather than a violent one, and a hundred grand or so would have bought Brandon's way in.

That does, however, pose a problem.

"Have you had any dental work done?" I ask.

"What? No. I got that all taken care of before I came here, like they told me to."

A thought occurs to me. "What exactly did Conrad say to you? When he started the blackmail."

"That he knew what I'd done. That I thought I'd gotten away with it, but I hadn't, and if I didn't sell him more booze, he'd tell everyone."

"Did he give any details?"

"About *how* he'd tell everyone?"

Dalton sighs, softly this time.

"About what you'd done," I say. "To prove that he actually knew something."

Silence.

"You think he was bluffing?" Brandon says finally.

Dalton thumps his head against the ground. Cypher throws up his hands.

I shush them and say, as gently as I can, "Did he ever say anything specific about what you'd done?"

"Well, no, but that was the point, right? I was paying for him to keep my secret, and there's no point in telling me what I did—and risking someone hearing—when I already know what I did." He pauses. "He was bluffing, wasn't he?"

Ironic, really, that Conrad's lies nearly got him killed by his target. He'd wanted to freak Brandon out, and he'd succeeded beyond his wildest dreams.

"We will take care of Conrad," I say. "But the best thing you can do is stand as witness against him."

"Everyone will hate me if I do that."

Even I have to fight the urge to sigh by this point.

"No, everyone will blame *him*," I say. "He tricked you. They'll understand why you tried to . . ." Bury him alive? Nope, no one's understanding that. "Why you tried to stop him before he hurt others."

"That's right. I did stop him, didn't I?" He pauses. "I'm kinda a hero."

Oh, just ask Phil how big a hero you are. Better yet, ask Isabel.

"You kinda are," I say. "Now let us come down there and help you up."

"I've got it." He pushes to his feet. "It's not that far down. I can climb it."

He puts one foot on a small rock, and before I can warn him, he shifts all his weight onto it, and it pops from the soft ground. I jump up, imagining him falling backward, the one thing that could indeed seriously injure him. Instead, his feet scrabble to find a hold, and he slides right over the ledge. He has time for a single second of terror before his feet splash into the shallow river.

He goes still. Then he looks around slowly, leaps up, and

bolts. He gets two long strides. Then his ankle gives way, and he pitches forward, howling in pain.

"He's all yours," I say to Dalton as I pass him a handcuff strip.

NINETEEN

Dalton goes to get Brandon, but before he can, Brandon is stung by a water insect, and then freaks out over that, tries to run, gets his foot trapped, falls face-first, and nearly drowns because he doesn't realize it's so shallow he could just lift his head to breathe. . . .

No, none of that actually happens, though I wouldn't be the least surprised if it did. Today is truly going down in the books as our most ridiculous wilderness pursuit ever.

By this point, Brandon is just tired. He's used up all his adrenaline stabbing people, running for his life, being treed by a moose, falling off cliffs . . . By the time we reach town, we need to give him a shake-up. If anyone saw us dragging a semiconscious suspect in, it wouldn't matter if the guy confessed on the steps of the town-square podium, he'd clearly be making up shit out of sheer terror after whatever we did to him in the forest.

I tell myself it isn't that bad. Residents don't hate us. Most at least. They either support us or they're confused by what's going on and understandably concerned. Yet it's like any performance evaluation. Ask ten people to rate us, and we'll get a bunch of high numbers, a few middling ones, and two who only gave us a one because zero wasn't an option. Statistically, we're doing great, but if twenty percent of our residents think we're liars and killers, we cannot stop feeling the sting of that.

We rouse Brandon into a sensible state, and then Dalton escorts him into town as I follow along, chatting with Cypher. No big deal, see? Brandon's fine, and we only need one person to bring him into town.

We escort him to the station, where he'll be held in the cell until the council can be notified. Then I sit at the desk to write my notes.

I grudgingly have to hand it to Conrad for a mildly ingenious scheme. He found out that some people here *aren't* victims in hiding. He wonders how he can use that information. His first thought? Booze!

It isn't as if we're all borderline alcoholics up here. It's just that there's a huge list of things we don't have and can't get, things we took for granted in a world where we can think *I'd like to take up cycling again* and have a new bike within hours. Rockton compensates for that by making sure residents get plenty of the things we *can* supply: books, clothing, hobby supplies, pastries, coffee, and so on.

What lies in the middle is the very short list of things we have and you're only allowed to purchase in limited quantities no matter how many credits you've saved up. The most prized item on that list is booze. Our tight regulation only exacerbates the problem. People want what they cannot have. Of course, loosening the restrictions would lead to binge drinking and all that goes with it in an isolated community.

What did Conrad want? Extra booze. Hell, he'd even pay for it. So he blackmails the bartender and gets those extra bottles of wine to enjoy on his front porch.

What next? What is the other tightly regulated and highly

desired commodity in Rockton? Sex. Yet even if he'd found a woman who'd bought her way in, she obviously hadn't fallen for his "I know your secret" shtick without proof.

But he then meets Gloria, former alcoholic teetering on the edge. Excellent. Just go back to Brandon, buy more booze, and seduce Gloria.

Now what else did Conrad want? The right to work a day or two a week as a dentist, without filling in the extra time stocking shelves.

To get that, he needs to blackmail someone in charge. Jen has a dental appointment, so let's see what she knows. There he hits the jackpot. His designated nemesis is a murderer. Ka-ching!

The problem there is that Anders isn't in a position to determine Conrad's work orders. Nor would he cave to blackmail. So it's time for a little personal revenge. Make the bastard pay with public exposure.

Conrad won all this from discovering that some of our residents are criminals.

I look up at Dalton, who's stoking the station fire. "How often have people figured out that criminals can buy their way in?"

"Figured it out and complained? Never as far as I know. Took me years."

"Because it probably wasn't happening before that. Or not in large enough numbers to notice."

He shrugs. "Maybe. But whenever it started, it's not as if anyone's going to stand up in the Red Lion and announce they were a violent criminal."

"Or even tell their friends and lovers."

"If you're trying to figure out how Conrad knew, I'd check his patient file."

"You think someone other than Jen talked under the influence." I tap my pen on my notebook. "I suppose, but . . ." I look toward the thick door separating us from Brandon's cell and lower my voice. "I feel guilty as hell about what I did, and I've still never talked, drunk or sober. There is a third option. Plenty of people in town *do* know criminals can buy their way in."

He frowns. Then he swears.

Who knows criminals can buy their way in?

The criminals themselves.

I would love to stride into the clinic and confront Conrad. Get confirmation of Brandon's story and confirmation that Conrad himself is here because he committed a crime.

Others keep quiet in hopes they're the only one . . . or because exposing Rockton's secret would expose their own. Why did Conrad take that risk? Because he wanted stuff and he thought he was entitled to it and he doesn't think he should be held accountable for his actions. Almost makes me wonder whether I'm wrong about the violent part, because otherwise, he fits the mold for our white-collar criminals.

I can't ask Conrad anything, though, while he's unconscious. So I make my case notes and then I pay a visit to Phil.

I didn't wait this long to check on his condition, of course. I'd visited April while Dalton got Brandon settled in the cell. Anders had been right about Phil's brachial artery. It'd been nicked, by which I mean cut instead of severed, though I'm sure April would tell me I'm being semantically imprecise. Minor surgery had been required. Anders had assisted. Phil is fine and resting at Isabel's. I visit him there and update him. He's still groggy, and he'll probably need Isabel to repeat my update later. As for Isabel, she's doing as well as I'd expect, which means she's quiet, very quiet. She takes in my retelling of Brandon's confession and says little. I suspect it'll be awhile before we have a full-time bartender at the Roc again.

The rest of the night passes without incident. Morning comes, and I'm at loose ends, waiting impatiently to wrap up this case. I need to talk to the council and tell them what Conrad did. I also need to tell them what Brandon did and have them decide what we should do about both.

In my mind, the case is closed, and yet I can't officially close it until I talk to Conrad. Speak to him. Speak to the council. Speak to the town. Steps that must be completed in order, however much I want to just barrel through in the vain hope of getting back to normal life in Rockton.

It's dinner hour when April finally determines that Conrad is waking. This doesn't mean he'll pop up, ready to talk. We don't even know whether he'll be in any mental condition to talk even when he's fully awake.

I hover in the clinic until April kicks me out, and then Dalton and I eat dinner on her back steps as we await updates.

Here my sister shows her sadistic side. She doesn't mean it, of course. Once upon a time, I'd have thought she did. I know better now.

When she leaves us on that back porch for two hours without a single update, it's only because she has nothing to say. Telling us *that* would be a waste of time. We're left to stew while playing with the dog, trying to distract ourselves, getting a wee bit crankier every time someone slinks behind the clinic to ask whether there's any news.

The only person we don't snap at is Anders. He's trying to play this cool, but I know how much he needs confirmation that it was Conrad, if only so he can stop looking into faces and wondering whether they're the ones who exposed his secret.

He knows about Jen's role in it. She didn't want that, obviously, but after a long conversation earlier today, she agreed that Anders needed to know. She just didn't want to be the one to tell him. I did that for her, and he spent the next few hours trying to speak to her as she kept ducking him. She doesn't expect he's hunting her down to give her shit. That's not Anders. He wants to tell her it's okay, and he understands this wasn't her fault, and somehow that's worse. She's escaped into the forest for a couple of days with Cypher, which seems best for all.

It's nearly nine when April finally comes out to say that Conrad is ready for questioning. He's still groggy and may not fully understand the consequences of what he's saying. In a court, his confession would be thrown out, and I'd be severely reprimanded. Luckily, we don't have courts and my superior officer is overseeing the interrogation.

Conrad confesses. Or maybe "confess" is the wrong word. Even in a judicial setting, there's usually an air of guilty shame to it. Confessing one's sins. Unburdening one's soul. Conrad brags his way through it like the villain in a B thriller. He's very pleased with his scheme, and furious that Brandon had the audacity to try to kill him for a bit of falsified blackmail.

"I didn't even have anything on him," he complains. "It's not my fault he was stupid enough to fall for it."

"Like you fell for his note promising information he didn't have?"

Conrad squints at me. "What's that supposed to mean?"

Yep, he's a little muddled, and I'm sure when this is over, he'll insist on retracting his confession. Too bad. Phil gave us his cell phone to record this interview. That will be all the evidence the council needs. We aren't torturing or threatening Conrad. I don't ask leading questions. He's just not in a mental state to screen his answers.

There's nothing new in those answers. It is exactly as Gloria and Brandon said. Of course Conrad still tries to justify and downplay his culpability. To him, he did nothing wrong. In fact, he'd been the one wronged and if we had only given in to his demands to only be a dentist, he wouldn't have had to resort to all this.

I don't ask what crime he committed down south. I only care in the sense that, if I'm wrong, I need to know how else he realized Rockton admits criminals. I'll confirm this with the council. They'll never admit to it, but if they tell me there's no need to keep digging for a leak, I'll have my answer.

I still ask Conrad how he knew, just for the hell of it.

"Because I'm a smart man," he says. "I figured it out."

"Did someone tell you?"

He looks offended. "I said I figured it out. No one needed to tell me anything."

Yep, he figured it out all right . . . because he was one of those taking advantage of the loophole.

We end the interview shortly after that, and Dalton gives instructions for Conrad to be moved back to his duplex with a militia guard assigned as his personal-support worker. The clinic is too small for him to stay in the main room, and he's well enough to go home, as long as we can keep an eye on him.

And with that, the case is solved. We know Conrad exposed Anders, and we know where he got the information. We know he didn't have any more stories to expose. We also know who tried to kill him for his bluff. Case closed, and we can enjoy our first restful night in days.

The next morning, we have time to put the pot on for coffee before there's a knock at the door. It's Kenny telling us we've been summoned to a breakfast meeting with Phil and the council. We finish the coffee, but that's as far as our foot-dragging goes. I'm actually fine with talking to the council today, because I have good news. We know who posted the sign. We know he didn't have any more information. And we don't even need to worry about whether or not we should punish him for revealing Anders's secret, because he's been punished already. The guy who did that is in the cell awaiting judgment. I'm feeling damn proud of myself, and while I'm sure I won't even get a "good job" from the council, I look forward to telling them that all situations have been resolved.

We take the long way to Phil's and stop by the stable yard to give our horses a good-morning carrot. As I'm feeding Cricket, Mateo comes out from the small barn. He's the backup stable keeper, temporarily elevated to the main role in Maryanne's absence.

"You didn't see Jolene on the way over, did you?" he asks.

"Haven't seen much of anybody," I say. "Is there a problem?"

He shakes his head. "She's just late for her shift, and I was really hoping for my coffee by now."

"Go get it," I say. "The horses will be fine."

He nods and lopes off, and we continue to Phil's house, where breakfast waits. We settle in, and we've just begun eating when Tamara calls in.

Tamara is—as Phil once was—a faceless voice on a radio. The only radio that can contact the outside world, and only this one particular number. The council isn't there in the background. I used to think they were at least listening in. They aren't.

Phil has explained how it works. While council members can be there by videoconference, they usually tell their liaison what to say and that's it. All the times we argued with Phil, there was no council listening and considering and making judgment calls. Just Phil, under orders to deliver their word, listen to our inevitable complaints, and reiterate their stance. Phil was—and Tamara now is—the human equivalent of an AI teleservice bot. They can provide information. They can listen to us and attempt to give appropriate responses. But they have zero volition. Zero ability to make decisions.

Tamara's first words, though, surprise me. "Before we get into the matter of this latest attempted murder, the council would like me to share information on Conrad. Specifically, his background. I am aware that Detective Butler believes he is there under a false cover story."

"And Detective Butler is wrong," Dalton mutters, too low for Tamara to hear.

"Detective Butler is correct," Tamara says. "Conrad is indeed one of our special cases, where we chose to allow a nonviolent white-collar criminal into Rockton for a fee that allows us to accommodate true cases of need."

"White-collar?" I say.

"Yes, we categorized his actions as such because they did not cross our threshold for violent activity."

"There's a threshold?" Dalton whispers.

I smile at him and shake my head. All she means is that whatever Conrad did, it's low enough on the violence scale for them to reclassify it as white-collar crime.

"While resident stories are privileged information," she continues, "I have been given permission to share Conrad's as proof of our good faith. He was accused of blackmailing several former lovers with photographs and videos of an indiscreet nature."

"Blackmail?"

"Yes, for money. It was also alleged that, in two cases, he blackmailed them for sexual favors, but he denied that. Our findings concurred. We would never have permitted a resident into Rockton with a known history of sexual coercion."

Also not true, but we say nothing.

"His crime was blackmail," she says. "Devoid of any violent actions."

I want so much to say something. Conrad violated the trust of former lovers and threatened them with public humiliation. If a guy gave me the choice between a broken bone and my naked body splashed across the internet, I'd snap my arm for him. But I clamp my mouth shut.

"Blackmail, huh?" Dalton says. "Okay, I get that. It's not like he could come here and pull that shit on . . . Wait . . ."

"We're aware of what he has done."

"Are you?" Dalton says, rising from the sofa, as if she's more than a voice in a box. "He blackmailed our bartender and panicked him so much the guy tried to kill him. He also used that blackmail to induce a recovered alcoholic to have sex with him. Then he actively sought blackmail on any figure of authority, only to use what he had to wreak chaos in my town and put a huge dent in the ironclad trust we need to run it."

"We understand that, Sheriff Dalton."

"Do you? Do you really?"

Her voice sharpens, words bitten off. "We do. As you will see if you allow me to continue talking."

Dalton grumbles, but it's for show only. He's made his point, and even if it fell on deaf ears, he feels better for having made it.

"All right," I say. "So we've solved the case of who put up the sign and the case of who tried to kill that person. The question now is what to do with Conrad and Brandon."

"Moot."

There's something oddly like satisfaction in her voice, and the hairs on my neck prickle. I've heard that tone before. I was being a pain in the ass to the lead detective on a case, convinced that he was ignoring evidence out of prejudice against a suspect. Monday morning, I went to update him on my progress, and he told me not to bother. I'd been reassigned. This exact same note had been in his voice as he said it, paired with a smug little smile as he'd awaited my reaction.

"The point is moot because . . ." I begin.

I hate saying the words. It feels like reaching out to a cobra, allowing it within striking distance. I'm making this easy for her when I should just shut down this meeting—feign an emergency or bad connection—and get the hell out of here. But I can't slam the door and lock this particular cobra out of my life. I need to hear this. We all do.

"It's moot because we're shutting down Rockton."

TWENTY

Silence. Three long beats of it before anyone can speak, and when someone does, it's Phil.

"I beg your pardon?" he says.

He pulls off all the surprise and outrage we couldn't manage. He makes it sound as if he hasn't known this for two months now, as if he bought the council's story that our decreasing numbers were a temporary adjustment.

Dalton takes my hand, and with every sentence Tamara says, his grip tightens. I barely hear her exact words, only the gist of it washing over me. That gist is that this is our fault. All our fault. Starting with Anders for telling the truth. Then on to Dalton and Phil for failing to mitigate the damage, and me for not arresting Conrad for breaking into Anders's chalet, which would have meant Brandon never tried to kill Conrad or attacked Phil.

"Detective Butler was gathering the evidence needed to arrest Conrad without the whole damn town accusing us of scapegoating him," Dalton says. "The only way she'd have done it faster is with a fucking confession."

"Then you should have gotten a confession."

"How? Beat it out of him? If we'd applied *any* pressure, we'd have been accused of being the power-hungry bastards he claimed. So which was it? You wanted us to get a confession? Or to mitigate the fucking damage?"

"It took too long," she says briskly. "If Deputy Anders had consulted us before confessing, we could have bought Detective Butler more time to solve the case. It would also have bought you and Phil more time to calm the residents. As it stands, they've lost faith in you."

"Based on what?" Dalton says. "The fucking poll you didn't fucking conduct?"

Phil clears his throat. "Eric has a valid point, Tamara. I'm not sure how the council can assess the damage when I haven't been asked to report on my conclusions. If I had been, I would have said—"

"Unnecessary."

"I would have said that the damage, while concerning, is already dissipating swiftly in light of—"

"Unnecessary. The point is that every move you three and Will Anders have made only deepened the damage."

"How the—" Dalton clamps off the profanity. He takes a moment, and when he speaks again, his tone is even. "I don't understand how we made things worse. Enlighten me."

"Unnecessary."

Dalton rocks forward. I brace for him to grab the radio. He doesn't, because there's no point. We see that now. We told ourselves, for a brief moment, that if we debate the matter with logic, we can win.

We know better.

Unnecessary.

It's an ugly word, dismissing us, dismissing Rockton, dismissing everything we've done here. Yet it is also accurate. Our objections are unnecessary because the council has made up its minds, and their explanation is nothing more than an excuse.

They were already shutting us down. According to Émilie, the internal explanation was the hostiles, an explanation that also blamed us. We'd "riled up the hostiles" by killing their leader in self-defense. We fixed that problem. I solved one of Rockton's biggest mysteries—how the hostiles were created—and only a couple remain in the forest, and we haven't seen them in months. Our reward for that should have been a reversal of the shutdown orders. It wasn't. As Émilie suspected, the hostiles were an excuse. The council continued quietly shutting us down while telling Émilie they'd stopped.

Excuse upon excuse. The truth is greed. The council and those who invest in Rockton have wanted an increasingly better return for their money. Any pretense that Rockton is a philanthropic endeavor went out the window when the four original investors—Émilie, her husband, and another couple—dropped to just Émilie. The council started with bringing in more white-collar criminals and ended with sending us bona fide serial killers.

They say we can't handle the responsibility. That we've lost the trust of our residents. After all, no former sheriffs had this problem, did they? Except no former sheriffs had to deal with this situation. They had white-collar criminals and maybe the occasional low-risk violent criminal. It's only been in the last few years that the number of those violent criminals has increased, along with the risk they pose.

The obvious answer should be to confront the council.

You're the ones sending us these criminals. You're the ones endangering our people. You're the ones lying to us. You've sent us man-eating tigers and expected us to control them with the same tools we use for house cats.

I've asked Phil what would happen if we told the council

we knew the truth. He says they'd ship us out. Exile Dalton, exile me, exile Anders and anyone else they suspect knows, all the while denying everything.

They've overreached, and it's all gone to shit. They got greedy, and this is the result, and with all the trouble we "cause," Rockton is no longer a viable asset in their investment portfolios. It doesn't matter what we do or say. Our protests are like those of factory employees thinking they can stop their plants' closure by working harder.

All protest is, in Tamara's words, unnecessary. All explanation is unnecessary because they don't owe us shit. We are the foremen in their factory, and they can close our shop without explaining themselves to us.

"How long do we have?" I ask finally.

"We'll begin extracting residents in two days," she says. "There will be twice-daily pickups of seven residents each, who will be transferred to a private luxury property, where they will remain, as our guests, as they are debriefed. This is where you will get your wish, Detective Butler. We'll take Brandon and Conrad on the first flight. We would like you to devise the exit lists, with known troublemakers being removed as quickly as possible. Two dozen residents will remain a month after the others depart, for which they will be provided generous recompense for helping with the cleanup effort."

"Cleanup effort?" I say. "You mean removing supplies?"

"I mean removing everything. Rockton is being dismantled in its entirety. By the end of August, the town will cease to exist."

TWENTY-ONE

Dalton and I go straight home after that. Phil murmurs something about calling a meeting, but he doesn't try to get a response from us, just says he'll handle it.

We take the forest route and go in our back door. Dalton walks through, and I nearly let the door shut on Storm, padding along silently behind us.

We head to the living room and sit on the sofa. Just sit there, hip to hip, hands entwined, Storm stretched at our feet.

I don't know what to say. That's always the worst thing about having a loved one in pain. Wanting to say, "I'm here," and knowing that every variation on it sounds trite and incomplete.

I'm here for you. Whatever you need, just say it. What can I do to help? I'm sorry you're going through this.

We need new words, fresh words, words that can cut through the pain and express how much it hurts to watch them suffer.

I want to fuss. Take action.

Do you need coffee? Tea? Something stronger? Is the temperature in here okay? I could open a window. Fresh air maybe? How about a pillow? Would you like a pillow?

All laughably ridiculous. Dalton is barely even here right now; he doesn't need a damn pillow.

Bigger action then.

I will solve this for you. I will . . . leave you here, alone and in pain, while I stride into the town to make myself feel like I'm fixing something I cannot fix.

"I'm sorry," I say finally.

"We knew."

"I'm still sorry. I'm so, so, so—" My voice cracks and the tears come, hot tears of pain and confusion and grief.

Dalton reaches over and pulls me to him, and I crawl onto his lap, hold him as tight as I can, and cry onto his shoulder.

I'm sorry.

So incredibly clichéd. Yet what more can I say?

I'd have done anything to avoid this. Rockton is your life. Your mission. Your purpose. I've made it mine, but it was yours first, yours most of all.

"I don't know what to do," he says.

I open my mouth to say that we'll figure it out. That isn't what he needs, though. I mean it to be reassuring, but it's even more empty than those trite phrases I can't bring myself to repeat.

Of course we'll figure something out. Dalton would never give up so easily. He's saying he doesn't know where to start. He'll figure it out—we both will—but in this moment, he needs to be allowed to experience grief.

This is loss. A monumental loss for him. His life has been founded on unstable ground, and he has always known it, and the only way he's been able to deal with that is to accept the instability of relationships in his life.

People come and go. He stays. Rockton stays. That is the true bond in his life. Dalton and his town. He's devoted his adult life to it. He knows nothing else. Wants nothing else.

I need to let him have his grief and not jump in to fix it. So I just sit there, holding his hand and letting him feel whatever he needs to feel. When he's ready to talk, he will.

An hour later, we *are* talking . . . about training Storm to signal when she locates whoever's trail we've put her on. Yes, it has nothing to do with the current situation, and that is the point. It doesn't matter whether we stay in Rockton or not, this is still training we might want for her. That makes it a safe topic of discussion while we distance ourselves from the rest. We get twenty minutes of that before Anders is at our door.

I open it, and he's standing there, hands in his pockets, looking exactly like I felt an hour ago, not knowing what to say.

"How's he doing?" he asks.

I make a face and shrug, and he nods, understanding Dalton is doing as well as can be expected.

"So," Anders continues. "Phil called a meeting."

I sigh so deeply my knees quiver as I lean against the doorframe.

"Yeah," he says. "That's why I volunteered to come get you. Say the word, and I will make your excuses."

"No," Dalton says as he walks from the living room. "Phil told us that he was calling a meeting, and we didn't stop him."

"Give us ten minutes to freshen up," I say, and wave for Anders to come inside.

We're walking through town, the three of us moving fast enough that everyone knows we're on a mission, and no one interferes.

"Phil mentioned they're blaming me," Anders says, his voice low. "My confession."

"Phil should keep his damned mouth shut," Dalton grumbles.

"He also said they're blaming you and Casey and him and everyone but themselves. And that all that is just a smokescreen for the fact they jumped on this as an excuse to tell you what you already knew. That they were shutting us down."

Dalton grunts.

"I'm not looking for you to tell me it isn't my fault," Anders says. "I'm just saying that I realize they said that, which means they may want me on one of those early flights as a troublemaker."

"They'd better not try," Dalton says.

"If they do, we'll need a backup plan. Probably me disappearing into the forest. I could, uh, stay in Brent's old cave but, uh, I'd really rather I wasn't sent out there alone."

Dalton nods. "Tyrone and Jacob are both close enough to call in."

"Hopefully, it won't come to that," Anders says. "But I think we need to be prepared for who they might include on those early flights and what we're going to do about it."

We're in the Roc. We need to go around the back, because Isabel has locked the front doors. I see the patio still in disarray, chairs knocked over. I imagine residents trying to help clean it up and Isabel shooing them away.

I stare at the mess, and it seems symbolic of what is to come. Is there even any point righting the chairs? Clearing away the glass? Scrubbing the blood from the wood? Any point in finding someone to tend bar when everyone will be gone within a fortnight?

I pause there, staring at the blood on the deck. It nudges a thought deep within me, one that doesn't take form, and I shove it aside.

Anders holds the door, and we go into the darkened room. All the blinds have been shut, and it smells of stale beer. It's never smelled like that before. It might look as rough as a Western saloon, but Isabel keeps it in tip-top shape, with the sawdust swept and replaced regularly.

Another task that has now been rendered moot.

Unnecessary.

The room is so hushed that it takes a moment to realize anyone's there. I glance around at the faces. Kenny. Isabel. Phil. Mathias. Petra.

Kenny walks over to us. "April couldn't make it. I only told her that the word came down and the closure is happening faster than we expected, and she suddenly had a lot of cleaning to do and couldn't possibly join us."

I nod.

"I figured it's best to leave her to that for now," he says. "Would you agree?"

I nod again. The news has thrown my sister off kilter, and that is disturbing to her in a way I can only try to comprehend. She will deal with the disorganization through organization. Controlling what can be controlled.

There are two empty chairs at the front table, and Dalton heads there. I start for a seat at a table with Petra and Mathias, but Anders brushes past me with, "You're over there, Case."

When I hesitate, he dips his chin, acknowledging that I'm uncomfortable taking a seat at the front when he's been here longer. Except for Phil, everyone has been here longer. When I've charged forward, putting myself in the center of town business, it's always been as Dalton's supporter. Or that's how I intended it. Now it feels as if I've stepped above my station.

"Take it," Anders says. "We need you up there."

I'm still slow to move, even as Dalton frowns my way, wondering why I'm not already sitting beside him.

Even after I sit, no one says a word. Dalton glances my way, and I realize he's waiting for me to begin. I may not feel I've earned this spot at the head table, but what I have earned is Dalton's trust. He trusts me to speak for him.

When I lead the town meetings, I've always been very aware that I'm speaking on behalf of the law-enforcement agency of Rockton. A PR rep, nothing more. Dalton isn't comfortable in the role of communicator, and in Rockton, he shouldn't play that part. He is the voice of absolute authority here, and the person on that podium must be more conciliatory, more reasonable. More feminine? Maybe it seems so, but Anders could do the job just as well.

Dalton's projected image means he should not be "lowering himself" to explaining anything to the residents. It's also personality. Even here, among friends, he'd rather I ran with this meeting. He trusts me to run with it, and so I must.

"Phil has explained the situation, I'm sure," I begin.

"I've relayed the conversation with Tamara, in as much detail as I can recall."

I pass him a small smile. "In other words, you've relayed everything. So that's where we stand. The council has finally admitted they're shutting us down, and they're using the current situation as an excuse."

"Reminds me of my first summer job," Isabel says. "My employer concocted a firing-worthy offense against me, when the truth was that she just didn't like me very much. My real crime was that I'd made the unforgivable error of pointing out all the flaws in her business model."

"Yep," I say. "We've been complaining too much about these criminals they keep tossing our way. We're endangering their business model. Émilie has said that she suspects they aren't shutting down the business model. Just the town. Relocating."

"To a new place, run by suckers who don't realize they're dealing with serial killers," Kenny mutters.

I shrug. "Or maybe being paid enough that they don't care. Rockton has evolved into something different, and we aren't the right kind of law enforcement for it."

"They need jailers," Dalton says. "Not cops."

"Or we could be mistaken, and they've decided that a town like Rockton isn't profitable enough to sustain in any form. It doesn't matter, because whatever they do, none of us will be on the invitation list."

"Is there anyone here who'd go to a new Rockton under those conditions?" Petra says.

Muttered epithets and eye rolls all around.

"I'm presuming we have two options," Isabel says. "We accept this, or we try to stop it. Is there any point in stopping it?"

"I believe there is," Phil says. "We have the infrastructure here. The town is built and well established. The alternative is starting from scratch."

"Which will be both difficult and expensive," Isabel says.

"Very. It makes good fiscal sense to work within the current parameters."

"The current parameters being living among killers."

Phil's gaze slides to Anders.

"I don't mean Will," Isabel says. "I have no issue with him nor any issue with anyone here who might have something in their past, something worse."

"Why are you looking at me, Isabel?" Mathias asks.

"Pure coincidence, I'm sure. I'm talking about the dangerous offenders who've been sent here and continued to commit dangerous offenses. We've had serial killers, rapists, unrepentant murderers, for whom being here only solidifies their sense of entitlement. They aren't being punished for their crimes. They received a free pass to a wilderness town where they can do as they like."

"I wouldn't say it's free," Phil murmurs. He lifts his hands. "Which is not your point."

"My point is that I'm not going to live in this damned town anymore," she says. "You were almost killed by a man who tried to attack me for the terrible crime of trusting him. Yes, Brandon doesn't have a history of violence, but he was driven to his actions by Conrad, a known blackmailer who came to a town ripe for blackmail. As I know very well, having used it myself to extend my stays."

"You are looking at me again, Isabel," Mathias says. "If you continue that, you may make Philip jealous."

"Phil knows exactly why I'm looking at you, since he's the one who negotiated both our blackmail-infused extensions." Isabel turns to us. "I've had enough, and I frankly do not understand why we are trying to keep Rockton alive. This ship is sinking, Eric. I am very sorry to say that. But it's sinking, and the council isn't willing to make repairs. It hands you teaspoons for bailing out the water, and then complains when we have flood damage."

Silence. Beside me, Dalton holds himself tight, listening. I'm thinking of that blood on the back patio. It caught my eye and dragged with it a sense of deep exhaustion.

Blood soaked into the wood of this town. Blood we'll never get out, and all we can do is replace the boards, knowing it does nothing to solve the problem.

Not every murder here has been the council's fault. Stop-

ping the inflow of unrepentant criminals wouldn't solve everything. But it would untie our hands. Let us chart our course,
not rely on navigators a thousand miles away who don't give a
shit where we end up.

Isabel turns to Phil. "I understand the infrastructure issue. I
really do. If someone offered me the Roc instead of building
a new saloon at my own expense, obviously I'd take the exist-
ing structure. But this isn't that. They're offering me a free bar
built on quicksand and infested with rattlesnakes. This town
is poisoned. We cannot save it."

She turns to Dalton. "I know how hard that is for you to
hear, Eric. You're the one with the greatest stake in this. But
this entire town is built on quicksand, infested with rattlesnakes, and it's about to be set afire."

Dalton grunts. That's it. Just a grunt.

"Could we buy it?" Kenny asks. "I have no idea where we'd
come up with the money, but it'll cost them to dismantle this
place. We can offer to take their rattlesnake-infested town off
their hands."

It's Petra who shakes her head. "Émilie has tried to buy
Rockton multiple times. She made them a massive offer when
the dust settled on the hostile issue. They turned her down flat."

"Liability issues," Phil says. "To extend Isabel's metaphor,
they will be afraid that if they let us take the rattlesnake-
infested town someone will get bitten and—" He waves a
hand. "Forget the metaphor. They're afraid that if your version
of Rockton was exposed, it'd come back on them. This isn't a
rattlesnake-infested town. It's a highly illegal operation."

"They think we'll screw up, and they'll be caught in the
fallout," Kenny says. "Better to burn it down and salt the
earth."

"Yes," Phil says. "You say they'd need to pay to dismantle
it. To them, that's insurance."

"We need to build a new Rockton," I say.

Everyone turns my way, and I feel the weight of those eyes as I continue. "When I first came here, I told Eric that if the council ever shut us down or kicked us out, we'd rebuild. Our own Rockton. Our own rules. I came to realize just how naive that was. As Phil will happily tell us, there is so much infrastructure involved here. Not just the buildings, but the procedures and policies. We can copy those—at least the ones that work for us—but it's like thinking we can open a bed and breakfast in the middle of the wilderness and people will somehow find us. I don't even know how to *think* about that part. We need to find people in need without risking exposure, and we need to ensure we aren't tricked into admitting exactly the kind of people the council has been sending us."

I take a deep breath. "But Isabel is right. There's poison here. We can't keep living like this. She called it a sinking ship, and we're being given teaspoons for bailing. It's worse than that. It's an ark, and we're being given teaspoons to bail or we risk the lives of people who trust us to keep them safe. If we fight to keep the council's version of Rockton, we're complicit in what they do to those people."

I realize what I've said and turn to Dalton. "I didn't mean—"

"No, you're right. We've been trying to keep the boat afloat, and the damage keeps getting worse. At some point, we need to evacuate and save who we can. We've reached that point."

Dalton lifts his head to look out at the others. "Does anyone think we're being premature here? Well, other than Phil. We know where Phil stands." His gaze lands on Petra. "You thought we were acting in haste before. Still agree?"

She shakes her head. "I hoped my grandmother could fix this. She can't. To me, that was our only chance. Émilie buys Rockton, and we run it the way we want. The way it was always supposed to be."

"Anyone else?" Dalton says.

Headshakes all around. He turns to Phil. "You want to state your case for staying?"

Phil's quiet for a moment. Then he says, his voice soft, "I don't believe I have one. Isabel and Casey are right. We're trying to save a sinking ark, when what we need to do—what *you* need to do—is build a new one."

TWENTY-TWO

Build a new ark. A new Rockton. Is it even possible? I don't know. Right now, we must focus on dismantling this one.

Having made our decision, we move quickly. We need to, if the first flight out is in two days. Also, moving quickly will keep us busy. There will be time later to plan "New Rockton." We still have a town to shut down, and we need to make that as painless as possible for the residents.

That isn't easy. I keep thinking about the new town. Who will join us? Isabel, Mathias, Petra, Kenny, Anders, and April have committed to giving it a shot. Who else? Maryanne? Sebastian? Would Nicole and Jacob at least want to live there part-time? And what do we do with someone like Jen? Even if we dared offer her a spot, would we trust her with the secret? Yet if we didn't, and she found out, it would be worse. Would we want to start a new Rockton already admitting residents we don't trust? Isn't that the first step down a slippery slope? And then there's Diana. I don't even want to think about Diana.

What will we need to run it? Émilie has promised to back us financially. Part of me wants to refuse and do it myself—I inherited over a million from my parents. But we trust Émilie, and I'm not sure that having me finance the town will be any more comfortable. How would I expect people to treat me if I own the town?

Stop.

Just stop.

I can't, though. My galloping mind will not be reined in. So after some of the others leave and it's just me, Dalton, Phil, and Isabel, I make notes to get them out of my head while the others plan the exodus schedule.

Brandon and Conrad are on the first plane out. That goes without saying. Is it wrong that I want to add Marissa? I'm still angry at her defection. She hurt Anders, and I want her gone.

They do add Jolene to the list. That reminds me of what we heard this morning, but like Dalton said, she's probably holed up somewhere, sleeping off a rough night. She *is* trouble, though, so she goes on the first plane. Ted, too. And possibly Gloria. Get help for her alcoholism, in recognition that Rockton—by way of Conrad—set her back.

A few other troublemakers are added to the first two planes. Then Phil and Dalton divide the town into essential and nonessential workers. We won't use those terms, because they're the ones we've used to assess privileges and this is a different thing. Bakers, like Devon and Brian, aren't considered essential, because they can be easily replaced. Oh, I'd argue that no one can truly replace Brian, but the point is that baking is a teachable skill in a way that medicine is not.

We are at the point, however, where we cannot train a baker. Or even a new shop clerk. We must look at what we'll need to keep running, and in that context everything changes. We may not need a doctor if others can perform first aid. Hell, I'm damned sure we don't need a police detective.

April and I will stay to the end. We have a loophole here—the council wants us to assemble a team to dismantle the town. We'll find work for everyone that we need to stay.

In two weeks, we'll be down to that final team. That means reworking a lot of schedules. We must eat as much food as possible and won't have to gather more. No need to repair buildings or clothing. No need to construct new furniture or restock the general store. It will require a complete rethinking of how we run the town. First, though, we must tell them what's happening.

We've discussed this all before. If we cannot save Rockton, how will we tell residents that it's closing? Some will be champing at the bit to leave. To them, this isolated life is a prison sentence, and they've already decided they'd rather just face whatever they did down south. Yet another area where the council has failed us. Greed took over, and they misrepresented the living conditions here. They were like time-share promoters, pumping up the allure of the Canadian north while downplaying the reality of two years in an off-the-grid town.

Maybe I'm too seduced by Rockton myself to see the reality, but I believe those eager to leave will be in the minority. There are many residents who'd be happier if Rockton were, say, on a tropical island. Yet they came here for a reason, and they are not ready to leave.

Yet it's more than that, too. People are here to hide. And now we're about to shove them back into the world before they are prepared to face it again. We've discussed how to do that, should Rockton close, and all of our plans were careful and considerate. Need-to-know basis only until we've run out of options. In those scenarios, though, we would be fighting to the bitter end. That is no longer the plan. Also, in those scenarios, our residents were relaxed and content, and they trusted us. Again, no longer the situation.

We cannot afford to be secretive. We cannot even afford to be cagey. Cards on the table. Everyone must know, and that will itself be chaotic, but the alternative would be worse.

So we call a meeting. Shut down every place of business, tell people to drop what they're doing and come to the town square for an emergency meeting.

They come with the reluctance of teens being summoned to the school office. They think they're in trouble. Now that Conrad and Brandon have been caught, Dalton is going to lay down the law. Time to shape up and forget this criminals-in-hiding nonsense. Anders was a special case, and the rest was just panic whipped up by troublemakers.

They come with grumbles and dragged feet. They arrange themselves before the podium, like kids summoned to a disciplinary assembly. They've all misbehaved, and they're about to get a lecture, and they're trying to joke with each other about time off from work, but really, they just want this over with.

I have been elected speaker for this afternoon's session. I don't remember the poll, but apparently, I won. Or lost. Yep, I definitely drew the short stick on this one. I will deliver the news, and then Dalton and Phil will move forward to answer questions.

I climb up, and while some of the noise dies down, it's far from silent. People shift. People mutter. There is a rift here. A deep and—if I'm being honest—unfixable rift. There are those we could win back, those who are paying attention, those who are glancing at Anders with quiet smiles and nods, telling him that they've moved beyond their initial fear and confusion. But I have underestimated the depth of discontent. I think we all have.

In the past year, the tenor has changed so much. The rapid turnover made that easy. Far too many people who don't want to be here. Or don't deserve to be here. It's the rest I worry about, and it's for them that I choose my words with care.

"Everyone knows we've had a rough last few days, but that's not why you've been called here this afternoon."

This gets their attention. The shuffling stops. Eyes turn my way.

Someone shouts, "We all get ponies, right? Tell us we get ponies."

"You wouldn't fit on a pony, Neil," someone shouts back, to be met with good-natured hoots and laughter.

"How about a party?" someone else says. "If you want to make it up to us, we could go for a big summer bash. Free booze for all."

I bristle a little at the "make it up to us" part, but I keep my smile pasted on as others joke and laugh and agree that yes, a party is always good.

"You know," I say, "that might not be such a bad idea. How does Friday sound?"

I glance over at Phil and then Isabel. Isabel hesitates, and I can see her working her head around the free-alcohol part. But then it hits: the moment when she realizes it doesn't matter. That she's about to be sitting on a very large stack of useless credits and useless alcohol.

"Why not," she calls. "Friday it is. Free booze for all."

"Within limits," Dalton cuts in. "We'll raise the nightly maximum by one drink. But it'll be free. It'll all be free."

Shouts greet that. Whoops and laughter and then one voice cutting through the rest, saying, "You're serious, right?"

"Fucking serious," Dalton says.

The laughter slowly fades, and a sense of discomfort seeps

in, as some begin to realize that we don't do this for any other occasion.

"What's wrong?" a voice calls. "What's happening?"

"Nothing's wrong, per se," I say, raising my voice to be heard. "I do have news, though. News that will make some of you very happy." I take a deep breath. "The council is shutting us down."

"Shutting down the Roc?" someone shouts. "Can they do that?"

"Not the Roc," I say. "Everything. They're closing down Rockton."

TWENTY-THREE

There is chaos after that. We control it as best we can, and of course, I second-guess how I delivered the news, but in the end, I don't think there was a better way. It is what it is, and they deserved to know. I make that clear, and there's self-interest in that—well, self-interest on behalf of all of us.

We didn't want to hide this from you. We want you to know and understand and be prepared. We know we lost your trust, and here we hope to regain a little, even if it won't be needed for long.

I also blame the council. I totally blame the council. Fuck them, as Dalton would say.

Fuck the council.

I have spent two years smoothing things over for them. I've always been aware that, whatever our grievances, we cannot let the town see the schism. It's like your parents arguing. Worse, it's like divorced parents arguing, while the children are living with one parent yet reliant on the goodwill—and financial support—of the other. We could not drag our residents into our disputes. Better for them to think all is progressing with no more than the usual relationship bumps.

Now I am like the parent who has been covering for their

former spouse all this time. Protecting the kids from knowing that their other parent is an abusive bastard who doesn't give a shit about them. There's no need to smooth anything anymore, and I am not letting Dalton take the blame. Not letting Anders take it either, whatever bullshit story the council spun.

I'm sure there are residents who will still blame us. Who will still blame Anders. But I get the feeling that the Venn diagram between "thinks Rockton's leadership is corrupt" and "doesn't want to be here anyway" is close to a perfect circle. Maybe those residents should thank us for our "incompetence."

More, though, are in shock. That's the tough part. Seeing those faces. Seeing their worry and disbelief and fear. Mostly the fear.

The questions come then. Endless questions, some about the practicalities of moving out, others about what comes next, and still others about whether this is definite. Is there no way of stopping it? No chance to reverse the council's decision?

These are the hardest questions to answer. They'd have been easy before. Yes, we're fighting. Yes, we still have hope.

But we've moved on, and there's guilt there. We know there is no hope for Rockton, but we feel as if we should still fight for the residents who are afraid to go home again, for those who aren't ready to go home again. It's like telling desperate factory workers there's no chance of keeping their workplace open, while we've already secured a position elsewhere.

This is for the best, though. That's what we'll say, in the days to come. We'll say it to them, but mostly to each other.

Isabel was right. We've been trying to save an institution that doesn't deserve saving. Keeping Rockton open would help these people, but not all those to come, as the situation worsens.

So we talk. Talk, talk, and talk, until Phil reads the list of names for the first two departure flights and asks those people to

join him at the Roc for further instructions. Then the meeting is adjourned.

Adjourned but not over. Phil gets to escape with his small
group. We're stuck, like politicians at a press conference without security to escort us out. They have questions. So many
questions about their personal situations.

"Talk to Phil." That's what Dalton says, and it feels cruel,
dumping it onto Phil's shoulders, but that will be his job here.
Direct questions to one person so residents don't get conflict-
ing answers.

We're making our way from the crowd when someone
snags my sleeve. It's Neil, who works in maintenance.

"You'll need to speak to Phil," I say.

"It's not about the closure," he says. "It's about Jolene."

I inwardly sigh. Can I just say "screw it" and "I don't care"
for the next two weeks? No. Well, I could, but I won't.

"What's she done?" I say.

Even as I speak the words, the memory from this morning
twinges. I'm about to answer my own question when he says,
"No one's seen her today."

"I heard something about her not showing up for work. I
presume she hasn't been seen since?"

"Right. Mateo came by this morning. I live right next
door to Jolene. I'm on afternoon shift, so he woke me up asking about her. I said I hadn't seen her, but I kept an eye out.
She's . . ." He shrugs. "Jolene's not the most popular person in
Rockton, but she's been nice to me. I had food poisoning a
couple of months ago—my own fault, leaving food out—and
she brought your sister to my place, picked up soup for me,
checked in on me."

"When's the last time you saw her?"

"Yesterday evening. She was heading out for the evening.
When Mateo came by, I figured maybe Jolene was sleeping

someplace else. But she still hasn't shown up for her shift, and I started thinking about the time I got that food poisoning. I could barely get out of bed to answer the door. I know you guys have keys for everyone's place."

"You want us to check on her."

"Please."

"I'll go do that right now."

I glance at Dalton, who's already taking the skeleton key from his pocket. When Neil leaves, Dalton hands it over and says, "Go have a look. And take . . ." His gaze barely starts to scan before Kenny says, "I'll escort Casey."

Under normal circumstances, a welfare check doesn't require backup. Considering Jolene isn't a fan of law enforcement, it's wise to have backup that can also serve as a witness, if things go wrong.

I tell Dalton I'll be back as soon as I can, and then Kenny and I head for Jolene's place.

Jolene's apartment is in the same building as Ted's. She lives just above him, and opening the door into her place, I'm reminded of his. The layout is nearly identical. Will we change that in the new Rockton? Or does having the same layout mean no one gets pissy because someone has a layout they prefer? One thing Dalton and I have discussed is having fewer apartments and more multi-resident homes, with private bedrooms and shared living space.

And that has nothing to do with this welfare check on Jolene.

I hope it isn't food poisoning. Neil said his was a food-storage issue, but it's still the last thing we'll need.

I push my head through the open door. "Jolene? It's Casey. Detective Butler. I've been asked to check in on you."

When no one answers, I step just inside the door and try again. "Jolene? I'm just checking that you're all right."

Still nothing. I turn to Kenny. "Can you follow me inside, please?"

"Watch your back?"

"More like bear witness that I don't disturb or damage or swipe anything."

"Ah. Got it. Yeah, Jolene can be . . ." He trails off before saying more, his gaze going inside, as if remembering she might overhear.

We continue inside. The living room is a mess. That's the first thing I see, and I pull up short, tensing. The place looks as if it's been ransacked. On closer inspection, I'm not so sure. There's a blanket on the floor, a dirty mug and plate on the table, and clothing strewn about. That could all be messy house- keeping. There are also open drawers, a spill, and what looks like . . . Is that blood on the wall?

I yank my gaze from the wall and turn toward the bedroom instead. "Jolene?" I call. "I'm coming into your bedroom."

I rap on the half-closed door first. No answer. I push it open to see the room in equal disarray. The bed isn't just unmade— half the sheets hang onto the floor. Occupants have the choice of a double or single bed. Single makes it harder to have over- night guests. Double, though, takes up the entire small room. Jolene opted for a single bed and a dresser, and the drawers are open, contents spilling out.

One thing is clear. Despite the disarray, Jolene isn't here. By now, of course, I expect this. Or I'd been hoping for it, because after all my calling, if she was here, she was either unconscious or dead. I still do a quick check of the tiny bath- room and kitchenette. Both look like a tornado struck, but it's obvious Jolene isn't here.

"She sleeps out a lot," Kenny says.

When I turn, he lifts his hands. "That's an observation, not a judgment. I slept out a lot too in my first year and . . . er, that's more than you need to know."

"Yes, but I catch your drift, and I'm not judging either way. Plenty of that going on here. I presume Jolene is popular."

"Uh, have you seen the town stats, Casey? All the women are popular. Even—" He cuts himself off. "And it would be rude to say more. Point is that any woman who wants to be popular will be, especially when there are plenty—like Petra or April—who don't want anything to do with that side of the social scene. Or you and Isabel, who already have someone. Hell, these days even Jen—" He stops. "And I'm putting my foot in it again."

"Straight men vastly outnumber straight women," I say. "And many of those women aren't into hooking up, so those who are—like, perhaps, Jolene—could probably go their entire two years and never spend a night in their own bed."

He chuckles. "Yep."

"Any thoughts on who Jolene has been seeing?"

"I can share names on the understanding they didn't come from me. I don't go looking for that kind of information, but the kind of guys Jolene prefers aren't the kind who stay quiet about it. She seems fine with that, but it still feels wrong sharing it."

"Got it. I'll take a list then. Lovers and friends if you know names."

"Not so sure on the friends, but I can make a start on the lovers." He pauses. "I'm not on the list. Just in case . . ."

I look over, as innocently as possible. "In case what?"

His cheeks redden. "I know you discuss cases with April, and I, uh . . ."

"One, my sister wouldn't care if you'd slept with Jolene. She'd simply say that sex is a natural instinct and if done safely and respectfully, it's a healthy outlet. Two, if the fact you're no longer 'sleeping out' has anything to do with April, you might want to make an actual move on that."

His mouth opens. Shuts. He busies himself looking around. "Jolene's apartment is a bit of a mess, huh?"

"Yep."

"Any chance . . . Well, I hate to think anything happened to her, but it *is* a mess."

"Exactly what I'm thinking. Would you stand guard while I run and talk to Will? I want to take a closer look around, but I'd like the militia to start knocking on doors, seeing whether Jolene is behind any of them."

I'm trying not to overreact about Jolene. I don't want to declare her missing, and half of that is just the damned inconvenient timing. We wrapped up the case, and with that, I declare my work as Detective Butler done. The others will need help with a million things over the next couple of weeks. We absolutely cannot afford to have a missing resident.

On the way back to her place, I stop at both the stable and the laundry—where she normally works—and chat to her coworkers. They all say she's not exactly employee of the month, but she doesn't skip out either.

It seems Jolene shared a few things in common with Conrad, besides jumping on the "Anders is evil" bandwagon. She got the temporary stable position because she has livestock experience, and I don't know what exactly it is, but I'm guessing something like a veterinarian or horse-farm owner. Something relatively prestigious, because she's made it very clear that the laundry service is beneath her.

Unlike Conrad, Jolene didn't try to shirk her duties. She understood that her skills weren't useful here, so she just made sure everyone knew she'd been "someone" down south, while otherwise sucking it up and doing the work.

What's the chance she randomly chose today to skip out? Maybe it *wasn't* random. According to her coworkers, she'd been more than Conrad's groupie. Not lovers, but friends or at least drinking buddies. She's been seen at the Red Lion and the Roc with Conrad, Gloria, and a few others. Including Ted, who hadn't divulged that relationship when we'd talked. Even Marissa had been part of the group at one point.

As a detective, I feel as if I should be more aware of the relationship webs in town. Yet keeping tabs on that feels like indulging in gossip. Who's sleeping with whom. Who's drinking with whom. Who's fighting with whom. The case against Conrad happened so fast that I didn't have time to delve into any of his relationships. The Marissa one is certainly a shock. I knew he'd been interested in her, but she certainly never suggested they'd hung out socially.

All that goes in my back pocket. The point is that Jolene had been friends with Conrad. Had his near-death experience knocked her off track? Or, as someone who believed in his cause, had she been disillusioned to realize it was all self-interest? Needed a day off to think and reflect?

I will allow for the possibility then that Jolene is uncharacteristically playing hooky from work. She could even be lying low. After all, she was Conrad's fiercest supporter, and now it turns out that he only had that one tidbit, about that one special case. In her place, I'd be hiding my face, too.

Back to her apartment for a search while the militia scout around town. I leave Kenny outside Jolene's place to question anyone walking past. I've barely made it through Jolene's apartment door before Dalton appears with Storm at his heels.

"I'm going to see whether she can track Jolene," he says. "She's better with you, but you're better at this." He waves around the apartment.

I shake my head. "No need for that yet. You have plenty of other things to do."

"And plenty of other times to do them. My head's a mess and, right now, nothing seems more tempting than accompanying Storm on a pointless tracking exercise."

I walk over and kiss his cheek. "Then you absolutely should do that. If Jolene doesn't turn up in a few hours, I'd have needed to do it myself."

He nods.

I rub his arm. "I won't ask whether you're okay, because I know you're not."

"I'll *be* okay. I'm shifting my brain over to the idea of Rockton closing. To the certainty of it. Part of me wants to yank back, like I'm touching a hot iron. But part of me is . . ." He purses his lips. "Relieved, maybe? If that's the right word?"

"Well, half of me is running around in a panic, like Chicken Little seeing the sky falling. The other half is madly thinking of all the things we can do better."

He kisses the top of my head. "Yeah, we can do a lot of things better. I'll focus on that. I have some ideas."

"I'm sure you have a ton of ideas. Let me search this place, let the militia do their rounds, and let Storm do her tracking. One of us will find Jolene. And then we'll spend the evening at home, getting drunk and making plans. Or getting drunk and getting naked and forgetting all of this."

"How about getting drunk, making plans, and *then* getting naked and forgetting all of this?"

I smile up at him. "Sounds just about perfect."

★　★　★

I find a piece of Jolene's discarded clothing. That's certainly easy—it's all over the apartment. Then I set Storm on the scene and send them off.

I spend two hours searching Jolene's apartment. That sounds more impressive if I don't mention that I periodically pop out to check on the progress of the militia, as if they wouldn't run to tell me if they found her. I also check on Dalton and Storm, as if they wouldn't come to tell me if they found a trail. I can't help it. In my current state of mind, I can only focus in twenty-minute bursts. Then my thoughts wander to the demise of Rockton, and I need fresh air and a mental shake-up before I can resume my search.

Apparently, I'm not the only one distracted. At the two-hour mark, Petra raps on Jolene's door.

"I come bearing coffee and cookies," she says.

I walk out onto the porch, and we sit on the step, with Kenny eating a cookie behind us.

"I won't ask what you found," Petra says as she sips her coffee.

"Does it matter?" *Does any of it matter?* I don't say that. It sounds too much like whining.

I continue, "I don't think I need to keep my investigations quite so confidential anymore. Her place is a mess, but I think that's mostly just Jolene."

Petra turns her face up to the sun. "She's the kind of house-keeper who only washes dishes when she runs out of clean ones?"

"Yep. But the problem with messy housekeeping in a crime scene is that it could hide legitimate disturbances. Are the drawers opened because someone searched through them? Or because she just never closes them?"

I stretch my legs. "The place seems ransacked, but on closer inspection, I see no obvious evidence it was." I glance over at her. "Want a look?"

"Sure."

We head inside, still eating cookies and drinking coffee. It's not as if Jolene will notice the crumbs when she returns.

I have no idea exactly what Petra did before she retired. I call it "special ops," but I suspect she'd wrinkle her nose at that. From the way she goes through Jolene's apartment, though, it's obvious she has some experience with this or at least with ransacking a place and then covering her tracks.

When she finishes, she shakes her head. "I see nothing that couldn't be messy housekeeping. If someone went rummaging through her drawers, they'd be more likely to make the amateur mistake of closing them back up again. There's a mark on the wall, that could be blood."

"It's not. I used an ultraviolet light on it. I'm guessing ketchup or tomato sauce."

"Well, that makes sense. I don't see obvious signs of a search or a struggle."

"In other words, Jolene's going to pop up in a few hours and give me proper shit for going through her things."

"Maybe, but you don't need to worry about that anymore, do you?"

I sigh. "True."

She lowers her voice. "Have you talked to Diana?"

It takes me a moment to make the segue. Then I curse under my breath.

"Yeah," she says. "Diana and I aren't exactly pals, but you might want to talk to her about the town closing."

I sigh. "All right. Time to temporarily forget Jolene. I have house calls to make."

TWENTY-FOUR

Two hours ago, I was mentally bitching at having to search for Jolene while I was busy thinking about Rockton closing. Now it's the opposite. I'm caught up in the mystery of Jolene, and balking at needing to divert to deal with Rockton-closure issues. Or maybe that's an excuse. Compared to speaking to Diana and April about the closing, I'd rather keep hunting for Jolene.

I find them both still in the clinic. Which is awkward when I need to have two very different conversations.

"Inventory?" I ask as I walk in to find April holding a clipboard while Diana bends to count something in a drawer.

"Yes," April says briskly. "I realize we will not be allowed another supply trip into Dawson City, and so I am taking inventory in the event that I need to begin conserving resources."

"Ah."

She turns to me. "If that sound is meant to imply that I'm overreacting to the news, I am not. I have become accustomed to having an abundance of supplies, and I cannot afford to give away bandages or painkillers willy-nilly, only to run out of them days before the town closes."

"I wasn't implying any form of judgment, April."

She sniffs and goes back to work. It's true. I wasn't judging her choice of activity. Merely registering it and understanding that this is what she needs right now. Tasks. Work. Focus. Not conversation. That can wait.

"Well," I say. "If there's anything you need . . ."

"Diana."

I nod. "Diana, could you leave us alone for a few minutes?"

"I mean I need Diana. I require her services."

I look at Diana, who's sorting through the drawer, her gaze fixed on her task. She's hurt. Hurt that she had to hear about Rockton's closing from someone other than me. I get that. It's why I'm here. Making amends. Yet I bridle, too, at the thought that I should need to make amends.

With Diana, I will be forever trapped between feeling as if I'm being a bitch punishing her for past betrayals and feeling as if I'm being a pushover by not severing our relationship permanently.

"Diana?" I say.

"Hmm?" She continues sorting and organizing.

"We'd like you to stay in Rockton until the end. Of course, that's up to you. I could make arrangements if you wanted to leave, but if you're willing to stay, you'll be compensated."

"I'll stay."

"Good. I'd like to talk to you later, if you have time."

One shoulder rises in a shrug. "Sure."

I turn back to April. "There, you have Diana."

"For now," she says. "But I'll need her after that."

I tense and shoot April a warning look that she doesn't catch.

I clear my throat. "If you have any post-Rockton job offers for Diana, that's something to discuss at a later time. Right now, we're focused on shutting down Rockton. Diana, would you give me a moment with my sister, please."

Diana rises. She wipes her hands on her jeans and turns to go. Halfway to the door, she glances back and says, "You're restarting Rockton, aren't you."

"Restarting . . . ?"

She gives me a look. "I'm not stupid, Case. There's no way in hell Eric is giving up that easily. If you guys aren't fighting this closing tooth and nail, it means you have a backup plan. A backup plan would be a new Rockton. That's what April means. She'd like me there."

This time, my glare at my sister does the job.

"I said nothing," April protests. "I merely mentioned that my need for Diana will not end with the closing of this town."

And with that, she confirms Diana's suspicions. I resist the urge to sink to the floor and put my head in my hands.

I look at Diana.

"Guess I deserved that," she says, and reaches for the door.

"Diana."

She lifts a hand. "I'm not going to tell anyone, Casey. Whatever else I've done, I've kept your secrets."

She passes me a knowing look that raises the hair on my neck. She catches my expression and shakes her head. "That wasn't a threat. I wouldn't—" She stops. Considers. Restarts "There was a time when I would have done that to you. The threat, not the actual betrayal. I wouldn't now. I heard nothing here, and I can speculate on nothing, should I be asked."

"I *would* like to talk to you." I glance at my watch. "When are you free?"

She fingers the doorframe. Then she says, "You're busy. I know that. So let's say tomorrow. Also, you might want to talk to the others before you speak to me. Let them know that I know and see what they want to do about that."

"I will. And I am sorry you heard about the closing second-hand. We've suspected it for a while, but the word just came down this morning." I pause. "Also, you haven't seen Jolene, have you?"

"Jolene?"

"She's missing."

"Last time I saw her was yesterday afternoon. She was outside the canteen, talking to Marissa."

"I heard they're friends."

Diana leans against the doorframe. "I wouldn't say that. When Marissa arrived, Gloria reached out. Invited her to join a bunch of them for drinks. I was there a couple of times but . . ." She scrunches her nose. "Not really my scene. Conrad and Jolene are always complaining. Solidarity through sniping and bitching can be fun for a bit of stress relief, but it gets old fast. I don't know what Gloria sees in them."

"I got the impression Gloria is quiet."

"She is. I guess that'd be it. Like the quiet girl in school who hangs out with whoever will hang out with her. Also, like I said, snarking and sniping can be fun. They glommed on to Marissa when she first arrived, but it didn't last. She'd have a drink with them now and then, same as me. She stopped when she got together with Will."

"Have you hung out with them recently?"

"Only as part of a larger group. They'd gotten bitter. Grumbling about work and rules is one thing, but eventually, that's *all* you're doing. They became obsessed with what a shithole Rockton is and how everyone in charge is incompetent. I checked out then. I don't have time for that."

"Did they know you and I are old friends?"

She hesitates. Then she says, "I may have mentioned it."

"Did they ask for dirt on me?"

Now she's shifting, uncomfortable. "Yes. That's another

reason I cut out. Conrad asked, and I pretended I didn't think he was serious, and then my drinks got stronger."

The hairs on my neck rise. "Damn."

She looks up at me. "I should have told you. I didn't make the connection between that and the sign about Will. Conrad and Jolene jumped on it, and I figured that was just them being happy to help drag one of you guys through the mud. Never imagined they started it. Guess I'd make a lousy detective, huh?"

"Others heard them bitching and didn't make the connection either. If you see Jolene—or hear anything about her—let me know. And breakfast tomorrow?"

"Sounds good."

She's about to leave when April says, "I need your help with this inventory, Diana."

"I think Casey wants to talk to you."

"She can talk to me later. This must be done today."

Diana and I exchange a look. It doesn't need to be done today. Or even tomorrow. April's really saying she doesn't want to talk, as I presumed.

"I should go check in on the search for Jolene," I say. "April, can I ask you to please not talk about any future plans—or hint at any future plans—to anyone?"

"Who else would I tell? Diana is here, and Kenny already knows."

"Kenny knows," Diana murmurs. "And Petra presumably."

"Of course," April says before I can silence her.

"Petra knows because of Émilie," I say. "We need Émilie's guidance here."

True, but also partly an excuse. If we're looking for current residents who'd be good founding members for a new town, Petra is on that list. She's a smart woman and a skilled fighter, yet she's perfectly content doing whatever job needs doing.

"Tell me Jen doesn't know," Diana says. "Please tell me Jen doesn't know."

"Jen does not know." *Now, let's hope Diana doesn't realize Jen hasn't been in town since the word came down.*

April says, "The others are Will, Isabel, and Phil. Also Mathias, though I'm not quite sure why."

"Don't ask," I mutter. I turn to Diana. "Obviously, I wouldn't have shared that list with you. Nor would I have shared the possibility of a replacement town. Not without consulting the others."

"I know," she says. "I won't go up to Mathias and offer the secret handshake."

"Thank you. I'll see you tomorrow for breakfast."

No one has found Jolene. Storm picked up her trail, but when it wound all through town, it became clear it was from yesterday. That's the thing about a place this small—you easily cover it in a day of regular activity. All the competing scents meant that Storm kept losing the trail and then picking up what could either be a continuation of it or a different trail from a different time.

Eventually Dalton gave up and took Storm for a walk along the border path. She didn't find any trace of Jolene's scent.

No easy end to this search, unfortunately, which means no quick end to our workday. I interview Jolene's drinking buddies next. While there seems little point in talking to Conrad, I do it anyway. He's still under house arrest with his militia nurse/guard. He confirms that he hasn't seen Jolene since before his near-death experience.

I'd planned to talk to Ted, but Gloria has told Anders that she's eager to speak to me about Jolene. That seems promising.

It's not. Gloria hasn't seen her since yesterday. She'd invited Jolene to dinner at the Red Lion, but Jolene had other plans, so Gloria went on her own and ended up dining with a couple of residents who invited her over. That smacks of pity—the rumor mill is in full swing, whispering that Conrad used Gloria—but whatever the reason, it was a nice gesture.

As for Jolene's "other plans," Gloria knows nothing about them. Jolene had been cagey, and Gloria wasn't sure whether she genuinely had somewhere else to be or she just didn't want to have dinner together.

That's all Gloria can tell me. She'd asked to speak to me mostly just to express her concern and offer her help. She considers Jolene a friend. I'm not sure that goes both ways, but that isn't Gloria's fault. She's standing by, ready to join the search party.

I ask her the same question I put to Conrad.

"Did you ever know Jolene to venture into the woods?" I say. "For a walk or anything."

She laughs. "Definitely not. I tried to get her to go on one of Maryanne's nature hikes last month, and Jolene looked at me like I suggested skydiving. She hates it here. She always says it's like being trapped on an ice floe in the Arctic Ocean. I've pointed out that we're not trapped—that's why I suggested the hike—but walking in the wilderness is not her idea of entertainment."

I'd gotten the same from Conrad. Jolene hates the forest, and to her, this town might as well be surrounded by an impenetrable wall. She didn't sneak into the woods for a walk and get lost. She didn't wander out for a little peace and quiet either.

I speak to Ted next. He insists he hasn't been part of "that group" in a month. Apparently that's his excuse for not mentioning he'd been friends with Conrad when we first spoke.

When he feared he'd be "outed" after Anders, it was because he damn well knew Conrad was probably behind it and suspected Conrad had dirt on him.

Ted confirms what Gloria said. No forest trips for Jolene. Otherwise, he has nothing for me and really wishes I'd move along. He's scheduled to take the first plane out, and he's already packing.

"Gloria mentioned that Jolene had plans last night," I say. "Gloria invited her out to dinner, and Jolene was busy."

"No, Jolene was making a half-assed excuse not to have dinner with Gloria."

"There was friction there?"

He looks over from folding his clothing. "Friction with Gloria? I'm not certain that's possible. She's . . ." He sets down a shirt and says, "Jolene considers Gloria boring. Gloria is shy, and Jolene interprets that as dull."

"Jolene likes more dynamic dinner companions."

"No, Jolene likes dinner companions who reflect well on her. Who make her look good. Gloria didn't add to her social cachet. I believe she likes Gloria well enough, but Jolene is very image conscious. For example, she dislikes *you*, but she'd have jumped at an invitation to dinner."

He folds another shirt and then pauses. "That does remind me of something, and I'm hoping you will take this piece of information and leave me to my packing."

"What is it?"

"Marissa. She used to join us for drinks, before she moved up in the world by sleeping with Deputy Anders. Jolene took the defection hard. Marissa was well liked, and Jolene enjoyed being associated with her. When Marissa took up with Will Anders, her social status climbed even higher, and Jolene couldn't share in the reflected glory."

"Uh-huh. What does this have to do with Jolene going missing?"

"You say she told Gloria she had other plans for dinner. I saw her with Marissa early that evening. If Jolene did have plans— and wasn't just giving Gloria the brush-off—I'd start there."

TWENTY-FIVE

Two people saw Jolene with Marissa last night. I'd like more than "saw them together" before I speak to Marissa, but this will have to do.

I spot Marissa and try to wave her down; she pretends not to see me. She retreats into her apartment and then doesn't answer when I knock.

"Marissa?" I call through the door. "You don't need to speak to me if you don't want to. I can just keep investigating Jolene's disappearance and keep asking myself why you—the last person to see her—are avoiding talking to me. You're due to leave on the second plane. I'll go to Phil right now and tell him to move you to the last one out, to ensure you don't escape in the midst of an investigation—"

She pulls open the door. "I wasn't avoiding you, Casey. I'm busy. What's this about Jolene?"

"Two witnesses saw you speaking to her last night. So far, you were the last person with her."

Her face screws up. "Jolene?"

"She's missing."

"I heard she didn't show up for work. No one said anything about her being missing."

"She hasn't been seen since last evening, when she was spotted with you. I'm also surprised you haven't come around to give me shit about interviewing Conrad without you being present. You *are* his lawyer, right?"

"I was his legal representation in potential harassment by local law enforcement."

I snort.

Her eyes narrow. "Yes, obviously it wasn't harassment. Your professional interest in him was warranted."

"You could have just trusted that, having seen no evidence that we harass any residents, regardless of the trouble they cause."

"I was retained to represent Conrad in his case. It's now apparent that he has no case, so I am no longer his legal representative."

"His guilt only became certain after he confessed—a confession I obtained without checking with you. I interviewed him in the clinic while he was recovering from head trauma. Questionable tactics."

Her brows rise. "You're admitting it?"

"Why not? The town's shutting down. It's not as if you can file a complaint. I also recorded the interview, presuming you'd raise hell. Yet you haven't asked us about it."

"Your point?"

"Just that it's interesting. You were dead set on representing the guy who attacked you. Then you lost all interest in his case after he was nearly killed." I wave a hand. "Not that it matters. I'm here about Jolene."

She's obviously flustered when she says, "I don't know anything about Jolene."

"I'm not asking whether you do. I'm asking what you two were doing together last night."

"Nothing."

"You were seen talking. Two witnesses—"

"I mean that we were doing nothing. We talked. That's it."

"Talked about what?"

Her lips tighten, as if locking down a response.

"Marissa," I say. "I was asking in hopes that whatever she said might give me a clue to her whereabouts. That's it. But now that you don't want to answer the question, you're going to force me to look deeper at you as a suspect. You get that, right?"

"A suspect in what?"

I throw up my hands. "Who knows. She's disappeared."

"Well, since she isn't in town, maybe you should start looking outside of it. That's the obvious answer, isn't it? Will said people are always sneaking out. That's why the militia patrol constantly. Not to keep animals out but to keep residents in."

"You've known Jolene to go for walks?"

"I don't know her well enough to say."

"I heard you were drinking buddies. Before you got together with Will and started hanging out with us."

She speaks in careful, measured words, as if I might not be clever enough to keep up. "I'm new here, relatively speaking. I wanted to socialize. Gloria offered me a seat at their table. They'd invite me to one of their places for a beer. I stopped before I got together with Will. I was having a drink alone when Will first joined me."

"I'm not accusing you of dumping Jolene and her friends for us. I'm just asking whether you've ever known her to go into the forest for any reason. Because so far, the three people I've asked that have said that she hates the forest and has never left town."

"Maybe? I don't know, Casey. I was just suggesting you look there. You're the detective."

"Do you want to reconsider telling me what you two were talking about?"

"No, because it's none of your business. If you find that suspicious, so be it."

She shuts the door. The lock clicks into place.

Yep, I find that suspicious. I find everything Marissa has done in the last few days suspicious. But I'm going to need more information before I push her on it.

With no time to waste cooking dinner, it's a quick meal at the Red Lion. It's been nearly twenty-four hours since anyone has seen Jolene, and we know she almost certainly hasn't wandered into the forest. That means she's here, somewhere. Time for a door-to-door search.

Before dinner, we ask Anders to round up the militia. We're down to a half dozen members, so we also recruit Petra. After dinner, we meet them all behind the station, where we can explain the plan in relative privacy.

We don't want to alert the town, in case someone is . . . hiding Jolene in their house? I don't know. We had a case last year where a suspect tried to trap me under floorboards. Permafrost means that there's a gap under every building here, some exposed and some not. There are other places to hide a person, too. Or a body.

We head out in pairs. Dalton, Anders, Kenny, and I all take a less experienced militia member with us. I get Sebastian.

I've volunteered to search the chalets. That includes ours. While I don't think anyone hid Jolene under our floorboards, it's worth checking. It also gives me privacy for speaking to Sebastian.

"So the town is closing," I say as he climbs up into our attic.

"Yep." He shines a light around and then crawls in.

"What has Mathias told you?"

"He said I should talk to you," he calls back. "Which I'm guessing is why we're partnered together. Don't expect him to take the initiative if he can leave it to you."

I wait for him to come back down. "How do you feel about the closing?"

His brows lift, as if I've asked how he feels about self-immolation. "Uh, I came here to escape. To be someplace where I'm just a guy, no history shadowing along after me. I've barely gotten a year out of the deal."

"The council will refund your money."

"Really not what I was hoping for."

We check the crawlspace next. As I'm holding open the hatch, I say, "Would you like options?"

"Depends on what they are."

"The First Settlement would take you in."

He goes quiet. I hear him scuffling around in the crawl-space as the flashlight beam moves. Then he comes back up.

"I've been thinking about that," he says. "One, I don't like the way Edwin runs the place. Two, I don't want to live out here permanently. I'm not even sure I want to live out here long-term, but if I did, I'd need to be able to fly in and out, like you and Eric do. Three, of course, is Felicity. Moving into her town seems a recipe for trouble. Like that weird schoolmate you start hanging out with at lunch, and the next thing you know, he's joining all the same after-school clubs as you."

Sebastian shoves his hands in his pockets. "I've been that guy. Done that creepy stuff. I was desperate for friends and this"—he taps his head—"means I didn't quite know how to go about it properly."

"You seem to be doing well with Felicity."

"I learned my lesson. That lesson means I shouldn't move into her town. Especially when they'd only let me because I'm fresh blood. Fresh DNA for the gene pool." He shudders.

"So you and Felicity . . ."

He shoots me a hard look. "Did you hear the part where I'm playing it cool? That includes not even suggesting I might like her as more than a friend. As soon as I move to the First Settlement, they'll start making wedding plans."

"Would you like other options?" I ask.

"If they involve staying up here."

"Would that be contingent on how close you are to the First Settlement?"

He doesn't answer for a moment. Then he says, "I don't need to be next door to it, but I'd want to be within a day's walk. Or a few hours on a dirt bike. Otherwise . . . Well, I'm not going down south, if can help it. The alternative would be to live near Baptiste and Sidra for a while. Not ideal. We're friends, but they have a baby, and they don't need me hanging around. I'd do it before I'd go home, though."

"All right. I'll see what we can figure out."

We complete our search. There's no sign of Jolene anywhere, and all we did was stir up anxieties. We also get the same question Marissa asked. Why aren't we searching the forest? We turn the question back to them. Have they ever seen Jolene in the forest? Close to the forest? Heard her talk about going into the forest?

No, no, and no. Before dinner, I'd also checked the logs

of every excursion. She's never joined one. There's zero indication that she's set foot outside our boundaries since her arrival.

Still, the residents will expect a proper forest search. Dalton rails against the waste of time. I let him have his moment of strenuous objection, knowing that if I hadn't suggested it, he'd have been out himself searching for her come morning. It must be done.

We organize search parties to set out at 7 A.M. Then Dalton and I spend the next hour with Storm, circling the town again on the border path. It's mostly for show. The entire search will be mostly for show. Finding someone in the forest is a logistical nightmare. It only works when we can actively pursue them—as we did with Brandon—or they haven't gone far—as with Conrad. When we have no proof Jolene entered the forest, let alone know where to find an entry trail? It will be an exercise in futility.

So where is she? That's the question I cannot even begin to answer. Could someone be holding her hostage in town, stashed in a place we didn't search? I guess so. But why?

Dalton thinks she's hiding. Intentionally making us search for her. Causing trouble. Again, I don't see her motive. Is it possible she wandered into the woods? Got drunk and stumbled out there alone despite hating it? Maybe, but I don't see it.

By the time we call it quits for the day, it's too late for our fantasy evening of relaxation and conversation and sex. We manage one drink in front of the fire, conversation meandering aimlessly, and then it's off to bed, where we don't have the energy for anything more than quiet talk, cuddled up together until we drift off to sleep.

The knock comes at 2 A.M. I rouse from a dream where Dalton and I are enjoying an overnight in Dawson City, and someone comes banging on our door in the middle of the night. I lift my head, blink, and realize I'm at home in Rockton. The knock comes again, more urgent now.

Then the front door slaps open.

I bolt upright, my sleepy brain screaming that we have an intruder.

Yeah, an intruder who signals their entry by knocking.

I roll out of bed as Dalton wakes with a gasp, as if he missed the knocking but somehow senses intrusion.

I'm already out of bed and yanking on Dalton's T-shirt, which covers me enough to leave the room. As I do, I smack straight into Storm standing in the doorway, having not so much as growled.

"Good watchdog," I mutter.

She glances over and grunts. Feet pound on the steps. I throw open the door just as Anders hits the top step.

"Problem," he says between deep breaths. "Big problem."

TWENTY-SIX

"I couldn't sleep," Anders says, his voice hushed as the three of us jog through the forest, Storm at our heels. "I heard something. At first, I thought I was being paranoid. I was downstairs in the living room reading a book. I had the back windows open, and I was pretending it was for the night air, but really, I was listening for trouble."

"And you heard it," I say.

"I heard something."

He cuts around a tree. We're circling along the border path, heading toward his end of Rockton.

"I thought I caught a voice. That's when I went outside. Grabbed my gun and stepped onto the back deck. It was quiet. Then I heard something in the woods. I went to investigate and . . ."

He slows. He hasn't told us what he found. He's too agitated.

Storm whines. I drop my hand absently to her head. I'm peering into the forest as we continue forward at a walk.

Dalton sees it first, muttering, "Shit."

I follow his gaze. It takes a moment, my eyes still adjusting. Then I make out a figure sitting at the base of the tree. I pick up my pace. I'm not worried about startling the person. I know I can't.

I recognize the figure in a blink. It's Jolene. Dead. Sitting at the base of a tree, eyes closed, throat slit.

Around her throat hangs a wooden sign. A sign with a single word burned into it.

Killer.

We stand there, looking down at Jolene's body in the glare of Dalton's flashlight beam. I lower myself to one knee and check her body temperature.

"Well, we found her," Anders says. "Tell me I wasn't sitting in my house, listening to her being murdered, while telling myself I was hearing things."

I straighten. "You weren't. She's cold." I borrow Dalton's flashlight and shine it on the ground. "There's no blood. She was dead when she was brought here." I bend again and shine the light on her face. "Her throat might have been cut here, but her heart had already stopped beating. That's conjecture, of course. April can confirm. I don't think, though, that if your throat is cut, you're going to die with your eyes shut. Not unless you're heavily drugged."

I rise. "And I'm wildly theorizing because it gives me something to do, rather than deal with the fact that this is, as you say, a very big problem. Bad enough she was murdered after residents didn't think we were looking hard enough. But that sign . . . ?" I shake my head. "We do not need that."

"Do we know whether it's true?" Anders says. "That she killed someone?"

I glance at Dalton, who grunts and says, "That wasn't her official story. We had no reason to investigate her."

"Which means this could be a shot in the dark," I say. "Or it could be someone who knows her backstory better than we do. It's not Conrad or Brandon. Brandon's locked up. Conrad is under watch. I'll check on that, of course."

Anders shakes his head. "Conrad or Brandon would have needed to break out yesterday to kidnap her and then break out again to pose her body tonight. Storm's been by here a few times. She'd have scented a body."

"Her body definitely wasn't here last night. But that only rules out Conrad and Brandon if she's been missing because someone was holding her captive."

"Ah, okay. The other possibility is that she was in hiding herself. Then she was killed. That would only require Conrad or Brandon to sneak out tonight."

"All speculation," I say. "I only even mention them because of the sign. Even Conrad admits he didn't have any more background on anyone. Jen told Conrad about you, and she's been out in the woods somewhere with Tyrone. This seems to be a one-hundred-percent new case, unrelated to yours."

I glance at Dalton. "So the question is what we do about this."

He grunts. That's no answer. He isn't ready to give one.

I continue, "Conrad almost died for claiming he had more dirt on people and threatening to expose them. Marissa was attacked for being in Will's place after he was exposed. Now the town is shutting down. People are on edge. If we tell them about this?" I point at the sign. "We're going to panic everyone who has secrets of their own, and we're going to panic everyone who was ready to accept that Will's case was an exception—the *only* exception. It's the absolute last thing we need while trying to close the town."

"You think we should cover up her death?" Anders says. "Inform the council, but otherwise keep treating her like a missing person?"

"I still need to investigate her murder. I don't think the

town has to know what happened. Either we hide it entirely or we just hide . . ." I point to the sign around Jolene's neck.

"I'd agree we're sitting on a powder keg here," Anders says. "Casey solved the case two days ago. Yesterday we told them we're shutting down. People haven't even had a chance to breathe."

I glance up at Dalton. "We can hide her body and let me investigate her death under the guise of investigating her disappearance. I'd rather not do that, though. I'd like to admit she died and just not mention that sign."

He nods slowly, still processing.

"Whatever we do, there's also the question of what we tell the council." I pause. "Or does that even matter now? Either way, they can't do anything worse than shut us down. They're sure as hell not going to ship us out early and shut down the town themselves."

"Well," Anders says, "if there's any advantage to accepting what's happening, here it is. For the rest of our time here, we are out from under the council's thumb. They can't threaten to shut us down. Can't threaten to kick us out. Can't threaten to split us up. Remind me why we didn't do this a year ago? Oh, right. Because it involves starting an entirely new town from scratch. Still, I kinda like this part."

"Yeah, and I hate to be petty and vindictive, but fuck them." Dalton tilts his head. "First time I think I've ever said that and meant it. Feels good." He looks back at Jolene. "Doesn't solve this problem. Just means we don't need to factor them into our decision. Also means we can't blame them if we make the wrong choice and royally fuck up."

"Not necessarily," I say. "Why don't we let them make the decision? My inclination is to hide the existence of the sign. I suspect they'll agree. Let them feel like they made the call. We can always ignore their decision if we don't like it."

"Works for me," Anders says.

"I would also suggest we bring in Phil before we do anything, including moving the body."

"Tell him what we plan," Dalton says. "See whether he sees any issues we're missing. Quietly move Jolene to the clinic. Inform the council. Get their take on it before we tell the town anything."

"It's not perfect," I say. "But perfect would have been Jolene sitting there, dead drunk. We didn't get that."

"Fuck, no. That'd be too easy." Dalton exhales. "Let me get Phil. Will? Stand watch. We don't want anyone seeing this. Casey? Start your crime-scene work. No one touch that sign until I'm back."

While Dalton's gone, I do a preliminary examination of the body. I'm very careful, knowing April will have my head if I interfere. I need to examine Jolene in situ, though, and as soon as Phil has had a look, we'll move her to the clinic.

I inspect her slit throat in the beam of my flashlight. I'd love something to poke at it with, to get a better look, but I came running in an oversized T-shirt and sweatpants. I'm lucky I grabbed a flashlight.

The wound is consistent with my theory that it was slit after death. Blood loss is minimal. I'd say she was dead when this happened and had been dead long enough for her heart to stop pumping and her blood to start settling.

Still using only the flashlight, I examine her for other signs of injury. With her head, I'm looking for blood-slicked hair that reflects in the flashlight beam. There's none on the visible parts of her skull. That doesn't mean she wasn't hit in the back.

Or it could have been a blunt-force blow that didn't cut into the scalp.

Her eyes are shut. I prod one lid up. The whites of her eyes are dotted with red. Strangulation? Suffocation? When I shine the light full on her face, her skin seems slightly darker, another sign of asphyxiation.

I move the light over her clothing. It's all dark. Jeans. Black T-shirt. Dark sneakers. Is that intentional? Was she doing something that meant she didn't want to be spotted? Given the lack of clothing options in Rockton, though, it could be unintentional.

Her arms are bare in the short sleeves. Her wrists are ringed with abrasions, suggesting a soft binding that she'd struggled against. Struggled hard. Her nails are ripped and torn.

I shine the light up and down her body, looking for cuts in the fabric or darker spots that suggest blood. I bend and shine the beam on what looks like a dark line in the crook of her elbow. A darker line than the usual crease. I consider. Then I pick up a stick and poke, ever so gently.

Dirt.

There's dirt caught in the crevice, and now that I'm staring hard, I see dirt dusting the fine hairs of her arms. I move the light beam to her jeans. Dirt crusted in the seams. I lift my flashlight to shine it full in her face, forcing my attention beyond the gash in her neck.

There's a spot of dirt at the corner of her mouth. A smear of it at her hairline. Grains in her eyelashes.

How would dirt get there? I have a very good idea, but for now, I'm keeping it to myself.

TWENTY-SEVEN

Isabel insists on coming with Phil, and I think Dalton is just too tired—physically and mentally—to argue. Isabel is understandably annoyed at us for dragging Phil out of bed when he'd been stabbed a few days ago. She thought Phil might die because he leaped in to protect her. Now she needs to protect him in any way she can, including making damn sure we don't shift responsibility from our shoulders to his.

Two months ago, I told Phil that he needed to make choices, after he complained about us keeping something from him. The problem was that if we'd told him, he'd have needed to decide whether to tell the council and therefore he might prefer to not know. That's even more critical now that Rockton is shutting down.

Phil's job isn't real. Rockton doesn't exist, and so the council doesn't exist, and so his job—the one he's had since being headhunted in university—doesn't exist. He hasn't said he'll go with us to a new Rockton. He's made it clear that he probably won't. So if he pisses off the council, where does that leave him? Thirty-one years old with a blank résumé and zero job experience. They promised him a sizable bonus in return for his work here—as if it's work and not exile—but he can hardly take them to court if they refuse to pay up.

Dalton faces the same issue, having never worked elsewhere. For him, it's worse. He doesn't exist himself. The council insists his ID is real, but we don't trust that they're telling the truth about that.

The difference is that, for Dalton, the council lacks leverage. Sure, he'd like to be able to hop on a plane to Vancouver for a holiday, but it'll hardly be the end of his world if he needs to drive instead. Even if we can't rebuild Rockton, he'll find a new life. We'd find it together. If we were somehow forced to stay in these woods forever, while it wouldn't be our first choice, we'd be fine. Phil would not.

Stuck between that rock and hard place, Phil has decided that he understands if there are things we don't bring to him. He's not sticking his fingers in his ears, but he won't complain if we bypass him on matters that don't concern him.

This is different. We're telling the council about Jolene. The only sticking point is that we're asking for his advice on that. If he says we shouldn't tell them, then we won't . . . and he's in the awkward position of knowing something the council doesn't.

The easy solution would be for him to insist we inform the council, regardless of whether that's the right call. We trust he won't do that, and he doesn't. He considers the matter. He asks questions. He considers some more.

"What are you suggesting then?" he asks. "That we destroy the sign or quietly take it into evidence?"

"Option two," I say.

He nods. "It is entered into evidence, but we do not openly admit to that when we communicate Jolene's death to the residents."

"Yes."

"And when residents ask whether it's connected to her involvement in Conrad's case? Her support of him?"

I take a deep breath. "That's where we cross a line, which I'd like to do as nimbly as possible. I will say we are considering the possibility of a connection while reminding them that both Conrad and Brandon have been in custody since Jolene disappeared."

Isabel wordlessly pivots to Anders, who sighs.

"Yeah," he says. "The fact that I was at home, fifty feet from where Jolene was found—*and* I'm the person who found her—is not going to help me here."

I shake my head. "Conrad exposed you. Gloria helped. Jolene was not involved in any way."

"Except as one of the loudest voices calling for Will's head on a pike," Isabel says. "I know it makes little sense for Will to murder her out of spite, but even one voice raised against Will can incite others. That's how conspiracy theories start. I would suggest we leave out who found her. No one ever asks about that."

"Agreed," I say.

"Someone is still going to raise Will's name as a suspect."

"And I'll assure them that I'm investigating all avenues. Unless you have a better idea."

"I wish I did," she says. "I'm merely bringing it up so Will won't be blindsided."

Anders shakes his head. "These days, I'm prepared to be blamed for everything from murder to stale muffins."

"Anything else?" I say. "Angles we're missing?"

We look at one another.

"Oh, I'm sure there are many," Isabel says. "This is a hornets' nest of trouble, and even if we think we've gassed all the little pests, one or two are bound to be hiding inside, ready to sting."

"Ready to bite us in the ass," Dalton mutters. "All right then. Phil? How do you want to handle telling the council?"

"I will notify them immediately. That will mean leaving an urgent message for Tamara, which she will certainly not bother answering for hours, but the timing of the message will be on record."

"And then we keep quiet on the murder until we hear back from them?" I say.

"We do."

The next step is getting Jolene's body to the clinic. We're still a couple of hours from dawn, but that comes quickly at this time of year, and we want Jolene inside by then. Even this late at night, the occasional resident is out and about, usually sneaking home from a lover's place. Isabel leaves with Phil, and I stand guard just inside the edge of town while the guys transport Jolene to the clinic and in the back door. I meet them there.

Jolene's body goes on the table. The rear door is relocked and Anders stands guard while I return to the crime scene. Dalton gets the thankless task of waking my sister. In my defense, I *am* the detective, so I should be the one on crime-scene duty. Also, if there is one person that April will not grumble at for a 3 A.M. wakeup, it's Dalton. I suspect, though, that she'll still inform him, as gently as possible, that given the status of the patient's health, it could have waited for morning.

Once Dalton has delivered April to the clinic, he returns to me while Anders assists April in preparing Jolene for autopsy.

When Dalton arrives, I'm still examining the crime scene. He takes over important tasks such as holding the flashlight.

The first thing I look for is blood. I hadn't seen any earlier, but now I take a closer look with an ultraviolet light to check whether any of the dark soil might be blood-soaked. I find zero evidence of blood at the scene. Either her throat was slit elsewhere or she'd been dead long enough that slitting it here produced only enough blood to stain her shirtfront.

Next is footprints.

Dalton takes a break from flashlight holding to help with this. He finds where someone walked through the brush—broken branches, etc. Once he points out the path, I'm able to locate two footprints from a standard-issue rubber boot. Both are only partial prints, but I measure them anyway. It'll be easy to get samples and maybe narrow down a rough size. Right now, I'm going to say it's a medium men's, wider than the women's model.

Now comes the big question. How did Jolene get here? Okay, there are multiple questions in that one. Where was she for the last twenty-four hours? What happened to get her from "missing" to "dead"? Right now, though, I want to know how she got *here* from wherever she'd been.

It's possible that someone escorted her here and then killed her. Escorted at knifepoint? All she'd need to do is shout to bring someone running. I'll need to check for signs of a gag, but I'm reasonably certain she died hours before her throat was cut. While it's possible she walked here and was murdered—and her killer returned later to cut her throat and try disguising cause of death—that seems overly convoluted.

"Any signs she was dragged?" I say.

Dalton shines the flashlight to crushed vegetation a few feet away.

"You could have pointed that out before I spent the last five minutes pondering how she got here."

"You're the detective. I hate to interfere."

I pull a face. Then I rise and follow his flashlight beam.

We're in an open area, so it's not as if her killer had to drag her through thick bush, leaving an obvious trail. There's that patch of crushed vegetation, and when I kneel, I see evidence that someone has swept away signs of dragging.

"So the crime scene is that way," I say. "Let's grab Storm and—"

Anders comes running at a jog. "April's ready for the autopsy, if you want to be there."

I look from the trail to the distant clinic.

"The scene's not going anywhere," Dalton says. "I'll have Kenny guard the area. You go sit in on the autopsy."

"You're wrong about this case," April says as I walk into the clinic. Okay, she actually says it in April-speak. "Your preliminary conclusions regarding the death of this woman are mistaken, Casey." Also, "I will ask you—again—not to speculate on cause of death. You have me here for that."

"For speculating on cause of death?"

She skewers me with a look. "For determining cause of death."

I walk to the table and look down at Jolene's corpse. "So what have you determined?"

"Nothing, obviously. I have yet to perform the autopsy. I have drawn only preliminary conclusions."

"Ah, speculating, you mean." I wave off her protest. "I'm teasing you, April. I'm not sure, though, how you know my preliminary conclusions when I haven't even spoken to you yet."

"The slit throat is not what killed her."

"Yep. Her heart had stopped before the cut was made, right? That's why she wasn't sitting in a pool of blood. Also, it explains her expression, which is not indicative of a violent death. If my throat was cut, I'd die with bulging eyes and my hands frantically trying to stop the blood flow."

She shakes her head. "It is entirely possible for a person with a slit throat to realize their death is imminent and close their eyes to surrender to it. That is what I'd do."

"Yeah, not me." I grip my throat and bug my eyes, and the barest hint of a smile tweaks her lips. "So I'm wrong then? Jolene didn't die *before* her throat was cut."

"No, she did. Eric failed to impart that portion of your speculation." She sets down her clipboard to look at me. "That was very fine detective work, Casey."

"Uh-huh."

"I'm paying you a compliment."

"And I'm waiting for the rest of it. The part that starts with 'However . . .' "

"I was giving you a moment to savor the compliment first."

Now her lips definitely do twitch, and I clap a hand on her shoulder. "I appreciate it. Now get to the part where I screwed up and should refrain from practicing medicine without a license."

" 'Medicine' does not quite seem the right word. 'Forensic medical science' is better." She walks to Jolene. "My preliminary finding is that yes, she died before her throat was cut. Her heart, as you say, had stopped. I thought first that perhaps she had been strangled." She looks over at me. "That would be clever, would it not? Strangle your victim and then cut their throat to cover the signs of strangulation?"

"Practicing detective work without a badge again, April? We'd still see strangulation in her eyes and organs. It could, however, cover marks left by the murder weapon, which might be useful. That isn't what happened here, though. I checked the sides and back of her neck for ligature marks."

"You are correct. She was not strangled. I will know more once I perform an autopsy."

"Drug screening, too, please."

"You think she was drugged, then."

"I think nothing. Just covering all the bases while allowing the doctor to do her work."

I give a little bow, and she rolls her eyes. Then she says, "I'm presuming you'd like to be present for the autopsy? I was going to ask William to assist."

"Better not."

Her brows shoot up. "Surely no one would suspect him of this crime."

"He said earlier that, right now, he expects to be blamed for everything from murder to stale muffins. He's not wrong."

She frowns. "How would he be responsible for stale muffins?" Her eyes widen. "Unless he left open a bag while removing one to poison for Conrad's breakfast tray."

"April . . ."

"Not that William would ever do that. I was simply trying to come up with a scenario in which he was responsible for stale muffins." Her gaze lifts to mine. "Stale muffins *and* murder. At once."

"Uh-huh. So, are we doing this autopsy tonight or not?"

She checks her watch. "Do you think the bakery would have muffins ready yet? I'm quite peckish."

I hand her a scalpel and then open the back door to find Anders standing guard.

"April wants a muffin."

"But not a poisoned one!" she calls.

His brows rise.

"Don't ask," I say. "Just see whether Eric will grab muffins and coffee. Stat."

TWENTY-EIGHT

April conducts further preliminary examinations. Then we pause for coffee and muffins before we begin the autopsy. Dalton has joined us by then, and we eat and drink and talk while poor Jolene awaits the knife. I suppose it's better than pausing for coffee halfway through, though we could have done that, too. You don't grow up in our family without an iron stomach.

If it seems at all disrespectful to eat first, one must remember that an autopsy can take two to four hours. Under my sister's meticulous care, we're looking at the far end of that. We have questions that need answers, and she's not giving them until she's absolutely certain of her facts.

Fact one is—as suspected—Jolene's heart had stopped pumping blood before her throat was cut. She'd died, and then her body had rested enough for the blood to settle. It'd been moved upright—probably at the tree—and her throat had been slit.

Why slit her throat? Almost certainly it was intended to cover up how she died. Did the killer not realize the lack of major blood loss would give it away? Or did they think that with a neurosurgeon for a coroner, we wouldn't figure it out?

We easily figured it out. Just as April easily figures out the cause of death.

Suffocation.

"Lack of oxygen," April says. "That is all I can conclude for now. She was deprived of oxygen and perished."

From there it's on to other injuries. There's a bit of chafing on one cheek, which suggests a gag. Her ankles show the same marks as her wrists, though the abrasions are more superficial. Bound hand and foot while fighting madly, mostly with her hands.

As my sister continues her examination, I return to Jolene's hands. To those ragged nails. I turn Jolene's hands this way and that. They're clean. Same as her feet, which had been wearing crew socks.

"There is a contusion on her skull," April says. "It's a hard blow."

"Enough to knock her out?"

"It's a hard blow. That is all I can say. It could have rendered her unconscious. Or it might merely have stunned her."

"Mind if I run a comb through her hair?"

"I can point out the contusion, Casey, and I will shave the area to take a closer look, although I can already tell you the head injury did not deprive her of air." She pauses. "No, I should amend that. The injury itself would not have caused suffocation, but it is possible that she collapsed from it and then suffocated, if the fall led to an obstruction in her airway. That would make it manslaughter not murder, correct? If death occurred unintentionally?"

"Mmm, debatable. If you hit someone intentionally on the head, particularly with that degree of force, you can kill them. We'd have no way of judging intent from the blow. Arguing for a lower charge would be the lawyer's job. But I don't think that's how she died."

"You believe I'm wrong about the cause of death?"

I have to smile at her expression. "No, April. I agree that she suffocated. I just don't think it happened as the result of a fall. I'm asking whether I may comb her hair because I'm looking for detritus. I've noted dirt in skin creases. Which could be explained by lack of easy showering facilities, but there's also some on her face. May I comb her hair to check for more?"

April fetches me a medical comb as I take a blank sheet of paper from a clipboard. Then I carefully comb a section of Jolene's hair. Grains of dirt speckle the white page.

I formed a theory back at the scene, and nothing we've uncovered here has disproven it. The opposite, in fact; April's findings and my examination support that initial theory. If I pause to think, it's because I don't want to be wrong in front of April.

I scan Jolene's body over one more time, double-checking my findings. Then I say, still with great care, "Have you seen anything inconsistent with Jolene having been buried alive?"

"What?"

And there it is, her tone just sharp enough to make me flinch.

"It's a theory," I say, my voice as calm as I can make it. "Her wrists and ankles seem to have been bound. Her nails are ragged. There's no dirt under them—her hands are clean—which may suggest they were gloved or that her killer cleaned them, removing the most obvious sign of burial. There's dirt in skin creases and embedded in clothing seams, as if her killer did a quick but imperfect job sweeping it away. Dirt in her hair, too. The cause of death was suffocation, which is consistent with burial. The only thing that doesn't quite fit is that I'd expect a more violent death."

"The medical evidence is not consistent with what I would

expect to see in a violent suffocation. And I cannot imagine anything else if one were buried alive."

"What if Conrad had died?" I say. "If he hadn't been found in time?"

"I don't see what that has to do with . . ." She slows. "Oh. Yes. You mean that he would not have shown signs of violent death if he'd died without waking. Agreed, but Jolene was clearly awake at some point. She *did* struggle."

"So, based on the evidence, you would conclude that it is not possible someone buried Jolene alive."

"I would find it highly coincidental for a second person to be buried alive so soon after the first. Particularly when the original offender is imprisoned?" She peers at me. "Are you suggesting Brandon escaped from his cell and murdered Jolene? One might think he would have the sense not to repeat a failed attempt."

Before I can answer, she says, "Though he did succeed this time, so perhaps all he needed was a little experience."

When I pause, she says, "That was a joke, Casey."

"Ah, good. Thank you. I'm not suggesting Brandon did this, though I'm not suggesting he didn't either. If Jolene was buried alive, that's not a coincidence. It's a copycat."

"A copycat killing?" Her eyes widen. "I read one of those in a novel. It happens then?"

"It does, which is why police conceal some details in crimes that get a lot of media coverage. It helps them weed out the perpetrator from the copycats."

"But why resort to copying the methods of another? Are there not enough to go around? I am hardly the most creative person, but I can think of at least a hundred ways to murder someone."

"I'll remember that." I point at Jolene. "Back on topic. Is

there anything you found here that would preclude this being another burial?"

"There is not," she says.

"Thank you."

I'm back at the crime scene. Or, at least, the spot where we found the body. The militia have ensured no one goes into the forest. It's now early morning, and people have noticed our attention, so they've started lingering in the area, trying to figure out what's so important. They're probably also wondering why we've postponed the search for Jolene, and some will connect those dots. I'll deal with that later.

Kenny keeps onlookers out of sight while Dalton and I bring Storm back to the scene. Dalton takes a crack at tracking first, and as I might have expected, we don't need the dog's nose. Dalton follows signs that are mostly invisible to me. Within twenty feet, he reaches the end, and with it, we find a scene that sets the hair on my neck prickling.

If I'd seen this spot a week ago, I'd never have noticed it. Even yesterday, I doubt I'd have paid much attention. Now, with what I suspect happened to Jolene—and what I know happened to Conrad—the signs are unmistakable.

Disturbed ground.

It's been hidden even better than the place where I found Conrad. Instead of just yanking a tree branch onto it, someone has gone to the effort of not only filling the hole and packing it, but scattering vegetation over it. At a glance, I'd have passed it by. Yet the trail leads here, and so I find signs that someone has dug and refilled a hole.

"We're going to have to dig it up," I say. "If there's any evidence, I'll need it."

"Another baseball cap, maybe?"

"Let's hope not. But in light of that, I'll want excavators I can trust."

I consider my options. Of the militia who'd been here when I arrived, only Kenny remains. We need him elsewhere.

"Let's get Sebastian on it,' I say. "And Petra if she can be spared."

TWENTY-NINE

My plan is to assist in and supervise the excavation. That goes to hell when Phil comes to say that the council needs to speak to me. Not him. Not Dalton. Me.

"I'll take over here," Dalton says as we stand beside the spot, where we've just begun excavation. "Dig carefully. Sieve everything. Treat it like an archaeological dig. Right?"

"Thank you."

I follow Phil through town. As we walk, I notice Ted on his porch, his gaze tracking our movements. I glance over, and he retreats inside.

"Detective Butler," an out-of-breath voice calls behind me.

I turn to see Gloria jogging from the general store, her face taut with worry.

She catches up and lowers her voice. "I know you canceled the search. I was part of the first party heading out. They say something's going on in the woods. Is it . . . ?" Her mouth works, as if she can't form the words. Then she swallows and says, quietly, "Is something wrong?"

I hate moments like this. I can't tell her the truth, but I can't lie either. I'm forced to retreat into "I can't comment," and as gently as I say it, her face still contorts with grief. She knows what that means, but she only backs up, stumbling a little.

"All right," she says. "I'll wait."

"We'll call a meeting as soon as we can."

She keeps nodding as she turns and then hurries straight for her apartment.

"Can we have someone pop by the general store?" I ask Phil. "Tell them Gloria won't be back to work. I know we already stole Petra today . . ."

"I can't imagine people are doing much shopping," he says. "Unless they're looking for souvenirs."

I give a little laugh at that. "Yeah, we could probably make a killing on Rockton T-shirts right now. Maybe you should invest in snow globes."

"I'll get on that. I'll also speak to the general store."

He ushers me into his chalet. It takes a few moments for him to get Tamara on the line. Once he does, he tells her that he has a couple of errands to run, but he'll be back in twenty minutes, should we need him. Tamara assures him we will not.

"The council is very concerned about this latest murder," Tamara says, after giving Phil a moment to leave.

I don't think I'm imagining the emphasis she puts on *latest,* as if we're living in Murder Central. Which, all things considered, we might be. But that would be the fault of the people who keep sending us the damn killers.

"I'm also very concerned," I say. "Particularly about the accusation made on that sign."

"Irrelevant."

"How do you figure that?" I ask.

She pauses. Randomly snapping *unnecessary* had shut me up the last time, and she expected more of the same.

When she recovers, she says, "This sounds like victim blaming, Detective."

I have to bite back a laugh at that. I also need to award her a point. She may barely know me, but she's hit a weak spot there. I'm that kind of cop, the kind who's very careful not to blame victims, especially women.

"Yeah, no," I say. "That would only apply if I were suggesting I'd treat Jolene's case differently if I discovered she *was* a killer. I believe my record there speaks for itself. You guys keep sending us criminals, and I keep treating them like normal citizens until they fuck up. So let's drop the bullshit where you pretend the council only sends us white-collar criminals, okay? We only played that game to avoid giving you ammunition against us."

Silence. Then, "I realize you're under a lot of stress, Detective Butler—"

"Fine, let's play *that* game instead. You've never knowingly let in violent criminals. They just get past your background checks. I'm asking about Jolene for a reason. Because her murder and that sign take us right back where we were two days ago. Will's case seemed to be a one-off. Is it? Or are others in danger? The answer to my question doesn't affect how well I investigate. It does affect *what* I'm investigating, though."

"I don't see how."

"Jolene's murderer left a sign on her body accusing her of being a killer. If she did kill someone down south, even accidentally, then her murderer knew that. Others could be in danger. It also provides me a place to start looking—who might have this information or who might she have told? On the other hand, it could be a red herring. Maybe her killer stuck that sign on her to send us in the wrong direction. With the limited time we have available, we can't afford to run down the wrong path."

She's quiet, and I make the mistake of thinking she's considering my words. That she might actually give me a tidbit, if only telling me that they'll look into Jolene's story and let us know if they find any murders in her background.

"I think we are misunderstanding one another," she says finally. "When I say the council is concerned, I don't mean they are concerned you may not catch Jolene's killer. They are concerned about the timing."

I hesitate. "Because with the exodus we may not catch her killer before they leave?"

"No, Detective Butler. I mean the timing of her death. It's convenient, don't you think?"

I blink, and my mouth opens, then shuts, my brain whirring madly. There's a trap here. I sense it, and I suddenly wish I were not alone on this side of the radio. I need someone to help me see the trap before I fall in and pull us all down with me. I need Dalton. I'd settle for Phil. But I don't have them, and that is when rage begins to twist in my stomach.

Tamara insisted on me coming without Dalton. Without Phil. Yes, this is about a criminal case, and I am the town detective, but why separate me from my ranking superiors?

Because I'm the weak link. I'd like to say it has nothing to do with me being a woman, but I suspect that would be naive. That's how it goes, isn't it? A situation arises where our gut tells us a man wouldn't be treated the same way, and yet there is that voice in our heads, from all the times we've cautiously brought up the possibility of sexism and been told we're overreacting, imagining things, playing the feminism card. Same goes for being a person of color. We're told it has nothing to do with the shade of our skin.

That little voice means I won't say for certain that the council wouldn't pull this shit on a man, but I suspect it. Strongly suspect it. I have been the conciliatory feminine balance to Dalton's bulldozer masculine approach. That made me the one the council preferred speaking to, which suited Dalton fine, but did it also make them see me as weak? Typically feminine traits being labeled lesser?

Whatever the reason, I am the fall guy here. A trap has been laid, and without the men to protect me, I am expected to stumble into it.

How is the timing of Jolene's death "convenient"? It takes me a moment to get there. I'm focused on the fact that it'd been damned inconvenient for Jolene. I may not have liked her, but she did not deserve that. And yes, there's the uncomfortable admission that the timing is inconvenient because we have other things to do and does it even matter who killed her? If no one else is in danger—and we don't expect her killer to suffer any consequences—does it matter?

But that's not what Tamara means, and I need to unwrap my brain from those sticky thoughts and reach farther. Get into their mindset.

Shit.

Fucking hell, no.

I need Dalton here, to voice all the explosive profanity that erupts when my brain finally makes the connection.

My mouth opens. I shut it fast, because I realize how it will look if I blurt my thoughts here. How they can willfully misinterpret them.

The council is saying that the timing of Jolene's death seems suspicious because it happened after they announced we were closing down. We'd just solved the Conrad situation, and suddenly, with this murder, we've ripped the lid off the closed-case file and shouted, "It's not over!"

You can't shut us down because the problem isn't resolved.

We have a new murder to investigate, one that could have significantly larger implications, and if you shut us down, the killer will escape justice.

They think—

No, they don't "think" anything. They know better. They're simply implying it.

Implying that we killed Jolene.

Killed her to stall the closing of Rockton.

I weigh my options and realize none will save me here. If I figure out what Tamara means, is that because we actually killed her? If I don't figure it out, am I just playing dumb when the answer is obvious?

"I'm not sure I understand," I say carefully. "I think you're implying that *we* hung that sign on Jolene, which makes no sense if Phil relayed my suggestion correctly. We don't want the sign to be made public. Therefore, why would we have written it in the first place?"

"Because the sign isn't for the town, Detective Butler. It's for us. Clumsy 'proof' that the cases are connected. Also, there are members of the council who fear Sheriff Dalton would go farther than simply crafting a sign."

"Eric?" My voice rises in genuine outrage as I sputter. "What are you suggesting? That Eric *murdered* her?"

"Perhaps it wasn't Sheriff Dalton. While some on the council fear that his passion for Rockton might lead to an eruption of his temper, others argue that it would not be him. He might be fully committed to Rockton; other residents are fully committed to *him*. Loyal to him. Others who have taken lives in the past."

"If you're implying that Will would—"

"No, that wasn't our candidate, though now that you've mentioned it, we should consider him, too."

Fucking hell. Think before you speak, Casey. There are land mines everywhere.

"Okay," I say. "So who . . ."

A chill that ripples along my spine. *Think. Take two seconds and think.*

"Wait," I say, my voice slow and even. "If you're implying that I would kill for Eric because I have in the past, I would like to point out that I shot a known murderer who was an eminent threat to Eric's life. I shot someone to save him. This is not the same."

"That is not what we meant, Detective Butler, though now that you've mentioned it, we should also keep *that* in mind. You have killed for Eric Dalton."

She's enjoying this. Whatever Phil's faults when he sat on the other end of this line, I never got the feeling he enjoyed making our lives hell. Just doing his job. The equivalent, as I've said, of an AI mediator.

Tamara is different. There is glee in her voice, as much as she tries to mask it. She doesn't know me. She has no reason to wish me ill. Yet she enjoys making me squirm. Enjoys laying out the land mines and watching her blindfolded victim stumble into one after another.

"Can we cut through the bullshit, Tamara?" I say. "You have something to say, and you're beating around the bush when I have a murder to investigate and a town to shut down. Just tell me what you're getting at here."

"What I'm getting at is that you came to Rockton to avoid being charged for a murder you committed."

"What?" I knew this was where she was heading, but I still inject proper outrage into my voice. It helps that she's mangling her facts, and I don't need to manufacture my entire reaction.

"Uh, I have no idea what they told you," I say, "but I came here because I was being *accused* of a boyfriend's murder. The guy died when we were in university, and his mobbed-up grandfather apparently decided I did it—ten years after the fact—and sent his goons after me. As it turned out, that was a setup. I was tricked into coming to Rockton, believing I was being falsely accused of murder. The key word there is *falsely*."

"If you say so," she murmurs.

To my surprise, I laugh. I'll be pleased about that for a long time to come, like those rare moments where you actually manage the perfect comeback. The laugh is genuine because she's grasping at straws here. We've gone through days of residents being subtly and openly accused of vague crimes. Hell, Conrad got himself buried alive doing it to Brandon. This is the same.

Yes, I killed Blaine Saratori. No, she doesn't know that for a fact. Can't know it.

Yet even as I laugh, a little voice warns me to be careful. She may be bluffing, but there is a real threat here.

"I did not murder my college boyfriend," I say, "and I did not murder Jolene. I'm fine with shutting down Rockton. We all are."

Now she's the one who laughs.

"Believe what you want," I say, "on all counts. We have an actual murder here, and I need to know what the council wants me to do about it."

"Nothing, Detective Butler. They want you to do nothing."

"I'm supposed to tell people Jolene was murdered, and we don't care?"

"No, you will tell them that she suffered a fatal accident in the forest. She went for a walk and was attacked by wild animals or fell into a gorge or whatever works for you. Make up your own story."

"It's going to need to be a helluva story, given that everyone I interviewed yesterday says she hasn't set foot in the forest since she arrived, and she planned to leave without *ever* doing so."

"Then you will have a creative challenge ahead of you. For those who know the truth, convince them to keep quiet. If you fail, then when you leave Rockton—and you *will* be leaving—you can expect to be arrested for the murder of Blaine Saratori."

THIRTY

Phil came back as I was finishing the call. I couldn't speak to him. Just asked him to please tell everyone who knows about Jolene to keep quiet about her murder until I can talk to them. They were already doing so. This is just a precaution.

From there, I go straight to Dalton, who's in the police station waiting for me.

"I need you to come home," I say as I walk in.

He's on his feet in a second, and with Storm trailing after us. Once we're home, with the doors locked and the windows all shut, I tell him what the council threatened.

I expect a profane outburst. I *want* that. Instead, he stares at me in shock and then sinks into the sofa cushions.

"Fuck," he says.

My heart hammers double time.

"They can't know," I say. "Right? I never admitted to it. I played it as a false accusation that could ruin my career."

He nods. "That's what I was told."

"But you suspected otherwise. Right from the start."

He rubs a hand over his mouth.

I lower myself beside him on the sofa. "You always knew the truth."

"*Suspected*," he says. "But I'm a paranoid son of a bitch who already knew they let in killers. I hadn't made up my mind about you. Nothing the council told me suggested you actually did it."

"Because they wouldn't say that. Not to you. You aren't supposed to know they let in real criminals."

He says nothing because there's nothing to say. Nothing to dispute this. After a moment, he turns to me.

"You're the detective. Can they pin this on you? I'm sure you've thought of that."

I nod slowly. "Many times. It was presumed Blaine was killed by the same guys who beat me. They attacked us because Blaine was selling drugs on their turf. He escaped. I got the beating, and they caught up with him later. That makes sense."

"It does."

"And since they never found those guys, it's the kind of case where the detectives consider it solved. I don't know what evidence they had. I would guess it was very little. I was questioned at the time, but only to see whether I could give more details on my attackers, presuming they'd also killed Blaine. I'd been the victim of a brutal attack, and I'd never openly blamed Blaine for it. I wasn't a suspect. Ever."

He relaxes. "Okay, then. They can threaten to give your name to the police, but it wouldn't go anywhere."

"How much does that matter?" I say as I turn to face him.

He frowns.

I continue, "I'm not afraid of going to prison. That wouldn't happen unless I confessed. It's the threat that matters. It could keep me from getting a job in law enforcement, which I don't expect to ever need again, but I want that option. It's also possible that they don't plan to tip off the police at all. That the threat is about Leo Saratori."

"Blaine's grandfather, right? Organized crime?"

I nod. "That was the reason I came here. I wasn't afraid of being arrested. I was tricked into thinking Saratori was after me, hurting people close to me. That's the real danger."

"Not while you're up here."

When I don't answer, he says, "Yeah, I know that isn't your point. You mean that we can't ignore the threat. It's not as good as the council seems to think, but it still has teeth."

"Yes."

He leans back against the sofa. "So we take the threat seriously. We do as they say. Don't investigate Jolene's death as a murder. Investigate it as an accident. She went into the forest and died, and we're trying to figure out how that happened when we know she hated the wilderness."

I nod slowly.

He continues, "The council doesn't need to know you're investigating her 'accident.' If they have spies we haven't turned?" He shrugs. "What does it matter?"

He puts one arm around my shoulders. "That'll be our motto for the next few weeks. *What does it matter?* We need to shift our thinking that way. We're like lab rats who've been electroshocked into submission. Don't do this, or we'll get in trouble. Don't do that, or they'll ship us out. Doesn't matter now."

"Even if they have a spy here, it isn't worth giving me shit for investigating Jolene's so-called accidental death. The point is that I'm not causing trouble. I'm not making waves. The town is shutting down as expected, and I'm doing nothing to stop that."

"Yep. So let's come up with a fake-death story for Jolene, bring in the others on it, and start spreading the word."

The story we come up with is as simple as possible. Early this morning, a member of the militia reported finding Jolene's body not far outside the town borders. Cause of death remains unknown, but we are considering it death by misadventure.

Anders and April obviously know the truth, but if anyone asks, "No comment" would be their usual line anyway. Kenny knows we found Jolene's body, and he probably suspects it was murder, but he isn't going to ask us to confirm that. Petra and Sebastian know Jolene was buried alive, which is very obviously not "death by misadventure," but they won't tell anyone. That closes all loopholes without us needing to ask anyone to lie.

We do not call a meeting. There has been quite enough of that, and from recent experience I must accept that our residents are no longer the ones I've dealt with in the past. Someone will question us, just for the sake of making trouble, and it'll go downhill from there.

We send the story out with a few key people who will pass it along, and if any rumors start, well, it's back to our new motto: What does it matter? Those most likely to spread stories are already scheduled to leave tomorrow. Let them talk. No one's going to care.

I have a list of residents I want to speak to now that Jolene's disappearance turned fatal. It might even help that I'm not saying she was murdered—it'll keep suspects from getting defensive.

Step one is to check on Brandon and Conrad. Is there any way either of them got out?

The answer seems to be no. There's always doubt, but not a reasonable amount. Brandon has been in the cell the entire time. Anders and Dalton themselves have been bringing his meals and taking away his chamber pot. They have the keys to the cell, which have been on their person the entire time.

Conrad has been in his duplex, under guard. Someone has been inside his room the entire time, meaning he didn't sneak out his window. We've had problems with guarding residents before, and in his case, it was easy to say that he needed round-the-clock "medical" care.

I speak to everyone who has watched Conrad in the last twenty-four hours. He's gone as far as the bathroom, but never for more than ten minutes. Is it possible his guard fell asleep and he slipped out to meet with Jolene and murdered her? Possible, but unlikely. Conrad's bluster is long gone, and he just wants out of Rockton, preferably before he has to face anyone who believed in his fake cause.

Next up? Marissa. The last person to see Jolene, and the person whose behavior puts her at the top of my suspect list. I had to check out Brandon and Conrad, but that was just ticking off boxes. It's Marissa I want.

And it's Marissa I don't get.

I spend the rest of the damned day chasing her. Which is ridiculous in a town this small. Or it would be under normal circumstances. With the impending closure, everything is in disarray. Tomorrow, two planes will arrive a few hours apart, and each can carry seven residents. Two more will follow every day until we are down to the skeletal closing-up crew. That's over ten percent of our population disappearing daily. We'll be at half capacity in five days and down to that cleanup crew in just over a week. Also, anyone who's leaving soon does not expect to spend their final days working.

What does it matter?

If I don't show up for work today, what are you going to do? With-hold credits I won't need? Throw me in that tiny cell with Brandon? Give me a stern talking-to?

We excused all tomorrow's departures from their jobs. An-other twenty percent of our workforce just didn't show up. And yet everyone expects to be able to buy coffee at the bakery or lunch from the canteen. They expect their trash to be picked up and their toilets to be emptied, but you can be damned sure that the people in charge of those jobs aren't showing up to work.

Also, while I'm doing my interviews, someone has the bril-liant idea that no one should need to pay for *anything* this last week. In theory, we'd be fine with that. But it would need to be instituted with care, because we still need to get through the shutdown. This person went around claiming Phil and Dal-ton declared everything free, and the result was chaos. People grabbing stuff from the general store just because they could, and then more people grabbing stuff because they feared the store would run out.

What does this have to do with interviewing Marissa? Well, first, I can't find her. I'm told she was reassigned after the Red Lion closed, but the people at the canteen, where she's supposed to be working, haven't seen her. I'm tracking her down when the "Everything is free!" run on the general store begins, and then spills over to the canteen, and that's where it definitely needs to be halted or our cleanup crew is going to be very hungry. I can imagine the council's response if we said we needed a couple of extra days to go hunting. They'd tell us we can eat after we leave.

Once the looting is stopped, the town detective—me—needs to find who started it. That's two hours of work while Anders and Dalton are busy trying to ask—Anders—and intimidate—Dalton—residents into returning what they took.

The perpetrator turns out to be someone I barely know, a resident who arrived six months ago and hasn't caused any trouble. He's caused trouble now, though. Seems that was intentional. Not that he wanted free goods. He just realized that the first two flights out were full of difficult residents and decided to become one in hopes of earning a seat. Instead, I move him to the last flight and warn that if he does anything else, he'll be held behind on the cleanup crew. Someone needs to empty all the toilets into the sewage holes one last time.

I finish that and head to report in to Phil and Dalton. I'm halfway across town when a voice hails me, and I inwardly cringe. If I've been looking for Marissa, I've been avoiding someone else. Someone who has been trying to get my attention.

"Hey, Gloria," I say as I turn. "How are you doing?"

"Do you have a moment to talk?" she says.

"I'm actually in the middle of something. Can we chat later?"

Her face droops with disappointment, but she nods and murmurs, "Sure."

"If you have anything new to tell me about Jolene, I'd appreciate it," I say. "But if you're hoping I can tell you anything more, I'm afraid I can't."

"It isn't that."

I slow my pace. "Isn't about Jolene?"

"In a way? Tangentially?" She swallows and her gaze darts around. "I'd rather talk about it in private."

"Sure," I say. I glance at my watch. "If it's urgent, let's do that now. This can wait."

She chews her lips, considering. Then she gives a decisive shake of her head. "It's not urgent. Just come speak to me later."

"Are you sure?"

She nods. "I have a few errands to run, but I'll be home after dinner."

THIRTY-ONE

The rest of the afternoon passes in a blur. It's only when I'm in the station, waiting for Dalton to be ready to eat dinner, that I finally have time to go back through my evidence from Jolene's death.

Disappeared two evenings ago. The last definite sighting we have is when Ted spotted her talking to Marissa.

Nothing in Jolene's apartment proves she did—or did not—return that evening. If she returned, there's nothing to suggest she was forcibly removed, which would be tricky given that her building is close to the center of town.

She's known for not wanting to venture into the forest. That means she wasn't waylaid there while out for a stroll. Yet a dislike for the forest wouldn't preclude her from going in for a reason, such as the kind of meeting that got Conrad buried in his shallow grave.

Either way, it's more likely she went into the forest voluntarily, rather than being dragged there, and the only reason for her to go in is to meet her killer.

No, stop there. The person Conrad went to meet—Brandon—tried to kill him. That does not mean Jolene's killer was whoever she went to meet. Also, I must remember that Jolene knew how Brandon lured Conrad to his near death. No anonymous note would do. This would be from someone she trusted. Or allegedly from someone she trusted.

Jolene goes into the forest. She meets someone. That person or another knocks her over the head, following Brandon's playbook, and then continues following it by burying her alive. Unlike Brandon, her killer succeeds.

Here's where I don't like my theory. A mental chafe says this isn't adding up.

Brandon did not intend to bury Conrad alive. He intended to kill and then bury him. While he claims to have thought Conrad was dead, he may have just not wanted to admit a crueler truth: that when the head injuries failed, he couldn't bring himself to finish the job and decided to just bury Conrad and let nature take its course.

It's clear that the premature burial was either an accident or a panicked attempt to finish a botched job. So why copycat the attempt? It's not as if someone heard what happened and said, "Great idea!" It's not as if they hoped to frame Brandon either, with the guy in jail at the time. Burying someone alive isn't quick or efficient.

Slow and torturous *could* be the point. But why then dig up the body and cut her throat postmortem?

I'm missing something here. I'm sitting at the desk, staring at my notes, when it hits. I'm missing evidence. I haven't looked at what Sebastian and Petra found at the dig site. While Dalton had initially been helping them, he'd had to go tend to another matter before they finished.

Earlier, I'd seen Sebastian in passing, and he'd made an offhand comment about something being "weird, huh?" but we'd been pulled into our separate chaos vortexes before I could pursue it.

I'm out of the chair so fast that Storm looks up with a startled grunt. I give her a distracted pat as I pass, and she pads out of the station behind me. I'm barely off the front steps when Dalton appears.

"Dinner?" he says.

"Er . . ."

"Not dinner."

"If you're hungry, go on without me," I say as I head for the lockup. "If you're not, I could use your help. I totally forgot to look through what Sebastian and Petra found."

Anders put the evidence in the lockup—a secure building that mostly serves as a gun locker. Dalton unlocks the door as I flick on the lantern. Normally, I'd take the evidence back to the station, but I don't dare do that when I'm technically not investigating a murder.

The bag is right on top of the "Killer" sign. A clear baggie, with three items inside, each within yet another bag.

One is a key. I make a note to check whether Jolene's apartment key was on her. I'm guessing this is it, but it'd be damn embarrassing to realize the killer dropped their key in the hole and I ignored it.

The next item is the one Sebastian probably thought was odd. It's a Saint Christopher's medal. While it's possible Sebastian just didn't recognize it, I'm guessing he actually did. I know from childhood friends that Saint Christopher is the patron saint of travelers, which makes sense for someone here. He's also the patron saint of luck, and yes, there's irony finding that in the grave of someone whose luck clearly ran out.

For me, the third item is the odd one. A three-inch length of scratched and dented thin copper pipe. Scrap metal. To Sebastian—and even Petra—it would be debris. We find that sort of stuff whenever we need to dig.

These days, Rockton is as close to zero waste as we can get.

When we buy products down south, we're always looking at how the packaging can be recycled and, when possible, discarding extra waste there.

This certainly isn't the way Rockton used to work. Our town is a microcosm of the greater world. In the past, people looked at this vast wilderness—or planet—and saw endless resources for use and endless room for waste. After a few decades of townhood, Rockton began to realize they were running out of easy dumping space *and* polluting the land and waterways.

While some of the old dumps have been dug up and disposed of properly, the surrounding land is riddled with crap that was either tossed away or buried. Finding a piece of old copper piping is hardly a surprise.

And yet . . .

I show it to Dalton.

"Looks like piping used when we rebuilt the canteen maybe seven, eight years back. There's a box of scrap in the workshop. Kenny uses it whenever it comes in handy."

"So some could have been tossed into the woods during construction."

"Yeah. We tell people not to do that shit, but some still do."

"Okay, random trash is one explanation. However, maybe I'm overthinking it but . . ." I sit back on my haunches, bag in hand. "I can't figure out why Jolene's murderer buried her alive, rather than use a more reliable way of killing her. It's possible they thought it actually seemed like a good idea after Brandon tried it, but then why dig Jolene up and cut her throat?"

I shake my head. "I can come up with explanations. Or fall back on the classic: criminals don't always make sense. But . . ." I lift the bag. "I want to see whether April can test this for saliva."

"Saliva?" His brow furrows, but before I can explain, his eyes widen. "You think that was in Jolene's mouth. A breathing tube."

"I want to measure the burial hole—how far down the soil was disturbed. Using that and her size, I can tell whether it's feasible, but I think it is."

"Bury her alive with a tube in her mouth to breathe through." He shakes his head. "Fucking stupid, if you ask me. How long can you hold that tube before you gasp or cough or pass out. As soon as it falls, you aren't going to be able to breathe anymore."

"Precisely."

I measure the hole, which is shallow enough that this tube would have allowed Jolene to breathe. Then I consult with April, who informs me that there is no easy way to test for saliva on the pipe. I figured that, but I hoped she'd know some workaround. She doesn't, and I can no longer say I'll send it south for DNA testing.

I think back at how many times I said that since I arrived. At least a half dozen. How often did I actually do it? Never. We always caught the perpetrator before I could send the sample out. I could be proud of that track record, but I must also remind myself that if the cases had taken place elsewhere, I'd have still needed the testing as evidence for trial.

I'll check the pipe for fingerprints, but my theory will doubtless always remain a theory. A plausible one, though. There is dirt clogging the end of the pipe, which is consistent with it slipping and cutting off her air. There's also a scratch inside the back of Jolene's throat that could have come from the pipe falling in.

Time to take another shot at talking to Marissa. That's when I remember I promised to stop by Gloria's. It's almost nine, and I can't expect Gloria to wait for me. Is it possible I'm postponing that conversation? Fearing she'll ask about Jolene, questions I can't answer? Yep, but I won't let it go until tomorrow. I agreed to stop by after dinner, and so I'll go there tonight.

Right after Marissa.

Except Marissa is not home. Or she is, and she's not answering her door. This interview I *will* tackle tomorrow. First thing in the morning.

I'm turning from her door when I spot a pair of boots tucked off to the side. Rubber boots. That's not unusual. The Yukon is quite dry, but we still get enough summer rain—usually in short bursts—that everyone makes use of their rain boots. Between thaw and freeze, it's not unusual to just keep them on your front porch.

What catches my eye here is that I know these weren't here a few days ago. It hasn't rained. No need to bring them out if she was keeping them indoors. Yet here they are, and there's dirt on the porch, where it's fallen off the bottom of the boots.

I walk over and crouch beside them.

Definite dirt, suggesting recent wear. I pull a glove from my pocket and lift a boot to note the size. Eight. Men's boots, too, which doesn't mean they aren't Marissa's—the men's are wider and some women find them more comfortable. As I'm setting the boot down, I notice a hair inside. I pluck it out. Dark brown. I have evidence bags in my pocket from earlier, and I tuck it into one.

I eyeball-measure the width of the boot's toe and compare it to my notes. I haven't gotten around to seeing exactly what size footprint I found, but this is a reasonable match. I rise and turn toward the general store. I should get the key from Dalton and measure sample boots.

No, I need to speak to Gloria first. Get that over with, and *then* I can measure boots.

Gloria lives in the next building. I rap on her door, and there's a click before it swings open at my touch. It'd been closed, but not pulled completely shut.

I hold the knob so the door won't open as I knock again, louder now. When she doesn't answer, I push the door a few inches and call, "Gloria?"

No answer. I glance around, considering. My first reaction is to find someone who can confirm that I am only entering Gloria's apartment for a welfare check. Then I remember our mantra. Does it matter? Nope.

Right now, no one cares what we do, short of hurting residents. Even if they did, what's the council going to do? Fire me for violating a resident's privacy? Yes, they've made their threat about exposing me, but they'll save that in their hip pocket for a real emergency. A resident accusing me of breaking and entering hardly qualifies.

"Gloria?" I call. "I'm coming in. Your door was ajar and I'm concerned. We were supposed to talk tonight."

My voice is loud enough for a couple of passing residents to glance over, which is the point. Yes, I've just convinced myself that it doesn't matter, but in my gut, I still don't want anyone accusing me of impropriety.

I ease inside. The first thing I notice is that the hall-closet door is open. Wide open. As if Gloria grabbed her shoes and left in a hurry? I file that aside and continue in. I do a quick sweep to be sure she isn't unconscious on the kitchen floor or asleep wearing earplugs. She is not.

I slow for a second sweep. It's easier here than in Jolene's apartment. Gloria's is immaculate. So when I see a folded piece of paper on the kitchenette table, it grabs my attention.

It's a page torn from a standard town notebook. The writing is shaky and uneven. The quick-and-dirty way to disguise handwriting is to write with your nondominant hand. That's what this looks like.

The note reads:

> THEY'RE LYING ABOUT JOLENE. IT WAS NO
> ACCIDENT. WE CAN'T LET THEM GET AWAY WITH IT.
> YOU'LL SEE WHAT I MEAN.

The note ends there. I frown, and then I see faint markings through the paper. I turn it over, and there's a map. It's crudely drawn but labeled in that same shaky hand, leading to an X.

Leading to the spot where we found Jolene's body.

I stare at the map, my brain chugging through the implications. Why send Gloria there? It's not as if we were hiding where we found the body. Enough people saw us guarding the area to have a rough idea of the location. Yes, this pinpoints it exactly, but what could Gloria find there that would prove Jolene was murdered?

Nothing.

Not a damn thing had been at the scene, even when we found her body. No weapon. No blood. No "proof" of murder.

There's nothing to find because that's not the point. The point is to get Gloria into the forest, alone. What would possibly lure her in? Not a note to a secret meeting, that's for damned sure.

But this? Proof that her friend had been murdered? A map luring her to a spot that seems safely close to our borders?

I look at the open closet door, and there is no doubt that Gloria got this note and went running.

Went running straight into a trap set by whoever delivered this note.

A note sent by someone who knows exactly where Jolene's body was found.

Because they put it there.

THIRTY-TWO

I round up Dalton and Storm. As we hurry along, I explain, keeping my voice low. Dalton's reaction is the obvious one. "What the fuck was she thinking?" Everyone in town knows Conrad was lured into the forest. Yet we believe someone still managed to lure Jolene in to her death. And now someone has lured in Gloria. At some point, you really need to start questioning the IQ level of our residents. Yet while I understand Dalton's frustration, I also see how this happened, and I can't blame the victims for seeming to follow this lemming pattern.

Conrad was desperate for stories to share after he pretended he already had more. Easy lure there.

I have no idea how Jolene ended up in the forest, but she's not alive to tell us, which could mean there was no note involved. Someone asked for a private forest meeting, and she agreed because Conrad's attacker was in prison. Also, it suggests she knew whoever lured her in well enough not to think twice.

Now we have Gloria, who'd been very obviously upset over Jolene's death. Who may have suspected it wasn't misadventure, knowing how much Jolene hated the forest. Gloria, who'd wanted to speak to me. Gloria, whom I had been avoiding.

I have guilt here, but I need to set that aside. The point is that I don't blame Gloria for investigating. It was close enough to town that she'd have felt safe.

We check the site first, on the off chance Gloria is there. Maybe I'm mistaken. Maybe someone other than the killer and ourselves knew where Jolene's body had been found. Someone got a glimpse of her corpse and knew "death by misadventure" didn't cover a slit throat.

Gloria is not there, and there's no sign of anyone around. I'd grabbed a scent marker from Gloria's apartment. That hadn't been easy. We shut down the laundry this morning, but she'd obviously taken a load in the day before, and her hamper had been empty. I'd grabbed the hand towel from her bathroom. If that's not enough for Storm, then we'll retreat to Gloria's apartment and proceed from there. Storm sniffs the towel and then snuffles around, and in a moment, she's hot on the trail.

We spend the next half hour following Gloria's trail as darkness falls. Storm has it, and then she loses it, as whoever took Gloria does the one thing Brandon didn't: walks through water, effectively hiding their trail. Storm picks it up again where they exited, but that takes a bit of time.

There are no other diversions. Whoever took Gloria ran through one stream and decided they'd hidden the trail well enough.

We get another fifty feet before a scream rings out. We run, twisting and dodging trees, flashlight beams swinging in front of us, cutting a swatch of jerky light. I'm behind Dalton, both of us running as fast as we dare in the shadowed forest.

The first shriek had been surprise. That dies down, and

we hear garbled panic that sounds like "No! Go! Get away!" Then a growl. An animal growl.

Dalton pulls away, running faster. I struggle to keep up, but if he hears me fall behind, he'll slow. My foot catches in the undergrowth, and I stumble. He starts to turn.

"Go!" I say. "I'm fine!"

The voice comes clearer now. Female. Gloria? It sounds like her. She's telling someone—something?—to stay back, to go away.

Dalton stops short, hands going out to hold me back as a sharp wave orders Storm to stop. I move up beside him to see what he does. It *is* Gloria. She's backed against a rocky hillside. In front of her is a snarling gray canine.

I think "wolf" but the coloring is wrong. Then the beast snaps, and I see freckles on its pale muzzle. Wolf-dog. An Australian-shepherd-and-wolf mix, like Raoul. A pup from an earlier litter? This dog is older, more wolf in size and shape, big and powerful.

It snaps at Gloria, who bats her hands as if to fend off attack. She's streaked with dirt. Blood drips from one hand, and there's more smeared on her shirt.

"Go!" she says. "Shoo!"

She kicks. She means it as a threat, and that's exactly how the wolf-dog interprets it. But for a predator, threat can mean different things. When cornered by an animal, you want to show them they shouldn't mess with you. From Gloria—an average-size human already smelling of blood—that kick doesn't scare the wolf-dog. It pisses it off.

It's not unlike when I'd been attacked in that alley all those years ago. I tried to disarm one of our attackers and that set them all off. Should I have *not* fought back? I can't say for sure. It's the second-guessing every survivor does. If I hadn't tried to disarm them and I'd still been attacked, I'd have been forever cursing myself for not taking my shot when I saw it.

Gloria kicks at the wolf-dog, and her foot doesn't land within a foot of it, but it's all the canine needs. It lunges, and before we can act, Storm races out and slams into the wolf-dog's side. A battering-ram strike. The wolf-dog goes flying into a roll. It scrambles up, but Storm has parked herself between the wild dog and Gloria. I have my gun trained on the wolf-dog, and Dalton has run forward, ready to intercede in case of a fight. The wolf-dog doesn't notice us. It's too busy staring at the mountain of black fur in front of it.

The wolf-dog's nostrils dilate as it sniffs the air. I swear I see its brain processing.

Huh, it looks like a bear, but it smells like a dog.

Wolves are big, and this one isn't much shorter than Storm. It's all legs, though, with a muscular but slender body. Storm is pure mastiff bulk.

She lowers her head and growls. It's a warning, one that says she has no interest in fighting—she's just here protecting her people.

"Move along now," Dalton says.

The wolf-dog's head swings his way. It notices me in that sweep and then glances over at Gloria.

Not one terrified human woman, but three humans and a very big dog. I've seen movies where wolves don't care about those odds. They still leap in, fangs flashing. Yet even with just Gloria versus the wolf-dog, the wild canine hadn't been committed to attack until she lashed out. Now, it looks between us and back at Storm. Then it grunts, and its gaze moves to a tangle of brush.

Dalton follows its gaze and nods. "You'd like your dinner to-go, huh?"

I ease around and see what Dalton does. The reason the

wolf-dog went after Gloria in the first place. Again, we might see movies where healthy wolves attack at random, but it's rare enough to be almost unheard of. In that clump of brush I see fur and blood. Gloria stumbled on the wolf-dog with its prey, and it mistook her for a meal thief.

"Okay," Dalton says. "We're going to leave you to your dinner. Gloria? Can you carefully walk sideways until you're behind Casey?"

Gloria nods, chin bobbing, eyes wide. She does as he says, and at the same time, Dalton moves to stand beside me.

"Storm?" I call.

She glances over out of the corner of one eye. She knows I want her to retreat, but it takes her a moment to figure out how to do that without exposing herself to attack. She sidles until she's given the wolf-dog room to return to its meal.

The wolf-dog creeps back to the brush, grabs what looks like a mangled hare, and dashes into the forest.

"I—" Gloria begins.

"Hold that thought," Dalton says. "He seemed to be alone, but we're going to put a little distance between us first."

We do that, moving until we reach a clearing. Then I turn to Gloria.

"Are you okay?" I ask.

Her mouth opens, and she bursts into tears, her eyes widening in horror before she rubs her hands over her face. I move closer and put an awkward arm around her waist in a quick hug of reassurance.

"Are you okay?" I repeat.

"I . . . I think so. I was so proud of myself for getting away, and then I realized I was in the middle of the forest, with no idea which way to go. I remembered walking through water, and I heard water running so I started that way, and then I saw the dog. I could see its face and those freckles, and it looked like Raoul, so I thought Sebastian must be taking him for a walk, and I ran over and . . ."

A sharp breath. "I got right up to it before I realized it wasn't Raoul. I shrieked and that made the wolf—the dog—whatever it is—jump and snarl. I backed up, only I backed against the rock and . . ."

She swallows. "What *was* that? It looked like Raoul, but it looked like a wolf, too, and I remember someone saying Raoul is part wolf."

"He is. We rescued him as a pup. There are feral dogs out here. Some escaped from Rockton, and some might have escaped from other people. They breed with the local wolves."

She gives a strained half laugh. "I'll have to tell Raoul I met his brother or uncle." She wraps her arms around herself and shivers convulsively.

"Gloria?"

She looks up at me, her eyes not quite focusing.

"What are you doing out here?"

"Doing?" She stares at me. Then she makes a noise, half groan, half bitter laugh. Her face falls into her hands. "Oh God, I'm losing it. I'm really losing it. I'm babbling about wolves and dogs when . . . when . . ."

"How about you sit down?" I tap her arm and point to a fallen log.

She nods mutely and moves to sit. I take a spot beside her.

"I found the note on your table," I say.

She looks up sharply and then nods. "I got it, and I took off. I didn't think." She glances over. "I'm sorry, but I felt as if I wasn't getting the whole story about Jolene, and I needed to see for myself. I realized I shouldn't go running into the forest, but then I saw that the place indicated on the map was barely past the town border. If anything went wrong, I could scream, right?"

Another bitter laugh. "I didn't have a chance. I was kneeling, looking for whatever clue I was supposed to find when someone pressed a knife to the back of my neck." She reaches back, and there's dirt-coated blood there, with a tiny scrape. "She told me to walk and said if I screamed, she'd kill me."

"She?"

Gloria nods. "I couldn't recognize the voice. It was muffled, and she barely said ten words. Definitely a woman, though. She told me to walk and . . . Oh God, this is embarrassing. I did as she said. I didn't fight. Didn't scream. I let her lead me into the forest. I kept thinking I could talk her out of it. That's what I did. Talked and talked when I should have been fighting back."

Which is why she lashed out at that wolf-dog. Exactly as I said, a survivor of violence will question every move they did and did not make. Gloria failed to fight her human attacker, and so she'd fought the wolf-dog.

She continues, "We got to a spot and stopped, and I started to turn. I wanted to see her, to talk face-to-face. That's when I noticed the hole. Before I could even react, she jabbed me with something." Gloria rubs her upper arm, where there's another blood-smeared spot. "Then she shoved me hard, and I was so surprised that I fell. I went to get up, and she kicked me, and then everything just went black."

She shivers, and I let her have that, not pushing or prodding. She'll continue when she's ready.

I think I know what happened—I figured it out when I saw her dirt-smeared clothes—but I'm going to wait. Dalton does the same. He's behind us, as if standing guard, but really getting out of her line of sight. Letting her feel as if it is just the two of us.

"I woke up in a hole," she whispers. "I couldn't breathe. I went wild. I've been thinking about what happened to Conrad and what that would be like to be buried alive. I remember when I was young, I read about how it used to really happen, and it terrified me. Then it happened to Conrad, and I could barely sleep. What would it be like to wake up like that? Buried and trapped? I'm surprised I didn't think it was just a nightmare. Thank God, I didn't."

She rubs her throat, shaking convulsively, as if remembering that moment of waking up, gasping for air, realizing what had happened.

"I fought," she says. "There was a rope on my hands, but I didn't realize that, and I just pulled, and my hand came free. I could scrape and claw, and that's what I did. Went wild clawing at the dirt. Then I could breathe."

She takes a deep inhalation, as if reliving the moment. "Once I could breathe, I calmed down. I stayed under the dirt for a few moments, listening to be sure she was gone." A dry chuckle. "By then I was calm enough to realize she might be there but not thinking straight enough to realize that if she was, she'd have seen or heard me digging."

She shifts on the log. "After a few minutes, I started working my way out. She must have dug one end of the hole deeper, because I couldn't get my legs out at first, and I panicked. But I eventually got free, only to realize I had no idea how to get back to Rockton. It was getting dark by then. I knew I had to get away from the hole—in case she came back to check on me. I remembered the water we walked through. My shoes were still soaked with it." She lifts one foot. "I heard water and headed that way, and then stumbled on that dog-wolf."

I take a few minutes to provide some victim support. There's always part of me that wants to jump ahead and ask more questions and start investigating. That part feels cold. Yet on the few occasions when I've *had* to jump straight into an investigation,

I've been equally champing at the bit to offer support instead. Two warring sides. Tend to the victim with quiet sympathy and tend to the victim by solving the case.

I give Gloria the first and then ease into the second. The obvious initial question would be "Can you tell me anything about your attacker?" I already know that she didn't get a look, and pressing the point will only panic her. Instead, I ask if she can help us find the spot where she was buried.

"Of course," she says. Then she freezes, panic flashing as she looks around. "If I can find it I should have paid attention." She straightens. "No, I can find it. I'm sure I can."

She stands quickly, and then gasps, wincing in pain.

"Gloria?" I say.

"I'm fine. Just . . ." She touches her side and winces again. "That's where she kicked me. When I took a deep breath, it hurt."

She starts to inhale, as if to test it, before I can stop her. Pain flashes over her face and then she doubles over, dry heaving.

"Eric?" I say. "We need to get her back to town."

"No," Gloria says, raising a hand. "We have to find the spot. I'll be fine, just give me a moment."

Gloria tries to sit back on the log, but misses. I catch her arm and steady her.

I look at Dalton. "I was going to ask you to take her, while I search with Storm, but I think we're both going to need to help her get back."

"No," she says. "This is important. We need to find that spot." She rises and straightens. "There. I'll be—"

Another wave of pain as she doubles over, and I catch her again. Dalton takes her other arm over her protests.

Gloria's face contorts, as if she's infuriated by her own weakness. I understand that. She wants to lead us to that spot so I can catch her would-be killer. The truth, though, is that it's unlikely any case-breaking evidence will appear at the scene, and certainly not any we won't be able to find just as easily tomorrow—*more* easily, in the daylight.

We note this spot to begin our search and then we're off, helping Gloria back to town.

On the way back, I remember to ask Gloria what she'd wanted to tell me earlier. It was about Jolene. Gloria had taken coffee to her apartment the morning after we found Conrad. She heard Jolene inside arguing with someone. Jolene didn't answer the door, and when Gloria asked later, Jolene said it was none of her business. The person she'd been arguing with? A woman. That's all she knew, the conversation having been too muffled to recognize the voice.

A woman argued with Jolene the morning before she vanished. Jolene was last seen talking to Marissa. Then a woman tried to murder Gloria.

I really need to talk to Marissa.

I leave Gloria with April and head to Marissa's apartment. She doesn't answer her door. Dalton offers to open it with the skeleton key. I consider. Consider some more. That seems the obvious course of action. Charge into her apartment and haul her to the station for questioning.

And yet . . .

Marissa has done something. She may have murdered Jolene. She may have attempted to murder Gloria. Or she did something completely unrelated.

I know she's not innocent—her behavior has been too suspicious. But I need more evidence before I get her into a room for questioning. She's a lawyer. Unlike Brandon, she's not going to break down and confess when confronted with flimsy evidence.

She's been seen around town, which means she isn't missing. Just avoiding me.

Dalton gives me permission to bag her boots before we leave her apartment. Back at the station, I examine her boots and the hair I took from them, along with a sample hair from Jolene. It's a match insofar as I can tell without DNA. The boots are also a match for the size and tread found at the scene. That seems damning, but it's still circumstantial. Next I write up all my questions about Marissa—all the things she's done in the last week that strike us as suspicious.

"I don't like it," Dalton says when we're done with our list.

"Yep."

"Is it wrong that there's a little part of me that would like to see her guilty of something?" he says. "Proof that Will's better off without her?" He leans against the station wall. "Not murder, though. I'd rather it wasn't murder."

"Agreed. Still, something is definitely up." I skim the list. "There's nothing here that lets me go in hard. I think I'll keep the boots in my back pocket and insist on an interview. Where was she when Jolene disappeared? Where was she tonight when someone kidnapped Gloria? Softball it until I have more. Like a lack of alibis." I glance up at him. "Agreed?"

He nods. "First thing tomorrow, you interview her. If she holes up in her room, we'll go in after her. If she ducks you, we'll get every damn person looking for her."

"Tomorrow is also the first exit day."

"Don't remind me."

"Sorry. I just mean . . ."

"That it's a damned inconvenient time for investigating a murder, and it's not going to get any better."

I nod. "I'm also trying not to freak out over what happened to Gloria. The more chaotic things get, the less likely we'll be to realize anyone's missing. Perfect environment for anyone bent on murder."

"Yep."

THIRTY-THREE

First thing the next morning, I am not knocking on Marissa's door. I'm at April's place as she gets ready for work. I brought breakfast, which she's eating as she scans her schedule.

"How's Gloria?" I ask.

April doesn't look up from her reading. "As well as can be expected. She appeared to have experienced only minor injuries, but I am concerned about her abdominal pain. I will be examining her again this morning. I expect it's muscle soreness from being kicked, but I will remain concerned until the pain eases." She looks up then. "I hope you intend to find whoever did this to her."

I bite back a sarcastic reply, and settle for staring at her until she says, "Yes, I worded that poorly. Obviously you intend to. I mean that I hope you do. We do not need a serial entomber on the loose right now."

"Pretty sure no one ever needs a serial entomber on the loose. Or would that be serial vivisepulturalist?"

Her brows rise.

"Vivisepulture is the practice of burying alive. Don't ask

276 | KELLEY ARMSTRONG

me how I know that. I probably read it in a book. I may also be saying it wrong, and 'vivisepulturalist' is almost certainly *not* a word."

"But it could be, as that seems to be what we have here. Have you confiscated all the shovels in town?"

When I don't answer, she says, "That is the obvious first step, Casey. You must remove all the tools that could be used to bury people alive."

"I'll get on that. For now, I have a laundry list of tasks. The planes start departing today."

She nods, her gaze sliding away.

"Is there anything else you'd like to talk about, April?"

She shakes her head. Then, when I'm at the door, she says, "Do you think we can do it?"

I turn.

"A new Rockton," she says. "Do you think it's possible?"

"I think if it is possible, then we can do it."

"It's important," she says. "To people. It's been . . . It's become important to me."

"Me, too."

She exhales softly, as if she expected the ceiling to collapse at her admission. She straightens her shoulders.

"Then we shall do it. A better Rockton, where residents are not buried alive. Or shot. Or murdered in any way."

"That would be wonderful." I smile at her, and then I slip out while she returns to her schedule.

I've just settled in the station when the door opens. I don't look up. I know who it is by the angry slap of sneakers.

"Hello, Marissa," I say. "Nice to see you this morning."

"You're a vindictive bitch. Has anyone ever told you that?"

There's no real anger in her voice. Annoyance, yes, but mostly exasperation, and I may be wrong but I think I detect a hint of grudging admiration.

"Vindictive seems harsh," I say as I look up. "I'm not out to get you, Marissa. I'm just doing my job."

"By sending someone to inform me that I'm now on the *last* flight out?"

I shrug. "You're part of an active investigation, and I've been having trouble interviewing you. I thought a little incentive might be in order." I wave at her. "It worked, didn't it?"

She glowers at me. "So it's a threat? Talk to you, or I'm stuck here to the bitter end."

"No, the bitter end is for the cleanup crew. Your exit was delayed. That's hardly catastrophic. Unless you're in a hurry to get out. A hurry to get away. Or get away with something."

"What exactly are you accusing me of, Casey?"

"Honestly? I don't know. You're just acting very oddly, and now there's the Gloria situation."

She hesitates. "What Gloria situation?"

"Someone lured her into the forest, marched her away at knifepoint, and buried her alive."

"W-what?" She stares at me. "You're joking, right?"

"I don't see how that'd be funny. It certainly isn't for Gloria. Fortunately, she managed to escape."

Marissa sinks into the chair I brought in from outside. "How is she?"

"Physically okay, it seems. Emotionally, though?" I shake my head. "She was a wreck last night, as you might imagine. Knocked out and then waking up to realize you've been buried alive?"

Marissa looks sick. Then she sits there, staring into nothing.

"Gloria," she says finally. "God, who would do that? Gloria is . . ." She looks up. "She's like that nice, quiet girl who hangs out with the assholes. You know what I mean? There was always that clique in school, not quite the popular kids, but they thought they were, acted like they were, and kids like Gloria made the mistake of believing their advertising. In return, they treated her like shit."

"Did you know she was a recovering alcoholic?"

Her lips tighten. "Those *assholes*. Conrad knew, I bet, didn't he? He was always pushing her to drink, and when they hooked up, I did wonder . . ."

She shakes her head. "I should have done more than *wonder*. I should have talked to her. But by then, I'd moved on, and I cut her out of my life with the rest of them. It was a shitty thing to do. I'd see her in town, and my gut would clench, and I'd pretend not to notice her. I didn't mean it. I just . . ." She swallows. "I had to get away from them, and she felt like part of 'them.' Except she wasn't. They were toxic, and she'd been poisoned."

Marissa exhales. "I'll speak to her now. Try to make up for it."

"That's great," I say. "However, I didn't call you here for Gloria-emotional-support duty."

She's so lost in her thoughts that it takes a moment before her head snaps up. "You think *I* buried her alive?"

"Here's what I know. You were the last person to see Jolene. You were spotted by multiple parties speaking to her, and then she was found dead in the forest."

"I thought that was an accident."

I look at her. Just hold her gaze and say nothing for a moment. Then I continue, "You may be looking for your rubber boots."

"My what?"

"Your boots. They were on your front porch. They are now in evidence, because while I was trying—repeatedly—to speak to you, I noticed them on your porch and realized they looked about the right size for treads found near Jolene's body. They match exactly. A hair found inside one also matches Jolene's."

"What? Slow down. My rubber boots—"

"Where were you at eight last night?"

"I . . ." She blinks. "Eight? I—"

I plow on. She's asked me to slow down, and that's exactly what I am not going to do. This isn't a normal interrogation. This is going toe-to-toe with a professional, and I need to hit her as hard and fast as I can.

"Someone heard a woman arguing with Jolene the morning before she disappeared. Then you were seen talking to her later, the last person who did."

"I—"

"You took on Conrad as a client when all evidence suggested he broke into Will's place. That he hit you over the head. Yet you agreed to represent him? That made no sense."

"I—"

"How many times have you said you can't understand why I keep giving Jen more chances? Why we let her on the militia? She's a pain in my ass, the first to snarl an insult my way, but I still argued her case for an extension because she's turned out to be a valuable member of the militia. You told me you wouldn't be able to look past her insults, and yet you turned around and accused me of railroading Conrad because I don't like him? Of framing him as revenge for speaking out against Will?"

"I—"

"Sure, it's a valid legal tactic, but then we loop back to why the hell you agreed to represent Conrad in the first place. You aren't a lawyer here. What was he going to pay you in? Credits? You've said before that you don't need a better-paying job because you don't spend the credits you have."

"Yes, but—"

"You interfered in our investigation and made the overall situation worse, Marissa. Which is not like you. Not at all."

"I was taking a leaf from your book, Casey. Trying to see past Conrad's flaws and realize he was entitled to representation."

"In a town that doesn't use lawyers? That has no real court system because it has no real punishments? The worst that could happen was that he'd get shipped out. If there was no evidence he was the one who hit you, he'd be assigned to shit duty for a few weeks. Hardly ten years of hard labor."

She doesn't answer that. She can't.

"Speaking of Conrad," I say. "When you took him on, you could have mentioned you'd been drinking buddies."

"I never hid the fact that I knew him."

"Maybe not, Counselor, but you seemed to engage in a little bit of creative obfuscation. I get that you moved on from their friend group. I get that you realized they were toxic and therefore might not want to let on you'd hung out with them, especially if you were dating the deputy and realized they'd caused some problems for us."

"Right, so—"

"So you wouldn't feel the need to volunteer that you'd been drinking buddies. At least not until I found it odd that you agreed to represent Conrad. That was the time when you'd use the past connection. Sure, he's a jerk, but you'd been friends at one time and therefore you felt obligated. I'd have understood that. Yet you preferred me to just think it was suspicious."

"I—"

"And yet, after feeling obligated—I presume—to represent him, you did a half-assed job of it. You went in blazing, but when he was nearly murdered, you disappeared. Didn't insist on being there when I interviewed him. Didn't give me shit for interviewing him without his lawyer present. You shrugged and wandered off."

"Maybe because my client turned out to be the guy who exposed Will. We might not be together anymore, but I still care."

"Except you *didn't* care when you agreed to represent Conrad *knowing* he was at the head of the mob against Will. Also, you didn't know what Conrad had done when we first brought him back to town. But you failed to so much as check in on him."

No response. She's realized she should take the best advice a lawyer can give: stop talking.

"I've been trying to speak to you about Jolene's death," I say. "I've been chasing you down since yesterday, and you've been dodging me."

She meets my gaze. "I want to go home, Casey. I've made a mess here, and I just want out."

"Well, if that mess involves murdering Jolene, I'm not sure I can help you."

"I didn't kill Jolene. Didn't bury Gloria. I've just . . . I made a mess that started the first time Gloria invited me to have a drink with them. I felt like the new kid in school looking for a place to eat lunch. Here was someone offering me a seat at her table. Everything in Rockton was so different and over-whelming. Part of me wanted to hide in my apartment for two years, but I knew I couldn't do that. I'd go stir-crazy. So I jumped at the first offer of friendship, and I made a terrible mistake."

When I don't comment, she continues, "Then one night, they're drinking at Conrad's place, and I can't take the grum-bling anymore. I go into the Roc, thinking I'll grab a beer to go, and instead I end up drinking it with Will. Just a beer and conversation. Then he says you guys will all be there the next night, and I'm welcome to join you." She gives me a wan smile. "So I traded up. Found a social group more to my tastes and got a boyfriend in the bargain. Look at me. New girl to prom queen in a month."

She shifts in her chair, gaze going to the window. "Then it all crashed down. I overreacted seeing you with Will, and when he told me about the sign, that just carried over. Like I was still upset about you two, so I used the sign as an excuse for pushing him away. By the next evening, I'd already come to my senses and went to Will's place hoping to work it out. Instead, I was attacked, and before I can even talk to Will, guess who shows up on my doorstep, demanding my help . . . or else?"

"Conrad."

She gives a bitter laugh. "No, Conrad is a buffoon who lacks the brains to properly blackmail anyone. Look how he screwed up with Brandon. Conrad suffers from the white-dude delusion of thinking that because life has been a little easier for him, it's proof that he's a little better than everyone else. It almost got him killed. No, he didn't blackmail me into representing him. Jolene did."

"Jolene?"

"Oh, she made it sound as if she was playing errand boy for Conrad. Passing along his message. That's how she operates." Marissa pauses. "How she operated, I guess. Past tense. Jolene liked to keep to the shadows. I wouldn't be surprised if she was behind the whole Will thing."

"Conrad's covering for her?"

She snorts. "Taking credit from her, more like. Anyway, she came to me and said that Conrad told her if I didn't help him, I'd be next on the hit list."

She waits. Seconds tick by. Then she says, "You aren't going to ask what I did?"

"Does it matter? Whatever you tell me could be a lie. I can't look it up online. The council certainly won't confirm it. As far as they're concerned, we're already closed. What matters is that Jolene allegedly blackmailed you into representing Conrad."

"Allegedly?"

"Can't confirm that either, can I?"

"True, but I'm going to tell you my story anyway. Maybe I still give a damn what you think about me, Casey. Down south, I was on the partner track. One of the founding partners mentored me. I was late getting into law, but she picked me out as a first-year and made me her pet project. That day, we were at lunch together. Driving back, she hit a cyclist. She panicked. Begged me to say I was the one driving. Turned out, while we'd been having our long lunch, she'd done a line of coke in the bathroom. Or maybe she just said that. Flustered and in shock from the accident, I agreed. There were no witnesses, so we'd say the guy swerved in front of us. He'd been thrown from his bike, but he seemed fine. We tell the police our story, which the cyclist refutes, but whatever. Twenty-four hours later he's in the morgue. Brain injury. He wasn't wearing a helmet. My boss tells me to stand strong, she has my back, and now they can argue that mental confusion explains his testimony."

There's a noise outside, and Marissa stops short, but resumes when it moves on. "Next day, we discover there's footage. CCTV camera on a nearby auto-body shop. It shows the accident was clearly the car's fault. What it *doesn't* show? Who was driving. Or us climbing over each other to switch places. I'm about to be charged with vehicular manslaughter, and my boss swears she'll fix everything. The next thing I know, I'm fired, and the family of the man killed is planning to sue me. My old boss shows up and says she'll send me here to Rockton. So sorry she couldn't save my job. She tried. Totally went to bat for me."

Marissa rolls her eyes. "Yeah, I wasn't buying that. I even recorded our conversation, but she was careful. She pretended that she'd asked me to drive after she had too much wine, and maybe I'd hit him because I was in an unfamiliar car, and she felt *so* bad. I consulted a lawyer friend, and he told me I was screwed, which I already knew. Since the charges hadn't been laid and I hadn't been served by the family, the best thing I could do was disappear for a couple of years and try to sort it when I came back. Or start over somewhere else. With charges looming, I didn't have time to think, which I'm sure is what my boss wanted. Next thing I know I'm here."

"You were framed by your boss."

"I was."

"And Jolene threatened to expose you as . . . ?"

"A naive idiot?" Marissa gives a short laugh. "Sadly, no. I'd told her the general facts—that I pretended I'd been the driver in an accident where the victim died. She *knew* I hadn't done anything. It didn't matter. What mattered was that, as far as anyone down south was concerned, I hit and killed a cyclist. She threatened to say that I'd hit a guy while drunk after a three-Cosmopolitan lunch, and I'd fled up here before the family could sue me. Typical lawyer, right? Cold, greedy bitch."

I tap my pen against my notebook and say nothing.

She continues, "Representing Conrad seemed a small price to pay for avoiding that. I never said I'd represent him *well*. I figured I'd go through the motions, blow a bunch of smoke, and let you guys take him down. That's why I didn't go to his bedside before he'd confessed and then . . ." She shrugs. "My client was guilty. Nothing more for me to do."

"Except . . ."

"Jolene didn't drop it. That's what people saw us talking about. She gave up all pretense of doing it for Conrad and said I owed her."

"Owed her what?"

Marissa throws up her hands. "Who knows? She was probably planning to make me stew for a few days before she told me what she wanted. Then she disappeared, and I wasn't exactly crying over that."

"Nor over her death."

She meets my eyes. "Nope. I didn't kill her, though."

"Where were you at eight last night?"

She doesn't answer.

"Marissa?"

"At home reading, which does not help. I was alone. I didn't go out again after seven, so no one saw me that evening."

"And the boots."

"My rubber boots are in my closet."

"They're in evidence."

"*Mine* are in my closet, which you may escort me home and confirm. I think I recall seeing a pair on my deck yesterday, but it's a deck I share with three other residents, and I'm not territorial about space. If someone else's boots were on my side, I'd barely notice."

"What size do you wear?"

"Women's nine, but my rubbers are men's eight because I have wide feet. Presuming those are women's boots, they aren't mine."

She looks at my expression.

"They're men's?" she says.

"Size eight."

"Then either that's one hell of a coincidence, or I'm being framed."

"Let's go check your closet."

THIRTY-FOUR

Marissa's boots are in her closet. Size eight. Men's. She knows that doesn't prove as much as it might seem. Rubber boots aren't exactly a highly rationed item. She could easily have two pairs. It also means someone else easily could have gotten hold of a pair similar to hers and planted them on her porch.

I find Dalton deep in preparations for the first departure. The plane is on its way, and this first dispatch will be the toughest. Both Brandon and Conrad will be on it, which is both awkward and kind of satisfying. There are two planes leaving today, and we could have sent one on each, but we want Brandon out of that cell where he needs constant attention we can't afford to give. Conrad insists on taking the first flight, and we also can't afford the manpower to keep guarding him, especially since we're shorthanded without Jen. Of course, Conrad doesn't know Brandon will be on the plane, too, but hey, that's not our problem. It does mean, though, that Dalton and Phil are both on the scene, helping with the last-minute preparations and preparing for issues that arise from sending a full flight of troublemakers off together.

I tell Dalton that I'm going to find the scene of Gloria's burial, see what I can get from it. I'm not taking Gloria—not with her abdominal issues. On the way back last night, she'd provided enough information that I should be able to find it on my own.

Dalton is distracted, and Storm and I get ten steps away before he calls after me.

"Butler!"

I turn.

"Take someone with you. Take . . ."

He looks around. Everyone in the area is bustling about, carrying luggage or the unneeded supplies we'll stuff into extra cargo space.

I wave it off. "I'll be fine."

He hesitates, and I lay my hand on Storm's head. "I've got protection. I'm also going to do a quick hunt for Jen. We need her back."

He reluctantly nods, and Storm and I head out.

We should have gotten more details from Jen before she disappeared in the forest with Cypher. We'd been wrapped up in everything else, and when she'd asked to leave, Dalton had only been half listening. I know she said she didn't have militia duty for a few days—she'd banked time recently pulling extra shifts. We thought she deserved a break, and with everything going on, it was best if Cypher wasn't hanging around Rockton, making people even more suspicious.

Have you seen that guy? He's the former sheriff. If that's who they hire around here . . .

Valid point, honestly. Just not one we'd needed anyone making when anti-law-enforcement tensions were already running high.

There are a few good camping spots not far from town. Dalton and I have used them when we want a break but don't have time to go farther in.

Storm and I check the spots and find no evidence of camps, current or recent.

Wait, Cypher was hunting that moose. While I'm sure he'd have happily taken time off to visit with Jen, I doubt he'd have abandoned the hunt altogether. I'll head that way, which will bring me within a kilometer of where I need to be to pick up Gloria's trail.

I stick to the path. Even after nearly two years of hiking these woods, I'm not sure I could easily find my way back. Dalton's taught me the landmarks to use if I get off the trail, but I still rely on paths and my pooch, and in case of an emergency, I have flares in my pack.

I get as far as I dare before I need to cut over to where we found Gloria. There's a path that'll take me in that general direction. I've gone around a quarter of a kilometer when someone whistles. I stop, and a few moments later, Cypher comes tromping onto my path.

"Thought I caught a glimpse of your pup there," he says. He looks up and down the path. "You alone?"

"We couldn't spare anyone," I say. "Which is why I was really hoping to run into you guys. Is Jen around?" I pause, and then say, "They're closing Rockton. Immediately. First flight is leaving any minute now."

"Fuck."

"It happened after you guys left. In a week we're going to be down to a skeleton crew. I'll explain more later. Right now, I need Jen."

He doesn't answer. Doesn't even seem to have heard what I said.

After a moment's silence, he says, "They aren't bluffing then. It's happening. Rockton's closing."

I resist the urge to say yes and hurry this conversation along. I'm so wrapped up in my own concerns that I haven't realized what I just told him. That Rockton is leaving. That we're all leaving. That Jen's leaving.

"I'm sorry," I say. "We can talk more about it on the way. Eric and I have plans. Contingency plans. Right now, though, I really need Jen."

It takes him a moment to snap fully back. Then he peers at me. "Jen?"

"Uh, yes. Your girlfriend? She went with you into the forest." My gut seizes. "Wait. Please tell me she went with you."

"She did. But I haven't seen her since yesterday morning. I needed to pick up the moose hunt, and she wasn't interested in coming along. I left before dawn. She was heading back to Rockton."

"You let her leave on her own?"

He gives me a look. "I don't 'let' Jen do anything. I offered to walk her back, but we weren't more than two hundred feet from town. We could *hear* Rockton. Not like she'd go wandering off the path, and we don't need to worry about hostiles anymore. Are you sure she didn't get there?"

I consider and then shake my head. "It's been chaos in town. I just presumed she hadn't returned." I look back toward Rockton. "Can you go check? I really need to examine a crime scene out here."

"Crime scene?"

"It's Rockton. Crime never sleeps. Can you check on her, please?"

He agrees, and we go our separate ways.

★   ★   ★

I can't stop thinking about Jen. I wish I could have gone back to Rockton with Cypher. I'm not in the right mental place for this search.

Part of me is back in town, waiting with Dalton for that first plane to land. It feels wrong to be anywhere except at his side, as if I've abandoned him at the bedside of a dying relative.

Part of me is also with Cypher, thinking of everyone we're about to leave behind, all the relationships we've worked so hard to foster.

And part of me is consumed with thoughts of Jen.

It starts with the role Jen played in all this. She told Conrad about Anders, and that's not her fault—it could have happened to me just as easily—but the fact remains that she is involved. Could that make her a target of whoever killed Jolene and attacked Gloria?

Before I can pursue that, my distracted brain jumps tracks back to Marissa and what she told me. Let's say Jolene was blackmailing Marissa. Marissa takes her hostage and buries her, reenacting Conrad's near fate because Gloria almost certainly wasn't the only one having premature-burial nightmares after that. It's the perfect torture method.

Bury Jolene alive. Put that pipe in her mouth so she can breathe. Then come back, dig her out and confront her about the blackmailing. See how far I'm willing to go? See what I'm willing to do? Now back the hell off. Agreed?

Only Marissa digs Jolene up, and finds her dead. Cleans her up, drags her to that tree, and cuts her throat. Hangs that sign to throw suspicion in another direction.

Huh, Jolene must be another killer, like Deputy Anders, and now someone took the law into their own hands.

The problem is Gloria. Whoever buried her didn't seem to intend for her to survive. Was Gloria helping Jolene with the blackmail? Did Marissa leave that out so I'd think this piece of the puzzle didn't fit? Did she overdo her shock and horror at hearing Gloria's fate?

As I think, Storm finds the spot where Gloria stumbled over the wolf-dog, and we pick up her trail from there. It's a well-laid one that Storm easily follows, and so my mind drifts back into its thoughts, circling to Jen again.

What if Jen and Conrad lied when they said she only talked about Will?

What if there's another story she divulged, one that might provide perfect blackmail fodder . . . against Jen herself.

We have no idea why Jen's here. Despite her behavior, everything she's done has been petty criminality, with no reason to dig deeper.

Imagine Jen, under the influence, reveals her past to Conrad, who tells Jolene and possibly Gloria.

When Storm whines, I look up to see we're at the stream where she'd tracked Gloria last night. Damn it, I missed the burial site.

I give Storm a pat and a few murmured words of praise. "Sorry, girl, but we're going to need to do that again. I messed up."

I set her back on the trail, and I struggle to focus on her work. I manage it for about two minutes before I start thinking about Jen again.

I've been dismissing her as a suspect because she wasn't around. Yet she *was* close enough to commit the crimes.

Cypher said Jen presumably left yesterday morning. He himself had been up and gone before dawn. If he saw a Jen-size lump in the blankets, he might have just left. Either way, she'd have had time to hurry back to Jolene, dig her up, realize what happened, and get her to her final resting spot before dawn.

Storm whines, and I look up to see the spot where we found

Gloria and the wolf-dog. I curse under my breath and kneel to rub Storm's ears.

"I'm so sorry, girl. I'm distracted, and I'm not doing my job. One more time, and I promise I'll pay attention."

We start back the way we came, and I fully focus on the task. Twice I must have walked right past the burial site. I won't do it again. I keep my eyes open, scanning the ground for any sign of disturbance.

A crashing sounds in the forest. My hand falls to my gun, and I glance at Storm, who growls softly, only to whine at the end, as if apologizing for the growl. It's a person, then. Someone she doesn't care for.

"Who's there?" I say.

"The big bad wolf," a voice calls. It's familiar, yet I still tighten my grip on my gun, starting to pull it from its holster.

"Jen?" I say. "What are you doing out here?"

She appears, tramping through the undergrowth. "Looking for you, obviously."

I slide my gun from the holster, as quietly as possible, and keep it down, so when she catches up, she barely glances at it, presuming I had it out all along.

"Looking for me?" I say.

"Uh, yeah. You wanted me, right? Eric said you'd headed this way."

"And you came out on your own?"

"Do I look stupid? I came with Ty, obviously. He's the one who said you needed me."

"Where is he?"

She throws up her hands. "Nearby, I presume. He was with me until a few minutes ago and then he saw a moose track. Damn idiot and his damned moose. How the hell is he supposed to bring it down without a gun?"

"So he's within shouting distance?"

"I presume so. He wandered off, and I said I thought I heard you and he just kind of . . ." She waves her hand. "I'm not even sure he heard me. Obsessed with that moose."

"If I shout for him, he'll come?"

She shrugs. "He should. Why? You need him? Go ahead and shout. Better make it loud, though. His hearing's going."

When she takes a step toward me, Storm growls.

"Yeah, yeah," she says. "Never going to forgive me for that, are you?" Another step. Storm growls louder and that stops Jen short.

"What's with the pooch?" she says. "I know I'm not her favorite person, but that sounds serious."

"Where were you last night?"

"What time?"

"Around eight."

She eases back, thinking. "Talking to Will. I caught up with him just after eight. Been trying to talk to him all day."

"Trying to talk to Will about what?"

"The town closing." She looks at me. "No one who knows Eric is ever going to think you guys are throwing in the towel that easily. If you aren't fighting to keep Rockton open, it's because you have a backup plan. It's all hands on deck shutting down, not even the slightest show of resistance. You have other plans. I want to know what they are."

"So you asked Will."

"Yeah, and he said he"—she air-quotes—"isn't 'at liberty to discuss that.' Which means there's a plan. He said if I wanted, I could join the cleanup crew. Stay and help tear down Rockton. I said hell, yeah. Not exactly my idea of fun, but I figure the people who are sticking around are the people who have a shot at a seat on the ark. You guys just want to make sure we're prepared to row our asses off first."

"Will offered you a spot on the cleanup crew?"

"That's what I said. The conversation lasted from about eight ten until close to nine."

"He never mentioned it to me."

She leans against a tree. "I got the feeling you were a bit busy, solving that so-called misadventure Jolene suffered." She snorts. "Obviously she was murdered. Point is, you're busy. Do you even know who's on the cleanup crew? Who all has been asked to stay?"

I don't. Not beyond those who are part of our plans for a new Rockton. I do remember Dalton saying they'd fill the crew with residents they might want to invite to join us. I hadn't been part of any further conversations. I'd been caught up in my investigation and happy to let Dalton make decisions.

"I can see where you're heading," she says. "I didn't kill Jolene. Didn't bury Gloria alive. I'm not sure what you think my motive is, but I'm sure you have one, because 'just pissing Jen off' isn't really your style. Sadly. Grudge matches are so much more fun when the other person fights back."

"Are they?" I arch my brows.

Her eyes roll up in thought. "Nope, I lied. It's fun to needle you, Butler. You're like one of those carnival games, where you throw balls at the clowns, and they bounce back up. The trick is to hit them just right so they fall down and stay down. I haven't quite found the right spot on you yet, but I will."

"Go back to Rockton, Jen. I'm working here."

"I was joking, Butler. You have no sense of humor."

"No, you need to improve your jokes. Also improve your tactics. That one's old and stale. If someone takes offense?" I pitch my voice up. "'I'm just kidding. Is it my fault you can't take a joke?'" I shake my head. "Go on. I'm busy here."

"And I'm here to watch your back. Also, I can't just mosey off to Rockton and leave Ty looking for me out here. I'm not sure I could find my way back either. Do your work. I'll keep quiet."

When I don't answer, she says, "You're supposed to tell me not to strain myself."

"Sorry, *my* jabs are a little fresher than that."

"Ouch." She waves me on. "Go. I'll follow."

THIRTY-FIVE

I do not like having Jen behind me. I keep my gun in hand, as if that's just what I do in the forest. I also make her stay ten paces back. I don't disbelieve her story, but I don't completely buy it either.

I'm walking behind Storm, surveying the area, when Jen says, "Mind telling me what I'm looking for?"

I'm about to snap that she isn't looking for anything. She's supposed to be watching my back. Instead, I pause and then say, "Storm is following Gloria's trail. We found her over there. Her captor led her through water. There's about a hundred and fifty feet between those points where it must have happened."

"Where she was buried."

"Right."

"She didn't tell you where it was?"

"She gave me a few landmarks—a dead tree, a boulder—but I've found three dead trees and two rocks she could have considered boulders. Storm and I were just following her trail, looking for a hole."

"And you can't find one?"

When I glance back, her hands shoot up. "That wasn't an insult, Butler. Not to the pooch or her trainer. I'm just curious. I don't know how this works."

I resume walking. "Storm should slow at any spot where the trail tangles. For instance, where Gloria's captor knocked her out and dragged her into a hole. However, if the entry trail and exit trail overlap, Storm might skip the tangle and just keep going."

"Because she knows the exit trail is usually the important thing—where Gloria went afterward."

"Right."

Jen goes quiet as we continue. Two minutes later, we're at the stream again.

"Is it possible—again, not insulting anyone here—to ask her to *find* a tangle of scents? Or to show you where Gloria stopped?"

"It's not something we've trained her for. For us, it's all about taking us to where a person is *now*. Tracking missing people. That's hard enough in this terrain."

I crouch in front of Storm and think as I pet her. Then I straighten. "The problem is that the waypoint should be obvious. It's not as if Gloria pulled off to pee and rejoined the trail two minutes later. She was hit on the head and dragged to a hole that couldn't have been far from where she fell. With the number of times Storm has followed this section of the trail, she should have diverted at least once."

I glance down at Storm. "She clearly knows she's missing something, and she's a smart dog."

I rub the back of my neck. "Maybe I'm overthinking it. She knows where the trail leads so she's skipping any side paths."

"Or maybe Gloria was buried on the other side of the stream?"

I squint over at the running water. "Possibly? Gloria said she walked through water with her captor. That was to foil any tracking, but Storm eventually found the exit point, which is here. Then Gloria says she woke and heard the water, knew that was the way back and headed toward it."

I pause and look both ways. Then I shut my eyes to listen for the water. To Jen's credit, she doesn't speak. When I look again, I say, "Okay, so it seems as if she woke and walked *away* from the water, but with my eyes closed, if I was farther from it, I could see how she'd make the mistake."

I glance at Jen, who shrugs and says, "You're the detective. It's way too complex for me. What exactly do you hope to find at the scene anyway?"

I pause. Then I say, "What did you hear about Jolene?"

"That she died of misadventure."

"That is the council's ruling."

"Huh," she says. "Let me guess. Her misadventure was that she stumbled into a person-shaped pit and dirt magically covered her."

"Something like that. But I didn't say it. The council has been very clear on the ruling, outlining dire consequences if we contravene it."

"Dire consequences worse than shutting down Rockton?"

"Yes. Nothing must get in the way of closing. Nothing. But if Jolene did trip into a person-size hole and dirt fell from the sky to cover her, that falling dirt also conveniently put a small length of pipe in her mouth to allow breathing."

"Wait? You're saying—Yeah, yeah, I know, you're not saying anything. But if you were, you'd be saying someone not only buried Jolene but let her think she'd survive? Gave her a way to breathe for a while? That's cold."

Jen shakes her head. Then she says, "You want to see if the same thing was done to Gloria. If there was another pipe. What did she say?"

"That she was fully buried and couldn't breathe. Which is why I want to check—because that means it could be a separate incident. Also, finding the site might give me other evidence."

A rumble sounds overhead. We both look up, squinting in the direction of Rockton.

"Da plane, boss," Jen mutters.

The first exit flight is arriving in Rockton. With it, something in me collapses.

"Screw this," I say. "I've been out here too long already. Eric needs my help, and I'm chasing a killer who won't be prosecuted. I can't even tell the council that I caught Jolene's killer because they don't want to hear about it. So why the hell am I bothering?"

I glance over to see Jen standing there, and I wrinkle my nose. "Ignore me. I'm tired and frustrated. Let's get back to town where we can do some actual good."

"How about one more pass?"

I sigh, and with that sigh, everything in me seems to droop.

"The point, I think," Jen says slowly, "isn't about punishing the killer. It's about finding them. Letting them know they didn't get away with it. Also making sure there's not another Gloria, one who won't survive."

"One more pass," I say, holstering my gun. "Then I'm following April's advice and confiscating all the shovels."

This time, when I walk the route, I don't rely on Storm's nose. Instead, I channel Dalton and use whatever tracking skills he's managed to impart. Any footprints on the trail itself are lost beneath our own. Same goes for any signs of passage. What I want are signs that someone left the path. They should be here.

Gloria's captor led her at knifepoint off this game trail and neither would have been trying to hide the signs.

I spot them this time, which suggests I just wasn't looking
very hard before. There's a place where crushed undergrowth
suggests someone left the trail. A footprint confirms it. I follow
and find a few more footprints. Storm noses them and then
grunts, as if to say, "So this is what you were looking for."

When Jen moves in behind me, I wave for her to stay clear.
The last thing I need is more footprints.

"I see disturbed soil over to your left," she says. "That's
what you want, right? To find where she was buried?"

I nod and follow her gaze to see scratch marks in the dirt.
I take two steps and then stop as I realize it really is just
scratch marks. Some creature—wolverine or bear—pawed at
the ground, disturbing the soil.

I tell Jen that and pick my way around the site. The burial
spot should be impossible to miss, yet I'm not seeing it. All
I have are maybe a half dozen partial footprints in one area.
Beyond that? Nothing. There also isn't a dead tree in sight, or
a rock larger than my fist.

I circle the spot looking for the place Gloria and her captor
left it. There's nothing. Not a broken twig. Not a crushed
plant. Not a smudged footprint. I spend ten minutes making
increasingly larger circles and when I glance back, I can easily
see my own signs of passage, but that's it.

That isn't possible. Gloria's captor led her off the trail, and I
can see that. There's no sign that's the spot where she knocked
her down—certainly not where her captor dragged her—but
there is also no sign that they moved past that small clearing.

I call Storm over and have her circle searching for a scent.
She finds none.

I return to the small clearing and crouch at the footprints.

They're Gloria's. They're all Gloria's. I checked her soles so I could eliminate the tread. She was wearing sneakers that she brought to Rockton with her, meaning her attacker's would have a different tread. Yet all I see are Gloria's prints.

I walk to that disturbed bit of ground and bend. From a distance, it had looked like animal scratching. There are clear claw marks. Four of them. Yet they aren't sharp-ended, and I've seen both wolverine and bear claws. They're fearsome weapons, and incredible tools for digging that leave deep ridges. Here I see multiple sets of four clearly delineated lines raking the earth.

I reach out as if to scrape at the spot, and my fingers fit perfectly into a set of four grooves.

I push to my feet. "We need to get to Rockton. Now."

THIRTY-SIX

Jen doesn't ask for details. Maybe the answer is obvious enough that she doesn't need to. I start sprinting back to Rockton, and I make it about a hundred paces before Cypher hails us. I don't stop. Jen does, and the murmur of their conversation reaches me as I keep going.

My damned leg won't allow me to run all the way to Rockton, but it's not as if we're ten miles deep in the bush. Even doing half at a quick walk, I'm back in ten minutes. I burst into town just as the roar of a plane fills the air.

First flight out. Right on schedule.

A reminder that I need to move quickly or my quarry will escape.

I enter town closest to the clinic. My sister is on the front porch, heading out.

"April!" I call.

She turns, sees me, and waits. Just waits. I grumble that she should see how fast I'm moving and at least meet me halfway.

"Gloria," I say as I catch my breath. "Have you figured out what's wrong with her stomach?"

"No." My sister's tone is as calm as if I had ambled over,

asking out of idle curiosity. "She continues to complain of pain, which is concerning."

"Did you get her flight bumped up?"

"I asked Will to do so last night. She departs first thing tomorrow morning."

I turn to Jen and Cypher, just emerging into town. "Can you grab Eric? Bring him here?" Back to April. "I need to speak to you."

I might think she hasn't noticed my emotional state, but the fact that she doesn't argue tells me she has. She waves me inside.

Once the door closes, I say, "Is there any *proof* of internal injury?"

April frowns. I brace for a lecture on questioning patient reports, but her brow smooths as she says, "You're wondering whether she's malingering. There is faint bruising on her torso, but my ultrasound could not detect any internal damage, which as you know, does not negate the possibility."

"Other injuries?"

"A small spot on the rear of her neck, which you saw. Also one on the back of her arm, which you also saw."

"The knife tip and needle."

"Yes."

"Any bruising around either?"

April shakes her head. "Both were fine this morning."

"Additional injuries?"

"None. She complained of a twisted shoulder. I found nothing, but I had someone bring ice."

"I saw her nails last night. They were dirty and seemed ragged. Yes?"

"Yes. One was broken, two were slightly damaged, and there was dirt under them, consistent with digging out."

I consider my next question, unsure how to frame it. In the

end, I just ask, "Did you notice anything *else* consistent with being buried alive? Any further proof?"

"You think she lied?" She pauses and then murmurs. "You seemed to suspect she was faking. You didn't just mean the stomach pain, did you?"

"I did not."

April walks to the counter and picks up her clipboard. "I also checked inside her mouth for any signs of what we found with Jolene."

"The tube."

"Yes. Gloria appeared confused by that."

"Confused or concerned?"

April takes a moment before answering. "She asked what I was looking for. I find it hard to gauge sincerity or detect body-language cues that might override her words."

"Right. Sorry."

"No need to apologize, Casey. I understand that would be a valuable skill in detective work." The faintest smile. "Which is one reason why I should not trade my stethoscope for a badge."

She consults her chart again. "I asked whether she felt anything in her mouth that might have aided with breathing. At that point, she became agitated, which I presumed was from triggered trauma. She said that you had asked the same thing. She wanted to know why. Naturally, I couldn't mention Jolene, so I ignored the question."

"Good. Thank you."

"Had you suspected she lied about being buried, I would have searched for dirt particles in her nostrils. I will say that I did not observe any offhand. Nor did she complain of having inhaled or aspirated dirt. In short, I found nothing that contradicts your theory." She peers at me. "You don't seem surprised by that."

"There was no sign of a second party in the area where she was taken. No sign of anything like a grave. Just a spot where someone had dug fiercely in the dirt."

"Damaging her nails and ensuring they'd be dirty."

"Also scraping up enough to smear on her clothing. Last night, when I suggested we find the spot right away, she experienced sudden stomach pain."

"Which convinced you to bring her back. She then presumed you'd be unable to find the spot on your own."

"I almost didn't. So the only evidence we have is those pricks to her skin, which could have been self-administered, yes?"

"Yes."

The door opens, and Dalton walks in, his face drawn. Seeing me, he straightens and finds a faint smile.

"Hey," he says. "You wanted to see me?"

"I think I know who killed Jolene. I need more proof, but I can definitely accuse Gloria of misleading police."

"Gloria?" he says slowly.

"Jolene was blackmailing Marissa. I thought that could be a motive for Marissa. She kidnaps Jolene and buries her alive with that pipe in her mouth. Once she's scared the shit out of her, she'll let her go. Except the pipe displaces and Jolene dies, and Marissa frantically tries to make it look like a murder."

"And Gloria?"

"Remove Marissa from that solution and substitute Gloria. Marissa's smart—she'd see all the flaws in that plan. Gloria is just inspired by what Brandon did to Conrad and tries to duplicate it as torture. Marissa wouldn't think for a moment that we'd be fooled by the slit throat. Also, she wouldn't panic like that. Gloria doesn't know better, and she *would* panic."

"But Gloria was buried . . ." He doesn't finish that sentence. Just shuts his eyes and whispers, "Fuck."

"There's no pit and no physical evidence. I believe she

smeared dirt on herself and roughed up her nails and poked a couple shallow holes in her skin. She must have planned to stumble back into Rockton after destroying her scent trail in the water. Instead, she got turned around, headed in the wrong direction, and interrupted a wolf-dog's dinner."

"Then faked stomach pain so we'd bring her straight back without investigating the scene."

"And continued faking it to get an earlier flight out. Gloria also questioned why April was examining her mouth. She seemed agitated, suggesting she knew how Jolene died and was worried we'd found the breathing tube, which wouldn't match her own burial. We need to keep her here. She's due to leave tomorrow."

He's quiet. So quiet that my heart starts to thump.

"Eric?" I say.

He looks up at me. "Phil bumped her up to the first plane. Gloria's already gone."

THIRTY-SEVEN

Five minutes faster. That's what I keep thinking as we jog to the airstrip, where Phil is preparing for the next flight.

If I'd run faster, if I'd figured it out faster, if I'd talked to Dalton faster, I could have stopped that plane.

It isn't true, of course. I can imagine myself running onto the airstrip yelling "Stop that plane!" to no avail. The council's pilot would have ignored me. They have their orders, and their orders would include a warning not to let us stop them from taking off.

Gloria played her cards perfectly here. Severe stomach pain that April couldn't diagnose, which was guaranteed to spark my sister's fear that she's not providing perfect care in this imperfect environment. I doubt Gloria knew that. She just got lucky.

April wanted Gloria on an earlier plane. Phil did that, but Gloria kept pressing, according to Dalton. Her stomach really hurt. Wasn't there some way to get her on the first flight? Dr. Butler seemed quite concerned, and maybe she was mistaken, but Dr. Butler didn't seem as if she was a specialist in that sort of medicine . . .

Yep, all the right cards slapped down, one after another. The last thing Phil wanted was a medical emergency. Nor did he want Gloria pestering him for the next twenty-four hours. So he rearranged the flight to open a seat for Gloria.

We reach the airstrip. The first flight is gone, and the next doesn't leave for two hours. The only people there are Phil plus a couple of residents trucking in extraneous supplies for the next flight.

Phil's so enrapt in his clipboard that he doesn't even notice Dalton telling the trio of workers to put their stuff down, head back to town, and take a break for thirty minutes.

Phil doesn't see me until I'm right in front of him. Then he gives a start, as if I erupted from the earth.

"Gloria killed Jolene." It takes all my willpower to say those words without the usual string of qualifiers. *I think she might have possibly killed Jolene.* Yes, I could be wrong, but any doubt I inject into my wording is a crack for him to grab and rip open.

Ah, well, unfortunately, she's gone, so you won't be able to interview her. Too bad. So sad.

That doesn't reflect well on Phil, but right now, he has a job to do, and he will want to shove aside any interference with his core mission.

Gloria is gone now. Not our problem.

Before he can open his mouth, I continue, "She faked her own burial to throw off suspicion. Possibly also to frame Marissa. Her primary goal, though, was to arouse our sympathy and concern. Let her get on that first flight. Let her escape justice."

Phil looks west, in the direction the plane went. "Which it seems she has." He lowers his clipboard. "Do you want me to notify the council? That would be the obvious next step, but knowing they've ordered you not to investigate—and threatened you against doing so—I'll understand if you'd rather we kept this between us. The important thing is that she's gone and no longer a danger to our remaining residents."

"No," Dalton says as he walks up. "The important thing to us is that she flew out of here thinking she got away with murder. Also, while she's not a threat to the remaining residents, she's on a plane with Conrad."

"Yes, I realize that was imperfect, but she said she was fine flying with Conrad, despite what he did to her." He stops and his eyes widen. "Oh."

"Yeah, *oh*," Dalton says. "She was damned quick to reassure us that she was fine with it. Maybe getting the hell out of here isn't the only reason she wanted on that flight."

We're at Phil's, trying to contact someone on the receiver. The council will not be pleased to hear that I investigated, but I can smooth that over. Ironically, in trying to deflect possible suspicion, Gloria provided me with an excuse for officially investigating. Not looking into Jolene's murder, which the council prohibited, but looking into the attempted murder of Gloria herself. It's easy to hide Jolene's fate, relabel it as misadventure. But there's no way of telling a survivor—a living witness—that they imagined being buried in a hole.

And so I investigated Gloria's case, detached from Jolene's. I'd only planned to make a show of investigating. Instead, I discovered that Gloria not only faked being buried alive but seems to have killed Jolene. Now she's on a plane with the man who seduced and betrayed her, and she *really* wanted to be on that flight.

My story is valid. If the council still wants to be vindictive and expose me, I can do nothing about that. Yes, Conrad is an asshole, but I can't risk him dying because I did nothing. While I'm not certain Gloria even plans any revenge, it's a fine excuse for what I really want: her to know she didn't get away with it.

Phil punches in whatever he needs to do to call Tamara. Then we wait. And wait. And wait. Finally there's a beep and Tamara's voice comes on with "We are unable to take your call at this time. Please leave a message and—"

Phil jabs the button to disconnect, his face darkening.

"That's not normal, right?" I say.

"It is not."

He calls again and gets the same message. It's definitely Tamara, and her tone is light with mockery. When Phil speaks, it's through gritted teeth.

"Hello, Tamara," he says. "This is Phil. The plane left approximately twenty minutes ago. We have an urgent situation on board. One of the passengers—"

A beep cuts him short, and the call disconnects. He stares at the receiver, fury mingled with disbelief.

"Yeah, that's a big ol' 'fuck you' right there," Dalton says. "You were a pain in the ass to work with, Phil, but you never seemed to enjoy being a dick."

"I did not." The words are clipped. "I derived no satisfaction from denying your requests. In my defense, you were equally a pain in the ass, Eric, but only because my understanding of the situation was skewed. Tamara has no such excuse. She knows exactly what Rockton is dealing with."

"And she doesn't give a shit. Enjoys waving her middle finger at us. At you, most of all, I bet."

Phil makes a noise in his throat and retries the call. As soon as the beep to leave a message sounds, he says, "Gloria murdered Jolene. She may be planning to kill—"

The ending beep comes, and Phil's hand swings back to smack the receiver. Dalton catches it, and they exchange a look.

There is no doubt that beep came sooner than the last. Meaning someone—no, not someone—*Tamara* is on the other end, listening and deciding she's having none of whatever nonsense we're pulling.

I say, "Her orders must be to ignore communications from Rockton. They're presuming we'll pull a stunt to stall the closing."

"You may be giving her a little too much credit there," Dalton says. "But whatever the reason, they aren't going to get our message."

"Then I don't know what to do," Phil says. "Except hope Tamara realizes what will happen if someone is hurt after we tried to warn them. While I don't expect her to feel guilty, she will lose her job and that is a serious threat, presuming she is in the same position I am."

"There's one more thing we can do," I say, looking at Dalton.

"Follow that plane?" he says.

"Exactly."

THIRTY-EIGHT

Phil argues the entire way to the hangar. Surely, Tamara will pass along our message. She might have initially cut him short, but she'll reconsider and pass it along, blaming technology for the truncated message.

We are taking a risk here. That's what really concerns him. The council expects us to fight the closing of Rockton. If we defy orders and follow that plane, and they decide we've concocted this whole scenario as an excuse, we will pay the price, like children who sneak out after being grounded.

What is Gloria going to do on a plane, anyway? That's Phil's argument. Is this really about stopping a viable threat? Or is that just an excuse because we cannot drop the matter? Because *I* cannot drop this. I've solved this crime, and I'm going to make damned sure everyone knows it, whatever the cost.

We're in the plane now, buckling up, when I say to Dalton, "What if he's right?"

"Doesn't matter."

"Yes, it does, Eric. I do believe Conrad could be in danger, but that wasn't my original concern. I just didn't want Gloria thinking she got away with it."

He flips switches, starting the plane. "Then they should have answered that damned call. Taken the fucking message."

He's been calm, but anger sparks from his words. Anger and outrage and insult. Shutting down Rockton so quickly disrespects him and every sheriff who has come before him. The way they treated us before the shutdown was bad enough. Now we've gone from disinterest and disrespect to outright mockery and contempt.

Dalton is furious. He stood by and let them close us down. Shut his mouth and did his job. Watched residents kicked out after we'd promised them sanctuary. This is his breaking point. The council is refusing to listen, refusing to treat him like the exemplary employee he has been, and so he will take matters into his own hands. He must.

Phil doesn't try to stop us from leaving. He's registered his concerns, and he can only hope we'll bear them in mind. I will.

The plane left over twenty minutes ago. Dalton can track it. His plane is equipped for that. The council made sure it had the best radar possible, because Dalton needs to know when there are other planes in the vicinity.

It's a larger plane, heavily weighed down with passengers and supplies. Yet their head start makes it unlikely we'll catch up, and even if we do, what then? I presume Dalton would attempt to hail them. I suppose he can only get within range. Otherwise, though?

Otherwise, we are following them to their final destination. To where the council is holding them. We can say that we haven't been forbidden to go there, but we both know they do not want us there.

That's our real fear with this expedition, even if we haven't voiced it. If we need to go all the way to wherever they'll be taking the residents, it will look like spying. Checking up on them. Not trusting them to do the right thing by our residents.

All of that is true. More fears left unsaid, pushed aside by the sheer volume of work needed to decommission Rockton.

The council said residents will be moved to a private location, a northern resort they've taken over for the next few months. That was the carrot to get the residents to come along nicely.

Yes, your stay is being cut short, but not only will we reimburse part of your payment but you'll be moved to far more luxurious accommodations. Hot showers! Baths! Electricity! Running water! Even Wi-Fi with some restrictions. Most of the comforts of down south living provided while you prepare to re-enter modern life.

More than one resident had grumbled about why they weren't given that from the start.

Phil says the council will follow through on about seventy-five percent of their promise. It won't be the luxury resort residents expect. More like an abandoned one hastily aired out and patched up, with decent solar power and well water.

Do we believe Phil? I know *he* believes it. I'm even reasonably sure he's right, though the accommodations may be rougher than he imagines. After all, if it's too good, won't residents ask to spend the rest of their stay there? The council would rather have them eager to return home.

Still, we are afraid that we are sending our residents off with no way of checking on them. Washing our hands of our responsibility in our eagerness to be done with old Rockton and on to the new one.

Yes, we may be hoping to see where the plane ends up. This provides a good excuse for doing so. Yet it also comes with the risk that the council will see it as distrust and punish us for it.

Dalton flies west. The plane headed that way. Not surprisingly. West takes you closer to Dawson City and Whitehorse. Closer to Alaska and the west coast.

We don't speak. I stare down at the endless forest to keep from straining to see a plane I know I won't spot.

"Got it!" Dalton says.

I look over as he taps the radar. I've been trying not to look at that either. He knows what he's doing, and I can't be pointing out every blip. There have been blips, tiny ones that I presume are bush craft. Now he's pointing to a larger dot heading due west.

"Can you radio them?" I ask.

He makes a face, and that says he doesn't want to try just yet. We have closed part of the gap between us, but only enough for them to appear on the radar.

"They're still . . . out," he says, intercom static swallowing the rest, and I presume the missing words tell me how far away they are. To a non-pilot like me, the exact distance would be meaningless anyway. He's only saying what I already realized. He wants to get closer before hailing them. Now that we see them, we can.

A plane isn't like a car, where you can hit the gas and kick it into turbo. There are more delicate maneuvers required, such as figuring out the other plane's height and trajectory and speed, and attempting to narrow that gap as safely as possible.

I wait as patiently as I can while Dalton does his thing. As he hits the radar touch screen, numbers fly past. The other plane's velocity? Height? Distance? I'm not even sure how much of that is possible to get from radar. Dalton and I had talked about training me to fly. That was before Phil arrived. Phil has his license, which means he's Rockton's backup pilot. I still want to learn, in case of an emergency, but it is another on a long list of skills I haven't had time to acquire.

When Dalton's screen jabs grow more insistent, I know something's wrong. I glance over to see him frowning. He squints out the windshield, but I see nothing on the horizon. More jabbing. More frowning.

I bite my tongue against asking what's wrong.

Dalton's lips move in a familiar phrase. "What the fuck?"

I bite my tongue harder. He smacks the radar, not a hard bang but a smack of annoyance, as if it's malfunctioning. Then he returns his attention to flying, his face tight.

We ease downward and pick up speed, and I'm squirming in my seat now, desperately wanting to ask what's wrong. Then I see a dot flying below low cloud cover. It drops and then veers to one side. Another drop before the nose rises again.

Dalton's on the radio, identifying himself in a machine-gun patter, his voice strained but calm.

"Are you in distress?" he asks. "Do you require assistance?"

Dalton pauses to listen to the radio channel. The line between his brows deepens, and I know he's not getting an answer. Ahead, the growing dot continues to move erratically.

Dalton repeats his identification along with coordinates.

"I am close enough to assist," he says. "Please respond."

His brow fissure only grows. The plane is listing to one side now and starting to circle.

"Fuck it," he snaps. "This is Eric Dalton, sheriff of Rockton, the town where you just picked up your passengers. I am here to assist. Please respond. I can see you are in fucking distress, and I am trying to fucking help."

His jaw works, as if grinding his teeth.

"If you can hear me and cannot respond, you are losing altitude fast. You are—Fuck!"

The plane has completed its circle and is coming straight for us. Dalton acts quickly but calmly as he moves us to one side. When the other plane circles into our path again, Dalton lets out a string of profanity.

"Are they intentionally—?" I begin.

Before I can finish, the other plane veers and drops. It's not trying to hit us. It's out of control.

The gap between us has closed enough for me to see the plane clearly. We might not be moving at jet speeds, but that is still far too close. Dalton works fast to get us out of the way.

"Can you hear me?" he says, his voice louder. "Can you see me? Something is wrong with your plane. You need to land."

He switches to the intercom and turns to me. "Look out your side. Any clearing. Even water."

I'm already looking, and I see nothing but trees. Dalton's doing the same while talking steadily, as if the other plane is in mild distress and not about to crash.

"There!" I shout. "Two o'clock. A burn site."

Dalton sees it and starts machine-gunning instructions to the other plane. He tells it where to go. Then he tells it to follow us, and we'll lead it in.

Is he getting any response? Any at all? I suspect the answer is no, but there is nothing Dalton can do except talk and lead.

He turns our plane toward the burn site. It's a long patch of wilderness scar tissue, blackened stumps that will not be perfect for landing but will be better than crashing through fifty-foot pines.

Soon we're ahead of the other plane, and again, it isn't like a car, where I could just twist around and see what they're doing. There are windows, but I'm squinting out them, unable to catch more than a flash or two of what seems to be the plane behind us.

"Are they following?" I ask, when I can't keep silent any longer.

"I don't know," he says grimly. "They're behind us, but they're all over the place."

"I am going to land," he says, the change in tone telling me he's speaking to the other pilot. "If you are listening, follow me. And if you aren't listening, I hope to hell you can see me and figure it out."

I want to ask if there's enough room to land, if even we can do it safely. The answer must be yes. He wouldn't risk it otherwise.

We start to drop, and Dalton's focus shifts entirely to our plane. I keep straining to see the other one, only catching glimpses of it when it flies into view. Dalton's right. It's behind us. That's all we can tell.

As we fly lower, I can see the burn site better. It's recent. Not much regrowth. There's also a bare patch of rock, one that seems to grow blessedly larger as we descend.

We're in a small plane, almost half the size of the other one. We can land here easily. Taking off will be tougher, maybe even impossible for them. Not a concern right now. We just need to get down, and within a few heartbeats, I feel the tap of the tires on rock. Then we're rolling along.

"I'm taxiing as far as I can get," Dalton says. "Giving them all the room they need."

Our plane rolls toward the forest. It comes to a stop. Then Dalton's eyes go wide.

"What the—? Out! Out now!"

I yank off my belt, and I'm reaching for my door when he shouts "No!" and grabs me with both hands, hauling me to his side. Something flashes outside the window. It's the other plane, coming down right beside us. Dalton drags me out his door, and we run for cover.

THIRTY-NINE

Metal screams, an endless shriek. Dalton throws himself on me, and we hit the ground, rolling on the forest floor together.

I am waiting for the crash. There isn't one. Just that scream of metal. Then it ends, and we lie there, Dalton's arms around me so tight I can barely breathe.

Finally, he exhales with, "Okay, okay, okay," quiet reassurance, as much for himself as for me.

"I should have let them crash," he mutters as he lifts his head. "That was close. Too fucking close."

I say nothing. My heart slams against my ribs so hard I'm not sure I could speak if I tried. When we rise, we're both shaking. I take a deep breath, and his echoes it.

"Are they . . . ?" I trail off before I can ask whether they're okay. He can't answer that. Neither of us can until we go out and see.

I should run to see what I can do. But my knees are quivering, and a tiny voice whispers that I do not want to go over there. I do not want to see what has happened.

The first time I climbed into Dalton's plane, he'd given me two sedatives from the town doctor, who'd heard that my parents died in a small-plane crash. I'd been confused for ten seconds before shame washed over me. The doctor provided the tabs presuming riding in a small plane would be traumatic for me. I'd felt not one iota of concern, and that shamed me.

I could have died moments ago. Died as my parents did. Now there is a plane out there, and that scream of metal—and the silence that followed—tells me the passengers are not okay. The daughter inside me realizes she's about to see a re-flection of her parents' death, and it will be terrible.

"I've got this," Dalton murmurs against my ear. "If I need medical help, I'll call you."

I shake my head. "Absolutely not," I say, though my voice comes out as a croak. I lurch forward. My knees are still fluid, and I realize with a dull detachment that one of them hurts. I must have cracked the kneecap at some point. I grit my teeth, but I do accept Dalton's offer of a supporting arm as we make our way from the forest.

The first thing I hear is an ominous creaking. Metal groan-ing. Then a human groan. A soft cry. I pick up my pace. All I see at first is our plane. It's where we left it, and when we get around the other side, I note with relief that our plane is un-damaged, the other one skidding mere inches past the wingtip.

That other plane is ahead. Half submerged in burned forest. The front end . . .

There will be no survivors in the front end. It plowed straight through dead trunks, ripping one from its roots. The other trunks were larger, and they did not give way. The entire nose of the plane is mangled metal, and there's a still-standing tree in the first row of seats, the plane wrapped around it.

The metal has been ripped open, and we can see inside through the gash. One cargo door is open, too, hanging as the plane lists to one side.

"Hello!" Dalton calls. "We're—"

He stops so abruptly he almost whips me off my feet. I follow his gaze. He's looking toward our plane.

I'm not sure what I see at first. Then I am. It's a body.

I do not know who it is. I only know that I don't have to run over and check for vital signs, no more than I need to rush and check on the pilot and whoever sat in the copilot seat.

Dalton tugs my arm, drawing my gaze away. "Can't help him," he murmurs. "But there may be others we can help."

Are there? The groaning has stopped. The soft crying continues, but in my heart I am afraid we are already too late. The crash is horrific. If there are survivors, I'm not certain my rudimentary medical skills will help anyone.

"Our radio's working, right?" I say to Dalton as we continue toward the wreck.

"Should be."

"Let me do this then, while you radio for help."

He hesitates, and I know what he's thinking. Radio whom? The outside world? Will we really summon help at the cost of exposing Rockton?

Maybe we should continue our mantra of "What does it matter?" It does matter, though. That caution is entrenched in us.

"Call Phil," I say. "Even Tamara can't ignore this."

He nods, but he doesn't leave, just stays at my side while glancing toward our plane.

"I'll be fine, Eric," I say. "Bring help. Please."

A squeeze on my arm and one last look toward the wreckage before he lopes off.

I take out my gun. Pure instinct when walking into an unknown situation. I continue toward the plane while trying very hard not to look at that body to my left, trying hard not to identify it as someone I knew.

The crying stops abruptly and that yanks me back.

"Hello!" I shout. "It's Casey. Detective Butler. I'm approaching the plane."

No one answers. No one did for Dalton either. The groans have ceased. So has the crying. All is silent. Eerily silent.

Then, "Casey?" It's a woman's voice, coming from the wreckage. It's weak and tremulous, but I recognize it in a heartbeat.

"Gloria?" I call back.

Snuffling answers, and I pick up my pace, fingers wrapping tight around my gun. I say her name again, but only get more snuffling. Ten paces from the plane now. I'm parallel with that opened cargo door, and I can see inside. Someone's crying again, the sound rising to a keening.

"Is that you crying, Gloria?" I say.

"N-no." Her voice comes from the darkness. "It's Ted. He's hurt bad. There's . . . there's something . . . through him." Her voice starts to shake. "Something went flying, and it's right through him, Casey. Through his stomach. He passed out, but he's awake now and making that . . . that noise."

I take my penlight from my pocket and shine it into the dark interior. The plane seats eight. Pilot up front, with a seat for either a copilot or another passenger. The council had, of course, wanted that seat for a resident. Behind them are two benches, each seating three. The door I'm looking through opens just behind the last row. I can see nothing but that seat, and I'm viewing it from the rear.

"Where's Ted sitting?" I ask.

"What?" Her voice is sharp. "He needs *help*. We all need help. I'm bleeding. Brandon's unconscious. So's Sylvia."

"I know, but you landed in a very precarious position," I lie. "I need to be careful. Eric says the damage may have perforated the plane's . . . I don't remember what it's called, but it could release some kind of chemical. He's gone to call for help. So I'm going to come in slowly. I'm hurt, too. I was getting out of our plane when yours crashed and the force caught me."

As I make up nonsense excuses, I peer through the cargo door. At first I see nothing but that rear seat. Then my breath catches. There's something poking through the vinyl. Something bloody. I shine the light, and my gorge rises as I see a metal rod piercing the back of the seat. Blood drips from it, and I know Gloria is telling the truth. Something impaled Ted.

The low keening rises again, and it is clearly coming from that seat.

I clench my fists against the urge to run to his aid. My caution might cost a man his life, and later I might discover that I'd been wrong about Gloria. That she might have faked her own burial, but she didn't kill Jolene, that I'd misread the evidence and misread her reaction to April's questions. I might discover that the crash was actually a tragic accident, unrelated to anything I'm investigating, and my paranoia cost Ted his life.

"I think I see him," I say. "I'm going in behind the seat to see whether I can pull the object free from there."

Gloria buys this, which proves she lacks even a rudimentary knowledge of first aid. All that matters is that she believes me. I make a few thumping noises, as if climbing in.

"Tell me what happened," I say, and then I carefully slip along the wrecked body toward that other opening, where the impact ripped the metal.

"Conrad," Gloria says. "Conrad happened. He got the pilot's gun and, oh God, I thought he was going to kill me, Casey. He pointed the gun at me, and the pilot tried to stop him and Conrad shot him."

I keep easing forward, my gaze fixed on that opening, watching for any movement within.

Gloria has paused, as if waiting for my reaction. I say nothing, and she continues.

"Conrad shot the pilot, and Neil said he could fly the plane. Except either he'd only taken a few lessons or he'd only flown them in video games, because he could barely keep the plane up."

Neil. The guy who'd been worried about Jolene disappearing. A decent guy, who never caused any trouble, so I can't imagine why he was on the first flight.

Because the council insisted. I remember that now. I'd overheard Phil and Dalton speculating that Neil was a VIP the council wanted to grant the privilege of an early exit.

That's when I see Neil, as if my memory conjures him in the flesh. I catch a glimpse of a figure through the ripped metal. A face twisted sideways, crushed against an equally twisted pilot's seat. I can't see more than that, and it is enough. He's obviously dead, as I expected. He's also in the pilot's seat, as Gloria said.

Have I screwed up here? Was it Conrad who lost it? I want to ask more. *Why did he try to shoot you? What did he say?* I can't speak, though, or she'll know I'm not where I said I was.

I'm close enough to the opening that I need to duck. When silence falls, I hear Dalton's voice. He's on the radio. I can't tell what he's saying, but his tone says he's trying to hurry through the call and get back to me. Any moment now he's going to come running, first-aid kit in hand.

I take another step. Movement stops me short, my foot twisting on the rock, boot giving the faintest squeak.

"Casey?"

I reach for a rock and pitch it at the back of the plane. I have no idea what the hell that's supposed to tell her, but some of the tension leaches from her voice as she says, "How is he? Can you get the thing out?"

As she speaks, I'm stepping forward, my gun in hand. The middle bench seat is right there. As with the rear one, I can only see the back of it. There's the squeak of vinyl, and then a head appears, and I yank my gun down just as Gloria looks around a seat back. She gives a yelp and falls back.

"Oh my God," she breathes. "Casey. You scared the life out of me."

Gun hidden at my side, I move forward until I can see her. The inside of the cabin is dark. The smell of blood hits me. Blood and piss and shit. The stink of death. Neil is right there, dead, in his twisted seat. There's another body crushed in the front, this one halfway through the broken windshield. The pilot? In the copilot seat there's a dead woman, her face covered in blood. A resident, but there's too much blood for me to recognize her, and all I know is that she's dead, and I take a split second to silently apologize for being unable to grant her a name yet.

My gaze then goes to the middle bench seat. Gloria is in the first seat, right beside me. I can barely make her out in the dim light, and when I raise my flashlight, she shields her eyes.

"I'm fine," she says. "Just pinned here. My seat belt saved me, but now it's stuck." She yanks at it uselessly.

I shine the penlight in, the weak beam fading fast in the shadowed interior. Brandon sits beside her. His eyes are closed, eyelids twitching. His chest moves quickly, as if he's breathing fast. Beside him is Sylvia, also unconscious. I don't know her well, only know that she'd been a thorn in Phil's side, with endless petty complaints that had earned her a seat on this flight.

There's only one person in the back bench. Ted. A metal rod pierces his chest, pinning him to the seat. His eyes are open and his mouth works, but he doesn't seem to hear or see anything.

"I'm going to try to help Ted," I say. "I couldn't get the bar out from the back."

Gloria only nods.

"First let me help you with that seat belt," I say.

"N-no, I'm fine. Help Ted. Please."

I shine the light around the cabin. "Where's Conrad? You said he shot the pilot?"

"Yes, and then he wouldn't get back in his seat. Kept yelling that Neil was going to get us all killed." Frustration seeps into her voice. "You need to help Ted, Casey."

"I am. I'm assessing the situation before I get back where there's not much room to move. If Conrad is in here some- where, alive and armed—"

"He's not. That cargo door opened on impact, and he flew out it."

"Who else was sitting back here?"

"Neil. There was someone else in the copilot's seat. I don't know her name. Casey, you really need to—"

"I'm going to wait for Eric. He's bringing the medical bag."

"Wh-what? Ted's hurt. *Dying*. You can't—"

Dalton's feet pound, cutting her off. Before I can move, she lunges. My gun flies up, but it's not me she's lunging at. It's Brandon. Her seat belt flies free, and she grabs him, yanking him in front of her as her right hand whips up, a gun pressing to Brandon's chest. His eyes open.

"I-I'm sorry," he says. "S-she made me keep my eyes shut and pretend to be unconscious."

"Shut up," she says. She raises her voice. "Sheriff Dalton? I know you're out there."

I glance over to see Dalton poised ten feet away, gun drawn.

She continues, "I also know you're going to pretend you aren't so you can sneak up on me. You have to the count of five to get where I can see you. Otherwise I kill Brandon. First

Brandon. Then Sylvia. Then Ted, if he's not already dead, and then your girlfriend here."

Dalton appears, gun raised. I've still got mine trained on Gloria, and she doesn't even seem to notice that. She spat her plans as if we're all just going to stand here and watch her shoot us, one by one. The only person really at risk is Brandon. That still matters. They all matter.

"It's okay," Dalton says, his voice calm as he lowers his gun. "You're in charge, Gloria."

I almost laugh when satisfaction crosses her face. I've got a gun trained on her, and yet she believes Dalton. He's the real threat, after all. The tough, steely-eyed sheriff. If he's listening to her, and he's lowered his weapon in surrender, then she has won.

"Sh-she killed the pilot," Brandon says, and this time, Gloria doesn't tell him to shut up. "She was pretending her stomach hurt so she had her seat belt off and was moving around, and she took his gun. Then she shot him. Shot the *pilot*. On a *plane* in the *air*."

Gloria scowls. "I didn't mean to. I was trying to sneak the gun out, so I could kill Conrad when we landed. Only the pilot noticed, and my finger slipped."

"Did it slip when you shot Conrad, too?" I ask. "Putting bullet holes in an airborne plane?"

"Right?" Brandon says, his voice going higher still. "Who does that? She almost killed us all."

"Shut *up*," she snaps. Then she looks at us. "Here's how it's going to work. You two will back off. Casey will lower her gun. I'll take Brandon. He's my hostage."

"Fine," Dalton says. "Take him and go."

"What?" Brandon squeaks.

I answer. "I need to look after Ted and Sylvia. I'm sorry, Brandon, but you got yourself into this."

Dalton and I back up. Gloria hesitates. She got her demand, and now she seems uncertain how to proceed. She looks out the opening, at the forest beyond, seeing the problem with her demand. Where's she going to go?

"I want immunity," she says. "You're going to fly me out of here and grant me immunity."

"Because you didn't mean to kill Jolene," I say.

"I didn't. You know that. You found the pipe. I only wanted to scare her."

"Because she was blackmailing you. Threatening to tell everyone what you did down south."

"I did nothing. *Nothing.* It was my husband. He killed that girl. I knew nothing about it, but she said no one would believe me, and she was right. No one believed me down south. They said I must have known. I didn't. I *didn't.*"

The gun fires. One second she's waving it, caught up in her words, and then Brandon jerks around and grabs for her and the gun fires.

"Stop!" I shout, my own gun rising.

Brandon has the gun, and Gloria is slumping to the floor of the wrecked plane, blood blossoming on her abdomen, her mouth moving.

Brandon turns the gun on me. I dive, and Dalton fires as Brandon does. The bullet whizzes past me. Dalton shoots again. Brandon falls back, the gun sliding from his hand.

I run to grab the gun. Brandon's on his back, his side and shoulder bleeding. His fingers flex, as if reaching for the gun. I stomp his arm hard enough to make him scream. Then I pick up the gun as Dalton walks over, his weapon still trained on Brandon.

"You shot me," Brandon says.

"You tried to shoot me," I say.

He doesn't answer. I doubt he has an answer. I remember

him going after Isabel on the patio, the rage on his face. I remember him attacking Phil. He's never apologized for that. This is a man who is very good at playing the victim, but that doesn't mean he isn't just as good at protecting himself, whatever the cost.

I glance at Gloria, who's writhing on the floor, clutching her bloodied abdomen. "Your stomach hurts *now*, doesn't it, Gloria?"

Her look is almost comical shock, as if she's unable to believe I'd say such a thing.

"I-I'm . . ." she begins.

"Dying?" I say. "Maybe. I could forgive you for Jolene. That was a mistake, and she kinda had it coming. I can also forgive you for sending me on a wild-goose chase and pretending you'd been buried alive. But I don't forgive you for shooting an innocent pilot and bringing down a plane. So I'm going to do as you asked and see to Ted. Maybe you and Brandon will survive. Maybe you won't. But I have priorities, and you're not it."

I climb over her and make my way to Ted.

FORTY

Ted does not survive. I did what I could, but that metal bar was the only thing keeping him alive. Removing it would have meant instant death. Instead, I gave him all the painkillers from our medical bag, and by the time help arrives, he's gone.

The woman in the copilot seat was someone I barely knew, like Neil. Also someone whose exit the council expedited, like Neil. VIPs, likely expected to pay for their quick departure. Instead, they paid with their lives.

Sylvia is alive. Brandon and Gloria also survive, sadly. Brandon would have likely been fine without intervention, but I still had Dalton stanch his bleeding once I'd ascertained we could do nothing for Ted. Then I'd checked on Sylvia and tended to Gloria, and later April said that without my help, Gloria would have died. Not sure what to think about that. I couldn't have just watched her die, so I guess I did what I had to do for my own peace of mind, and she benefited from it.

When Dalton called Phil, he'd been able to patch him through to the other pilot, the one making his way to Rockton. The pilot had picked up April and Anders and brought them to the site. Then the council took over and we returned to Rockton.

We suffered no consequences for our actions. Kind of hard to give us shit when we'd been right and Brandon—ever eager to save his own ass—happily confirmed what had happened with Gloria. The council simply cleaned up and moved on, and by morning, Rockton's evacuation was back on schedule.

And now, as August rolls toward September, our town is empty save for the dozen of us who saw the cleanup through to the end. Rockton itself is gone save for the tents we're using as temporary housing. We have dismantled our entire lives here, piece by piece.

Dalton stands in the old town square as the crew finishes taking the last timbers from our chalet. He's watching it come down, his face hidden under the brim of his hat. I walk up behind him, put my arms around his waist and squeeze.

"I've read about people seeing their childhood home demolished," he says. "I guess that's what this is like."

"No," I say, my face pressed into his back. "For you, it's more."

He's quiet for a moment. Then he says, "It was never really mine. Like growing up in army barracks. It was theirs, and I always knew it."

"They never let you forget it."

His grunt may be half laugh. He pulls me around in front of him, and I hug him tight, cheek on his chest as his arms wrap around me.

"The next house will be ours," he says. "All ours."

"And the next town will be part of this one," I say. "Right down to its DNA."

The council wanted the physical buildings dismantled, but there'd been little of value in the remains. Émilie had offered to dispose of them, her final act as director of the board. One of her granddaughters runs a construction company that specializes in reclaimed building materials.

The council jumped at the suggestion, probably high-fiving one another at the chance to skip the most expensive part of deconstruction. Her granddaughter really does have an eco-friendly construction company, so there was no need to question Émilie's motives. The materials are being stored at a secure site until we need them to rebuild.

They'll be in storage for at least a year. The building season in the Yukon is short, and there's already snow on the mountains. Next year, we'll find a site and prepare it. Then we'll spend a winter in temporary buildings to get a feel for the area and any dangers that might have us rethinking our choice of site. The following year we'll build a permanent town.

Some of the next six months will be spent on vacation. Dalton and I hope to get a bit of time off. Anders is going to stay with his sister's family for a month. Petra plans a six-week European backpacking trip. April will spend a few weeks attending symposiums, which is her idea of a vacation. The rest of the time we'll be flying into the forest looking at the terrain, poring over geographical surveys and historical records.

As for where we'll be based during all that, it's Émilie to the rescue again. She has leased a luxury lodge somewhere along the west coast. Ironically, it's the kind of place I suspect most of our residents expected to go when the council flew them out. They'd apparently ended up pretty much where Phil had expected: a rundown lodge quickly patched up for new guests. They are safe, though. We know that. Which is where our concern for them must end. Our focus is here, on these remaining residents.

Who is left? Anders, of course. He's ready to rebuild. Ready to permanently commit to New Rockton? We aren't asking that of anyone. Maybe, having confessed his past, he'll decide it's time to go back down south. I hope not, but that's just me being selfish.

Isabel is staying. I still don't know her backstory, but she has no inclination to return down south. While she'll never be joining us on hikes and campouts, she has found something in Rockton that suits her, and so she will stay.

Mathias is a similar case. I *do* know his backstory, and I know why he isn't eager to go back. He could, though, if he wanted. He doesn't. So he'll follow us.

Petra is another who simply seems in no rush to ever go back. For her, there is the allure of the forest, too. With a new town, she'd also have more freedom to come and go, and I think she'll enjoy that.

As for my sister, she has declared herself indispensable. I've tried to broach the subject of whether she *wants* to come, but I've discovered there's no way to do that without her wrongly concluding I'm trying to get rid of her. I must console myself with knowing duty would not keep her here if she really wanted to leave.

Kenny's coming, and I hope that's part of the appeal for April. I also hope *her* going is part of the appeal for him. I'm just happy to have them both along, two more friendly faces in our new Rockton.

Speaking of friendly faces, Jen got her invitation, at least to the lodge. From there, we'll figure it out. Where does that leave her relationship with Cypher? Unknown at the moment. We do plan to relocate in the general area of our old town, if that helps.

Relocating to that region would also help Sebastian. He's joining us, but I get the feeling if we aren't rebuilding close enough to the First Settlement, it may be a temporary stay.

As for Jacob and Nicole, they're coming to the lodge. That's best for Nicole's pregnancy. If they don't like the close quarters, Émilie has promised the setting is wild enough for them to make camp elsewhere. They'd also like it if we relocated in the rough area of the former Rockton, but if we can't, they'll move near wherever we end up.

Diana is still with us. She's coming to the lodge at April's request/demand. From there, we'll work it out, as we will with Jen, deciding exactly how far that invitation will extend. In Diana's case, I'm not sure she'd even go for New Rockton. We'll see.

Maryanne will be joining us. She's come back from her dental-surgery getaway and is helping with the deconstruction. I don't know whether she'd make New Rockton her home, but she isn't ready to leave just yet, and we'll give her as long as she needs.

Phil is coming to the lodge. That's all we know. I suspect it's all Isabel knows, too, and I also suspect he has no intentions of joining us in New Rockton. He just doesn't want to say so. He'll take the winter to help us and to be with Isabel, and then he'll head south. The council has promised him his bonus pay and a glowing reference. That's all he ever wanted, and I cannot fault him for that.

Devon and Brian are coming, too. We'd kept them on the cleanup crew, and they'd overheard enough for Devon to flat-out ask, as Diana had. They want to stay, at least for now.

We stand there, watching our house come down, board by board. Storm wanders over from wherever she'd been playing with Raoul. Both dogs have been off their food for a few days, barely tempted by choice cuts Mathias saved for them. They sense our tension, and they are confused by the changes happening around them.

I bend to pet Storm. "How about a walk?" I glance up at Dalton. "Our deconstruction shift doesn't start for another hour."

He nods, and we're about to leave when Phil strides over.

"Tamara is on the line," he says.

"And she can stay there," Dalton says. "Tell her you couldn't find us. We'll talk later."

"It's not just Tamara," he says. "It's the whole council. They have something to say to you."

"I'm sure they do."

Phil shakes his head. "Not like that. They think you'll want to hear this, and they seem quite pleased with themselves, which means they're about to play Father Christmas."

"A parting gift?" Dalton glances from the main tent to the forest. Then he grumbles, "Fine. I won't be pissy. Let them bestow their generous bonus on me." He looks at me. "What do you think? Five hundred bucks?"

"Gold watch," I say. "The traditional parting gift for a valued employee."

"Can I pawn it for five hundred bucks?"

I smile and wave for him to go with Phil, but he tugs me along, saying, "You gotta keep me from saying anything smartass. We're near the finish line. Just let us get there before I blast them."

"I will ensure your response is no more than mildly sarcastic."

Dalton opens the tent flap. It's a big canvas structure, nothing like the little pop-up tents we use for our overnights. Anders was in charge of telling the council what we needed, giving us a sturdy base camp we can use both now and for our New Rockton phase one. I'm sure the council expects the tents back, but I'm equally sure they won't notice if they don't get them.

This tent is our communal area, and it holds leftover chairs from old Rockton. We settle into two as Phil tells Tamara that Dalton is here.

"Hello, Sheriff Dalton," she says, as if greeting an old friend. "So glad you could join us."

"Not like I have anywhere else to be."

Her laugh grates across the airwaves. "True enough. Which is why the council called you in this afternoon. They would like to recognize your loyal service over all these years."

"This is where I get the gold watch, right?"

"If you'd like one. However, the council has another idea." She pauses. "May I presume Detective Butler is there? And that Phil hasn't left?"

"You presume correctly."

"Excellent. Is there anyone else in the tent?"

"No, ma'am."

"What I am about to say is, for the time being, for your ears only. Others may be invited to share the information, but for now, it is just you three. Primarily you, Sheriff Dalton, though we don't mind Casey and Phil listening in."

"All right. What is it?"

Another voice answers. A man's. "We've had a change of heart, Eric."

"About what?"

"Closing Rockton."

"Little late for that. It's scorched earth out there."

The man chuckles. "That's fine. We did need to shut down Rockton in its current incarnation. As it stood, Rockton had become a relic. From a time when people were less reliant on technology and didn't struggle surrendering it. A relic of a time, too, when a town like Rockton could comfortably remain hidden. That same technology your residents crave is also a ticking bomb threatening to destroy their sanctuary at any moment."

"Uh-huh."

"We envision a new form of Rockton. Not a town but a

place. You know where your residents ended up, yes? A wilderness resort, ripe for renovation and reuse."

"Uh-huh."

"That will be the new Rockton. River Valley Resort."

"Uh-huh."

"Right now, it's in need of repairs. All that will be done. We have quite a budget coming from a new investor."

"Uh-huh."

"I wouldn't say the end result will be up to luxury-resort standards, but it'd rate a solid four stars. There's a single building that can house nearly a hundred residents, with the essential employees being given brand-new private homes, a step up from the chalets. They'll have running hot and cold water, full electrical services, and unfettered access to the outside world." He chuckles again. "Well, unfettered for staff. Residents will, of course, be provided with very restricted access. Entertainment, yes. Communication, no."

He doesn't even wait for a response before continuing. "The beauty of this new concept, Eric, is that it doesn't need to be hidden. It will operate as a private lodge. Guests will pay for their stay and register under false names. We will cover their tracks and give them sanctuary. True sanctuary."

"Sounds like you've got it all figured out."

"We do, and as you may have guessed, we'd like you to be sheriff. We are offering you a full-time position with pay. We'll also offer the same to Casey. While River Valley shouldn't need a detective, I know she's your romantic partner, and you will require a security team. As for Phil, we'll be making him a separate offer, equally generous. Now, what we're—"

"No deal."

There's a pause. Then the man sighs. "I know you haven't been pleased with a few recent situations in Rockton, Eric, but we hope you'll see beyond our disagreements."

"I am. And I'm still not interested."

Another pause. The man's voice shifts, just a little, some of that bonhomie sliding away. "I might suggest you take time to think about this, Eric. Let me give you all the details—including salary—and then you can discuss it with Casey."

"I don't need to. It's a no. Hell, no. Fuck, no. Absolutely, no. I'm done with this sanctuary bullshit, and I'm done with you."

"So what's next, Eric? Live off your girlfriend's money? Is that the plan?"

"Nope, the plan is to start a new life down south."

"How? You have no ID except the fakes we made for you. You're a thirty-two-year-old man with no education and no work experience that you can put on a résumé. Do you even know what a résumé is?"

"I'll find out."

"You don't exist, Eric. Casey? Phil? Have you explained this to him?"

"I have," I say. "I've explained that there are people who lack a paper trail for various reasons. Either their parents chose not to register their birth or they grew up someplace like this. Émilie has given us Eric's parents' real names. DNA could prove his identity if needed, but really, it's just a matter of filing the paperwork. As for his education, he can get his high-school equivalency easily enough and then figure out what he wants to do. As you've pointed out, I have the money for him to take his time doing that."

"What about you, Detective Butler? Or Detective Duncan, I should say. Perhaps you shouldn't be in such a rush to come back here, given your past."

"You mean because Diana's ex tried to convince me that Leo Saratori thought I'd murdered his son? Yeah, that's not going to fly."

"You murdered—"

"No, I thought I was being *framed* for murder. I fled because Leo Saratori isn't the kind of guy who'd let a court decide my guilt or innocence. Now maybe you're threatening to tell the Saratoris that I killed Blaine, but I've decided I can take my chances with that. I'm innocent, and I'll find a way to prove it."

"All right." The man sounds as if he's gritting the words through his teeth. "Phil, perhaps you can talk sense into your colleagues. There is room for negotiation here, and you have always been an excellent negotiator. Casey and Eric should go and take some time to think about this, and we will discuss your package, Phil. We are delighted with what you did in Rockton and we think—"

"No deal."

"Eric, we've heard enough from you."

"That was me," Phil says. "Refusing your offer, whatever it may be. I quit. Effective immediately."

Silence. Then, "Do I need to remind you of the position *you* are in?"

"I'm going to guess that means I don't get my bonus? Or my references?"

"You have spent your adult life working for a company that doesn't exist, Phil. You have no references. You will be lucky to find an entry-level position. A job barely paying minimum wage. I'm offering you a six-figure salary plus bonuses, with room and board included."

"No, sir. You are offering me an extension on my term of indentured servitude."

"Indentured—? Did I imagine all those very nice paychecks we wrote you, Phil?"

"Yes, they were very nice, and each one locked me in tighter. Eric and Casey are refusing your offer because they've realized they cannot live with an ax over their necks, and neither will I. You have my resignation. You also have my silence, presuming you deposit my bonus in my account, as promised."

"Wh-what?" the man sputters.

"You heard me, sir. I am walking away. I will do so in silence if you pay me what I am owed. I would also propose you pay a bonus to every Rockton essential worker. I can draw up a list of suggested amounts, if you'd like."

The radio clicks off.

"Sir?" Phil says.

The lights on the receiver go dark.

Phil turns to us. "That went well. Don't you agree?"

"I agree it's a good thing we'll be done dismantling today," I say. "And that we can get the hell out by tonight. Might want to call Émilie and have her send those planes early."

"I will."

He walks to the receiver. Dalton and I slip out. We make it just past the tent before I turn to Dalton.

"How are you feeling?" I ask.

He smiles over at me. "Like a free man."

I put my arms around his neck and he lifts me up and twirls me around as Storm barks in alarm. I give him a fierce hug, and then we're off to tell the others it's time to go.